JAN

JAN

Peter Haden

Matador
9 Priory Business Park,
Wistow Road, Kibworth Beauchamp,
Leicestershire. LE8 0RX
Tel: (+44) 116 279 2299
Fax: (+44) 116 279 2277
Email: books@troubador.co.uk
Web: www.troubador.co.uk/matador

ISBN 978 1788039 109

British Library Cataloguing in Publication Data.
A catalogue record for this book is available from the British Library.

Printed and bound in the UK by 4edge limited
Typeset in 11pt Aldine401 BT by Troubador Publishing Ltd, Leicester, UK

Matador is an imprint of Troubador Publishing Ltd

To my granddaughter, Elle Haden.

FOREWORD

Jan Janicki was my uncle. He was born in Pomerania, northwest Poland. When the Germans invaded his homeland in September 1939, Jan made his way across Nazi Germany, eventually to join the Allied war effort in the United Kingdom. It was a remarkable journey.

As a young boy in post-war Britain, I had always wanted to learn of his escape. Some years later, my aunt eventually persuaded Jan to tell me his story. I was a teenager at the time and remember a sunny but freezing winter afternoon as we walked over white, hard-frosted fields in Worcestershire.

Life was not always kind to Jan. Because of the post-war regime in his homeland, he was never able to return to Poland. He sent frequent food parcels to his widowed mother – sugar, flour, coffee and so forth – without once receiving confirmation that even one had arrived safely. Jan and his mother were not to meet again.

Uncle Jan was a remarkable character – kind, humorous, incredibly hard working and perhaps a little flamboyant. Were it not for his influence, I might never have been commissioned into the British Army.

What follows is a work of fiction; although I confess to having drawn upon some of the information shared with me nearly sixty years ago. Above all, this book is intended as a tribute to Uncle Jan, and to the many thousands of Poles who fought with the Allies during the Second World War.

Peter Haden

(Colonel Ret'd A P Haden)

CHAPTER 1

Pomerania, Northwest Poland, 1936.
Near the Polish-German Border

He would take the headshot. Slowly Jan reset the back sight for 200 yards. Yards, not metres, because this Mosin-Nagant M91 bolt-action Dragant had been made in America, probably during the early years of the century.

Pan Janicki, his father, had "acquired" the rifle in 1920, fighting under Tukhachevsky when the Russians captured the railway line north of Warsaw, cutting off the Free City of Danzig. He had never confessed the detail of its provenance, but stripped and concealed in his pack, it had been brought home in triumph. It was his father's most prized possession. *'Dużo lepszy - much better quality,'* he would say, *'niż te produkowane przez Rosjan – than those turned out by the Russians.'* Lovingly cleaned, oiled and polished, the rifle was in perfect condition.

Jan worked the bolt action to chamber a 7.62 mm round. As he had been taught, he controlled his breathing. In… out… slow and gentle, then a half breath and a brief pause. His target could not have heard a thing, not at that range and with a gentle breeze tangentially in Jan's favour. But the head lifted, perhaps from some innate sixth sense. A small adjustment for deflection and his finger caressed the trigger. Squeeze, never jerk and he took the shot.

The boar died instantly under the spreading oak; its mouth still full of half-masticated acorns as the forelegs collapsed and it rolled to the ground. Jan realised he was still holding his breath. Taking the head shot had been a risk, but his reward

1

was a carcass undamaged by the heavy round. Some his mother would keep, but the rest Pani Janicka would butcher and sell in the local market for much needed zlotys. They were not rich, with just thirty hectares to support a family of five, but they had enough.

Stefan Janicki heard the shot, then waited for another. None came, and he smiled at the silence. A former sniper – which was how he had acquired the rifle from its previous owner in the first place – he had taught both of his sons to shoot. But even though he was only 16, the younger one was a natural – he rarely missed, although this was only the second time Jan had been allowed to hunt on his own. He had gone for deer or boar. Stefan walked to the barn and put a halter on their only horse, Kary, a fifteen hands gelding used for any purpose on the farm. He was strong and had a bit of a temper. He would skitter at the scent of blood, but would carry whatever Jan had shot back to the house.

Aniela ran out to greet them as they approached the single storey farmhouse. A year younger than Jan, they were still close, although he sensed that as his sister began to show signs of maturity they were beginning to grow apart; no longer the intimate playmates of their childhood years. Still, she always sided with him when Tadeusz, who was two years older than Jan, tried to boss his younger siblings around. "Tadzio", as he was affectionately known, had eventually given up trying to impose any kind of authority over the pair of them.

'Dzik – a boar,' she said seriously, then broke into her angelic smile. Jan had long since realised that when she grew up she would be a beauty. Dark, wavy tresses reaching her shoulders framed an attractive if determined face. 'A head shot, and just one round,' said Stefan approvingly, for ammunition was expensive, and Jan could not help beaming with pride. So when their father was not looking, Aniela stuck her tongue out at her brother, but she was still grinning afterwards.

She disappeared into the kitchen to help their mother. Stefan and Jan gutted the boar in the yard then hung the carcass in the barn to mature. It was almost dark when they, too, entered the kitchen to be greeted by the smell of *pieczeń wołowa na dziko,* Jan's favourite, a pot roast of marinated beef, rich with herbs and wild mushrooms and served with dumplings. Tadzio joined them just as it was ready to be served. Chairs scraped on flagstones as they pulled them from under the wooden kitchen table. But for all of them, it was a bitter-sweet occasion.

Jan remembered his father's words from a couple of weeks ago. '*Skończyłeś szkołę, musimy postanowić, co dalej* – You have finished school, and we have to work out what you are going to do,' he began.

'Aniela will marry and move away. Tadzio will inherit the farm, but it's not big enough to support two families after your mother and I are gone. When land is split into holdings that are too small, all you end up with is poverty. Even now,' he went on, 'if I didn't have my job, we would struggle.' Jan's father cycled for half an hour two days a week to work as a foreman in an engineering firm in Chojnice, the small town south of the farm.

They had been sitting on a bench in the sunshine outside the kitchen door. 'You know Herr Raschdorf was here the other day,' he went on. Jan nodded, sensing what was to come. Herr Raschdorf was a wealthy German estate owner who managed both a farm and an agricultural machinery business a few kilometres on the other side of the border. Jan knew that with so many men joining the Wermacht, the German army, many Poles had escaped starvation by working on the land in Hitler's Reich. They had no rights – they were not citizens – but the Germans were glad to have them.

Günther Raschdorf and his father had been doing business

for years – the German bought produce from the farm, mostly grain, fruit and potatoes for wholesale distribution. Usually he sent one of his men, but a couple of weeks ago he had appeared in person.

'*Günther to dobry człowiek* – Günther's a good man,' his father went on, '*jest uczciwy*, and he's honest. I told him about you. He knows you can turn your hand to just about anything on the farm, you can read and write, and you don't need to be told anything twice. I don't want to see you end up as a labourer in this benighted country.'

Jan noticed that his father sounded almost apologetic, as if the recession in Poland were somehow his fault.

'Anyway,' he continued, 'he's offered to take you on. It would be a sort of apprenticeship, training you up as a mechanic. You would learn metalwork and machining skills as well. After that you could stay with him, or perhaps think about setting up on your own. But either way, it's a better future than you would have here.'

He paused to let his words sink in. Jan leaned forward, elbows on knees, looking at the ground. Going to Germany did not worry him. He spoke the language. Athough ethnically Polish, just after the war, his parents lived in what was then "Bromberg". In 1919, after the Paris Peace Conference and under the Treaty of Versailles, the city had been renamed "Bydgoszcz" and became part of Poland. But over 80 percent of the inhabitants were Germans, so although Jan's family spoke Polish at home, he literally learned German playing in the street. When his father inherited the farm, they moved north and west near Chojnice, alongside the border with Prussia. A number of German families lived in the area – their children went to his school – so he still used the language.

But he was only sixteen. All right, he was big for his age. Not that tall, but like Tadzio and his father, he was heavily

4

muscled and thick-necked from labouring on the farm. Mainly it was the thought of leaving home – his mother and father and Aniela... even Tadzio... that concerned him. But on the other hand he could look after himself. Once he had caught two bullies, both boys older than he was, tormenting Aniela. Neither of them were fit to go back to school for the best part of a week.

Slowly he sat upright and turned his head. *'W Polsce nie czeka mnie nic dobrego, prawda ojcze?* There's nothing for me in Poland, is there father?' Stefan sighed and his head moved from side to side. 'All right,' said Jan, 'it's good of Herr Raschdorf. So what happens next?'

After the stew, his mother served him first in honour of the occasion: it was Sernik, a rare treat and again his favourite – usually his mother would sell their cheese rather than bake a cheesecake with it. There was even cream. Jan took a modest helping, but she seized the jug and poured – smothered – as much again. He could see a glistening in her eyes. Nobody said anything as they finished their dessert.

Afterwards, whilst his mother and Aniela washed up, Jan, his father and Tadzio sat at the table. Stefan went to the cupboard and brought out a bottle of wódka and three glasses. It was the first time Jan had ever been offered alcohol. Stefan poured but his mother stood behind her husband's chair and leaned forwards to put her arms around his chest, soapsuds still on her hands. She smiled at Jan. '*A gdzie mój?*' she whispered in her husband's ear. 'Where's mine?'

The morning dawned bright and clear with a hard frost. Jan washed at the stone sink in the kitchen. His mother had placed the cardboard suitcase on his bed in the room that he shared with Tadzio. It took only minutes to pack the few clothes he possessed. His father and Tadzio were already out on the farm.

Jan wasn't hungry, not after what was supposed to have been a celebration send-off meal last night.

He'd been excused from any farm work this morning so he took the Dragant to the workbench in the barn. Last night it had been given a pull through with an oiled rag to protect the barrel but now he stripped it completely. He took his time, but half an hour later it was back on the kitchen table ready for his father to look at before putting it away. Tadzio and his father came back just as the harsh rattle of a four cylinder diesel heralded the arrival of the Raschdorf Estate's three and a half tonne Büssing lorry, with the red lion emblem at the front of its long bonnet. Günther Raschdorf was in the passenger seat. Apart from the driver, there were three other men in the open back, huddled up against the cab and protected by wooden sides.

Günther jumped down from the cab. He spoke some, if limited, Polish as did many who lived just across the border. 'Pan Janicki,' he greeted Jan's father politely. '*Towar gotowy*? Is the load ready?'

'*Za stodołą* – behind the barn,' Stefan replied. 'Come into the kitchen and have a glass to warm you up. Jan can show your men where it is and give them a hand.'

'*Dziękuję* – thank you,' came the reply, '*i możemy się rozliczyć*, and we can settle up.'

'Are you sure it will be all right?' Stefan asked anxiously. 'Jan not having a passport?'

'Ja, ja,' Günther laughed, 'the guards on the border know that he could walk through the woods if he wanted to. Besides, every time I go back I give them a bottle of your polska wódka. They'll be more interested in that than noticing there were three men in the back coming here and four going home.'

Three quarters of an hour later Jan took his place, his case on top of a row of sacked potatoes, and the Büssing coughed back to life. His mother and Aniela came out to join his father

6

and brother in the yard. As he waved, he wondered when he would see them again.

His accommodation, about ten kilometres inside Germany, turned out to be a large loft room over a brick workshop, entered by a metal staircase that ran up the outside of the building. The only heating was an iron stove, next to which someone had kindly stacked a small pile of logs from the lean-to wood store outside. A single oil lamp stood on a table, and the bed was an iron frame with a good mattress on which were two folded sheets, a bolster pillow, a couple of blankets and a generous eiderdown. There was a wooden chair under the table, which had a few basic cooking and eating utensils and a washing bowl on it. An old, rather threadbare armchair had been set nearer the stove. Above the table, the one window looked out over farmland. There was a toilet in the workshop below

'We have our main meal at one o'clock,' Herr Raschdorf explained. 'Frau Raschdorf supervises the meal for all the hands and you take it in the barn attached to the house. Breakfast and evening meal you make yourself but Frau Brantis, our cook, will provide you with rations.'

Clearly if he did any cooking it would have to be on the stove. But he had his own room for the first time in his life. For Jan this was luxury. '*Dziękuję, panie Raschdorf* – thank you, Herr Raschdorf,' he answered politely, but then remembered where he was. '*Danke, Herr Raschdorf*,' he repeated.

And so began a period that, for a time, produced some good memories for Jan. He missed his family and the small farm in Poland, but he need not have worried. Herr Raschdorf was a good man. Every few months, when he visited either Jan's father or another farmer nearby, he made sure that Jan was included in the work detail and – if necessary – dropped off at home for a while to visit his family.

His immediate superior was Johann, who had been an

engineer in *die Handelsmarine*, the merchant marine, for many years. A short, rather sparse figure with only a whisp of hair left, Johann was a widower who shared a cottage with his daughter and her family in the village, walking the kilometre or so to the estate every day. He lived for his work. At first Jan watched as Johann serviced or repaired not only the estate's machinery but also tractors, ploughs, bailers and harvesters from most of the surrounding farms. In truth, he ran a separate, good-sized business within the estate, and Herr Raschdorf had been no more than truthful in suggesting that his mechanic needed an apprentice as an extra pair of hands.

The work was mostly mechanical engineering, but from time to time Johann would light the small forge and work in the smithy, making horseshoes or spare parts that could not be machined. Jan enjoyed these days, not least because the rising heat made his loft warm and cosy for the evening ahead.

But it was the mechanical and engineering work that he enjoyed most. In addition to his own estate machinery, Herr Raschdorf owned a magnificent black Mercedes Benz Cabriolet C, the most wonderful thing Jan had ever seen. Usually it was garaged next to the house, but occasionally it came into the workshop where Johann kept it in perfect order, teaching Jan how to service the huge, eight-cylinder, supercharged three point eight litre engine that produced a staggering one hundred and twenty horsepower. When the master had bought it, Johann told Jan, it had cost nearly twenty thousand Reich marks. On his meagre apprentice's wages, Jan did not think he would earn that much in his lifetime.

Jan proved adept at his work and slowly developed an easy working relationship with his mentor, who also taught him metalworking skills. After a few months Jan could mill and machine spare parts even to Johann's exacting standards. It was rewarding to look at drawings, take a solid piece of metal and turn it into a new component that would restore a valuable piece of equipment.

He also enjoyed going to the house barn for his midday meal. Although the first time he had been mortified when the cook took one look at his oil-stained hands and told him to go and wash at the pump in the yard. She also looked pointedly at Johann, who ignored her and sat down at the long, wooden table.

Somehow Frau Brantis and her maid, Karin, a rather thin-faced woman in her twenties who was still single, managed to produce a delicious stew with mounds of potatoes and on rare occasions even his favourite Schweinshaxe, a large pork knuckle roasted till crispy on the outside and fork tender within. The fifteen or so hands and servant girls who sat down each day were grateful that the master was generous. Even though the rest of the country was barely out of recession, they ate extremely well.

Most of the staff were friendly to Jan, although the daughter of the house, Renate, exchanged only the occasional greeting, perhaps because he was a foreigner. The family did not eat with the staff and workers, although they took the same food in the dining room. Jan did not much take to Helga, one of the housemaids married to a farm worker. A rather stout woman with straw-blond hair, she seemed to think that those who did not work in the house – her husband included – were somehow inferior. Berndt, the husband, a coarse and surly individual who always sat with his wife at one end of the table, usually ate his meal and walked off without saying a word to anyone. Unlike Renate, he had never once bothered to speak to Jan.

Frau Brantis, though, a jolly, dark curly haired middle-aged lady whose size obviously reflected the portions she served, could not have been kinder. She had no children of her own, and took it upon herself to look after the young apprentice separated from his family. Often, before he left, she gave him an extra portion in a small pot 'just to heat on the stove'. And there would be homemade bread thick with butter, or even a slice of apple tart that had not been produced at lunch but which he loved.

Most evenings Jan was alone, but he did not mind. He was free to walk the estate, which he enjoyed, and although he was last in line within the household, he usually got the Berliner Tageblatt to read, albeit that by the time it reached him the newspaper could be anything up to ten days old. 'The master buys it,' Frau Brantis told him, ''cause it doesn't have to reprint propaganda. Then that Herr Goebbels can claim we have a free press.'

But politics played no part in Jan's by now contented existence. He was learning a good trade and remained pretty much in ignorance of the Nationalsozialistische Deutsche Arbeiterpartei. But before long, the Nazis would raise a terrible cloud over his existence.

CHAPTER 2

France 1918 - The Western Front

'*Wie geht es Ihnen?*' asked the *Leutnant*, rather politely thought Günther, after he had saluted and reported for the first time to his platoon commander. 'Welcome to Assault Detachment.' 'I'm well, thank you, sir,' he replied nervously. But the young officer seemed a lot less fierce than the *Feldwebel*, the company sergeant-major who had grabbed hold of him as soon as he arrived with the rest of the replacements. Günther's overwhelming impression was that *Leutnant* Geiger was not tall but wiry – from his slim, athletic frame to the tight, blond curls. His rolled-back sleeves showed muscled, sinewy arms. Günther guessed that the *Leutnant* was only a few years older than he was, but lines striating sideways from his eyes gave him a war-weary, almost sardonic gaze. From his accent, Jan thought he came from Bavaria.

'How old are you?' his new commander asked. His voice sounded tired, almost resigned.

As it mattered, thought Günther. 'Seventeen, sir,' he said promptly. The officer looked at him for several seconds, as if seeing through the lie. Günther was a big lad for his age but it would be another month before he reached his next birthday and the legal age for enlistment. The recruiting staff sergeant hadn't cared – despite the transfer of nearly fifty divisions from the Russian to the Western Front, the German army was desperately short of men. The Allies had their colonies to call on, and now America was entering the war, two massive advantages not conferred upon the forces of Kaiser Wilhelm II. Unless the German Army could secure victory in the forthcoming spring offensive, or at the very

11

least a satisfactory armistice, it must inevitably lose the war. In 1914, a typical rifle platoon had eighty-one men divided into nine squads. Now it was down to forty-five.

'I'll put you with *Obergefreiter* Steinke's squad,' the officer went on. 'He's an old hand and he looks after his men. Besides, he's down to seven, so he'll be glad to have you, even if you are still wet behind the ears.'

An old hand he might have been, but like his new *Leutnant*, the corporal could only have been a couple of years older than Günther. They were seated on bales in a barn, several miles back from the front. The buildings were on a reverse slope so they couldn't be seen by enemy artillery spotters. Günther had been made welcome and introduced to his new companions, but more importantly had been given his first hot drink of the day, even though the *ersatz* coffee was brewed from a mixture of beets and tree bark.

'How are things at home?' asked his NCO, by way of conversation.

'Not great,' admitted Günther, 'although my folks farm, so we are better off than most. The British naval blockade has caused a lot of shortages. We have to make bread with potato flour – *K-Brot*, they call it. It's supposed to be short for *Kartoffeln*, but the powers that be insist that it's called *Kriegsbrot*. I suppose they think that "war bread" sounds better.'

'Couldn't you have stayed on the farm?' asked Steinke, curiously.

Günther shrugged. 'No point – they've taken all the horses, fertilizer is almost impossible to come by, and we're barely producing more than half of what we were in 1914. It's even worse in the cities – we've had people coming out at the weekends desperately trying to buy on the black market. Milk's gone from twelve pfennigs a litre to nearly forty, but folks can't afford it. Father's switched to butter and cheese because they're not regulated.'

In response to Steinke's next question, Günther went on to explain why he had volunteered. When the authorities arrived unannounced to commandeer the farm horses, he had been out riding. Seeing that they had visitors, and knowing the way things were going, he'd hidden Grane in a nearby wood. Named for his colour, Günther loved the seventeen hands grey. It would have broken his heart to see him put to the lash pulling a gun carriage, or even worse. But too many of the farm hands knew he still had the horse, and sooner or later, word would have got out. Besides, grain was too precious and what little they had went to the livestock. So, in the end, Günther had decided that his best chance of keeping and looking after Grane was to enlist in the cavalry and take his precious horse with him. Although if he had been honest with himself, the thought of joining the army and taking part in the victory had also spurred him on. So, much against his parents' wishes, he enlisted.

'Didn't work out then, did it?' commented the *Obergefreiter*. It was as much a statement as a question.

Günther smiled ruefully. 'Once I had signed on the dotted line, they told me that there wasn't much call for cavalry. These days, apparently, it's all trench warfare. It was either that or volunteer for the *Stosstruppen.*'

'Wise choice,' said Steinke laconically. 'At least we get to be used in small groups as infiltrators. Better to break through the Tommy lines than spend your life knee deep in mud in the trenches hoping not to get blasted by their artillery barrage.'

'They told me that we're considered crack troops,' volunteered Günther, 'and that we even get better rations.'

'Supposed to be true,' replied Steinke. 'But if what we get is better,' – he emphasized the last word – 'God knows what the poor sods in the trench warfare units have to put up with. By the way,' he went on, 'what happened to your horse?'

'Not sure whose horse he is, these days,' Günther said

sadly. 'The officer running the training depot took a fancy to him whilst I was there and rode out on him most days. But when I was posted here, they put him with the other remounts. Because I was good with horses and could ride, I was detailed off to go on the train with the handling party. But we had to ride for the last part of the journey – two days, travelling by night to avoid the Camels and SE5As.'

'And did you…' asked Steinke, 'avoid the Royal Flying Corps, I mean?'

Günther nodded. 'When we got to the remount depot, I managed to speak to the Quartermaster in charge. I explained about Grane and he said he'd do his best to look after him. And if he couldn't keep him at the depot for one of the staff officers, he'd try to allocate him away from the front.'

'Which is where we'll be going soon, if the rumours are true,' Steinke told him. 'The *Leutnant* thinks we'll be crossing the line somewhere north of St Quentin, so I would clean your weapon then after we have eaten try to get as much rest as you can.'

Steinke smiled as Günther dutifully stripped and cleaned his Bergman MP18. He had been given only a few hours instruction on the *Maschinenpistole* during basic training, so he was a bit slow and clumsy with it. But the sub-machine gun was new into service that year and it was issued only to *Stosstruppen*. Its 32 round detachable drum magazine could be blasted off in seconds if you weren't careful, but its fire rate of 500 rounds a minute made it ideal for clearing enemy trenches. On the range, Günther had been taught to use only short, three- or four-round bursts and he was pleased to be told that he was a good shot with tight groupings on target. Even so, as the prospect of using it in anger loomed ever nearer, he couldn't help feeling apprehensive. When the time came he just hoped that he wouldn't let his comrades, or himself, down.

On the twentieth of March, they were given two days'

worth of rations and the battalion moved up to a rest area just behind the *Siegfriedstellung* – or "Hindenburg line" – as Günther knew the British called it. They were about five miles north-east of St Quentin.

'Why only two days?' Günther had asked his NCO when they stopped for a break on the march.

'Because in two days, either we'll be through the Tommy lines and able to feed ourselves, or we'll be dead,' Steinke had told him. 'They're not going to give us rations we might not need,' he added bluntly.

Günther almost winced at the grim reality. But they were soon only a half kilometre or so from the communication trenches. Miraculously, Steinke managed to find them some dry ground inside a clutch of shelled-out buildings. They ate cold rations and settled down for a damp few hours rest.

The toe of Steinke's boot nudged him just before eight o'clock that evening. Günther stood up and shivered. He'd been warm enough with a blanket round his uniform, but his cape was wet from a thick, almost drizzling, mist. The platoon gathered round *Leutnant* Geiger. Günther felt anxious and tired from lack of sleep. But his platoon commander, he realised, had been up for even longer – he would already have attended the Company Commander's orders group. Now he was holding his own.

'Well men,' he began, 'tomorrow is the twenty-first of March and it's the *Kaiserschlacht,* our Kaiser's battle. The Americans are entering the war. Either we get through the British and French lines and roll up the enemy, or we lose. So, if you want to win, we have to go forward. Think of it like this: it's the only way home.' He had their attention. Several heads nodded in agreement.

'H hour is zero-nine-forty. That's when a mass of seventy-six first class German divisions will attack twenty-eight mixed quality British divisions across a front of eighty kilometres.

From zero-four-thirty-five hours, the Tommies will be hit by a mix of high explosive shells together with chlorine, phosgene, lachrymatory and smoke. If the explosives don't get them, the tear gas will irritate their eyes and when they take their masks off to rub them, as I can promise you they will, the other gases will hit their lungs. This will suit us, because unlike the French, who hold a thin line and keep most of the troops in reserve, intelligence tells us that the British have put about 30 percent of their manpower in the front line.' He grinned again. 'I hope they enjoy what we will offer them for breakfast.' This produced an almost inaudible grunt of approval.

'The barrage is a big bonus,' he went on, as if determined to lift their confidence. 'Unlike Herr Raschdorf here, who has only just consented to join us, most of you know that after a couple of hours of high explosive shelling the enemy will not know their arse from their elbow – it's like just coming out from the effects of a powerful anaesthetic.'

Günther managed a rueful smile at the leg-pull – he knew he was the least experienced of all in the platoon. If it amused his comrades, or took their mind off what was coming for a few seconds, that was fine.

'Also, we're lucky here,' Geiger continued. 'The British took over this section of the line from the French. The trenches are not complete. The Tommies have only had time to put in some strong points, machine gun posts mostly, and there are gaps. All we have to do is find them.

'Now remember, we are *Stosstruppen*. Our job is to get behind the lines and destroy their headquarters, their arms dumps and their communications. We bypass heavy resistance and leave it to the assault battalions behind us. But we have to be across "No-Man's Land" and clear of their forward positions before the barrage begins, otherwise we'll find ourselves underneath our own guns. Don't dawdle – we can't afford to hang about. I'm giving us three hours to cross our

16

own line, an hour to be across the Tommies' line and through, another two hours to be safely behind their lines, plus an extra hour for safety. We might not need all that time, but just in case, we move out in half an hour. And check your kit. I don't want to hear a single bump or rattle.'

Geiger paused to let that sink in. He looked up. 'This mist will hold, so at least the weather is on our side.

'I'll lead,' he went on. And I want *Obergefreiter* Steinke's *Gruppe* behind me. *Unterfeldwebel* Fuchs comes next with the light *Minnenwurfer* and *Flammenwurfer* teams. The other *Gruppen* follow on in line astern – the usual order. We shouldn't have to worry about the flanks in this weather' – he raised his head again to the thick, swirling mist – 'so we concentrate on getting through.'

Günther's admiration for his platoon commander went up in spades. *Leutnant* Geiger could legitimately have commanded from alongside his *Unterfeldwebel* and the mortar and flame thrower sections, but he was taking point – the most dangerous position of all. His task was to lead them behind the British lines. And it was a safe bet that the *Leutnant* knew his job.

The *Siegfriedstellung* had been built as a precaution just over a year ago. But the Germans had been forced to retreat behind it in 1917. As they advanced through the communication trenches, Günther began to appreciate the scale of the defensive position. It was not a single line but several, one behind the other, for a depth of about five kilometres. Duckboards covered the bottom of the trenches, but even so, the going, through water and glutinous mud, had been slow and tough. The stench was appalling. By the time they reached the shallower, front line with its pill boxes, machine guns and barbed wire entanglements, Günther was gagging and exhausted.

At twenty-five minutes past nine, *Leutnant* Geiger led his platoon through prepared gaps in the wire. From time to time star shells from both sides lit up the night, but the mist was so thick that visibility was down to a few yards. Often, they stumbled or fell as an unseen shell hole halted their progress. The stink from the mud was still dreadful – this was the ground of the first battle of the Somme in 1916. As ordered, Günther was on Steinke's right flank and a yard or so behind him. They advanced in a line of tight, three-man arrowhead formations, with strict instructions not to lose sight of the man in front. Geiger was on his own and at point. But there was hardly any ambient light. Apart from Steinke and the man behind him, Günther couldn't see a thing. The sound of machine gun fire came from and left and right – enemy Lewis guns, presumably – but the noise was sporadic. Mostly, the silence was frightening. His heart was thumping.

Geiger hit the mud. Steinke followed. Men behind him did the same all the way to the rear. The *Unterfeldwebel* came forward to within earshot of his platoon commander then ran back. When he returned, there were two men with him, connected by an umbilical hose. The man in front carried what looked like a long pipe with a slight flare at the front end. His comrade had a tank strapped to his back containing just over seventy litres of highly flammable liquid. They both lay down just behind the platoon commander.

Geiger pointed but Günther couldn't hear what was whispered. The two-man crew leopard-crawled forward and slightly right for a few metres, then an almighty jet of flame spewed out. At its tip, drops of burning liquid showered down. Not a shot was fired, but Günther heard the most distressed, animal-like screaming that seemed to go on forever, but in reality, probably lasted only for about ten seconds. Then there was silence. The *Leutnant* stood up and resumed his advance, MP18 at the ready. But there was no need. The enemy Lewis gun detachment had sheltered in a circle of sandbags. On the right flank, Günther passed closer than his platoon commander.

Uniforms were still smouldering; exposed skin and flesh had charred back to the bone. There was a sickly-sweet smell of roast pork. Günther dry-retched. But at the same time, he realized that if *Leutnant* Geiger hadn't spotted the pill box and neutralized it, he would probably have been their nearest and first target. At that range, they wouldn't have missed. Günther was not a religious man, but he crossed himself, and not for the first time, gave thanks that Geiger knew his trade.

They pressed on. Visibility was appalling but that was helping enormously. Without the fog, the enemy Lewis gun would have opened up long before the flame-thrower could have been deployed – its range was barely more than thirty meters. But their best defence was to pick out enemy forms in the wavy mist before they were spotted. Twice in the next hour Steinke deployed men on the left flank to engage a trench whilst the men behind came up with grenades. Several times they seemed to change direction, describing a wide half-circle around enemy positions that Günther never even saw. But suddenly there seemed to be no more opposition. *Leutnant* Geiger picked up the pace and walked upright, no longer crouching. There were no more trenches or emplacements. They were through!

They pressed on into the early hours of Thursday morning. The going was difficult, but not as bad as in the immediate area of the front. Suddenly, behind them, the earth seemed to explode. It vibrated and shook from thousands upon thousands of explosions that produced enough ambient light for them to be able to make their way more quickly. But the nearest rounds were landing way behind them. Even so, what it must have been like underneath the barrage and what it was doing to the British, Günther could barely imagine.

They came to what had once been a village, a small hamlet; its buildings now in ruins. *Leutnant* Geiger leant against a wall and waited for his platoon to catch up and gather round. He hadn't risked a road thus far, in case they encountered an enemy column, so he reckoned they were in no immediate danger.

'Keep the noise down,' he ordered quietly, 'and *Unterfeldwebel* – I want sentries out-facing. One section should do it, about ten metres away.'

'*Jawohl*,' acknowledged the platoon sergeant and turned to organise his men.

'The rest of you sit down – we'll take a break. Smoke if you want. I doubt they'll see us in this weather,' his thumb indicated back the way they had come, 'and they certainly won't hear us with that lot going on.' A few of the men grinned, but most were grim-faced. They had crossed the enemy lines and were safely beyond the barrage, but the real work had yet to begin. And they had been pushing it for some hours – all of them were pretty tired. *Leutnant* Geiger sipped from his canteen and his men were quick to follow suit. Most of them chewed on *Erbswurst* and hard bread from their ration packs. A few contented themselves with *Ingwerbonbons* of brittle ginger candy.

'Fifteen to twenty minutes,' he told them, 'just to rest the leg muscles so that we don't cramp up. Then I want to push on. We'll take a longer break this afternoon whilst I send out a few scouts. If we can find something suitable, it would be good to put in an action at last light.'

The ruins of the village were astride a narrow lane and no vehicle or foot traffic passed through whilst they rested. Geiger reckoned that he could afford to risk the unpaved road, which was little more than a cart track really and not likely to be used as a main supply route. They advanced without contact until first light, and although the mist thinned, it did not lift completely. By now *Leutnant* Geiger had swapped positions with his *Unterfeldwebel* – no one could stay alert at point indefinitely. Geiger estimated that they were at least eight kilometres behind the enemy lines. Suddenly the barrage, which had become gradually more muffled as they pressed on, rumbled to a halt. There was no birdsong. Come to that, there were hardly any trees, just a few blackened stumps. But it was eerie to be able to listen almost in silence. Günther thought of the massed divisions hurling themselves on and through the British positions. A lot of good men on both sides would die this day.

They passed through two more villages, each as blasted out as the first, till finally the *Unterfeldwebel* lifted an arm and stopped, falling into a crouch. He ran back to his platoon commander. Günther was near enough to hear what was said.

'There's a proper road up ahead. I didn't see them but a few vehicles went past. Lorries, by the sound of it.'

Leutnant Geiger didn't hesitate. 'Get the men off this track into that field. I'll take Corporal Steinke and watch the road for a while. See if you can find some sort of shelter, then send someone back here so that I'll be able to find you.'

'Sir, we might need a runner,' Steinke suggested. 'Shall I have Raschdorf come with us? He's a fit lad. Bit of extra fire power might come in handy, as well.'

Geiger, Steinke and Raschdorf walked along the edge of the field towards the road. The ground had been fought over more than once since 1916 but some of the vegetation was coming back, although the land had not been farmed. The beginnings of a replacement hedgerow ran alongside the edge of the field. Through it they could just make out the road, although the mist was still thick enough not to know what was coming until the vehicle was almost in front of them. Several lorries and horse-drawn carts went by over the next half-hour, and on one occasion a team of horses harnessed to a field gun.

'Notice anything?' the *Leutnant* asked them both. Steinke looked at Günther and raised his eyebrows.

'The carts going from right to left are all loaded,' he offered

21

tentatively. 'The ones going the other way are empty, apart from the wounded. Same with the lorries. One way, they're quite quick. Going back to the front, the engines are labouring and the suspension's down.'

'So, what does that tell us?' asked his *Leutnant*, who seemed to be enjoying himself testing the young soldier.

'Somewhere up the road,' Günther answered quietly, 'there has got to be a supply dump. We could try following the traffic – that should take us to it…' he trailed off, hoping he hadn't been too forward.

But Geiger was an intelligent officer who enjoyed bringing people on, finding out what they were capable of.

'Good man,' he allowed. 'So, here's what we'll do. Raschdorf, you and I will take off our packs. Just bring your water bottle and spare mags. *Obergefreiter* Steinke, you will take the packs back to where we have just come from. When the *Unterfeldwebel's* man turns up, find out where the rest of the platoon are and join them. Whoever's going to wait for us two will be better off back there, rather than any nearer the road. *Alles klar?*'

'*Verstanden,*' the corporal replied. All quite clear – understood.

It was bliss to move without the weight of a pack. Keeping just far enough inside the field not to be seen, they alternatively walked and jogged alongside the supply route. The occasional passing traffic told them that they were going the right way.

They heard the supply dump before they saw it. It was in a former farmyard on the other side of the road. There was a jumbled noise of lorries, men and horses, together with the sound of matériel being humped, hefted and loaded. But the mist was thinner.

'We'll stay here,' the *Leutnant* ordered. 'Don't want to chance being caught in the open.' They settled behind the remains of a small clump of trees. As the weather slowly lifted they could make out the size and shape of the supply dump, although they weren't near enough to make out the contents. It wasn't a huge area – maybe a couple of hundred metres across. 'Probably a regimental facility,' he told Günther. 'Not big enough for a higher formation. Suits us – anything bigger and we might not have enough men.'

'What do we do now, Sir?' Günther felt confident enough with his officer to put the question.

'We move back, into what's left of the mist. Keep these trees between us and the supply dump. As soon as we can, we turn parallel with the road and make our way back to the RV.' He looked at his fob watch. 'It's coming up to midday. We can have a rest and a meal and be back before last light.' He grinned and patted Günther lightly on the shoulder. 'When Tommy turns up later for his nightly supply run, he's going to be disappointed. And with any luck, when they face our lads in the morning, they'll be short of ammunition.'

CHAPTER 3

The *Unterfeldwebel* had chosen well. The ruins were isolated but the walls of the farm buildings gave good shelter. The lads had made a small fireplace from some rubble and brewed a much needed hot soup. Both *Leutnant* Geiger and Günther accepted a mug gratefully.

'We'll move out in a couple of hours,' Geiger opened his orders group for the full platoon. 'I want to get there before last light because that's when Tommy will stand-to – he always does. We'll attack before he's ready.'

He drew lines in the dust on the floor. 'Here's the road, and the supply dump is in a farmyard on the other side. It's not huge. We approach in file behind a clump of burned out trees on this side of the road. The mist is clearing, but in this drizzle, we should make it unseen.

'Number 5 *Gruppe*, I want you about a hundred metres to our left, astride the road. Your job is to stop any traffic approaching once the attack goes in. Similarly, you take out anyone or anything that escapes from the dump. Number four *Gruppe*, you do the same to our right.

'As soon as I can just make out the edge of the dump, the rest of us will form line abreast. This is also the emergency drill if we are spotted. But assuming we're not, I give the ambush sections time to set up then signal the advance. They can come in afterwards on my whistle.'

He looked round at his men. 'Once we advance, the aim is to kill as many of the enemy as possible. Afterwards, the ambush sections stand by in case there's a counter-attack – although I don't think that's likely – and the rest of us will take what we need and set fire to everything else. Any questions?'

'What about numbers, sir?' asked one of the junior NCOs. 'We'll have the advantage,' came the reply. 'Raschdorf and I think that there are about twenty manning the dump itself, but there might be a few more when we get there either collecting or delivering.'

He looked around. 'No more questions? Good. For now, get some rest. Don't forget, we move in about two hours.'

A few of the men managed to doze. But most of them just pretended – too keyed up at the thought of the coming action. Their luck held as they advanced across the final field. Geiger was amazed that whoever was in charge – almost certainly the regimental quartermaster – had not thought to put out extra sentries to warn of any approach in the mist. They would be facing trained infantry, but the QM's department tended to get the sick, lame and lazy. Even so, the mist was a blessing. It wasn't last light, by any means, but visibility was pretty poor in the gloomy late afternoon.

Had the weather been different there might have been a problem, thought Geiger. The British infantry were equipped with the famous Lee-Enfield. They placed huge emphasis on musketry. The bolt-action rifle fired a high-powered .303 cartridge from a ten-round magazine and a skilled infantryman could rattle off anything between twenty and thirty rounds in what was known as the "Mad Minute" – after the order to open fire had been given. In the early stages of the war, advancing German troops had reported coming under machine gun fire, when in fact they were facing the rifles of a British Expeditionary Force, many of whom were veterans who had seen action in the Boer war. The Lee-Enfields far outranged the Bergmann MP18s, but in this weather, they conferred no advantage.

Geiger signalled the advance. Amazingly, they were across the road and at the very edge of the supply dump before they were spotted. The British must have thought themselves safe this far back from the line because they had even piled arms next to where they were working, putting them butt down in circular groups that sloped inwards to join at the muzzle. There were sentries, but only within the area itself, and they had been too interested in what was going on behind them rather than conscientiously watching their arcs of fire.

Someone screamed for a general stand-to. The sentries engaged the *Stosstruppen* even as the Tommies dived for their weapons, but the nearest Germans threw grenades towards the grounded Lee-Enfields. Many of the British troops were killed by shrapnel before they could pick up, shoulder, aim and fire. Günther realized with a start that he was in action for the first time in his life. His heart was racing but time seemed to be standing still. Although he was looking around frantically, they seemed to be advancing almost in slow motion.

An enemy soldier stepped out from behind a horse-drawn wagon and aimed at the advancing line. Without thinking Günther fired a double tap and the man went down. He realised that for the first time in his life he had killed another human being. As they advanced relentlessly, firing at any enemy standing his ground, Günther saw bodies everywhere – some still, others moaning piteously.

Geiger led his men onwards, still firing, through the wagons and stacks of supplies. He checked their line, left and right, but in doing he was briefly distracted. A brave British soldier lying prone in the open carefully took aim. Both Geiger and Günther saw him, but Günther's weapon was pointing in the right directions – Geiger's wasn't. Without taking aim and firing from the hip, Günther sent a short burst at the enemy, whose head exploded into a cloud of red and grey mist.

When they were just over half-way through the dump, the British broke and ran out into a field on the far side. It was all over in less than five minutes. The Germans fired at the retreating Tommies but did not pursue them. Some went down but quite a few escaped, shrouded by the weather. Geiger regrouped his men in the centre of the dump, amidst the carnage, and used his whistle to bring in the ambush groups. One section brought in four prisoners, disarmed and their hands in the air. Amongst them was the quartermaster, a portly individual who clearly hadn't seen much exercise or hard fighting lately.

'Take off your boots,' Geiger commanded in good English. When they hesitated, he pointed his MP18 at the British captain. 'Give the order,' he commanded.

Grudgingly, the prisoners obeyed. 'What are you going to do, shoot us?' the quartermaster sneered. Geiger knew it was pure bravado – the man's hands were shaking.

'I can't spare men to take you back as prisoners,' the *Leutnant* replied. 'And we do not shoot men who have surrendered. I suggest you put down your boots and follow your comrades into that field.' He waved his machine pistol towards the rear of the dump. 'But do not come back, or you *will* be shot.'

Unable to believe what they were hearing the prisoners walked, hesitantly at first, looking over their shoulders, but when they saw that weapons were not being raised behind them they fanned out and ran.

'He didn't even ask about his own wounded,' the *Unterfeldwebel* observed in disgust.

'And our butcher's bill?' queried Geiger.

'One dead – Meyer – and three wounded, but only one seriously.'

'We'll have to leave him with the British,' said Geiger reluctantly. 'Make sure they are all well clear of the ammo stacks, then see if you can find them some cover and medical supplies.'

Unfortunately, the British ammunition was of no use, but Geiger's men did not need to be told what to do with the rations. They looted prized tins of food that had long ceased to exist in their own ration packs – tins of fruit jam, tea, Fray Bentos corned beef, meat stew and even vegetables. Steinke led his men to a stack of parcels waiting to be sent forward with the rations. Günther became aware of *Leutnant* Geiger standing next to him. He turned to face him.

'*Vielen Dank, Junge,*' his officer began. 'You saved me, back there.'

He thought the *"Junge"* was a bit rich, considering the relatively few years between their ages, but it was nice to be thanked.

'Can I offer you a piece of advice?' the *Leutnant* went on. For a couple of seconds Günther thought it was going to be about the action, but without waiting for a reply *Leutnant* Geiger grinned, patted him on the shoulder and said, 'Look for those addressed to officers. They'll have the best gifts from their folks back home!' With that he walked off towards where the *Unterfeldwebel* was settling the wounded.

The first parcel Günther opened contained a welcome pair of hand-knitted gloves, two tins of cigarettes, a letter and a small glass jar with a label pasted onto the lid on which someone had written "Potted Shrimps xxx". He hadn't a clue what the words meant, but what looked to be butter in the jar would be a rare treat. Captain Gryce-Jones would have to donate his parcel, but Günther left the letter well clear of the stack in the hope that it would eventually find its way to the officer.

In the space of twenty minutes all of them had two or three days' rations stashed away in pockets, packs and pouches. And most of them had at least one item of warm clothing, with gloves and scarves being the most popular. They looked an odd bunch, thought Geiger, mostly although not entirely dressed in uniform, but he didn't mind, and in any case their somewhat mixed attire would help confuse the British.

Some of the horses were wounded and had to be shot, but

from the carts that were being loaded they found four good mounts and harnessed them.

'Right, listen in,' growled the *Unterfeldwebel*. The *Leutnant* says we are going to press on, away from the front. We'll take the road, but it's a supply route so we'll get off it as soon as we can and on to the byways.'

'What happens if we meet the British?' asked one of the *Gruppe* NCOs.

'Play it by ear,' the platoon sergeant replied. 'But it's most likely they'll be Army Service Corps drivers with a few carts or lorries, so with any luck it'd be more of a problem for them, not us.' He paused… 'But if we do come up against anything serious, follow Standard Operating Procedures. Lead section gives covering fire, the rest of us retreat. Then it's fire and movement by sections as we disengage.' What would happen if the SOPs didn't work nobody bothered to ask.

'Right then,' he went on, 'I'm only going to say this once. If any of you lot have found any alcohol, put it on the cart. No more will be said. But if I catch anyone drinking after that, God help you, 'cause that's who you will be talking to next.' He paused for effect. 'The *Leutnant* says we can all share a tot later, but only when we have stood down for the night.'

Günther was surprised at the number of bottles – whisky, cognac and wine – that were laid out. The *Unterfeldwebel* grinned and raised his eyebrows, almost as if he approved of their foraging. 'I want a few tarpaulins, some more rations – not booze – and if possible a couple of medical kits to go on the cart. Quick now, see what you can find. But we must be out of here in ten minutes, regardless.'

They left to the glow of flames behind them and the crackle of small arms ammunition cooking off. Their luck held – they were soon off the main supply route and onto a maze of tracks and lanes with Geiger using his compass to make sure that they were heading more or less in the right direction, which was away from the lines and the follow-on assault divisions and towards Amiens.

The *Leutnant* sent out scouts as they moved on at a leisurely pace, and it paid off. About five kilometres from the supply dump they found the ruins of another farm, well back from the lane, with a roof that had a couple of holes in it but which was nevertheless more or less intact. More to the point, the ground floor of what had once been a reasonably substantial, two storey house was still dry. They covered the windows with tarpaulins, lit a roaring fire in the range and made themselves comfortable. The *Unterfeldwebel* organised the distribution of a well-earned drink. Apart from those due to go on stag – they would have to wait till afterwards – it was a couple of large tots of spirits or half a bottle of wine for each man. Günther was excused sentry-go because he had been out with the *Leutnant* on the recce. There was a hot meal, a couple of mugs of red wine and the bliss of several hours of warm, dry sleep.

November

They were in a barn virtually identical to the one in which Günther had first reported to his unit some eight months ago, but this one was considerably further behind the *Siegfriedstellung*. Morale had been very different, back then. Now after a summer of hard fighting they were tired from the long retreat – demoralised, hungry and filthy. After months of living in the field they were all infested with lice.

The platoon gathered around *Leutnant* Geiger, who had just returned from the Commanding Officer's briefing

'All right, men, this is what I can tell you,' he began. 'In fact, it's as much as I or anyone else round here knows for the moment.'

Avid for news, they listened in silence.

'We all know that the spring offensive, the much vaunted *Kaiserschlacht,* was a failure.' His voice failed to hide his disgust. 'Not to put too fine a point on it, it was a complete fuck-up.'

There were nods of agreement. The speed of the initial advance had taken the powers-that-be by surprise. The logistic plan – or lack of it – had failed woefully to support the forward troops. Virtually out of ammunition, they had stopped short of Armiens and the Allies were given time to get their act together. The Germans failed to take the town, with its prize railway links and marshalling yards. Eventually sheer lack of numbers had forced them back behind the *Siegfriedstellung,* which had been fatally breached by the beginning of October. They could fight the British, but not the British, the Canadians, the New Zealanders and now the Americans. The Allies had over five hundred tanks that were vastly superior to the few built by the Germans. They also enjoyed a huge advantage in artillery, the newly formed Royal Air Force had established air superiority and despite a desperate and ferocious rear-guard action by *Stosstruppen* the German army found itself retreating in disarray.

Leutnant Geiger looked at his watch. 'Gentlemen, I am told that an armistice took place with effect from eleven hundred hours this morning. The war is over.'

'Have we lost?' asked one of the *Gruppe* NCOs anxiously amidst the immediate buzz of conversation.

'We were forced to sue for peace,' answered Geiger, 'but technically the German Army has not been defeated in the field. I am told that we will be allowed to return behind our original pre-war borders.'

He paused to let the news sink in. His men were shaking hands and patting each other on the back in their delight at the end of the fighting. They were still alive, they could go home, and that was all that mattered.

He raised his hand to still their noise. 'There are a couple more things I should pass on,' he continued. 'The news only reached us this morning, but the Kaiser abdicated two days ago. He is reported to have gone to Holland. So, as of now, the Fatherland is a republic.'

Some of them nodded in acknowledgement, but this was less momentous than his previous news.

'When will we go home, sir?' asked one of the men.

'Don't know yet – maybe in a day or two. But we can make ourselves comfortable here for now. We need food and the chance to clean ourselves up and wash our uniforms.' He grinned. 'You lot look like a bunch of pirates.'

That night he posted sentries, just in case, but the shelling had stopped and they were not disturbed. For the first time in four years he did not order a dawn stand-to.

Last evening the *Unterfeldwebel* had sent out a foraging party. They had found a supply unit and despite protests had "*liberated*" a quantity of food and even a few precious bottles of schnapps. It was just after nine when *Obergefreiter* Steinke approached his officer, who had been seated alone writing a letter to his parents – although when he would have chance to post it, he had no idea.

'A minute, sir?'

Geiger waved a hand for Steinke to sit down. With the war over, he saw little point in standing on ceremony.

'Günther Raschdorf came to see me last night,' he began. 'I didn't bother you then, because we all had a lot of other things on our mind.

'He thinks we are pretty close to where the remount depot used to be. Says he knows it's a long shot,' Steinke grinned, 'but he wants permission to go and look – maybe find out what happened to his precious horse.'

'He's a good lad,' Geiger replied thoughtfully. 'He's done bloody well. In better times, he would have made a good officer. No reflection on you,' he added quickly for Steinke's benefit. 'You've done wonders with that *Gruppe*. I couldn't possibly have asked for better.'

Steinke suddenly noticed that Geiger was wearing the insignia of an *Oberleutnant*. Seeing the look of surprise, Geiger said, 'They told me yesterday. Offered to reassign me to a Company, but I told them now that the war was over I wanted to stay with the platoon.'

'Glad you have, sir,' he said solemnly, shaking Geiger's hand, 'and congratulations. Well deserved, if I can make so bold; it's thanks to you that most of us are still alive.'

'Now, about Raschdorf,' said Geiger, deliberately changing the subject. 'I don't see why he shouldn't take a look. Not a lot happening so the *Unterfeldwebel* can keep an eye on things here. But Raschdorf can't go wandering around on his own. Take the *Gruppe* and I'll come with you. It's not a bad day for a walk in the country. Besides, Raschdorf might need my help and I owe him.'

Günther had a good memory and a natural eye for land. He was certain that the depot was, or had been, just a couple of kilometres north of where they were. It was a relief to walk in the thin autumn sunshine without fear of being ambushed or machine gunned from the skies. He had been right. They found the depot just after eleven o'clock. From all the bustle and activity, it was obvious that the unit was preparing to move. A couple more days and it would have been too late.

There was no sign of the quartermaster but they found an ageing, rather corpulent *Oberleutnant* taking his elevenses in a makeshift, tented office.

'Von Horner,' he introduced himself. Geiger decided that he didn't look like much of an officer, and he probably wasn't a "*von*" either.

'Geiger,' he replied evenly. 'This young man left a seventeen hands grey stallion here in March. It's not an army mount; it belongs to him. Your quartermaster promised to try to keep him safe. The horse is called Grane – I'm told he is a fine animal. Perhaps you can tell us whether he's still here?'

Günther almost had a panic attack as he waited for the reply. Geiger noticed that the officer was not looking at him directly when he replied.

'There's no horse here that matches your name or description,' he said, 'but he would have been reassigned months ago.' Somehow his words and demeanour did not carry a ring of truth.

'That's all right, then' said Geiger pleasantly. 'Just tell us which unit or which officer took him, and we'll follow it up.'

'I wish I could help you,' came the response, 'but I don't have the records.'

'I've been in this man's army for a long time,' said Geiger, his voice not quite so relaxed now, 'and I've had a shitty war. But one thing I have learned is that supply units don't part with anything as valuable as a top-quality remount without a record and a signature. You lot spend all day on your arses filling in paperwork. And you're trying to tell me there are no records?' He looked pointedly at several battered filing cabinets standing on wooden boards behind the officer's desk. There was a heavy silence.

'Günther!' he deliberately used Raschdorf's first name, just to make it clear to *"von"* Horner that he took a close interest in the rights of his men. 'Go take a look round – see if you can find your horse.'

'Wait a minute, you can't just wander round my depot,' said the *Oberleutnant*, striding round the desk to intercept Raschdorf. Geiger stepped in front of him, stopping his progress instantly. Horner's hand had moved to the flap of his holster.

'I don't think so,' he said quietly, placing his own hand over Horner's. 'I have a full section of *Stosstruppen* outside. I'm sure you wouldn't want to see any unpleasantness?'

Horner hesitated, then backed off and sat somewhat heavily behind his desk.

'Tell you what, old chap,' Geiger went on, his voice falsely pleasant now. 'Why don't you shout for one of your men. A couple of mugs of hot coffee wouldn't go amiss, and perhaps something to warm my stomach.'

They waited, the coffee and schnapps long gone. It must have been a good twenty minutes before Raschdorf ran back, completely out of breath but his face lit up with joy.

Geiger didn't need to ask. 'Tack him up and put a sack or two of oats on his saddle. Then bring him here and we'll be on our way.'

Geiger and Steinke were alone with the officer. They waited in silence for about ten minutes until Günther returned.

'We're ready to leave, sir,' he told them.

The *Oberleutnant* moved to stand alongside his desk. Geiger stood right in front of him. 'You lied to me, did you not,' he observed, his voice acid with contempt. 'That horse has never been on the books. Grane is an expensive animal. You were going to sell him, weren't you?'

Horner could not look Geiger in the face.

'We're leaving now,' he went on. 'Don't try having us followed. We are *Stosstruppen* not supply depot lard-arses. I shall have a rear-guard. Anyone who follows will be shot. And then we'll come back for you. Do I make myself clear? *Verstanden?*'

Horner could only nod his agreement. They wouldn't be followed – Geiger knew Horner wouldn't have the courage.

Without warning, his fist took *Oberleutnant* Horner hard in the solar plexus. The officer doubled over, gasping for breath. 'That was for Raschdorf,' Geiger told him quietly, his voice without rancour. 'He is a private soldier. You are an officer. But you are not fit to lick his boots.'

Geiger turned and walked outside, Steinke on his heels.

The *Gruppe* were all laughing and making a fuss of the horse. Several patted Raschdorf on the back. One of them had found a carrot – Lord knows from where. Grane stood quietly, basking in the attention, his owner now holding a lead rein.

They attracted a few stares as they left the supply area, Günther walking his horse. But the *Oberleutnant* stayed in his tent and no-one tried to interfere with their progress. Geiger was as good as his word. He did drop a man off who eventually caught up with them. They had not been tailed.

'Good job you have been promoted, sir,' said Steinke as they walked.

'Why so?' queried Geiger.

'I would have had to close my eyes otherwise,' came the reply. 'You're not allowed to hit a senior officer. But when you hit that fat bastard of an *Oberleutnant* in the gut, you didn't.'

Back at the barn, Günther fed Grane then rubbed him down. His horse had lost a bit of weight but was otherwise in fair condition. Although the lack of gloss on his coat Günther put down to a wartime diet light on a few fats, vitamins and minerals. After a while *Obergefreiter* Steinke informed him that the *Oberleutnant* would like a word.

'What are you going to do now?' he was asked.

'How do you mean, sir?'

'Well, you have your horse, and I am genuinely pleased for you. But how are you going to get him home?'

Geiger saw that Raschdorf looked worried. 'Can't we take him with us, sir?' he asked anxiously.

Geiger shook his head. 'Sooner or later we will form up as a company, and eventually as a battalion. Grane will stick out like a sore thumb. Any officer senior to me could order you to hand him over – and if he were commandeered again, there would be nothing I could do. If you try to put him on a train with the other remounts, that's exactly what I can see happening.'

Raschdorf looked crestfallen.

'Look,' Geiger said kindly, 'I've been thinking about this. Have you ever heard the expression "the fog of war"?'

'Carl von Clausewitz, wasn't it, sir? *Vom Kriege*, published nearly a hundred years ago.'

Geiger was impressed. The response had been automatic. The lad was not showing off. The *Oberleutnant* raised his eyebrows. Günther Raschdorf was even more educated and well-read than he had realised. *Definitely should have been officer material*, he thought.

'So you have read *On War*,' he replied. 'Well done. I think we are going to take advantage of that fog right now.

'I am going to give you a document on our regimental headed paper. In case you are stopped by our military police, or the civil police come to that, it will simply state that you have been honourably discharged and given leave to make your own way back to Germany, and then home, with a horse that is your own property. I shall give my rank and unit and the order that if there are any queries they are to be addressed to me, my successor or our *Unterfeldwebel* for verification. Also, I'll sign over a unit stamp. That should cover you. If I do that, do you think you can make your own way home?'

Günther knew that it would be a hell of a journey, but realised that if he wanted to keep Grane it was probably the only way. He had to try.

The *Oberleutnant* produced a British map. 'Take this with you.' He unfolded it and pointed to a spot near Charleroi, in Belgium. 'We are here. Head northwest towards Liège, then on towards Cologne, or *Köln*, as we call it. You can follow the railway line for most of the time, but stay off the main supply routes,' Geiger went on. 'And as soon as you can, get hold of some civilian clothes. The locals are not going to be that friendly to a lone soldier in uniform, seeing that we have occupied their country.

37

'And by the way, you can hardly pass as a civilian carrying an MP18. Get a good night's rest,' he suggested, 'and come and see me immediately after breakfast. Do you have any money?'

Günther shook his head. He hadn't even thought about it. Most of his Army pay had been sent to his parents.

'I'll give you enough to see you through,' Geiger went on, 'and I have a serviceable Mark Six Webley .455 that you can have, together with a fair amount of ammunition.'

Günther didn't even ask how his officer came to be in possession of a British officer's revolver.

'The money's mine, by the way,' Geiger concluded. 'But I'll give you my address. My people have a hotel in Sonthofen – it's a skiing village up against the Austrian border. If and when you are able, feel free to send back the funds. But better still, bring them yourself. I can promise you three things: a holiday with good Bavarian food that won't cost you a *Pfennig*, some great skiing and the finest hangover you can ever imagine.'

Günther was dumbfounded by this generosity. 'Aren't you taking a hell of a risk for me, sir?' he asked. 'How will you account for my absence?'

'I'll put you down on the platoon roll as sent to a medical aid post,' said Geiger with a smile. 'I'll just forget to say which one. In all this confusion, I don't see it being followed up. I'll still have your weapon, so there's no problem accounting for it. And don't worry about Steinke, he already knows what I have in mind.' He paused. 'As for the risk, if it were not for you, I probably wouldn't be here today. So, let's just say I owe you and I pay my debts. See you in the morning. Dismissed!'

Günther could hardly believe what he had heard. Bursting with gratitude, he stood to attention, threw up the finest salute he could muster, about faced and returned to his *Gruppe* and Grane.

CHAPTER 4

He was out of the swathe of land destroyed by fighting and into disarmingly normal countryside. Günther had no idea how far it was. But he had a map, at least for part of the way, and also a watch. He knew that if you pointed the hour hand at the sun and bisected the angle between that and twelve o'clock, using what the British called Greenwich Mean Time, that would give him due south. And if he travelled by night under a fairly clear sky, there was always the pole star for north. At a guess, it was probably well over a thousand kilometres. But if he headed northwest, avoiding any major towns and villages, then as the *Oberleutnant* had indicated he would cross still-occupied Belgium and head towards Cologne.

Grane was in good but not top condition and on a journey like this could not be ridden hard. He would do what the British and Portuguese had done during the Peninsular war: ride fairly gently for an hour, then walk for the next. Also, he would avoid the main roads and stick to the byways or even, if necessary, travel cross-country – although this would be slower. If he could cover about fifty kilometres a day he should be home in a month. Certainly in time for *Weihnachtsfest*. Christmas at home – that was something to dream about! He could almost smell the pine scent and see green needles on the *Tannenbaum* that his father would bring into the hall. Then he thought of his fallen comrades who would never see a Christmas tree again.

From time to time, when his chosen path converged near a main supply route, he could see huge formed units marching in an orderly retreat towards the Fatherland. But mostly he was on his own. It was strange, after the mud and the blood and

39

the noise and the stench of war, to listen to birds singing, to see cattle grazing. The fields were harvested now and settling down to winter before the spring ploughing and the endless cycle that would start over. And again, not for the first time, he thought longingly of home.

That first night he and Grane slept rough. His comrades had given him a couple of extra capes that he fashioned into a horse blanket. At last light, they retreated into a copse. Grane still had almost two full sacks of oats and Günther ate sparingly from the field rations he had been given, then loose-hobbled Grane so that he could graze. The weather was kind – it was cold, even wrapped in his own blanket and cape, but at least it was not raining. Although he was still stiff with cold when he woke just before first light.

He was reluctant to risk seeking shelter, but after three days and nights there was no alternative. On the third night, it rained hard and he and Grane were soaked. They dried out partially during the day, but Günther knew he had to find shelter or their condition would deteriorate. On the fourth day, he risked pushing on as hard as he dared and at long last came to signposts written in German. By mid-afternoon he was confident that they had crossed the border. He was still in uniform, but would no longer be seen as the enemy by all he approached. Better still, he could ask for shelter in a barn without having to worry about a pitchfork in his stomach in the middle of the night.

He turned off the lane onto a track still wet from the previous night's rain. Grane's hooves made only a soft, squelching sound in the mud. About fifty metres from the small farmhouse he dismounted, thinking to appear less intimidating if he were on foot. But he took the precaution of releasing his holster flap and easing the Webley.

Still about fifteen metres from the cottage he heard a frantic scream. The front door was open. He drew the revolver and ran. There were two men in the kitchen-come-living-room. The cause of the scream was a small child, a boy of perhaps four or five years, lying unconscious on the stone floor against a wall. It had come from a woman, presumably his mother, who was on her back on the wooden table, her blouse torn, one breast bare and her skirts pushed up to her waist. An undergarment was on the floor. One man in a faded and filthy uniform, at one end of the table that was sideways on to the door, was holding her arms. The soldier at the other end had unbuttoned and let fall his trousers. The woman screamed again, struggling violently but to no avail. It took Günther less than a half a second to take in the scene. She was about to be raped.

Leaning against the wall behind the table were two *Gewehr 98s*, the standard German infantry rifle, with bayonets attached. Seeing Günther, the soldier who had been holding the woman's arms let go and dived for a rifle. Leaving his unit in such a hurry, Günther had not even had time to fire the Webley, let alone zero it. It took him half a second to cock it and there was no time to take aim. He shot from the hip just as the soldier turned to face him, his hand working the bolt. The round took the infantryman in the shoulder, making him stagger and turn away. Günther fired again. His second shot was more accurate and landed centre back. The soldier dropped without a sound, his rifle clattering to the floor.

Trying to pull up his trousers and run at the same time, the second man was halfway round the table when the woman started to sit up, putting herself between Günther and the soldier's body. This time he raised his arm and took careful aim. The shot blew the soldier's brains out.

The woman ran to the unconscious child, weeping and cradling him in her arms. There was blood on the sleeve of her blouse. Günther checked that the two men were dead then knelt beside her. 'Please, let me see,' he said gently.

41

He felt for a pulse with two fingers on the boy's neck. Not that strong, but steady. There was a nasty gash on his forehead that was still bleeding, but not too profusely.

'Put him on the table, find a clean cloth, and press it on the wound,' he ordered. 'I think he'll be all right, but that needs a stitch. My first aid kit is in my pack on the horse. It would be better to do this quickly, whilst he's still unconscious.'

'You can do this?' she asked, her sobbing now more or less under control. 'Are you a doctor?'

'No,' he said with more confidence than he was feeling. 'But in the *Stosstruppen* they gave all of us some basic first aid training. I'll be back in a minute.'

Lacking iodine, he poured schnapps into the wound and put in two stitches. The spirit and the needle roused the child, who whimpered softly. But it was a good sign. He applied more schnapps and asked the woman to bind the wound. 'Put him to bed,' he advised, 'and sit with him till he wakes up. He'll probably have a hell of a headache and he might be in shock. Keep him warm and try to get him to drink something when he can. I'll clear up in here.'

It was a good two hours before he heard footsteps on the narrow staircase that led directly into the kitchen. Günther had been dozing in one of the wooden chairs.

'How's the boy?' he asked.

'His name is Hans,' she replied, 'and he came round. Then he was sick. But afterwards he drank some water and now he's asleep. I think he'll be a lot better in the morning.' She looked round the kitchen and at the fire now burning in the range. There were neither bodies nor even bloodstains. 'What has happened?' she asked nervously.

'They're gone,' he responded. 'A couple of metres down, and nowhere near the house – I borrowed a shovel from the barn. They were deserters, almost certainly alone. Then I took the liberty of lighting a fire from your wood pile so that I could heat some water and clean the floor and the wall. There's no trace of them anymore. But I have saved one of the rifles so you will have something better for protection from now on.'

'I don't know how to thank you…' she began, wringing her hands. 'I don't even know your name?'

He smiled. 'Günther Raschdorf.' He stood, clicking his heels and bowing mock-formally. It raised a very fleeting smile in return.

'I'm Meta Bielefeld,' she replied. He thought she was probably a few years older than he was, nice-looking rather than pretty, of average height and quite slim. Unused though he was to contact with girls, he thought she had a good figure.

'That's a long way from here,' he responded, hoping to ease her tension. 'Bielefeld is in the Detmold district, isn't it?'

'*Ja*,' she responded. 'That's where my family comes from. But I was here on holiday. That's when I met Hans. His father –' her head glanced briefly upstairs, 'was killed in the war. Verdun. So, I have gone back to using my maiden name.'

'I'm sorry,' said Günther. 'A lot of good men died. Now, I'm not sure what for.'

There was a moment of silence. They both had memories. Günther spoke first. 'Do you have anything to eat?' he asked, 'Because if not, I have some rations we can share. Then would it be all right if I slept in your barn? It's a bit late now to be moving on.'

'Hans's – my late husband's – father is the local *Bürgermeister*,' she replied. 'He makes sure we have enough to eat. And as a farmer as well as being the Mayor, he sends a man over every day to help me with our little place here. Those savages must have been watching, because they arrived five minutes after my help left for the day. You have already lit the fire. I can make us a meal, if you can wait half an hour. And no, you can't sleep in the barn.'

Günther raise his eyebrows.

'After what you have done for us,' she went on, 'you will

43

sleep indoors. 'We only have two bedrooms, and I don't want to disturb Hans, but we can put a spare palliasse down here and you will be dry and warm.'

The thought of a mattress, albeit one of straw, reminded Günther that this would be the first time he had slept in comfort for over six months. Without further ado Meta bustled about. First, she went to a pantry and settled a bottle of beer in front of him. It was the first he had seen since joining the field Army. And it was so, so welcome. She put half a loaf of home-made bread and a crock of butter on the table. 'Help yourself if you're starving,' she offered. 'There's some stew I can warm up.'

Forty minutes later, after one bottle of beer and after a huge platter of meat and vegetables, a day in the fresh air and all that had happened afterwards, Günther could hardly keep his eyes open.

'Sorry,' he said, as his head jerked up from his chest. Meta smiled, relaxed now for the first time since he had seen her.

'I'm going to bring down that mattress,' she told him. 'Then you can go to sleep. Tomorrow, I'll heat up enough water so that you can have a bath. If you don't mind me saying so, you don't smell too good.'

'If I gave you some money,' he asked, 'could you go into the nearest town and buy some civilian clothes?'

She looked at him. 'No need,' she replied. 'You're about the same size as my Hans. We can sort you out in the morning. I'm not a useless *Hausfrau* – any alterations needed and I'll fetch out my sewing basket!'

He used his own blanket and, as a precaution, slept with the Webley under the edge of his pillow. But when he awoke, just as dawn was breaking, he realised he might not have heard much anyway – he had enjoyed the warmest, most comfortable night's sleep since reporting for active service all those months ago.

Meta bustled into the kitchen looking fresh and relaxed, seemingly none the worse for her experience the previous evening. She poked the range fire into life and added some wood.

'How's young Hans?' he asked.

'Much better,' came the reply over her shoulder as she stood at the sink. 'He seems normal, apart from his cut and a huge bruise, but I'll keep him in bed this morning and maybe let him up for a while later today. I'm going to give him a light breakfast of scrambled egg. Would you like some – I can put it on a slice of bread, or there's a toasting fork on the wall?'

Whilst she took Hans his breakfast Günther dressed and they sat at the table for their own meal. The coffee was *ersatz*, but still hot and welcome. There was a loud knocking. Günther dived for the Webley and cursed as she moved to open the door, right in his line of fire.

'It'll only be Carl,' she said. 'He always arrives about now.' But even so she stood well behind the door as she opened it, so that he had clear line of sight. Günther beheld a slim but wiry man who must have been in his late thirties or early forties. He looked shocked as Günther uncocked and lowered the revolver. Meta pulled him inside and he sat at the table, not taking his eyes of the soldier in the filthy uniform.

She poured Carl a cup of "coffee" and told him, without too much detail, what had happened.

Meta and Carl agreed that he would spend the day hedging and ditching, not too far from the house. After he had gone she produced a tin bath that had been hanging on a nail in the farmyard and started heating two huge kettles of water on the range.

'You can fetch some more,' she ordered as she poured the boiling contents into the bath. 'It takes four hot ones and then two cold. You might not need all that though, you're bigger than me and my little Hans put together,' she said, smiling.

Günther found the thought of a naked Meta in the bath just slightly disturbing, so without further ado he grabbed the kettles and retreated to the pump in the yard.

Fifteen minutes later she produced a piece of flannel, a thin but quite large towel and a small block of carbolic soap.

'I'll go and see to Hans,' she told him. 'When you are ready, call me and I'll come down with some things for you to try on. Just wrap the towel round you – don't you dare put back on anything you are wearing now.'

With that she left him to the first bath he had been able to take since March. After which he was clean and the water absolutely filthy with a fair scum of soapy filth on the surface. Standing, he used the remaining water in one of the kettles to rinse himself off.

She came downstairs to find him in front of the fire in the range, looking rather self-conscious with just a towel wrapped round his middle. Günther reminded himself that she had been married, so was probably a lot less embarrassed than he was. In truth, she did not look surprised at all. Matter-of-factly she held some clean, serviceable underwear against him. The long johns and long-sleeved vest looked about right. As did a pair of good working trousers, a couple of shirts and a jacket with large, square pockets. The latter looked as though it might have been her husband's Sunday best.

'I'm going to leave you to get dressed,' she told him. 'I don't think I am going to need my sewing things, so if they all fit well enough, I'll make you up a bundle with some more clothes from upstairs.'

'Please could you roll them,' he asked, 'so that I can tie them more easily onto Grane? But perhaps not just yet,' he added. Meta smiled as she turned away – then turned back.

'What are you going to do with the uniform?' she asked.

'Could we just wash out the jacket?' he replied. 'We could use it to wrap round the other clothes. I have some papers authorising me to make my own way home, and if I keep some of my uniform as well it proves what unit I was in and no-one could argue that I was a deserter.'

She instantly understood the wisdom of this. But also, it was good to know that he was quite different from the scum who had almost violated her.

Seated at the table, clean, no longer malodorous and dressed in his "new" civilian clothes, Günther felt more comfortable than he had at any time in the Army.

'What are you going to do?' she asked.

'In a few minutes, I'm going to go out and groom and feed Grane,' he told her. 'He could do with a rest, we have been living rough since leaving the front. Could I perhaps stay her for a couple of days? If you would rather, I could move into the barn. I won't use up your rations, I have my own, and I could work for the roof over my head – I'm a farmer's boy. And I can pay for my keep: I have some money.' In order not to hurt her feelings, he did not tell her that he was the son of an estate owner.

'No,' she said flatly, 'you'll stay in the house. Hans can move in with me and you can have his room. As for the rations, we'll make out. And to be honest, I would be glad to have you stay for a few days whilst our Army passes by – it would be a huge relief not to have to worry about what nearly happened last night.' She placed her hand on his then drew it back quickly, but it was a clear sign that she wanted him to stay.

He spent most of the morning in the barn with Grane. After a light lunch of bread and cheese, he suggested that he take the *Gewehr 98* and try his hand at hunting – this far back from the front the wildlife had not been decimated.

'Hans had a shotgun,' she told him. 'It's upstairs. Silly really, I should have kept it down here. But there are only a few shells – or whatever you call them. Would that be any good?'

It most certainly would. Even if he didn't have any luck with the rifle he might be able to pot a rabbit, and almost certainly wood pigeon as they were flighting home to roost.

In the event the rifle had the range for a good buck hare. As dusk came down he settled on the edge of a small wood. There were not many cartridges so he tried to line up the birds, one behind the other. Four cartridges later he had seven good sized pigeon. When he put his bag on the kitchen table Meta jumped and clapped her hands, making no effort to disguise her glee.

Emerging from the cellar, she had two bottles of red wine, one in each hand. 'Hans loved a glass of wine,' she recalled sadly, 'even though we didn't have it very often. And alone with our son, I couldn't bear to open any.' She placed a corkscrew and two glasses, green German ones with short, thick, twisted stems, on the table. 'I'll do a pigeon casserole tonight,' she said, 'and in the morning, I'll gut and marinade the hare. We only have root vegetables, though.'

Hans reached into his pack and produced two tins of peas. 'Don't tell anyone,' he grinned, 'but these have been donated by the British '

He watched as she efficiently lifted the skin and feathers above the breastbone, then snipped and peeled back so that she could cut away two whole breasts from each bird. The rest of the carcasses she plucked and drew then put into a stockpot. Nothing was wasted.

Hans came down in his nightshirt and woolly dressing gown for a light supper of the rest of the stew. A likeable and intelligent lad, he seemed little the worse for his experience. He asked question after question about the war until his mother decided that he had been up for long enough, and anyway, Günther deserved to enjoy a glass of wine in peace.

It took a while for the meal to cook, but eventually they savoured the gamey taste of the pigeon breasts poached in stock, with vegetables. 'Thank you,' said Meta simply, 'I haven't enjoyed a meal like that since before the war.' There was a sadness in her voice. But her spirits lifted as they finished the wine.

'Can you use a shotgun?' he asked as they washed up together, Günther drying the dishes. She shook her head. 'Not really.'

'If you like, I'll give you some lessons in the morning,' he offered. 'I should show you how to use the *Gewehr* as well. I doubt you will have any more trouble, but you could keep both of them near you at night.'

'*Ja, ja,* it makes sense,' she replied after a moment's hesitation. 'But first, in the morning, I have to do some washing. That blanket you used last night smells as bad as you did. And I'm not wrapping that filthy old uniform jacket round clean clothes.'

Later she lifted Hans from his bed and took him to her own room. 'I hope you don't mind,' she said, 'but I can change the sheets in the morning.'

He didn't. It was luxury. The first bed in over six months. Still with the Webley to hand, and with the *Gewehr 98* and the shotgun leaning against the wall, he slept the sleep of the dead.

He spent a couple of hours next morning in the barn, feeding and grooming Grane, checking and polishing his tack. He also stripped, cleaned and oiled the shotgun, Webley and *Gewehr 98* – the previous owner had not kept it in the cleanest condition. After lunch Meta took him to a field not far from the house, where they set up a target. After a few practice rounds she was able to hit a cardboard box fairly consistently at one hundred meters. But it was unlikely that she would ever need the weapon. The shotgun would be far more effective at close range.

It was a 16-gauge double-barrel hammer model, built around the turn of the century by the German firm, Kettner.

Typical of a serviceable but not overly expensive gun owned by a farmer, it had the advantage of being light in weight – ideal for someone of her build. Perhaps it had been a gift for a teenage Hans. He explained that it was important to pull the gun firmly back into the shoulder, otherwise she would be bruised by the recoil. Also – although there was nothing to practise on – he went through the theory of not stopping when she was tracking a moving target, but following through as she pulled the trigger. Unused to firearms, Meta's left hand was all over the place, so from behind he put his arms around her to correct the stance. Nothing was said, but Günther found the gesture strangely intimate. He stepped back the instant she was holding it properly. He let her fire off one cartridge, to know what it would be like, then they went back to the farmhouse.

'When do you plan to leave?' she asked, as she was making soup with vegetables and the stock from the carcasses of last night's pigeons. 'Before he went home Carl told me he spent some time watching the Army go past today. There are still a few units – companies or regiments or whatever you call them – but not as many as the last few days.'

Günther thought this through. 'Grane would be a lot better for another day's rest and a night in a dry barn,' he offered. 'Could we stay another day? But I would like to be on the way home again, perhaps first thing in the morning the day after tomorrow?'

'I'll be sorry to see you go,' she said thoughtfully, 'but I feel safer now and I shall be more careful in future. The door will stay locked, even during the daytime, and at least I now know how to use the shotgun.'

The following morning, he wrote a letter to his parents. 'I don't have a stamp,' he told her, 'but I want to leave you some money to help out… pay for my keep. Next time you go to the village, could you post it for me?'

Günther spent a couple of hours watching the main supply

route. Traffic was thinning all the time, till it was almost non-existent. There was nothing more to be served by delaying his departure.

Meta had made a special effort that evening. There was more wine and jugged hare, followed by a local cheese and fresh apples from the small orchard. The mood was relaxed and they chatted easily.

'What will you do,' she asked, 'now that the war's over, I mean?'

'Don't know,' he said honestly, opening his hands. 'But I'm interested in the way mechanisation is changing the way we work the land. I would like to learn more about it.'

In easy companionship, they talked of farming and nibbled at more apple and bits of cheese. Meta had fetched a second bottle of wine. Unused to the warmth and the alcohol, Günther was beginning to feel drowsy.

'Be back in a minute,' she said matter-of-factly, and disappeared upstairs. She was back after a couple of minutes, but offered no explanation.

The dishes done and the wine finished, they were both ready for bed. Meta lit a candle. Günther stood aside whilst she climbed the staircase, then followed. She was waiting on the tiny landing.

He started towards what had been Hans' room, but she took his hand. 'Don't think ill of me...' she said softly. 'I was married to a good man, but it has been a long, long time.'

Gently but firmly she led him into her own room. 'Hans is back in his own bed,' she said quietly, 'and in case you are worried, your revolver is on the bedside table and the other two weapons are leaning against the wall.'

He could just make them out in the peripheral loom from the candle.

Meta blew it out and stood in the moonlight. Slowly she removed her shawl then untied the cotton at the top of her blouse. Günther stood, transfixed, his heart pounding. 'I think this is your first time?' she asked softly, stepping out of her heavy skirt. Feeling like an embarrassed schoolboy, Günther could only lower his head.

'They say,' she said quietly, 'that you never, ever, forget the first time.' She was naked now. He could not take his eyes off the beauty of her body – the plump breasts and pale pink nipples, the tangle of ash-blond hair at her groin.

'You will live your life, Günther Raschdorf,' she told him, 'and I wish you all joy and happiness. But you will never forget your Meta, who thanks you so much.'

CHAPTER 5

When he opened his eyes Günther found himself alone under a thick quilt and blankets. Daylight streamed into the room. There was a large, floral patterned basin on a marble-topped stand by the window. Next to it stood a matching ewer full of water. He washed and dressed and found Meta in the kitchen. There was no sign of little Hans, who presumably was still in bed. The letter to Günther's parents was propped up on the mantelshelf.

'Are you hungry?' she asked. He wasn't, not after a feast of hare and vegetables. There was no mention of the previous evening. There seemed to be a mutual acceptance that it had been wonderful but a transient lovemaking. He smiled, and she smiled back. 'I have to tack up Grane,' he said gently.

When he came back into the kitchen there was a cloth bag on the table, the neck closed with a draw string.

'Take it,' she told him. There's some cold hare, a sausage and some bread and cheese. Oh, and a bottle of wine. Will you be able to open it?' He nodded – there was a small corkscrew on a rather fine pearl-handled pocket knife he had liberated when the *Stosstruppen* raided the supply depot. That and a Webley were all he had to show for eight months at war.

'I'm going now,' he said softly, picking up the bag. 'Thank you for everything.' She reached for his shoulders and pulled him down to her. They kissed, just once and tenderly, her lips no more than brushing his. Then she released him. 'I'm not coming out,' she whispered, 'take care of yourself, Günther Raschdorf, and think of me once in a while.'

'As you said last night,' he replied with a wistful half-smile, 'how can I ever forget you?'

He turned and walked into the farmyard. Meta was not in the doorway but he could see her through the window standing at the sink. Grane stomped a foreleg, anxious to be off after a few days in the barn. Settled in the saddle, Günther held his mount on a firm rein and gave a hesitant half-wave as they walked off. She did the same, then he was past the window and she was gone.

It was good to be on the road again, although he had left Meta and little Hans with a heavy heart. But she was young and attractive and would hopefully find happiness again. And in truth, Günther did not see himself as the proprietor of a farm that was little more than a smallholding. But he would always owe something to Meta Bielefeld.

It was cloudy, but thankfully not raining. Grane was fresh and they made good progress that day. Now, back in his own country, when he asked for shelter in a barn, he was often invited into the house for a night. Sometimes he stayed for two, to rest Grane and put in a day's work by way of payment. From time to time he bought oats to supplement Grane's feed. His own rations he either purchased from farmers or from a village shop when he was passing through. Only a couple of times was he asked by the local police who he was and where he was going. The papers he had with him, and the fact that he still had part of his uniform, were accepted without question. He bypassed the mighty cathedral city, although it would have been nice to have bought a small bottle of *Eau de Cologne* for his mother, and headed off through North Rhein-Westphalia towards Hannover. It was a cold, damp but mild morning when he and Grane trekked wearily up a long drive bordered on both sides by mature poplar trees. Stiff and cold, Günther eased his stomach onto the saddle and slid wearily to the ground. Home at last.

The front door flew open. His father stood there for a few seconds, but his mother lifted her skirts, raced down the steps and threw her arms around him, sobbing with joy. Dieter Raschdorf followed his wife and took Günther's hand from his mother's back, clasping it tightly in his own and embracing both with his other arm. He bellowed for a groom to take Günther's horse. Still holding each other, with Günther in the middle, arms tightly round waists, the three of them walked slowly up the steps and through the double doors of the big house.

Inge Raschdorf dried her tears on a handkerchief, stepped back and looked at her son. Dieter Raschdorf was not crying, but his eyes had welled up. 'Thank God you wrote to us,' he said. 'I tried every contact I could to find out what had happened to you, but all the Army were able to tell me was that you had gone into a field hospital and they didn't know which one.'

'There's a reason for that, Father,' said Günther, 'but it's a long story. Perhaps I can tell you later? What I need now is a hot bath and then perhaps an indecently large glass of your excellent *Jägermeister?*'

An hour later, wearing his own clothes, a tumbler half-filled with hunter's liqueur in hand, and toasting himself on a large padded fender in front of a roaring fire, Günther told them what had happened.

'And who was, or is, Meta Bielefeld?' his mother asked shrewdly. 'She wrote her name and address on the back of your envelope, in case it wasn't delivered.'

'A farmer's wife,' said Günther not too untruthfully. 'It was the first safe shelter I could find inside the German border.' If Inge Raschdorf was still curious about Meta Bielefeldt, she had the good sense not to show it.

Wisely, Dieter and Inge Raschdorf did not question their son too closely about the war. Only once did his father raise the subject. 'I just want you to know,' he said, 'that I was angry when you ignored my wishes and joined up, but now I am proud of what you have done.'

They left Günther to return to normality in his own good time. Mostly he went out riding or shooting on the estate. Christmas was a subdued affair – there were still shortages after the war – but his mother managed to find some carp for Christmas eve, they decorated the tree, there was roast pork on Christmas day and all the staff received a small gift to thank them for their service. Günther had eight months of Army pay, in addition to the allowance that his father had continued to set aside. Having established by post that *Oberleutnant* Gieger had been demobilised and was safely at home, Günther and his father went to the bank to arrange for the money that had been loaned to be returned. There was more than enough left over in Günther's account to buy a pair of earrings for his mother and a replacement *Meerschaumpfeife* for his father to enjoy, although he was not allowed to billow smoke in the drawing room. Inge would tolerate a decent cigar, but "not that wretched pipe thing"! She thanked Günther for his gift, which she loved, but told him that she had already had the best Christmas present in her whole life – the safe return of her only child from the war.

As the spring of 1919 morphed into summer, Günther took a more active role helping his father on the estate. One evening in late Autumn, with the harvest now gathered, the two of them settled into comfortable armchairs for a glass of cognac after dinner. 'How do you feel,' asked his father, 'now that you have been home for quite a while?'

'All right, I guess,' Günther replied, wondering where this turn of conversation was leading.

'Now that the war is well and truly over,' Dieter went on, 'I think we have to give some thought to the future. And in particular, what you are going to do with your life.' He hesitated for a moment. 'I don't mind admitting,' he went on, 'I was rather hoping that one day you would take over the estate.'

'Not for a long time yet, I hope,' Günther replied, 'but I

would like to be involved.' He paused, wanting to put things as tactfully as he could. 'Farming's got to change,' he offered. 'I saw this clearly in the war. We were beaten by greater numbers, it's true, but also by the Allies' vast superiority in mechanisation – in aircraft, in artillery, and most of all in tanks. If she is going to survive, recover and prosper Germany will have to become an industrial power.' He sipped his drink, then inclined the top of the glass towards his father to emphasise his next point.

'We lost a whole generation of men in the war. There's a shortage of manpower now, and if I am right then more and more families will leave the land and move to the cities – to industrial centres like the Ruhr. The labour that's left will become more expensive. If estates like this are going to survive,' Günther concluded, 'we must sustain our profit margins and the only way to do this is to keep labour costs down. We, too, will have to adapt. And that means we have to mechanise.'

'*Ja, ja,*' his father sighed reluctantly. 'I'm sorry to see the passing of the old ways, but I know in my heart of hearts that you are right. So, what do you propose?'

'Forgive me for asking,' said Günther, 'but this affects everything. How well off is the estate after the war, financially, I mean?'

'It was good and bad,' Dieter replied thoughtfully. 'There were problems. We couldn't get fertilizer, so productivity was down. But prices went through the roof. People came out from the cities trying to buy food and I finished up ignoring the regulations and selling straight from the farm. There was more good than bad,' he admitted, 'and right now our finances are pretty sound. Will that do for an answer?'

'In which case,' Günther replied, not wanting to press him further on a somewhat sensitive subject that had always been Herr Raschdorf senior's responsibility, 'could we afford for me to study engineering?'

His father mulled this over for a full minute. 'And afterwards,' he asked, 'what then?'

'You run the estate,' said Günther, 'and I will help but only when you want me to. At the same time, when I have learned enough, we start an engineering business. We sell farm equipment and set up a facility to service and repair it. The buildings and real estate we have already. A few years from now, we will have secured the future of our own estate and in terms of machinery there won't be anyone within a hundred kilometres of here who could compete with us.'

'Horses and men have worked the land for centuries,' his father replied wistfully. 'And Grane brought you back safely.'

Despite this rather nostalgic response Günther sensed that his argument had struck home. 'True,' he countered with a smile, 'but it took me over a month. If I knew how to fly, and if I'd had a Fokker tri-plane, I could have been home in less than a week.'

'Let's go and find your mother,' his father suggested, striking his knees and standing. 'But if you are going to study, it will have to be at the best place we can find. Normally I would have suggested the Königliche Technische Hochschule, the Royal College of Technology, in Hannover. But it must be the best part of six hundred kilometres away. Ideally you want to be able to come home for at least some of the weekends. After you have been away at the war, your mother is not going to thank me if you now disappear for a whole term at a time.'

Dieter told his son that his Christmas present that year would be a trip to Stettin, to see his tailor. 'You have grown out of just about everything you had before the war,' he told him, 'so you had better go and see old Reubenstein. He'll make you a decent outfit, a couple of suits, a hacking jacket and trousers, and you'll be needing something to go with a white tie. When you go to Stettin I'll come with you – make some enquiries. I know someone who might help... in fact I'm sure he will.'

He smiled at his son. 'You know, even at my age I'm sort of jealous, because it looks as if you are going to have to spend some time in the big city.'

Having spoken to his tailor, Dieter Raschdorf disappeared whilst Günther was measured. 'I think we can do a little better than this,' said Herr Rubenstein as he eyed the jacket that had been given to Günther. 'Does sir dress to the left or to the right?' he asked discreetly, as he ran his tape down Günther's inside leg. Afterwards, as instructed, Günther made his way to the *Ratskeller*, the municipal restaurant within the council building that was a source of pride to all major German towns and cities. He ordered a beer and waited for his father, who arrived about an hour later looking extremely pleased with himself.

'It is all in order,' he said with an air of self-satisfaction. 'I have renewed my acquaintance with Herr Dreher. He used to be an academic at the Mechanical Engineering faculty in Hannover. Now, he's the Director of a large engineering company next door to the shipyard. He's going to take you on as a sort of student-apprentice. He feels that you will probably need to study and work under him for at least two years.'

'What will that mean?' asked Günther.

'A much faster and more hands-on training than if you had gone to a technical college,' his father told him. 'They don't just repair ships, they do all sorts of general engineering as well. You will move from department to department, the shop floor, the tool making room, the drawing office and so forth. Also, he's going to arrange for you to have theoretical lessons two or three days a week. Some subjects he will teach himself, but he knows a whole raft of local academics who would welcome you with open arms as a private pupil. Most of them are retired and would be only too relieved to earn the money. I reckon that short of travelling hundreds of kilometres, this is the best engineering training that you could possibly have. In fact, it might even be better than going to college,' he concluded, taking a sip of his wine and sitting back still looking rather pleased with himself.

'Thank you so much,' Günther told his father. 'I'm grateful, but how on earth did you manage it so quickly?'

'Herr Dreher came out to the farm several times during the war, particularly towards the end,' his father replied. Things were really expensive by then and he was desperate to buy food that just wasn't available in the towns and cities. I helped him out as best I could. He gave me his card – said if ever he could return the favour, he would. He took my word for it this morning that your last school said you were pretty bright. So, all you have to do now is prove it!

'By the way,' Dieter continued, 'it's too far for you to travel each day. You'll need to lodge locally. Herr Dreher's secretary gave me a list of people who offer accommodation' – he handed over several typed pages – 'so you had better come back for a day or two and look for somewhere to stay, before you begin your studies in January.'

Not wanting to add to the expense any more than necessary, Günther took a single room at the top of a three storey house owned by the widow Hesler. She lived on the outskirts of the city, not too far from where he would work and study and just off the main road to Berlin. She took in lodgers and commercial travellers to make ends meet. Frau Hesler made clear the rules – he would have a key, but she would expect him to be home by eleven in the evening. There would be no entertaining of guests, and certainly no "ladies" – the way she stressed the word made her meaning even clearer – allowed in his room. She would provide breakfast and an evening meal, but if he was to be out for any reason she expected to be warned in good time. He would take lunch at his own expense at the factory and she understood that he would be going home most weekends. Payment would be for each term, in advance!

Frau Hesler was a rather well-built but not unattractive lady, prematurely grey, in her mid to late thirties. She had lost her husband in the war. But when Günther mentioned that he had served with the *Stosstruppen* he sensed that she warmed considerably. When he asked if it would be all right if he did not go home for the first weekend she agreed readily enough. 'You can come downstairs for a proper lunch on Sunday,' she told him quite kindly. 'I'll make us a roast. I haven't done that since my Ernst died.'

He worked all day Saturday, with just a sandwich at midday, trying to get ahead by looking at textbooks and thinking about his first assignment. But he fancied a small treat for the evening. He told Frau Hesler that he would not be in for dinner and asked her advice on where he could eat well but not too expensively. He would only want a main course and perhaps a glass of wine, he told her.

She recommended a restaurant in the local shopping district a few streets away. It offered traditional German cooking, but also – unusually – Italian food, an entirely new experience for Günther but popular with both residents of the port city and visitors alike. He ordered spaghetti with a meat and tomato sauce, something he had never tasted before. Not only was it absolutely delicious, with garlic and a strange herb, but the portion was huge and it was also cheap. All the waiters except one were men. But unusually, he was served by a young woman, who told him that the herb was oregano, not much used in German cuisine. She was strikingly beautiful. Quite tall and modestly dressed in a long black skirt, white apron and a high-necked blouse, this could not detract from an obviously athletic toned figure, high cheekbones, long, wavy chestnut hair and the greenest eyes he had ever seen. Günther was smitten.

Careful not to take advantage of his agreement with Frau Hesler, the following week Günther announced that he would be going home on Saturday morning, returning first thing Monday, but he would be out on Friday evening. He was unlucky. To his intense disappointment his was not one of her tables. But whenever he thought he could get away with it unobserved, he studied her.

Not wanting to be too obvious, and in any case Günther was reluctant to eat out more than once a week, he visited Giulio's every Friday for the next three weeks. Only once was she his waitress, when he managed no more than a few pleasantries, but finally his luck held. She was acting as the head waiter, showing customers to their table and generally helping with coats and hats on the way out.

She held his *Loden* for him, struggling with the heavy, dark green hunting coat. 'You make me feel guilty,' he told her. 'Where's Joseph tonight?'

'He's not too well,' she replied as he buttoned up against the February chill. 'I hope you enjoyed your meal,' she added with a smile. 'You're becoming quite a regular.'

Günther glanced over his shoulder. There was no one else about to leave. 'Look,' he began nervously, 'I would very much like to speak with you. Please don't think me too forward, but could we do that, just for a few minutes, perhaps after you have finished here?' It had come out as something of a nervous stutter. He felt rather foolish.

But to his relief she smiled. 'I finish here at ten, when we close,' she told him. 'If you don't mind waiting, you may walk me to the tram stop.'

'I'll be outside,' he said instantly, realising straight away that he must have sounded like an over-eager schoolboy.

'Give me back your coat,' she suggested, 'then return to your table. I'll arrange for you to have a cup of coffee – it will be on the house.'

Other people were curious, several were looking at him now. His face reddened. This was worse than anything that had happened in the war. But he did as he was told. She spoke to his waiter, who returned a few minutes later with a coffee and a small glass of yellow liqueur. It tasted of herbs. A few minutes after ten, she put on her own overcoat and waited for him by the door, his coat over her arm. This time he put it on himself.

'Did you enjoy your nightcap?' she asked as they walked away from the restaurant.

He was beginning to think she was a little more sophisticated he had thought. 'What was it?' he asked. 'But it was good,' he added quickly. He did not want her to think him ungrateful.

'The Italians call it *Liquore Strega*,' she replied. 'We only have it because we serve Italian food,' she added, letting him down gently.

Günther realised that this was going nowhere and they would probably be at the tram stop any time soon. He stopped and turned to face her. She also stopped and turned. He took her gloved left hand in his right.

'Look,' he said with more confidence than he was feeling, 'I would very much like us to be friends. Would it be permitted for me to be your escort one evening... or perhaps lunch, if you would rather?' he added quickly.

'It might be possible,' she replied. 'But I don't even know your name!'

'Oh dear,' he said straight away, 'I don't think I'm doing this very well. I'm not much good with girls – young ladies,' he corrected hastily. 'There weren't any in the war... I'm Günther, Günther Raschdorf, and I'm studying engineering.'

She had guessed that he was a student of some sort. But he seemed a little older and more mature than the ones she had met previously. If he had been in the war, that explained it.

'You can call me Hannah,' she informed him, and left it at that.

'And could we… meet and be friends, I mean?' he added quickly.

'That would not be entirely up to me,' she told him. 'You would have to speak with my father.' In truth, she could probably have said '*yes*' and got away with it, but she wanted to know how genuine he was.

'How do I do that?' he queried.

'You come to the house,' she replied, 'and just ask him. Will you be coming to the restaurant again, next week?'

He would. 'Then I'll give you an envelope,' she responded. Inside will be my address. Perhaps you might like to come for *Kaffee und Kuchen* the following Sunday afternoon?' Before he could reply they had arrived at her tram stop and it was in sight, already slowing, so she boarded and gave a half wave from the window. It was only after she had gone that he realised she had directed him right round the block rather than directly from the restaurant, obviously so that they could talk. If he had been a youngster he might have skipped back to his room.

He ate at the restaurant on Thursday evening the following week. For once he was lucky, and Hannah waited on his table. But she was busy, and they exchanged only a few words. This time he tried a spaghetti with a clam-based sauce – billed as *Spaghetti alle Vongole*. Again, it was delicious and not expensive. But when – with a lovely smile – she removed his plate, there was a small envelope underneath containing a card. On it she had simply written '*4 p.m., Hannah, 7 Gutenbergallee – take the same tram and the driver will announce the stop.*'

He thought for a while about what to wear. She was working as a waitress, so the last thing he wanted to do was embarrass her family by being overdressed. But he wanted to impress Hannah by looking his best. In the end, he settled for a good daytime but weekend suit of green, thorn-proof cloth.

They were almost at the end of the line and he was beginning to be a bit concerned until the driver intoned *'Gutenbergallee'* to his passengers.

As the *Allee* suggested, it was a broad, tree-line road also off the way to Berlin but right on the outskirts of the city. It was not what he had expected. For a start, it was clearly a well-to-do district with substantial three storey houses each set back from the road and well separated from adjacent properties. He found number seven, but there was no brass name-plate on the substantial, brick, double gate pillars. There was a separate pedestrian entrance to one side, which was not locked. He began to wonder whether she worked there as a member of the domestic staff, as well as working evenings in the restaurant. He decided to play safe and rang the bell to the servants' and tradesman's entrance round to one side. A maid in black uniform and white apron opened the door.

'Herr Raschdorf?' she enquired, bobbing a tiny curtsy.

'Ja,' he replied, removing his hat. 'To see Hannah, if you please.'

He would probably be asked to wait whilst she was summoned. Perhaps her father also worked here as a butler or something.

'Miss Hannah,' she said, emphasising the first word, 'thought you might announce yourself here. But she would prefer that you did not enter via the kitchen. If sir would like to go to the front door, I shall be waiting to admit you.'

'Er... yes,' he stammered, feeling rather foolish. By the time he got there she had beaten him to it. The door was open and she bobbed another curtsy.

'Please follow me, sir,' she invited. He was shown to a small drawing room expensively and tastefully furnished. Hannah rose from a silk covered chaise longue and held out a gloved hand. Automatically, as he had been taught, he clicked his heels and brushed it with his lips.

'I'm so glad you could come,' she said with a twinkle in her eyes. 'Forgive me, but I thought you might knock on the wrong door. I'm afraid Heidi was lying in wait for you.'

'I'm not sure I understand,' he said. It came out rather more firmly than he would have wished, but in truth his pride was feeling just that little bit dented.

She didn't explain. Instead, she took his hand in hers and pulled him gently towards the door. 'Come and meet Father,' she said simply.

Hannah knocked on a set of huge oak double doors. '*Bitte komm, Liebling,*' echoed a heavy male voice. Hannah led him into a large study, shelved and lined with books so that it was also a library. Her father was seated on a captain's chair behind a partner's desk. Courteously, he rose and walked round to offer his hand. He was wearing plain dark grey trousers and a fine black velvet smoking jacket.

'You are Herr Raschdorf,' he said pleasantly. 'My Hannah has told me of you.'

The use of the affectionate possessive was not lost on Günther. 'Good afternoon, Sir,' he managed politely. Another click and bow.

Armchairs and a sofa confronted a warm log fire. Hannah's father waved an arm. 'Please be seated,' he suggested genially. 'Thank you for coming to see me. I know you were invited for coffee and cake, so that's what you must have. But I'm not so fond of it myself. Perhaps afterwards, you'll join me in a glass?' He turned to his daughter. 'Hannah, would you be so kind?'

'Of course, *Vati*,' she replied, smiling at Günther as she swished her long skirts and walked out of the room.

There was a bell pull on the wall. She could equally well have used it. Günther knew that this had been pre-arranged.

'So,' the older man began, 'I understand that you wish to become acquainted with my daughter?'

'Yes, Sir.' Günther had recovered somewhat by now. He saw no point in being anything other than straightforward. Her father could either agree or ask him to leave.

'You will forgive me for wanting to meet you and being protective,' came the reply, 'but since my wife died, Hannah is all I have. I would not want her to be hurt in any way.'

'Sir, Hannah and I don't really know each other,' said Günther simply, 'but I hope I would never do that. You don't need me to tell you,' he went on, 'that she is both an unusual and a lovely young lady. I know I like her, very much, and I hope she will come to like me. That's probably all I should say, for the present.'

The youngster wasn't afraid to stand his corner, thought the older man. 'Hannah said you were in the army?' he asked. 'What did you do?'

'*Stosstruppen,*' Günther replied simply. 'But I was only old enough to join at the last minute – as a private soldier.'

'And how old are you now?' came the instant response.

'I shall be nineteen this coming April, Sir,' Günther replied without thinking. Then he realised that he had fallen into a trap.

'So, you were underage when you enlisted,' came the instant summation. Günther realised that Hannah's father had a mind like a razor. He wondered whether he had ever been a lawyer. Günther decided to let it rest – not to say anything.

'And what do you do now?' the older man asked. Günther told him in as few sentences as possible.

'And where do your people farm?' came the next question. But Günther recognised that this was no more than gentle probing from a kindly father concerned only for his daughter.

'East of here, Sir,' he replied, 'over towards the border.' The last thing he wanted was to come across as boastful, but that said he thought it important that he defended his family. Their situation had to be a concern for Hannah's father, who was only looking after his daughter's best

67

interests. 'We farm our own hectares, but some of the land is let to tenants.'

Those few words said it all. 'So, what do you propose with my daughter, young man?' he asked kindly.

'Would you allow me to take Hannah out for dinner... or lunch, Sir, if you would rather?' he added quickly.

'Either,' came the unexpected response. 'I'm not even going to lay down any stipulations. You seem to me to be the sort of young man who will look after her and bring her home at a respectable hour. And she knows what that is as well as you do,' he added with a smile.

'But there is one thing you must be aware of,' he went on, 'Hannah has not told you her surname. It is, as is mine: Rosenthal. We consider ourselves good Germans. But we are also of the Jewish faith.'

He stood and tugged at the tasselled bell-pull on the wall. 'I am not going to take coffee and cake with you, Herr Raschdorf, but Hannah will return in a few seconds and then, if you wish, refreshments will be served. Afterwards, if you are still here, please join me for something stronger in the drawing room. But if not, I would simply like to wish you well. It can't have been easy, but thank you for paying me the courtesy of this visit.'

With that, and without looking back, he left the room. A few seconds later Hannah returned. 'Would you like to stay?' she asked simply.

Günther smiled wildly at her. He was ecstatic. 'Of course, I would,' he told her, 'and your papa has invited me for a drink afterwards. He said I could take you for dinner... if of course you would do me the honour of accepting?' he added mischievously.

CHAPTER 6

They chatted easily over Kaffee und Kuchen. She was curious to know what he had done during the war. He told her why he had enlisted in the first place. Hannah found it rather endearing that it was as much the love of his horse as his wish to fight for the Fatherland that had moved him to become a soldier.

Also, he discovered, she had a keen interest in how the Weimar Republic was looking after its war veterans, not to mention the hundreds of thousands of families who had lost their breadwinner in the service of their country. Uppermost in Günther's mind, however, was how a waitress in a modest restaurant came to be acting as the lady of what was clearly a wealthy household. But something told him that it would be impolite to ask personal questions at this early stage in their acquaintance. As if to forestall the issue, Hannah rose to her feet and suggested that it might be polite to join Father in the drawing room, because he would welcome their company

Over a glass of fine Armagnac, it was settled that he would take Hannah out on Wednesday evening – that, she told him, was her day off. But as he explained, taking his leave late on Sunday afternoon, the only establishment that he had ever been to in Stettin was Giulio's, and he presumed that she would not wish to eat at the same restaurant where she worked.

'Would it be possible,' he asked her, 'for you to choose where we might dine? Somewhere you would like to go,' he added quickly.

'Not a problem,' she said simply. Hannah walked to the side of the fireplace and rang a bell. 'Herr Raschdorf's coat, if you please, Heidi,' she requested. He thanked Herr Rosenthal for his hospitality and Hannah walked him to the hall. Heidi held his Loden.

'Thank you for coming, Günther,' she said quietly. 'Perhaps you could call for me at seven on Wednesday?' There was a brief pause. 'I shall look forward to it,' she concluded, as Heidi held open one of the two double doors.

The following Wednesday Hannah was ready, well wrapped up against the cold, when he rang the bell. They took the tram almost to the Stadtmitte, the city centre. Gli Olivi was another German-Italian restaurant offering the cuisine of both countries. The menu, he noticed, was not dissimilar from that on offer at Giulio's, but whereas the latter was a basic, value-for-money eatery, Gli Olivi was decidedly upmarket. Giulio's served a house wine. This restaurant had a wine list as long as your arm, not to mention damask table linen, silk-covered padded chairs, silverware and crystal. Nothing he couldn't cope with, not that different from home, really, but whereas Hannah had a menu without them, on his version the prices made his eyes water.

Again, the conversation was light and interesting. But when he asked if she enjoyed working at Giulio's she simply said 'Yes' and changed the subject. Clearly it was not something she wished to discuss. He noticed that she barely glanced at the menu. Declining an antipasto, she asked simply for a breaded veal cutlet and salad. He could see that it was one of the least expensive choices. Wondering whether she was being considerate, he ordered the same. When he offered wine, the sommelier at his elbow, she smiled at him and asked for the house white – her usual, please. Günther was puzzled, he hadn't seen any house wine on the list, but by then the sommelier had whisked it away. He returned with a white burgundy and poured a little for Günther to taste. It was delicious and chilled to perfection. His hand invited the waiter to Hannah's glass. With the wine set in a silver bucket on a stand alongside their table, Günther was not inclined to lift the napkin and inspect the label. But he recognised the quality that his father also served. This was definitely not house wine. They both enjoyed a gelato. Hannah declined coffee, preferring to sit and talk whilst they finished the wine. Mostly she wanted to know about his life at home, and what he would do when his studies were completed. Time just dissolved, until it was half past nine and Günther had promised that she would be home at a respectable hour. He called for the bill.

The maître d'hôtel bowed. 'Herr Rosenthal's compliments,' he informed Günther, 'and he would be grateful if you would allow him the courtesy of being your host this evening.' He bowed again and walked from the table before an astonished Günther had chance to reply. He looked at Hannah, who in turn was looking at the tablecloth but could not conceal a faint smile.

'All right,' he said not unkindly, 'I'm embarrassed. But what's going on?'

'We should be getting back,' she said, glancing at her wristwatch. 'But Father said to bring you in for a nightcap. I'll tell you everything on the way home.'

The tram was almost empty. She sat next to the window and half turned towards him. It felt strangely intimate.

'You have probably worked out by now that we... that is to say Father... owns the restaurant,' she began softly. 'He also owns Giulio's, as well as a couple of bars in the financial district of the city. They also serve lunches but they don't open in the evening.'

'Which explains why you are working there, at Giulio's, I mean,' observed Günther.

'Not entirely,' she responded. 'You see, I'm an only child. I can hardly remember my mother – she died in childbirth when I was four. My baby brother didn't survive, either. To cope with his grief, father hired a nanny and threw himself into the business.

'He's a very enlightened man,' she went on. 'I was well educated, albeit privately, and he would have allowed me to go on to university. But I guessed what he really wanted, and when I asked if I could come and work with him, he was over the moon.' She smiled at the memory. 'But he's also wise. He insisted that I start at the bottom, otherwise, he said, I would never fully understand the business and sooner or later a member of staff would take advantage and steal from us. I'm in the middle of a training programme that he devised. I worked as a commis chef at Gli Olivi for a year. Believe me, if any of our kitchen staff over-ordered to take home or sell food, I would know in an instant. And if I say so myself, I'm not a bad cook, although I don't do it at home unless I want to try out a new dish.'

Günther began to see Hannah in a new light. Most girls – young ladies – of her social standing barely knew where the kitchen was. But he thought it best not to comment.

'I've also done Front of House,' she went on after a short pause, 'and as you know I do a spot of waitressing from time to time. I've worked in the bars, too, although Father took some persuading.' She laughed. 'It was good fun, but most of the city types think that just because you're serving drinks they can be over-familiar whenever they choose. My next job is to learn the office side, so that if father wants me to, and he says he does, one day I can help him to manage the business.'

She had chosen the restaurant deliberately to spare him the expense, Günther realised. And he knew now why she had barely glanced at the menu. In her time, she had probably cooked her way through the entire list. As for the "house wine", her choice had probably been given to the sommelier before they arrived.

It was a short walk from the tram stop to the house.

Günther stayed long enough only to enjoy a glass of Armagnac with Herr Rosenthal and to thank him profusely for his hospitality, particularly at the restaurant. Hannah showed him out herself, Heidi having long since been sent off duty. He paused by the door.

'Thank you for this evening,' he said quietly, 'I have enjoyed it very much. Could we perhaps meet again? And this time, you will be my guest.'

'I would like that too,' she said with a smile. 'Let me talk to Father – perhaps you could come for lunch or dinner one day soon?' She offered her hand, palm down. Günther's lips brushed it for just a half second longer than was strictly decorous but she did not seem to mind.

When Hannah rejoined her father, he wanted to know all about her evening. 'If you don't tell me,' he teased, 'I shall find out everything from the staff.'

'Well,' she said with a laugh, 'thank you for the kind gift of our meal. But all they could tell you is that we each enjoyed a Schnitzel, an ice cream and a bottle of your best white burgundy!'

He was not to be put off. 'Even if he's not one of us, he seems a well brought up young man,' he persisted. 'How did you get on?'

'Vati,' she said seriously, deliberately using the diminutive, 'I like him. In fact, I think I might come to like him rather a lot. Will that do for now?'

'Hmmm,' muttered her father under his breath, and poured himself another Armagnac. Hannah excused herself and went upstairs.

Günther reached his lodgings a few minutes after eleven. Fortunately, Frau Hesler had waited up for him. He placated her with a very edited account of his evening.

After a weekend at home with his parents Günther was disappointed when he visited Giulio's on Thursday evening

73

and she was not there. He had resolved to ask when he might see her again. But as he sipped his beer a waitress whom he knew only by sight came to his table.

'You are Herr Günther Raschdorf?' she enquired with a smile. Günther confirmed that he was. She reached for a pocket underneath her apron and offered him an envelope. 'My name is Irma. Hannah, Miss Rosenthal, said to give you this.'

He opened it immediately. In her own hand she had written:

Sorry to have missed you this evening.
I am working in the accounts office this week.
Father says please come for lunch on Sunday.
If for any reason you can't make it, Irma will let me know.
                                                                    Hannah

From the grin on his face, Irma, who was still standing there, guessed that there wouldn't be a reply. 'Thank you very much, Irma,' he said. 'That's fine... in fact, that's more than fine.' Still she stood there. 'There's no message,' he told her.

'I'm not waiting for a message,' she replied with a knowing smile. 'I'm waiting to see if you want to order.' The decor wasn't Gli Olivi, but the breaded cutlet tasted every bit as good.

Hannah was nowhere to be seen when Heidi showed Günther into the drawing room. 'You'll take a glass of fino?' her father asked. The sherry was very pale, very dry and just the right temperature. Günther resolved to raise an issue that had been troubling him since he had first met and rather fallen for Hannah. 'Will we have a few minutes to talk privately, Sir?' he asked.

Herr Rosenthal indicated that they would. 'I would like to continue to see Hannah,' Günther went on, 'and you have been very courteous in inviting me to your house. But you told me that you are of the Jewish faith. And I have to tell you that I am not. I would never want to hurt Hannah's feelings or see her under false pretences. So, with the utmost respect, I feel it is only fair at this early stage to ask if this might be a problem?'

To his utmost consternation, and he suspected also to her father's, Hannah had appeared and was standing in the open doorway. She had obviously heard everything. Before either of them could say anything, she joined her father on the sofa and placed her hand affectionately on his knee. 'May I answer, please Father?' she said gently.

Taking his silence for assent, she turned back towards Günther. 'My mother was religious,' she began, 'and she followed our customs closely. Although as a family we were Jewish, dear Father was not particularly observant, but he was happy to go along with Mama's wishes. Well... most of the time,' she added with a smile. 'So, we remembered Shabbat at sunset on Friday evenings, even though a certain person was berated for checking on his restaurant after our meal.' She paused, 'I can remember what father used to say: *"The good Lord doesn't have to earn a living. I am not so fortunate".'*

Günther noticed Herr Rosenthal's sad smile at the memory. 'We have not observed Shabbat for many years,' she went on. 'Father does not go to the synagogue any more, either. I think after my mother died he found it too painful. So yes, technically our faith is Jewish, but it is not that strong.'

'Let me continue,' said her father. 'And this is not directed at you, Günther. A couple of years ago Hannah asked me if I would prefer that she married someone of our faith. I told her that I would – if only for the sake of her mother's memory.' He paused to look directly at Günther. 'But I told her something else as well. It was that if ever there was a choice between observance of our religion and happiness, I would without hesitation want her to be happy.' He paused for a moment, as if gathering his strength. 'I have known great happiness, and for Hannah that has to come first. Does that answer your question?'

Günther was still searching for a reply when Herr Rosenthal moved to the sideboard and removed the silver and glass stopper from the decanter. 'And now,' he said, 'I hope Hannah will tell me that there is time for another glass of this excellent sherry wine before we eat.'

'You can pour me one too, please,' said Hannah, 'and whilst you two are punishing the sherry, I am going back to the kitchen to make a sauce.' She picked up her glass and walked to the door. 'Don't panic, gentlemen,' she said with mock irritation, 'I'll take my time and stir it slowly.'

Hannah rejoined them in time for Heidi to place a chafing-dish on the sideboard. On it were three poussins, spatchcocked and halved, covered in a cream sauce and surrounded by a selection of vegetables.

'You are honoured, my boy,' said Herr Rosenthal, serving himself after Hannah and Günther. 'She doesn't even cook for me these days!'

'I wanted to try out a new dish,' she replied. 'Tell me what you think of the sauce? Although whenever I take over the kitchen, cook goes into a sulk for at least the rest of the day!'

Her father put an index finger in the sauce on his plate and licked it off, smacking his lips appreciatively.

'Father!' admonished Hannah.

'Once a chef, always a chef,' he said simply. 'But the sauce is good – it has a hint of game.'

'I used a woodpigeon to make the stock for it,' she told him. 'I think it's more interesting than just a plain cream sauce and it flavours the poussins ever so slightly.'

Despite his daughter's protest her father did the same thing again. 'I like it,' he concluded, 'this could go on the German section of the menu in Gli Olivi.'

Hannah turned to Günther. 'I don't want to seem too pleased with myself or to be immodest,' she said with a smile, 'but in this house the praise doesn't come any higher than that!'

Günther had never tasted anything quite like it. 'Thank you for making it,' he said sincerely. 'It's absolutely delicious.'

The rest of the year nineteen hundred and twenty, after the horrors of war, was the happiest Günther had known. Most Sundays he was invited for lunch. Often, they walked in Stettin's parks and occasionally hired horses from a local stables for a hack into the country. By the end of the year, with Christmas approaching, Günther knew that he had to introduce Hannah to his parents. Actually, there was more to it than that – he also knew that he had met the woman with whom he intended to spend the rest of his life.

'She's a what?' asked his mother, when Günther told his parents that Hannah's family were Jewish.

'Calm down,' soothed his father. 'I'm sure they are also good Germans. And we should respect Günther's choice. If he is old enough to fight for the Fatherland, he's old enough to choose a wife. Have you asked her yet?' he turned to his son.

Günther shook his head. 'I wanted you to meet Hannah first,' he told them.

'And so we shall,' said his father kindly. 'If you would like to bring her here for a weekend, she will be made most welcome. Will she not, my dear?' he asked pointedly. 'After all,' he went on, 'my parents were not that pleased when I told them that I wished to ask you to be my wife. But we have been happy, have we not?'

Günther knew that whereas his father's family had been wealthy "gentlemen farmers", people who hoped that he would marry someone with the prospect of inheriting land, his mother's parents had been rather more middle-class and not of the same social standing.

'I'm sorry,' his mother said quietly. 'It came as a bit of surprise, that's all. So, bring your Hannah here,' she told him, 'and let's see if she approves of us country folk.'

They loved her. That Christmas he had arranged to stay in Stettin for the festivities, then they would go to his parents for New Year. Presents were opened on Christmas Eve. For some reason, Hannah noticed, her father absented himself for a few minutes when Günther handed her a beautifully wrapped small box. Inside was a ring – a large square sapphire surrounded by diamonds. 'Will you marry me?' he asked simply. She pulled him to his feet, threw her arms round his neck and whispered 'Yes, yes, yes!' in his ear. 'But have you spoken to father?' she asked anxiously.

He had. A while back. Herr Rosenthal had been delighted. His only comment, although there were tears in his eyes, was 'I hope she has the good sense to accept.'

They decided to wait until Günther had finished his studies before they married. In the meantime, Günther's father had a small but very pleasant cottage built on the estate. 'You'll take over the big house one day, my boy,' he told him, 'then you can let this one out for extra income. But it'll do for now.'

Towards the end of nineteen twenty-one, Hannah became Frau Günther Raschdorf. They could marry neither in Hannah's local synagogue nor the Raschdorf's local church, not that Günther's parents were regular attendees anyway. But as a favour and mark of respect for Herr Raschdorf senior, the civil ceremony was not conducted in the local Standesampt. Instead, the registrar formalised the marriage in the main drawing room of the Raschdorf residence.

Herr Rosenthal was clearly disappointed at not being able to host the ceremony himself, so when he took Günther's parents to one side and begged to be allowed to host the wedding feast they agreed instantly. A small army of chefs and assistants, together with a veritable cartload of provisions, descended from Stettin to the Raschdorf estate. After the ceremony, which was attended by only the immediate family, the wedding party and every one of the estate's workers and their family settled down in the barn for a meal that – even to Günther's parents, never mind the assembled guests – was of a standard most of them had never experienced, nor ever would again. It was the talk of the village for weeks.

Just before Christmas Günther's mother handed him a letter that had been addressed – fortunately – to the estate house. Opening it, he saw immediately that it was from Meta Bielefeld – she must have copied the address from the letter he left with her to post to his parents. She began by hoping that he was keeping well and wishing him greetings of the season. In a firm, educated hand, she went on:

> ...*I am also writing to tell you that by the time you receive this letter I shall be Frau Meta Holtzer. Klaus is older than I and lost his wife a few years ago. He has no children of his own, but has been very kind to Hans and Gisela – she was born in August just over two years ago, and I wanted a name beginning with this letter in memory of the help that you gave us. She is a beautiful little girl.*
>
> *Klaus is the assistant manager of a local bank, and he will sell his own house so that we can develop the cottage and land, which will become more of a country home than a small farm. Perhaps in time we may even be blessed with children of our own.*
>
> *Thank you again for all that you did for us. I shall always remember you – may you have a happy life.*
> *Meta*

From the date of her birth and the hint given so clearly, Gisela was his daughter, although Meta had made no claim upon him and was telling him that neither would she do so in future. It sounded as though Klaus was a man of some means and although he had known nothing of her life since 1918 Günther was relieved that Meta's future – and now that of his daughter – seemed secure. Wisely, he said nothing that might put his own new-found happiness at risk and simply filed the letter inside one of the engineering text books in his study.

But in contrast to the joy of his own marriage, Günther was keenly aware that it was a terrible time for the Weimar Republic. With the onset of war Germany had suspended the convertibility of its currency into gold. And whereas countries such as France had financed the war through taxation, Germany did it by borrowing from its own citizens, with the aim of making defeated allies make up the deficit afterwards. But the Fatherland lost the war, and the mark fell from 4.2 to the US dollar at the beginning to 8.9 at the end. As 1919 became 1920 it took 32 paper marks to buy one US dollar. Germany printed money to pay for imposed reparations, and by the autumn of 1922 a dollar cost 320 marks.

Initially the effect upon the unionised workers in the great industries that survived the war was limited – they could strike to secure a living wage. Business, able to borrow and then pay back in devalued currency, prospered, at least at first. But for the retired on a fixed income, and those working on the land or in unskilled employment, inflation was devastating. Over the second half of 1922 the cost of living index rose from 41 in June to 685 in December. The elderly, who before the war had set aside sufficient funds to ensure a modest retirement, were starving. Many committed suicide.

Günter's father held a meeting of the estate workers in the barn. 'I can pay you with worthless money, he told them, but for now we are all in a desperate struggle for survival. That said,' he went on, 'we have one priceless asset – the land. My proposal is that until this crisis is over, as far as is possible, we abandon the use of money. Together we will work the land and grow enough to feed ourselves. I will try to work out a fair and alternative system of payment, perhaps a little money but mostly in slaughtered meat, cereals, vegetables and milk, so that your families can at least have enough to live. This stupid crisis has to end some time, but until it does, no-one on this estate will die of starvation.'

The proposal was accepted gratefully. But during the spring and summer of nineteen twenty-two, in their newly built three-bedroomed thatched cottage, Hannah had other things to think about. It was neither an easy confinement nor a trouble-free birth, but almost nine months to the day after their wedding, Hannah gave birth to their daughter. Renate was a happy baby, but the local doctor did voice a fear privately to Günther that his wife might not conceive again. For her part, Hannah had insisted on a name that was German and not Jewish. Having read of the latest pogroms further east, she knew that there was an undercurrent of anti-Semitism. Hannah kept her concerns to herself but there was no harm in being careful.

One morning the local carter arrived with an item that Günther had ordered from Stettin. Feeding their daughter, Hannah watched as her husband assembled the delivery. 'It's a draughtsman's board,' he told her. 'I'm going to try to design something.' He watched, fascinated and utterly happy, as Hannah transferred their daughter from one breast to the other.

'Let's start at the beginning,' he told her. 'At the moment, we use horses on the estate. They are expensive to buy and they cost a lot to feed: you need at least two hectares to grow enough for each animal. This is land that you can't use for any other purpose, like growing profitable cash crops.'

'I thought steam engines were coming in,' she replied. 'Your father was talking about them only the other day.'

'So he was,' Günther agreed. But they are not very efficient. Some of them rely on a belt system to drive a threshing machine, but once they are up and running – and that takes a while – they are really just static engines. Others can move under their own power, pulling a plough, but they are just one-purpose devices – two wheels, an engine in front, a plough behind and a seat mounted up high and in between. Hannomag make one, the WD 80 horse power Grosspflug with a four-cylinder petrol engine, but it's a hell of a size, it costs a fortune and all it can do is plough. It's not very versatile.'

Hannah was aware of the Hannoversche Maschinenbau AG, one of the major engineering employers in that city. Come to that, its directors were occasional visitors to Stettin and hence to the restaurant. 'So what are you thinking about?' she asked automatically, her attention more on Renate than the drawing board.

'I'm going to design a four-wheeled pulling machine, a tractor!' he told her. 'It will have a pulley wheel, so it can power static machinery with a belt drive, like the steam engines in use now. But it will also be able to pull other devices, like a cart, as well as a plough or a rake. Maybe I could design some sort of drilling device that would even sow the seed. Men are leaving the land for the industrial centres anyway, so this way we save on labour, we free up land that doesn't have to grow food for horses, and when it's not being used a tractor would not need to be fed and groomed – it just sits in the barn. It has to be the future for agriculture,' he finished enthusiastically.

Günther used every last ounce of knowledge from his engineering course and then some. He welded a chassis and added two axles and four wheels – two large ones at the back to drive the machine over soft fields and two smaller ones at the front connected to a steering wheel. The clutch and drive mechanism was straightforward – the designs existed already. There were no gears, just a hand throttle. He chose an existing

Benzolmotor of around thirty-five horse power. The design for a six-bladed plough to be towed behind he gave to a local blacksmith, who welded and hammered it out in a week. What he did not tell Hannah was that he had used his own money to finance the prototype. If this design did not work, he would have used up every Pfennig he had to his name and would have to go cap in hand to his father.

The day for the demonstration was set. The first field had been harvested. Normally it would have been ploughed in the spring. But then, it would take a farm hand with a gang plough and five horses more than three hours to till one hectare. Plus, of course, the time taken to harness and then return and groom the animals – effectively a day's work.

Perhaps unwisely, thought Günther, his father had invited some of the tenant farmers to watch. Hannah was there, too, with Renate well wrapped up against the autumn chill. Günther had pre-positioned the plough. Cautiously he reversed up the tractor, attached the towing bar and set off. This was a bit tricky, because his rather simple clutch plate system moved the tractor in a series of short jerks, but eventually he succeeded.

The field was as well-ploughed as any horse drawn team could have achieved. But more to the point, when Günther jumped down from his tractor to shake hands with his father and kiss a beaming Hannah, he had ploughed the entire hectare in forty-five minutes.

The small group of half a dozen tenants were not men given to compliments, but Günther sensed that they were impressed. 'How much?' asked one grizzled old farmer bluntly, nodding at Günther's machine.

'Don't know yet,' he replied honestly. 'I'll have to cost it up. But you'll have a choice. You can borrow to buy your own tractor, paying for it with the extra land freed up because you don't have to fodder horses. Or you can rent the use of it, with a driver if you don't feel confident to do it yourself. But I'll give you all the financial facts as soon as I can. Had to make sure that *Die verdammte Maschine* worked first!'

'Your damned machine certainly does work,' his father told Günther enthusiastically. 'Gentlemen,' he addressed his farmers courteously, 'I knew that the money spent sending my son off to study engineering would not be wasted. You are looking at a very proud father. It's been a fascinating but cold morning. Please allow me to offer a glass or two of something by way of celebration and to warm us up.'

Hannah squeezed Günther's arm then walked off with the others, carrying Renate, to take her out of the cold. He was left on his own to unhitch the plough and drive the tractor back to the barn. So much for the joys of mechanisation, he reflected, with a wry smile.

CHAPTER 7

His father agreed to finance the business, providing capital in exchange for a share of the profits – as yet to be decided. Günther would help on the farm if required, but would concentrate on expanding the new venture. They already had a suitable building – a large, two storey brick barn. Initially they would use only the ground floor.

But Günther knew that this would have to be more than a one-man operation. It was the blacksmith who introduced his brother-in-law, Herr Schneider. 'Johann has been in the merchant navy for years,' he explained to Günther when they were discussing the project over a coffee at the forge. 'He wants out, before some idiot starts another war, but he's a top-class ship's engineer. Why don't you talk to him?'

Günther was impressed. Invited into the study at the cottage, Johann wore a plain, but good, suit together with a collar and tie. His wingtip shoes were so polished you could see your face in them. They discussed the drawings, which Johann could obviously read at a glance.

'That shaft is too long, Herr Günther,' he said straight away, stabbing at the connection from the front axle to the steering wheel with a permanently oil-stained index finger. 'It'll whip and break. Won't last three months.'

'So, what would you suggest?' queried Günther, knowing in his heart of hearts that the older man was absolutely right.

'Simple,' came the reply, 'put a coupling just aft of these steering rods that connect to the front wheels. Then you'll have no more trouble. And it'll cope better with the rough ground.'

Hannah came in with some coffee and *Stollen* but made no move to leave.

'This is good, Frau Raschdorf,' said Johann appreciatively. 'Did you perhaps make it yourself?'

'We don't have a cook, Herr Schneider,' she replied, obviously pleased at the compliment. Günther suppressed a smile. Clearly his wife would be addressed as 'Frau Raschdorf'. His father would be 'Herr Raschdorf'. But in engineering terms, Johann was far more experienced. So, it would be a courteous 'Herr Günther'.

'We are going to need machinery,' Johann went on, 'and a basic metal supply. I could work out what you will need, if you wish?'

'That would be a great help,' Günther agreed. 'Perhaps if you could give it some thought, then we could look at it together. But the set-up cost does worry me, I must admit. We are not exactly over-financed.'

'So, we don't buy new,' Johann replied. 'Small firms often close down. I have a lot of contacts in Stettin. Particularly amongst the shipyards. If you wish, I shall ask around. A good second-hand lathe here, a milling machine there – I can inspect them and it shouldn't cost anywhere near as much.' He paused. 'As for metal,' he went on, 'ships come to the end of their life and are broken up all the time. But there's nothing wrong with the bulkhead plating or most of the other parts. You wouldn't have to pay any more than the price they would fetch for scrap.'

Günther was fast realising that there was a world of difference between his level of knowledge and Johann's lifetime of experience. 'It's like this, Herr Günther,' Johann explained, sensing that his prospective employer did not fully understand, 'if something breaks at sea, you don't call in at the local dealer and buy a spare part. And you can't carry enough items to cover the whole ship. So, you have a couple of machines and a few bits of metal. If a bearing shell goes, or a connecting rod breaks, you make another. Then you fit it. Don't worry; we can build your tractor.'

'I'm new to all this,' admitted Günther. 'What about wages. How much should I pay you?'

Before Johann could reply Hannah broke in. 'We have to know what the start-up costs are going to be, and then work out the production costs, the selling price and the profit margin, assuming a reasonably low build number initially but a sensible increase after that. Herr Schneider, if you would start on the metal and the machinery, I'll do the sums and work out what would be fair to both of us. Then it will be up to you to agree.'

'You can do this, Frau Raschdorf?' the older man queried.

'I worked in my father's business,' she replied. 'I've been trained to keep books and accounts. He runs a restaurant, but it doesn't matter whether you're making and selling plates of food or tractors: the principle is precisely the same!' she concluded.

Over the next two weeks they prepared a business plan. The Raschdorf estate had bought what Johann referred to as 'one of them horseless carriages'. Which was in fact a 1918 Daimler Marienfelde 3 ton truck, made for the Army but never taken into service. Its four-cylinder gasoline engine gave it a top speed of around 50 kilometres an hour. When Johann offered to take it into the barn for a day and check it over, Dieter Raschdorf was only too pleased. 'What are you checking?' queried Günther, as his father walked back to the main house. 'I'm not,' came the reply with a grin. 'There's nothing wrong with this vehicle. But I need half a day to take the transmission apart. Compared with your tractor design, it has a much better clutch assembly. Then we can copy it,' he spread his hands palms uppermost, 'in which case we might need to change the design so that we can make it more easily ourselves. But that would be a lot cheaper than buying in complete units. There's a name for it,' he went on. 'It's called "reverse engineering".'

Günther was impressed. Without Johann, he doubted whether he would have had the skills, the contacts or the experience to put his design into production. His father called at the cottage that evening. Over a beer, Dieter Raschdorf announced that he wanted to buy a production model for the estate. 'We've already lost a couple of hands,' he explained, 'gone to work in the factories in Berlin. And some of the horses are getting on a bit. I have looked at the figures and your tractor would be a lot cheaper than hiring and buying replacements.'

'We'll come to an agreement,' Hannah replied, before Günther could say anything. 'We have to demonstrate the tractor at local fairs and ploughing competitions. Also, we should advertise. All this takes money. Let me look at the figures, but we should be able to sell you the tractor at a discount if you will lend it to us occasionally, as well as the lorry when we need to move it around. Günther and Johann can make a trailer,' she announced, without even bothering to consult her husband.

It took Günther and Johann three weeks to build a second tractor. The third was completed in two. They entered ploughing competitions as a form of advertising, as much as to win, although more often than not, they did. But what impressed everyone was that Günther completed the usual two lengths of a field before the horse-drawn teams were barely a quarter of the way up the first. Also, they handed out leaflets. Their first advertisement in a national monthly farming magazine resulted in nearly one hundred enquiries. By the end of 1927, the Raschdorf 35 production unit was making more profit than the entire estate. But as Günther, Hannah and Johann agreed, they were rapidly becoming overwhelmed – victims of their own success.

In the spring of 1928, they demonstrated the up-rated Raschdorf 40 at a major exhibition in Hannover. The well-dressed man who introduced himself was obviously a foreigner but spoke perfect *Hochdeutsch* – high German. He handed over his card and introduced himself as Charles Bloch, a Director of Derresford Inc., manufacturers of farm equipment and machinery in Plains City, Illinois, United States of America.

'You're an American,' said Günther, somewhat taken by surprise.

'First generation,' came the reply. 'But my parents immigrated from Hamburg before the war. The old folks still speak German at home.'

'So how can I help you, Herr Bloch?' Günther queried politely.

The American's head inclined towards the '40'. 'Been admiring your machinery. In fact, my company bought one of your late model 35s.'

'Thank you, but why would you have done that?' asked Günther.

'It won't surprise you to know that we are developing similar machines in the U.S.A.,' the American told him. 'John Deere and Fordson both market a tractor. But I'm sure you know that a lot of major companies from the U.S.A. are investing heavily in Germany's economy. We want to build tractors for Europe, too, and we want to do it in Germany.'

'So why don't you just import your own tractors,' said Günther, thinking out loud, 'or come to that, just build them over here?'

'Any number of reasons,' Bloch replied. 'Labour and transportation costs, an exchange rate that's highly favourable for export from here, plus a German product with a German name is more likely to appeal locally than something American, which is why, as we speak, I can tell you that there's a rumour General Motors are looking at Opel.'

This was interesting news to Günther, but what little time he had to read newspapers did not stretch to keeping up with the motor industry. 'The clincher is,' Bloch continued, 'your design is better. Sure, our engineers could tinker with it, but if we are going to do something in Europe we don't want to get dragged into any legal disputes. I am authorised to talk to you, to see if we can put something together.'

'I see,' Günther responded cautiously. 'What have you in mind?'

'We can hardly talk here,' the American countered. 'Can we set up a meeting, after the show?'

'I really need to get back to the estate,' Günther told him. 'Would you be able to come to the farm? We could pick you up from the station in Stettin. I think my father would want to be involved, as well.'

In truth, whilst he would be happy to involve his father, it was Hannah that Günther wanted in on any discussion. He was smart enough to know that whereas he might have the engineering skills, it was his wife who had the head for business. They had just installed the telephone in the main house. It was the only private one in the village. He gave Herr Bloch the number.

'That sure was a mighty fine lunch, Frau Raschdorf,' complimented the American, two days later, forgetting himself and speaking in English.

'Thank you,' she said simply. 'We can speak English if you wish, but my husband would be at a disadvantage. *Bitte, lassen Sie uns Deutsch sprechen.*'

Günther was more than a little impressed. His wife had mentioned studying English, as well as French, with her tutors. She sounded pretty much fluent.

Switching to German as she had requested, the American told her that he could not remember having such an enjoyable luncheon. 'I trained in my father's restaurant,' she told him.

'Then Herr Raschdorf is an extremely lucky man,' he responded with feeling. 'I have a good mind to send our cook over for lessons!'

They moved to the small drawing room for coffee. Günther's father had declined to join them, saying that he was feeling a bit off-colour, but they could speak later or tomorrow once they knew what the American was proposing.

Which was, he said initially, that his company wished to purchase the design rights. And they would compensate Günther handsomely if he would sell. A figure of twenty-five thousand marks was on the table – a sum that would almost set up Günther and Hannah for life.

Günther sensed that Hannah was not impressed. The American was surprised when her husband seemed content for her to reply.

'That *sounds* like a generous *opening* offer,' she said slowly, choosing her words and emphasis carefully.

'But...?' Bloch responded cautiously, seeking to draw out any reluctance.

'I know what profit we are making now,' she told him. 'After all, I do the books. So far, our chief engineer has taken on two more skilled men and an apprentice, and we can sell every tractor we make. So, the business is ripe for expansion. I would like some time to look at the figures in more detail, but I am not sure at this stage whether your offer really compensates for this.'

Listening to his wife, Günther had the good sense to keep quiet. For his part, the American realised that he was facing a highly intelligent and experienced businesswoman, not just the wife of some farmer-come-manufacturer.

'So we need another meeting, after you have had time to consider our offer,' said Bloch.

'Just give us a few days,' Hannah requested. 'But before you go, please allow me to float another idea. So far you have proposed only a lump sum.' She went on. 'There is an alternative, which is that you manufacture under license. That way you pay us an agreed sum for every machine you make to my husband's design. We would have to work out the details, but instead of paying us out with a lump sum you would be able to put the capital towards setting up your own production facility in Germany.'

The American's response was that he would have to cable his board, but such an arrangement might also be possible, although he wasn't sure.

'Give me forty-eight hours,' said Hannah. 'Then if you wish, we can meet in Stettin. My father still lives there.'

'Now,' she said, rising to her feet, 'let me be a better hostess. Would you like some more coffee, perhaps a glass of something?' She looked towards her husband.

'Have a brandy,' Günther invited, 'before I drive you back to the station.'

'When you are looking at the price, it's really not unlike buying or selling shares in a company,' she explained to Günther that evening after supper. 'There's a relationship between what you pay, what that share earns, and therefore how long it takes to recoup your original investment. It's called the price-earnings ratio. In this case he is offering us twenty-five thousand marks for the design – effectively for your business. But that's it – after that, no more earnings, ever.'

She paused to sip her wine. 'But let's assume a reasonable production quantity and a fee for us on every unit. I'll do the maths tomorrow, but if he makes a given number of tractors and we have a fee on each one, I can work out how long it would be before we get the twenty-five thousand anyway, and after that we still receive an income. My guess is that based on what he is offering now, we ought to break even in about three or four years and after that we would be in profit.'

As she set down her glass they were interrupted by a

frantic knocking on the front door. It was Frau Brantis, still in her cook's apron.

'The mistress says can you come quickly,' she gasped, still out of breath. 'It's the master – he's been taken poorly.'

Dieter Raschdorf was lying on a chaise long, a cushion under his head and covered by an eiderdown. He was breathing but unconscious.

'He collapsed just after dinner,' said Inge Raschdorf, her lips trembling with fear. 'I've sent to the village for *Doktor Dorn*.'

An hour later, with the doctor's permission, Günther – with a little help from the doctor and Hannah – carried his now semi-conscious father to bed. He and Hannah left the doctor and his parents and waited anxiously in the drawing room.

They reassembled three quarters of an hour later. 'I have given your father a thorough examination,' Dr Dorn began, 'and it is my firm diagnosis that he has suffered a stroke. This accounts for some difficulty with movement, particularly on his left-hand side, and also the slackness of his facial muscles on that same side. And his blood pressure is elevated. I have given him some medication, and he may need to be taken to the hospital in Stettin, but for now he is probably more comfortable where he is rather than being subjected to quite a long road journey.'

Günther took a moment to consider the news. 'So what is your prognosis?' he eventually asked. 'What would be for the best?'

'Your father might make a full recovery,' the doctor advised, 'but I think it is more likely that he will be partially but permanently affected. I hope he will be able to resume at least some of his former life, but I would be failing in my duty if I did not tell you that it is unlikely he will ever return fully to his former self.'

Günther glanced at his mother. Inge Raschdorf had not

spoken, but she was twisting a handkerchief, tears coursing.

'He should be comfortable overnight,' the doctor said gently, 'but I would like to return and look at him again first thing in the morning.'

'Thank you, *Herr Doktor*,' said Hannah, rising to her feet. 'We will take care of him for now. Let me show you out.'

Günther and Hannah managed to put off the meeting with Herr Bloch until the following Saturday, but on Friday they sat with Inge for a family discussion.

'Dieter has some mobility, and he is fully conscious,' she began, 'but there is no way he can return to running the estate. I have to nurse him and it has been difficult this week to do that – even with help – as well as take charge of the house and supervise a midday meal for twelve people.'

She turned to her daughter-in-law. 'Hannah, my dear, I have no right to ask this of you, and if you would rather not do as I am going to ask, I shall never hold it against you.'

They were together on a comfortable sofa. Hannah placed a hand over those of her mother-in-law. 'How can I help?' she asked gently.

'I have given this a lot of thought,' Inge began. 'I can't run the estate and this household as well as look after Dieter. I think it might be time for you and Günther to take over from Dieter and me. You don't have to decide now – you will want to talk things over privately. But my dearest wish would be that you move into this house, that you and Günther assume full responsibility for the Raschdorf estate, and I will look after Dieter in the cottage.

'Neither *Doktor Dorn* nor I have any illusions that Dieter will make a complete recovery,' she went on, 'but this would allow me to nurse him and in time he may be able to give at least some help to Günther. Then he would still feel that he was making a contribution, and I think that would be important to him, for his peace of mind.'

Günther was forestalled by Hannah's reply. 'Then if that's what you wish,' she said firmly, 'that's what we will do. Please tell me when you would like to move and Günther will organise everything. As for looking after your estate workers at lunchtime, I shall start on Monday. After all,' she said, to lighten the mood, 'I used to make dinner for nearly forty covers a night in the restaurant. I wouldn't be much of a daughter-in-law if I couldn't supervise a lunch for your workers!'

Günther was overcome with a mix of emotions – love, gratitude and an immense pride in his wife.

They took the train to Stettin the following morning. Her father met them with his new Adler, which he had – only just, said Hannah not too kindly – taught himself to drive. They had lunch at the restaurant with Herr Bloch, who compared the cuisine most graciously with that available in America.

Hannah had done the maths. Bloch had been cabling back and forth. Their preference, he opened, was still to buy the design outright, and he was authorised to push the offer up to thirty thousand marks. But the board would consider a license agreement for five years, although based on their projected figures and the royalty fees the Americans were prepared to offer, the Raschdorfs would probably not be in profit until after year four. The buy-out option, he assured them, was much the better deal.

For Günther and Hannah, with all the forthcoming responsibilities of the estate, expanding their business was a non-starter. But the American did not know this. The license agreement, she said firmly, was the only way for them to go.

And besides, she knew he was bluffing. Based on what was on offer, the payback time would be three and a half years, max. She in turn pitched for a ten-year agreement. They settled on seven. Günther had already told her that after five or six years the design would probably be obsolete anyway.

But Bloch insisted that Derresford would have the right to

modify the design as they saw fit, Günther and Hannah were happy to agree. 'But a small *quid pro quo* – three, in fact,' she threw in at the end. 'First, you have to grant us a dealership, so that we can sell and service your tractors in our part of Germany. It doesn't have to be exclusive, we'll compete with anyone. But this way, we both profit.'

The American gave his word. *After all*, thought Hannah, *if you were going to buy a tractor or have it repaired or serviced, who else would you go to rather than the man who had designed it in the first place?* She had already mentally sketched out the first farming magazine advertisement.

'And the second?' asked Bloch

'I shall want access to the books, just to be sure that everything is fair to both of us,' she said bluntly. 'And finally,' she concluded, 'you pay us in American dollars, directly from the United States to our account in Switzerland.'

'But we don't have an account in Switzerland,' Günther pointed out as soon as they were alone and on their way home.

'No, but my father does,' Hannah replied. 'If there's one thing we Jews know how to operate, it's the banking system. My father's cousin is head of foreign exchange at the Commerzbank in Frankfurt-am-Main. And if cousin Josef can open an account for my father, he can open one for you and me!'

Two weeks later, after the lawyers had argued over drafts to justify their fee, the paperwork was signed. The Raschdorf 40 would be produced and sold as a "Derresford". Günther's two mechanics declined the offer of a job on the estate and left with a month's wages to seek skilled work elsewhere. The apprentice opted to remain, but with the stated intention of joining the Army as soon as he was of age. To Günther's relief Johann agreed to stay on and set up the dealership and repair shop.

Dieter and Inge settled comfortably into the cottage and Hannah, Günther and Renate entered a new phase in their life.

CHAPTER 8

Little changed in rural Germany as the nineteen twenties gave way to the thirties. The estate ran smoothly under Günther's now experienced hand. At the turn of the decade, they were saddened by the death of Dieter Raschdorf, who suffered a second stroke having never recovered fully from the first. Shortly afterwards, Inge declared that the estate held too many memories and she could not just sit out her middle and later years in the cottage. She loved her family and would see them all from time to time, but she had been invited to live with her elder sister, also widowed, in her now too-large apartment in Berlin. They would be company for each other, and the city had so much more cultural life to offer than an isolated cottage on a farm almost on the edge of beyond.

If life was comfortable for the Raschdorf family, however, it was less so for many of their fellow countrymen. The depression that began with the October 1929 Wall Street crash in America had severe effects in Germany, where there were already additional burdens stemming from the enormous compensation the country was forced to pay after losing the war. Following the crash and desperate for capital, the United States government called in the massive foreign loans it had provided to Europe. Germany suffered more than any other country, with rising social hardship. By the end of 1930, four million workers – some fifteen percent of the population – were unemployed. Many more could work only part-time. Inflation, the scourge of the Weimar Republic a decade before, returned. But the production agreement signed with Derresford still had more than another four years to run. Every day Günther blessed Hannah's wisdom in insisting on payment in dollars to a Swiss bank. They had, by now, a very considerable balance.

By 1932, almost one third of the German workforce was out of work. With a promise to cure unemployment, on 30th January 1933 Adolph Hitler was appointed Chancellor of Germany.

'I can't help worrying,' Hannah confided again one evening. 'He's been blaming the Jews for the state of the economy, as well as losing the war, yet there are only about half a million of us in the country. Father says we can't be to blame – Jewish people are less than one percent of the whole population!'

'President Hindenburg must know what he's doing,' Günther responded, 'and somebody has to lead us out of this mess. That's why the NAZI party got one third of the votes in last year's elections to the Reichstag. Heaven knows, things are pretty bad. I'm hard pressed to keep the estate above water. If we have to,' he suggested, not for the first time, 'we could use a little of the Derresford money to help us out.'

So far, Hannah knew, Günther had not laid off a single estate worker. But when anyone left, they had not been replaced. And her household staff had been reduced to Frau Brantis in the kitchen, one scullery maid mornings only to help prepare lunch, and one maid in the house.

But the Derresford fund, as they called it, was one of the few subjects on which they disagreed. Like her parents before her, Hannah had always been acutely conscious of anti-Semitism. True, it was much worse in countries further east, but as long ago as nineteen-twenty, the twenty-five point Party Program of the National Socialists had signalled an intention to separate Jews from "Aryan" society and to deny them political, legal and civil rights. Now, more than ever, Hannah felt that their Switzerland fund represented a safety net that they would be unwise to bring into Germany.

'But you're Germans first, by nationality, and Jewish second, only by religion,' argued her husband.

'That's how a lot of our people think of themselves,' Hannah responded, 'my father included. But even so...' she trailed off, without concluding her argument.

In the end it did not matter, as events began to lend force to her concerns. It began towards the end of March with a phone call. Afterwards her husband came in from the hall and sat down, obviously deep in thought.

'Who was it?' she asked.

'Your father,' came the reply. 'He's worried about the *SA*.'

'I have read something about them, they're part of the NAZI party, aren't they?'

He nodded. 'Hitler started the organisation in 1921. Officially it was called the *Sturm Abteilung,* otherwise known as brown shirts because that was part of their uniform. Rumour has it that the Party got hold of them on the cheap because they were made to be sent out to our troops in the colonies, but when we lost the war, they were never used.'

'Aren't the *SA* supposed to provide security at party rallies?' Hannah queried.

'That's the official justification,' Günther confirmed. 'But they recruited from the lower end of society – a lot of them former soldiers unemployed since the war. Now, in reality, they're just a bunch of roughnecks that harass anyone they don't like and particularly Jews. They're so out of control even the *Reichswehr* is worried about them. And if our own Army is worried then things can't be too good.'

'So, what did Father have to say?' Hannah asked. 'Presumably that's why he rang?'

'He's been meeting with some of his Jewish business friends,' Günther replied. 'Apparently, there have been a number of instances where the *SA* have put notices up outside Jewish businesses, mostly shops, saying things like "Don't buy from Jews!" But there's a big boycott being organised for 1ˢᵗ April in all our cities, and your father is concerned that things might get out of hand. So far, most people have ignored the *SA* demands, but he's worried that his customers might get mistreated if they try to go into the restaurant on Saturday.'

'Has he spoken to the police?' she queried. 'Wouldn't that be the best thing to do?'

'Apparently, they sent a delegation,' he told her, 'but the police were not very reassuring. So, he's asked if I would be prepared to go over, just to be around in case there's a problem.'

'Surely not,' she said anxiously. 'You have a family and a business to run!'

'So does your father,' he replied. 'And he and his friends don't want to just give in to the *SA*. But he's not a young man any more, Hannah. And although he says all the staff will go in if they can, I think he could do with my moral support.

'Don't worry,' he tried to reassure her. 'I'll take young Otto with me.'

Otto Blecher, she knew, was a good worker. But more to the point he was young, fit and had a reputation. On more than one occasion Günther had spoken up for him to the authorities when he had been involved in fisticuffs after a night in the local *Bierstube*. Moreover, Otto lived at home in the village with elderly parents. During the terrible inflation years of the Weimar Republic, Günther's father had given him enough rations to feed all three of them. So Otto Blecher was fiercely loyal. Not too much comfort to her, but if Günther felt he had to go, young Blecher would be a useful man to have around. Although it would not stop her worrying, and she said so in no uncertain terms.

Otto and Günther left the estate early on Saturday morning, taking Hannah's small Opel. Otto confessed that it was the first time he had been in a "motoring car". They arrived soon after ten, parked in a side street and waited more or less opposite the restaurant until Herr Rosenthal arrived to open up. The staff used the rear entrance and the luncheon service proceeded without interruption. Hannah's father asked them to stay until the evening service was under way, but expressed his thanks and offered the view that perhaps the *SA* had not realised the owner of the restaurant was Jewish. The first bookings were for seven p.m.

Herr Rosenthal's hopes were dashed when four men in *SA* uniforms arrived – brown shirts, baggy trousers tucked into high boots and swastika armbands. The first customers were roughly pushed away – they were elderly, not of an age to confront their aggressors. By half past seven the restaurant was still empty.

'Do you want us to go outside and sort this out?' queried Günther. 'We can't go on like this – it's unfair and it's horrible.'

'I have phoned the police,' his father-in-law told him, 'but although they took the call half an hour ago, nothing has happened. I don't want you to get involved with a brawl in the street – I think I shall have to send the staff home and close for the night. We are shut on Sundays and Mondays, but perhaps I shall be able to open again on Tuesday.'

They locked up the front of the restaurant. The *SA* men were a few metres along the street. With Herr Rosenthal between Otto and Günther they had no choice but to walk past them towards either the Opel or the Adler. The four men moved to stand directly in their path. The one centre-right, about thirty and strongly built, threw out the NAZI salute.

'*Die Juden sind unser Unglück,*' he announced, '*Geh nach Palestina.*'

'We don't want any trouble,' Herr Rosenthal said quietly, holding up his hands, palms outwards, hoping to placate the four of them. But he could smell alcohol and some spittle had landed on the front of his coat. 'We are good Germans,' he added gently. 'We are not your misfortune and we are not able to go to Palestine. I have closed the restaurant, so please let us pass.'

The *SA* member in front of him side-swiped the hat from the older man's head. Herr Rosenthal quietly picked it up and held it to his chest in his right hand. He moved to walk past the person confronting him. But that meant he had to pass between two of them, the one to the front and the one a pace or so to his right – the one facing Günther. And this latter swung a vicious punch into the older man's solar plexus. Herr Rosenthal, unable to draw breath, fell to his knees.

Günther could have taken the hat insult – just. But his father-in-law was one of the kindest, gentlest of men he had ever known – a loving father to Hannah and a doting grandfather to Renate. It ran through his mind in an instant that he had not fought a war to see this happen to an innocent family, least of all his own.

Günther's *Stosstruppen* training clicked in automatically. He might not have been as fast or as fit as he had been at the age of eighteen, but he was strong from heavy farm work and no slouch. It was a split-second decision. With Herr Rosenthal down, it was two against four and he had no intention of finishing up on the cobbles under a jackboot kicking that all too often these days proved fatal. He had to put his man down and quickly. Rather than skinning his knuckles and bruising his fingers, Günther used the palm of his hand. A straight blow would have bloodied his opponent's face but possibly left him on his feet. He dropped slightly and pushing up with his knees, put all the force into his arm that he could muster. His palm went under the *SA* man's nose and connected in a rising arc. The danger, he knew, was that the bone might be driven into the man's brain. Which was precisely what happened.

Herr Rosenthal's first attacker was stupid enough to try to land a haymaker, turning towards Günther and signalling his intention with a slowness dulled by alcohol. Günther, who had been taught years ago that the human knee joint has very little lateral strength, spun to half-face him. Using the sole of his right foot he kicked viciously against the inner right knee of his opponent. The joint, jolted outwards, was crippled. A swift kick to the other leg and his man was on the ground.

Günther was vaguely aware of his father-in-law, now with a foot on the floor, both hands on one knee, trying to push himself to his feet. But his immediate concern was Otto. It need not have been. One of the *SA Sturm Abteilung* was horizontal and unconscious, his arms splayed out as if he had been crucified. The other turned to run, but Günther watched as Otto tackled him from behind, turned him and began rhythmically to apply a series of low stomach and solar plexus blows that put the uniformed thug on his knees, gasping for breath. Günther approached the *SA* man from behind, placed one hand on his chin, ran his other arm round the man's forehead and twisted, hard. There was an audible crack.

They had been fortunate. Because of the *SA* presence, the citizens had stayed clear of the streets, not wanting to be involved. Günther looked up at the flats above the shops and restaurants, but they were all either in darkness or lighted with curtains drawn. He was fairly sure there were no witnesses, or at least none that would wish to come forward.

'*Schnell*,' he hissed to Otto. 'Help me pull them round the corner into the alley.'

The *SA* thug that Günther had crippled was on the ground, moaning softly. '*Bitte, bitte,*' he pleaded, having watched the fate of his companion. But Günther knew that if they left a single witness his father-in-law was a dead man, and that would also apply to himself and Otto, because Herr Rosenthal would not be able to resist the *SA* interrogation that would surely follow. He despatched his second opponent. Seeing what he had done, Otto did the same with the remaining survivor, who mercifully was still unconscious. He was as wise to their situation as Günther. They eventually left four bodies in a pitch black passageway that led off an alley. It was far enough from the restaurant for there to be no obvious connection. Herr Rosenthal joined them, still a little doubled over and clutching his stomach, but otherwise none the worse for his experience.

'Can you drive?' Günther asked his father-in-law, who nodded to confirm that he could.

'I don't think you should go back to the house,' Günther told him. 'Come with us to the farm and stay overnight. We'll put you in mother's old cottage, just to be safe, and see how things look in the morning.

'Otto,' he instructed, 'please go with my father-in-law, just to make sure that he is all right. I'll follow in the Opel.' A few hours later the two vehicles drove on to the estate.

On the way up the drive, Günther overtook the Adler and flicked his tail lights so that it would follow. He had not wanted to arrive outside the main house in case any of the staff were still on duty. It was a two-minute walk. Hannah had heard the vehicles and was waiting in the hall.

'What happened?' she asked anxiously. 'Was that the Adler, and if so where's *Vati*?'

'Later,' he said, more brusquely than intended. 'Are there any staff still around?'

She shook her head. 'Frau Brantis went home some time ago.'

'All right.' He took a deep breath. 'A lot has happened. But your father's fine. For now, can you bring the makings of a simple hot meal to the cottage? Otto's gone home, so enough for just two of us – three, if you haven't eaten. And put a bottle of schnapps and a couple of bottles of wine in the basket, please. We'll tell you everything when we get there.'

'As you know you have to secure the back doors from the inside,' her father explained. 'They have good strong bolts.

But the locks and the shutter are on the front door, so you always have to leave that way. There had been four *SA* thugs outside from the beginning of evening service. No one was allowed in, so at around half past seven or eight I decided that the best thing would be to shut the restaurant and see how things panned out over the next few days.

'Unfortunately,' he went on, 'when we were leaving they attacked us. I was hit and fell to the ground. They would have kicked us to pieces. Günther and Otto saved my life.'

'What happened to the *SA* men?' she asked immediately.

All three of them were silent, until Günther said quietly, 'I'm pretty sure there were no witnesses.' Her right hand flew to her mouth, but she kept her own counsel.

They passed an anxious Sunday but were not disturbed. On Tuesday morning Günther insisted on accompanying his father-in-law back to Stettin. His housekeeper made no mention of any police enquiries, which they knew she would have done. Herr Rosenthal learned that Giulio's had not been targeted, only the better known Gli Olivi.

During the lunch service Officer Bosch from the local *Schutzpolizei* called at the restaurant. Like most members of his force, he was conservative by nature and although he broadly supported Hitler he had little time for the *SA* party thugs, who caused him more trouble than enough. There had been many acts of violence on Saturday evening and several people killed in the city centre. He would do what he could, but this case was not a priority.

He also knew Herr Rosenthal slightly. Bosch was neither for nor against Jews, at least not those like Rosenthal, and the respectable businessman had contributed generously to their local police charity in the past.

'I haven't come to eat, Herr Rosenthal,' he told them. 'Can we have a word, somewhere private?'

Günther followed them into the office. 'My son-in-law,'

Herr Rosenthal said briefly, making the introduction without mentioning Günther's name.

'What happened on Saturday night?' asked the policeman, not unkindly.

'I phoned you, or at least the police,' Rosenthal replied steadily. 'There were four *SA* men in the street. They would not let anyone enter the restaurant. But nobody turned up to help us.'

'So what did you do?' came the reply. Günther sensed that the policeman was sympathetic, although he was duty bound to make enquiries.

'There was no point in staying open, so some time between half seven and eight I locked up and left.'

'Was there any trouble?' he was asked.

'Yes,' Herr Rosenthal opened his hands. 'They knocked my hat off, and there was some abusive language. It was not very pleasant, but as you can see I am still here.'

'And then?' the policeman queried.

'I did what I usually do on Sunday morning, but as it was early I went there on Saturday night. We are not open on Sundays, so I drove to my son-in-law's estate to join them for Sunday lunch. It's something of a family tradition,' he finished quietly.

The officer looked at Günther, who simply nodded his affirmation.

'We found the bodies of four uniformed *SA* men about half a kilometre from here,' the policeman announced. 'But there was a lot of unrest and violence in the city on Saturday evening. Thank you for your help, Herr Rosenthal,' he said courteously, rising to his feet. 'I hope not to have to trouble you again.'

After he had gone Günther let out a long, slow sigh of relief. 'I think I can guess what his report will say,' he said very quietly. 'The *SA* were murdered, but it was hardly likely to have been the work of one elderly gentleman.'

'Maybe he has his suspicions, maybe not,' said Herr Rosenthal, 'and he might even know more than he's saying. But for whatever reason, I don't think he wants to take this case any further.'

But both men knew that they had been very, very fortunate.

They were together again in May for Sunday lunch, this time at the Rosenthal family home in Stettin.

'How's business these days?' Günther asked as they sipped sherry. This was their first family lunch since the day after the boycott, as Hannah's father had wanted to stay in Stettin for a while to see how things developed. Hannah was in the garden with Renate, who would soon celebrate her eleventh birthday. With her mother's good looks and light, copper-golden hair she was a lovely child, with every sign of being a beauty in the years to come.

'Things more or less settled back to normal, after that Saturday,' his father-in-law replied. 'The NAZIs are still calling for a boycott, but I don't think any of my regulars are taking notice. I don't like the law that they passed on the seventh of April, though.'

The Law for the Restoration of the Professional Civil Service signified the beginning of a campaign by the NAZI party against the whole of Germany's Jewish population, not just business owners. In practice, it meant that Jews could not be employed by the government, either as teachers, within the judiciary, or as administrators within any branch of government service. Most were fired. The only exceptions were those who had served in the armed forces during the war.

'What will you do?' responded Günther. 'I don't mean you personally, but the Jewish community in Stettin?'

'The new law won't affect me, employment-wise,' his father-in-law replied, 'and we are still talking about it. But there is going to be a lot of hardship. Almost certainly we will have to set up a charitable fund, and perhaps some sort of soup kitchen, to help out those families whose breadwinner has lost his job.'

'It's wrong, but the rest of the population doesn't seem to be making much of a fuss about it,' observed Günther. 'Perhaps because the economy seems to be picking up again, either that or they're scared of the *SA*... or both!' he observed wryly.

'But what's worrying Hannah most is the Decree they passed a few days later,' he went on. 'If someone has a parent or grandparent of the Jewish faith they are now a non-Aryan. It might affect Hannah, even though she's married to a gentile, and it also brings Renate into that category.'

Further discussion was prevented by the return of Hannah and Renate to the drawing room. The restaurateur's face lit up at the sight of his daughter and granddaughter. Lunch was served and they moved to the dining room. It was mutton slow roasted on a bed of rosemary and whole garlic cloves, some of which had then been crushed into the *jus*. With it Hannah's father served a very passable Chianti *classico*. Renate, spoiled as ever by her grandfather, was given a little wine to which her mother promptly added an equal volume of water before wagging her index finger at her father, but she was smiling fondly. With the French windows slightly ajar to the early spring sunshine, the conversation eased on to other things as they enjoyed a leisurely, family meal.

Life on the estate, and for Hanna's father in Stettin, passed pleasantly enough. But Hitler's government continued to pass a series of worrying and sometimes draconian laws. In May books were burned, not just in Berlin but throughout the country. In July, the NAZI Party was declared the only legal political party in the country. Before the year was out, Jews were prohibited from owning land and were not allowed to be the editor of a newspaper. Many businesses, particularly the larger ones, increasingly refused to employ Jewish men.

In August of the following year the 87-year-old President Hindenburg died, and Hitler became Führer with the powers of both Reich President and Reich Chancellor, powers endorsed by 90 percent of German voters in a plebiscite soon afterwards. However, most shocking to Günther and Hannah were the Nuremberg race laws passed in September nineteen thirty-five. German Jews were deprived of their citizenship and became merely "subjects" within Hitler's Reich. Moreover, they were forbidden to marry or have sexual relations with Aryans, or to employ young Aryan women as domestic help. But fortunately, anti-Semitism eased in nineteen thirty-six as Hitler's Germany prepared for the August Olympic games.

A few weeks after the games, Hannah's father dropped the bombshell that he was selling up. 'The writing's on the wall,' he told Günther as they walked the estate one Sunday afternoon. 'It's not as though they make a secret of what they are thinking. The latest talk is of denying us the right to the professions – we are no longer permitted to be accountants or dentists, or to teach Germans. And we are going to lose all the tax allowances that everyone else enjoys. If they are doing that to Jews as individuals, it can only be a matter of time before they come after our businesses.'

'Is it a good time to sell?' queried Günther. 'And what will you do then?' he added.

'I'll almost certainly have to settle for less than businesses are worth,' said Rosenthal, 'whether I sell to a Jewish or an Aryan German. The buyer will know why I'm selling up, and take advantage. But I'd rather be cheated a little now than lose out even more in the future.' He paused, then went on, 'As for what's next, I have to get out of Germany. If and when Hitler's gone, I might come back, but for now it's just not tenable. I'll stay in the restaurant business, but to a certain extent I'm going to have to build things up all over again. If I can get into Switzerland, that might be favourite. If not, I'll try for Britain or America. But I'm not going to stay here. Josef and I will go to Switzerland first, and make enquiries from there.'

'So your cousin's going with you,' Günther observed.

His father-in-law nodded. 'Josef is doubly at risk from the NAZIs,' he said. 'First, he is a Jew. And second, although he is a charming and educated man, he's not married – because he told me he is homosexual,' he finished bluntly. 'Added to that, banks are not taking on Jewish employees these days,' he went on, 'and Josef said that although his boss is sympathetic and wants him to stay where he is because he makes them a lot of money, Josef reckons that it is only a matter of time before the bank will be forced to show him the door.'

'Will you be all right for money?' asked Günther.

'*Ja, bestimmt,*' came the reply. 'Definitely, Josef is quite well off, and he has been putting his money into a Swiss account for years. It's been easy enough, with his job, even if the bank doesn't know about it. I've been giving him my spare money for a long time now, so my savings are over there as well. He'll move the proceeds from the house and businesses for me, then we'll go.'

Back indoors for tea, Herr Rosenthal had pretty much the same conversation with his daughter. 'I'll miss you and Günther and Renate terribly,' he said at the end. 'But it won't be forever. With any luck Hitler will be gone and I can come home.'

'We have some funds over there, as you know,' said Günther. 'If you need them, use them. Hannah can give you the account details.' He looked at his wife, who nodded her agreement.

Herr Rosenthal paused then took a deep breath before replying. 'I hope it won't be necessary,' he said at last. 'But thank you, Günther. My daughter didn't marry into the faith, but she married a good man.'

'What are your plans for this week?' Herr Rosenthal went on, to change the subject and lighten the mood.

'Not really sure,' said Günther. 'But Johann needs an extra pair of hands since the other two left and the last lad joined the Army. I need some fruit and vegetables for the wholesale business, so I'm going over the border on Wednesday to see a Polish farmer called Stefan Janicki. We are talking about his son coming to live on the estate as an apprentice.'

'It's ironic, really,' said Herr Rosenthal. 'I'm a German citizen. Or at least I was until a year ago. But I don't really feel I can live here anymore. And you need an apprentice, but he's going to be a Pole. God knows where all this is going to end up,' he finished sadly.

CHAPTER 9

Helga did not enjoy working for the younger mistress of the house. The older Frau Raschdorf had been lenient to the point of *laissez-faire*. But whereas Inge Raschdorf had not easily adapted to taking charge of a household rather larger than that of her own modest origins, Hannah had already managed her father's establishment. When they transferred to the estate house, she ran it in exactly the same way. Which was how she also ran the business: efficiently, and not least with careful attention to expenditure.

Moreover, at first there had been two other housemaids within the establishment. Now, six years later, Helga was on her own and much more closely supervised. To her, it was as if Hannah Raschdorf was determined to extract a full day's work from her maid.

'When she gives me a job, she even tells me how long she thinks it should take,' she complained bitterly to Frau Brantis. The cook nodded sympathetically, but privately thought that the younger woman had been getting away with it for far too long. Helga was even careless about her appearance, until the mistress had told her in no uncertain terms that she needed to tidy herself up. And Frau Brantis noticed that she was taking ever increasing helpings at the communal midday meal. Losing a few pounds wouldn't be a bad idea, either. Even so, the Raschdorfs had been kind to Helga. When her husband Berndt handed in his notice, announcing that he had got a job "away", she had been allowed to keep the tied cottage to which her husband returned from time to time, even though strictly speaking it went with his job and not hers.

Frau Brantis was not sorry to see Berndt Gross gone. One of the most uncommunicative men she had ever met, he would sit at the far end of the table day after day chewing his meal, more often than not with his mouth half-open. She wondered what on earth Helga saw in him. Still, the economy was picking up these days, and with it, the fortunes of the estate. Only the other day the mistress had confided that she was thinking of taking on another maid in the house, whilst the Master was looking for an extra hand who would also work part-time in the stables. But the only horses kept these days were for leisure. The estate was entirely mechanised, and whilst Hannah Raschdorf had kept her faithful Opel, Günther proudly drove his magnificent new Mercedes.

What neither Berndt not Helga had mentioned, however, was that Berndt Gross had joined the *SA*. With Adolf Hitler as *Oberster SA Führer* its membership now numbered more than four million. With Hitler's rise to national power, it became an official part of the government organisation, with *SA* members joining the police to arrest and torture their ideological opponents and even – from time to time – their personal enemies. Many victims, of course, were Jews.

The Chief of Staff, however, had once had ambitions to take control of the regular Army. For his pains Rohm was executed in 1934 after what became known as "The Night of the Long Knives", but the *SA* continued with its role of guarding concentration camps and generally terrorising the enemies of the Nazi regime. Berndt Gross grew with it, and in a few short years was promoted from the lowest rank of *SA-Mann* to that of *SA-Rottenführer,* or section leader. Gross was cunning rather than intelligent, and well named. He took pride in his uniform and his size meant that men feared him. Moreover, he carried out his duties to the letter and did not find them in any way distasteful. In truth, his new career gave him a sense of pride and status that had not existed previously in his life. And the money was much better – enough to fund his leisure hours in beer halls and brothels. For him, the later nineteen thirties were good years.

But it was the *Schutzstaffel*, under Heinrich Himmler, that gradually assumed prominence over the *SA*, so in 1938 Gross applied for, and was granted, enlistment as a regular, salaried member of the *Allgemeine SS*. The general duties branch was responsible for police and racial matters within the Reich. At the same time, because of his considerable *SA* policing experience, he was able to secure promotion to the rank of *SS Unterscharführer*, or junior group leader. But best of all was a plum posting to the regional headquarters in Berlin.

Although not affected directly, Günther and Hannah were only too aware of the progressive persecution of Jews during 1938. From March, when Hitler's forces invaded Austria, to October, when they occupied the Sudentenland, German Jews were increasingly debarred from commerce and the professions. Hannah clung to the hope that her marriage to a gentile, plus the fact that she had never announced or practised her religion, would give her a cloak of anonymity. It might have worked but for Helga Gross.

A new maid joined the household. Gudrun was a pleasant and intelligent enough young woman and a hard worker. Her father was employed in a small factory near the village, where she lived with her parents. Hoping that the new girl would join as an under-housemaid, Helga planned to re-arrange their duties to her own advantage. But to her disgust, Gudrun had been taken on as an equal. Helga was careful, therefore, in her approach. At first, she offered "advice" to the new girl. But the suggestions gradually turned into orders that she should "do this" or "do that".

Gudrun realised that she had to establish her position or her employment would be a misery. After one particularly curt instruction she put down the bucket of ash that she was about to take outside and turned to face Helga. The two women were about the same height, although Gudrun was younger and almost certainly fitter and stronger. And with three brothers in the family she had seen more than her fair share of rough and tumble. Unconsciously her fists bunched at her side.

'Helga,' she began quietly, 'we have to settle something. I have been given my duties by the mistress, and I am to look after the downstairs rooms. You are responsible for upstairs. And some duties, such as the laundry, we do together. But I am not your junior.' She paused to let the words sink in. 'So, neither am I yours to order around,' she went on, still pleasantly but nevertheless quite firm in her demeanour. 'If we are to work together, I think you must understand my position.'

'Of course, you're my junior,' retorted Helga indignantly. 'Look at you, hardly out of school. I have been working here for nearly fifteen years.'

'Your age, and the fact that you are a married lady, means that I must show respect,' Gudrun replied, still in the same firm but pleasant voice, 'and I would hope that I do. But nevertheless, we are both housemaids and my orders come from the mistress, not through you.' She paused, sensing the older woman's rising resentment. 'If there is any doubt in your mind,' Gudrun went on, 'I shall raise the matter with Frau Brantis, who has been here a long time and in status is undoubtedly our senior. But she will probably take the matter to the mistress. And if she doesn't, then I most certainly will,' she concluded.

Helga had always known that she did not have a great friend in Frau Brantis, although there had never been any animosity between them. But she also sensed that the mistress quite liked and approved of the younger girl. Knowing that this was an argument she could not win, Helga exhaled sharply in disgust and walked away. But inwardly she was seething. She resented the younger woman's position, but most of all she was furious that not only had she been bested in argument but thoroughly outmanoeuvred to boot.

Gudrun felt like shaking with nervousness but she would never show it. With forced calm, she covered the ash with a cloth, picked up her bucket and walked outside through the kitchen.

Helga was still fuming when she went home that evening to her cottage. She did not miss her husband, who had not been home for months since his transfer to Berlin. Neither did he write, and it was not often that he remembered to send any money. She knew he was taking advantage of the fact that her own wages were enough to live on and she did not have to pay rent. But she had married him only to escape from a violent and abusive father. Berndt turned out to be a disappointment. His lovemaking was quick and painful, with no thought for her whatsoever. And he did little or nothing to help around the house. So, the longer he stayed away the better, as far as she was concerned.

However, Helga would have welcomed some male attention. That Polish lad, Jan, was strong and good looking, and she often made a point of sitting next to him at lunch. Several times her thigh had "accidentally" touched his leg, but he appeared not to notice. And her suggestion that she could pay him to do a bit of heavy gardening work at the cottage had seemingly fallen on deaf ears. She would have to look elsewhere. All of which fuelled further her general feeling of dissatisfaction and resentment.

In November of nineteen thirty-eight, the son of a deported Polish Jew shot the German Third Secretary to the embassy in Paris. He died two days later. The news was widely reported on the wireless, the state-subsidised production of which had been encouraged by Hitler so that it could also be used to broadcast propaganda. That same night, *Kristallnacht*, saw the smashing of Jewish shop windows and widespread looting across the country. Hundreds of homes and synagogues were burnt down. Some ninety Jews were murdered and, in the days that followed, 30,000 more were arrested and deported to concentration camps.

The Nazis fined the Jews one billion marks in "retaliation" for the shooting in Paris. The following month a law was passed to enable the "Aryanisation" of all Jewish businesses, and later that same month Herman Göring took charge of resolving the "Jewish Question". Unexpectedly, Helga received news from Berndt that he was to be given leave and would be coming home for Christmas.

And Günther received another communication from Hannah's father, who had always written to him rather than his daughter, clearly thinking it to be safer. It had taken a year to sell the house and businesses, so the first message came at the end of nineteen thirty-seven – a postcard showing the Alps and with just the words 'Great Skiing!' in the message area. This letter was to tell them that they had managed to acquire citizenship, in part due to their wealth and also with the help of Josef's banker friends with whom he had been placing valuable business for years, and who hoped that they would receive further clients from Josef's contacts within the Jewish community still in Germany.

Hannah's father and Josef were in Zermatt, in the Valais canton not far from the Italian border, and since the new Gli Olivi served both German and Italian cuisine, it was doing well, with good tourist trade all year round. 'I have to work as a chef again,' he wrote, 'but it is surprising how much I still enjoy it. Josef does Front of House, keeps the books, and worries about everything else! He says it doesn't pay as well as banking but it's more fun. Most important of all, we are safe.' Hannah hoped that her father had not said too much in the letter, but on careful examination it did not look as though it had been opened.

Mercifully, the Raschdorf estate was untouched by the anti-Semitic events of nineteen thirty-eight. Despite some initial coolness, Helga and Gudrun continued to work together, but that did nothing to lessen the older woman's feeling of resentment. Helga was jealous of her employers' wealth and dissatisfied with her own position, Gudrun's status as her equal, and the fact that she was supervised in a way that had not been the case under the older Frau Raschdorf. She, to Helga's mind, had been a lady, whereas Mistress Hannah – who in fact had never treated her with anything other than courtesy and fairness – she saw as no more than a bossy young upstart.

It was just before Christmas when she took the laundry into the master bedroom. Her orders were to place the ironed and folded garments on the eiderdown. Mistress Hannah did not wish anyone to open either her own chest of drawers or that of her husband. These, and the two huge mahogany wardrobes, were out of bounds. And that was another bone of contention – the old Mistress had been happy to let her put everything away. Helga no longer felt herself to be the loyal, totally trusted servant.

She knew that Hannah Raschdorf was out – she had seen her leaving the stables for a hack round the estate. Typically, she would ride for about an hour and a half. Gudrun was downstairs, as was Frau Brantis in the kitchen. There would be no harm in taking a look inside the drawers – see what the snotty female had to wrap round her body. The top drawer contained underwear – some of it French and lacy and obviously expensive. She ran her fingers over the silk and "humphed" at the thought of the cheap flannel and cotton that she had to wear. The blouses in the next drawer down were of equally good quality, many diaphanous although some were of a stouter material suitable for outdoor wear. The bottom drawer contained woollens, including expensive cashmeres.

She pressed down with the back of her fingers, enjoying the springy softness of several layers of garments, clothes that she could never afford. But there was something hard lying on its side underneath the woollens and it was quite large – about thirty centimetres long with a round base at one end and several curved arms at the other. Quickly looking over her shoulder, although the door was almost closed and she knew she was alone upstairs, Helga lifted the woollens and set them to one side. At the bottom of the pile lay a candelabra. It had a central stem and three curved arms that stemmed from either side to form seven lamp or candle holders in a level row at the top. Helga gasped. She knew what it was from pictures she had seen – it was a Menorah, perhaps the ultimate symbol of Judaism.

Well, well, well... so the bitch had a secret. She smiled, and replaced the clothes on top. Helga had no idea what she would do with this information – she would have to think about it and for quite some time. But she suspected that it had a value far beyond her present imagination. Perhaps she would discuss it with Berndt... he would know what to do. He'd been home for a few days, now. Clearly, he had lost all interest in her sexually, for which she was quite grateful – he was doubtless getting what he wanted in Berlin. But to her surprise he had been reasonably pleasant, explaining that the barracks was pretty deserted for *Weihnachsfest* so a break in the cottage and some home cooking over Christmas would not go amiss. Lunchtimes he wandered down to the *Bierstubbe* to boast of his new status to his old drinking friends. Mostly he drank before and after his evening meal and fell asleep in front of the fire. At some stage in the night he would come to their matrimonial bed and snore like a pig. But she knew only too well, things could have been a lot worse. She told him about the Menorah.

'Can we talk for a few minutes,' Hannah asked her husband as they sat at the dinner table after their meal.

'Of course,' he answered automatically, although he was paying more attention to lighting his cigar.

'I don't want to worry you,' she said nervously, 'but I think Helga has been looking through my chest of drawers.'

'Why would she do that?' asked Günther.

'I don't know,' came the reply. 'Her orders are to leave things on the bed for me to put away. It might be something that a man wouldn't notice, but I am quite particular about how I place my clothes, one on top of the other. It's almost obsessive, but something I have done since I was a little girl.'

'And…?' he responded.

'Well, I just have this feeling – my things are not quite *exactly* as they were before. Nothing I can put my finger on, but I have an overwhelming intuition, if you wish.'

'You said when we first moved into the house that Helga seemed to resent your arrival,' Günther replied. 'Maybe you should think about whether you want to keep her on? After all, it's your home and you can do without having to put up with tension from the staff.'

'There's something else,' Hannah went on. 'You know I brought very little with me when we set up home together – not much more than my clothes and jewellery. But there was one thing: my mother's Menorah – it was her own mother's and her grandmother's before her. She was very observant, and to her it meant the world. I'm not religious, but it is one of the few things of my mother's that I still have, so it means a lot to me, too.'

'Where do you keep it?' asked Günther, fearing what the answer would be.

'I'm sorry, it should have been in your safe,' she said anxiously, unconsciously wringing her hands, 'but it's in my bottom drawer, under a pile of woollens, and I think the damned woman has found it.'

Günther thought for a minute or so. 'We don't know for sure,' he said at length. She shook her head uncertainly. 'Let's not cross bridges before we get to them,' he went on. 'Even if she has seen it, which she probably hasn't, in any case you are married to me. I don't think there's much that she could do with the information. It wasn't a good idea to leave it in a drawer,' he added not unkindly, 'and we *should* put it in my safe. Other than that, for now I don't think we need to be panicked into doing anything.'

The year nineteen thirty-nine was, if anything, worse for the Jews. In January *SS* leader Reinhard Heydrich was ordered by Göring to speed up their emigration. The following month, the Nazis forced the Jews in Germany to hand over all their gold and silver possessions. Hannah turned a blind eye to the instruction and left her Menorah in Günther's safe. In March German troops seized Czechoslovakia, with its Jewish population of three hundred and fifty thousand souls. The rest of Europe did nothing. And in July, Jews in Germany and Czechoslovakia were denied the right to hold any government positions.

Jan was within weeks of completing his apprenticeship. Unbeknown to him, old Johann had recently had a long conversation with Herr Raschdorf. 'The lad's as good as I am,' the former mariner told his employer. 'He can read drawings and use any machine in the shop. He's also a first-class welder and a good blacksmith. But it goes beyond that. He's borrowed all my books. He understands metallurgy, stress and structural engineering. And there's a good business head on those young shoulders. I doubt he's mispriced or made a loss on a job since we took him on. Best of all,' he concluded, 'the young devil has an easy charm and he gets on well with people, ordinary folk to wealthy farmer clients…'

'It's nearly three years now,' Günther replied. 'Tell him that come the anniversary, we'll promote him to fully-fledged junior engineer. The title doesn't mean much, really, but he'll appreciate the pay rise that goes with it.'

It was towards the end of the following month that Jan, thrilled by his forthcoming change of circumstances, took an early morning walk from the estate to the now Tarmac-surfaced road that led past the drive into the property. Woken by a dull rumbling sound that had started a couple of hours earlier, as he approached the road birdsong was silenced by the roar of engines and the metallic squeal of tracked machinery. He stood in amazement as a column of mixed wheeled vehicles, half-tracks and tanks drove past, left to right, west to east – towards the border with his native Poland.

Retreating from the dust at the junction of drive and road, he walked back to his room above the workshop, deep in thought. First, he told Johann what he had seen, then they walked to the big house, set much further back and away from the noise.

Günther listened then thought things over. Clearly the lad was worried. 'Do you want to take Lujza?' he suggested. The mare was a second-generation offspring of Günther's beloved Grane, now sadly no longer alive, but more of a chestnut than a Grey. 'I'll take Alger, and we'll ride after breakfast. See what's going on. You happy to leave in about an hour?'

With Günther astride his massive Alger they set off cross-country, about half a kilometre from and parallel with the road. But a good seven kilometres from the border they were halted by a *Wehrmacht* detachment that emerged from a hedge, rifles pointing at the ground but clearly instantly ready. Beyond the hedge, they could see perhaps a hundred vehicles of different types, and beyond them a massive field encampment.

'*Was machen Sie, und wo gehen Sie?*' demanded a young NCO.

'We are exercising the horses,' replied Günther politely, 'and we are from my estate over there.' He thumbed vaguely behind him over his shoulder. 'As for where we are going,' he went on, 'we have been riding this way since I was old enough to sit on a farm pony.'

'I'm sorry, *meine Herren*,' he told them, 'but the area behind me is now a closed military zone for our exercises. Please go back the way you have come. I expect your normal ride will be open again soon,' he finished, obviously trying to be helpful.

'*Danke,*' responded Günther, giving the young man the formal salute from his own army days. It was recognised, but the response was the stiff-armed reply of Hitler's Nazi party. '*Kommen Sie bitte schnell,*' he said to Jan, not wanting to use his name, as he right-wheeled his mount. The younger man followed immediately without speaking. His German was pretty fluent by now, but he had never succeeded in losing his eastern accent.

They returned to the estate at a gentle canter. Not until they had dismounted and Günther's groom had taken the horses did he turn to Jan.

'Well,' he exhaled, 'what did you make of that?'

'It looks like an army on the move, sir,' Jan responded. 'And it's hard up against the Polish border.'

'I'm going to ride out each morning,' said Günther. 'To a different place every day, a bit to the left, then a bit to the right. Not as near as we went just now, only so that I can see if they are still there. It's safer for me than it would be for you but I'll let you know what's happening. For now, you can tell Johann, but don't discuss this with anyone else.'

Jan bowed his head in agreement and went to help look after the horses. But he was troubled.

Ten days later, Günther looked at the fields beyond the

hedge that he and Jan had first approached. The ground was churned to mud but the fields were empty. A flight of German bombers passed high overhead, their black swastikas just visible. There was a faint rumble of what he recognised as artillery from somewhere in the distance. He set Alger at the hedge and went on for a kilometre or so, but other than the destruction left by a mixed armoured and infantry formation on the move, the countryside was empty.

It was, he realised, the first day of September nineteen thirty-nine.

CHAPTER 10

Jan was working on the clutch housing of an old Raschdorf 35 when the phone rang in a corner of the building boarded off to make a small office.

'The Boss wants to speak with you,' Johann told him. 'He said please go to the front door and Gudrun will let you in.'

Pausing only to give his oily hands a hasty scrub, Jan walked to the house and smoothed himself down as best he could. He was about to lift the knocker when the door opened. 'Please follow me, Jan,' she said pleasantly.

They walked through a large entrance hall and down a long corridor patterned with diamond-shaped black and white tiles. Gudrun stopped in front of an oak door. Inside it was more like a small library than a study. Herr Raschdorf rose from behind the largest desk Jan had ever seen.

'Please sit down,' he invited, his hand indicating one of two comfortable chairs in front of the desk. Günther took the other. 'Jan,' he went on, 'I have just got back from where we rode just under two weeks ago. The *Wehrmacht* is no longer there. Also, you must have seen the planes flying over.'

'I was in the workshop, Herr Raschdorf,' replied Jan. 'Although when I heard the engine noises I went outside to look. I did wonder…'

'It's also been on the wireless,' his employer told him. 'I'm afraid it looks as if that madman has invaded Poland. He got away with the *Anschluss*, and after Austria, England and France did nothing about the Sudetenland last year – or Czechoslovakia this March either, come to that. But this time he's gone too far. The British and the French will probably take a few days to make up their mind, but I suspect that the former, at least, will give Hitler an ultimatum. Either he withdraws from Poland, which I don't think he will, or Europe will be at war.'

'I know that's serious, Herr Raschdorf,' said Jan. 'But right now, I'm worried about my family. If those troops we saw headed east from the border, they would almost certainly have crossed our farm.'

'Which is why I asked you to come and speak with me,' Günther told him. 'I have always been on good terms with your parents and they have my respect. It suited all of us when I needed an apprentice and you had to carve out a career. And I might tell you, I think I have probably had the best of the bargain...'

Jan smiled at the compliment.

'... but I have always felt that I owed a duty to your parents – *in loco parentis*, as it were.' Jan did not recognise the Latin, but he knew that Herr Raschdorf had always honoured a certain responsibility to keep an eye on him.

'I understand your concerns entirely,' Günther told him. 'If I were in your shoes, the first thing I would want to do would be to cross back over the border and make sure that everything was all right. Am I correct?' he asked.

Jan could only nod his head in reply.

'So, this is what I'm suggesting,' his employer went on. 'I thought about going by road, but there is bound to be a lot of military traffic and we would probably get turned back at some stage, or at the very least held up and questioned. Instead, supposing we ride as close as we can to the border. The *Wehrmacht's* gone, so there shouldn't be a problem. And I doubt if the border even exists any more. Once we can assess the situation, take Lujza if you wish, and ride to the farm. I'll come back here.

'But I want you to know,' his employer emphasised, 'that whatever you find on the other side of the border, and even if our countries are at war, you will always be welcome on this estate. We look on you as part of the family now, and as such I have a duty to keep you safe.'

'Thank you, Sir,' Jan replied. 'I'm grateful for the ride to the border,' he added, 'but I would be a bit conspicuous on the other side – a Polish lad on a thoroughbred horse. I can walk to the farm in an hour or so, maybe a bit longer if I keep to the woods and hedges. I know the lie of the land… it would probably be safer. All being well, I would like to spend a night with my parents, then perhaps cross back over the border at dawn tomorrow.'

'That's what we'll do then,' said Günther kindly. 'Meet me at the stables when you are ready. Take some warm clothes, and I'll have Frau Brantis put some food in a satchel for you. We'll ride to the border, assuming that we can, then as Alger has already made the return trip once today, I'll ride Lujza back with my horse on a lead rein.'

'*Ich bin dankbar, Herr Raschdorf,*' Jan told him.

'Don't mention it,' said Günther. 'This has been your home for almost three years now – it's the least I can do. Let's just hope to God that things turn out all right for all of us.'

Before they mounted Günther handed Jan a sealed envelope. 'It's a "*to whom it may concern*",' he told him. 'If you get stopped by any of our people, the letter says that you are a valued mechanic working on my estate and that you have my permission to take a couple of days leave to visit your parents, but also that you will be returning to work for me afterwards. It might just come in handy…' he tailed off.

Jan placed the letter inside the leather satchel that Günther had also handed him – obviously a personal possession since it had the initials "G R" embossed on it. They took advantage of a mounting block and set off across Günther's fields to the east.

At what had once been the border, which was now just a mangled stretch of wire, they dismounted. Günther offered Jan his hand. 'Good luck,' he told him, 'and I hope everything is all right. My regards to your parents and come back as soon as you can. Most important of all, come back safe.'

'*Danke sehr*,' Jan replied. 'And once more, thank you for your kindness. I'm grateful.'

Günther mounted the smaller Lujza and took his own horse on the lead rein. Jan watched him for a few minutes then faced east and started walking.

Returning home, Günther was surprised to see a black Adler *Trumpf* parked in front of the house. The front door was slightly ajar. Gudrun ran to meet him as soon as he walked into the hall.

'I'm sorry, Sir,' she rushed to explain. 'There are two men in the drawing room. They say they are from the *Schutzstaffel*. I tried to tell them that you and the mistress were not here, she's gone to the village, but they just pushed past me. Frau Brantis was ordered to give them coffee and I was told to pour cognac, but when she told them that she took orders only from the mistress, and that she would give them coffee as and when the mistress asked her to, they shouted at us. We were afraid, so we did as they said.'

Günther was angry, but knew he had to stay calm. 'Don't worry, it's all right,' he reassured Gudrun. Even so, when he walked into the room he was surprised to be greeted by Helga's husband, his former estate worker Berndt Gross, now wearing a passably respectable dark suit. The other man was presumably his driver. They remained seated. 'Good morning, Herr Gross,' he said evenly, sitting opposite them.

'I am not in uniform, so you would not know,' came the reply, 'but you will address me as *Unterscharführer* Gross,' he said abruptly. 'I returned to this district on promotion. Specifically, I am with the *Allgemeine SS*. The racial division,' he added ominously. 'I have my credentials, should you wish to see them.'

Günther's heart rate increased – he could sense where this was leading. But he forced himself to appear calm. Opening his palms, he indicated that producing documents would not be necessary. In any case, he had heard of Gross' appointment through the village gossip.

'So to what do I owe this visit?' he asked evenly, thanking his lucky stars that Hannah and Renate had not been at home when these two louts arrived.

'My superiors have decided that you will support the war effort,' Günther was told. 'I have not come in uniform because we do not wish to cause speculation and talk amongst the locals. But your estate is conveniently adjacent to the border. As you will know, this morning the Third Reich began to take *lebensraum* from Poland. We require a vehicle repair facility – a workshop, if you like, where we can bring back damaged equipment from the front for repair and subsequent return to the field army. Your facilities here will eventually need to be expanded. This we confirmed with an inspection this morning. Also, this house will be able to accommodate the senior engineers and officers.'

'My facilities, as you call them, are in use already,' Günther replied. 'As you doubtless will be aware, I have an agricultural sales and repair business that I am not prepared just to abandon. Neither do I have the staff for what you suggest – at the moment, I have only Johann and one apprentice. They could not possibly cope with all that extra work.'

'You will be reimbursed,' Gross continued, as if Günther had not spoken. 'You might even find it more profitable. And you will be provided with workers – true, they will be *Untermenschen* from Poland, but you will not have to pay them, or feed them much, for that matter.'

'This is my family home,' Günther informed him, making a huge effort not to raise his voice. 'I am *not* prepared to share it with strangers.'

'What has been ordered is not a basis for discussion,' came the reply.

'I refuse,' said Günther bluntly.

'Herr Raschdorf,' responded Gross with false reasonableness, 'of course you can refuse. But I am from the racial department – we have done our homework and we know that your wife's former name was Rosenthal. You have married a Jew, and from that union you have a *Mischling*.'

Günther was mortified to hear his lovely daughter referred to as a hybrid human being. 'With or without your assistance and co-operation,' Gross went on, 'this project will go ahead. But with it, your family, provided that you fulfil your side of our agreement, will possibly survive the war. Without it, your wife and daughter will become inmates of Dachau. It is a camp where we place persons who are no longer desirable within the Reich – mostly intellectuals, homosexuals and *Jews*.' Heavy emphasis on the final word drove home the threat.

He paused to let his message sink in. 'I congratulate you,' he continued coldly, 'your Aryan blood has been dominant. Your *Mischling* does not look like a Jew. But impure as she is, she is quite beautiful, so I might offer her to the commandant of Dachau. Although if he does not want her, I suspect he will give her to his guards; perhaps after I have tried her out for myself, of course.'

Günther was halfway out of his chair when the driver whipped out an automatic, at the same time sliding the mechanism to chamber a round. Clearly Günther's reaction had been anticipated. There was no way he could close the gap without taking a bullet. Slowly, his hands still on the arms of the chair, he sank back into his seat.

'I am sure when you have taken time to consider, you will see the wisdom of my argument,' concluded Gross, rising to his feet. 'In the meantime, Helga will not work here any more, although you will continue to pay her wages in the form of a pension. And she will remain in the cottage. You can write the costs off against the considerable profit you will doubtless enjoy from your contribution to the war industry.'

He handed Günther a card with a name and telephone number. 'Phone this person within twenty-four hours with your decision.'

He left the room. The driver backed towards the door, still holding the automatic, then turned to follow. Günther remained in his chair, face in hands, knowing he had been utterly defeated. He was still there when he heard the sound of the Adler's engine and the scrunch of its tyres on the gravel.

Jan crossed what had once been the border without incident. He could hear heavy vehicle traffic off to his left, on the main supply route, but there were no longer any troops on the churned-up farmland. Even so, he tried to walk alongside woods and hedgerows that would give him cover at a moment's notice. He came across only one other person as he made his way home. An old man, scythe swinging from years of practice, was trying to salvage corn from round the edge of an otherwise flattened field.

'*Guten Morgen,*' Jan greeted him politely. The man took a step back away from the edge of the field and raised the blade waist high in a defensive gesture. Jan realised immediately the mistake he had just made from force of habit.

'*Przepraszam, dzień dobry – jestem Polakiem, nie Niemcem,*' he added hastily. 'Sorry, good morning – and I'm Polish, not German.' The farm worker lowered his blade but did not reply.

It was past midday when he reached the edge of the farm. A plume of smoke from just over the final rise made his stomach lurch with anxiety. As he approached he could see that the farmhouse was a burnt-out ruin, although the stone walls were still standing. Against all the odds, the barn was undamaged. He ran to the yard.

His father was lying face down in the mud. He, too, was horribly burned, as though someone had turned a flamethrower on him. Judging by the blackness on the outer walls, that was what had also happened to the main building. He called out, but there was no response. Pushing open the barn door, he found Aniela lying on the floor. She had been stripped naked and there was a mess of blood and semen on her inner thighs. Her stomach and lower chest were disfigured by several bayonet wounds – it would not have been an easy death. With tears in his eyes he gathered her garments and covered her as best he could… she and his father would have to be buried. He looked around for where someone might have left a shovel. From behind he heard the sound of a rifle bolt being flicked back and forth to chamber a round.

Slowly he raised his hands. '*Odwróć sie,*' said a familiar voice. 'Turn around.' He did just that. 'Jan,' gasped Tadzio, lowering the Dragant, '*co, u licha tutaj robisz?* What the hell are you doing here?'

'Have you seen?' asked Jan.

'Our father, yes,' his brother replied. 'Oh no,' he whispered, moving to kneel alongside their sister and uncover her face. Tears welled in his eyes. 'What have those animal bastards done to her?'

'They can't hurt her any more,' said Jan softly, taking his older brother's shoulders and lifting him to his feet. They hugged in a meltdown of greeting and utter misery. Feeling just a little more in control, despite his lack of years, Jan put his arm round Tadzio and led his brother out of the barn and away from the yard, so that they could no longer see the dreadful evidence of the *Wehrmacht's* passing.

'*Byłem z drugiej strony gospodarstwa.* I was right at the other end of the farm,' Tadzio told him, struggling to control his sobbing. 'Father said to take Kary and put in a bit of early ploughing. We knew about the Germans massing on the border, so I had the rifle with me in case they decided to search our house. When they came through, I took Kary into the woods. I knew it wouldn't be good when I saw the smoke. After that I just waited – they are not all that long gone… I think they must have found Aniela and then killed Father when he tried to stop them. In the distance I saw someone walk up to the farm. *Nie wiedziałem, że to ty.* I didn't know it was you…' he tailed off, no longer crying but leaving a misery of silence hanging between them.

Together they entered the remains of the house through the charred front door, on the other side of the yard. There had been little inside to burn. Already the smoke was clearing. But the thatch had gone, the stone walls were still hot and everything was covered with ash. The building was no longer habitable. Tadzio went to a stone in the kitchen floor and lifted it with the aid of the Dragant's bayonet. Underneath was a small cloth sack of coins and a couple of boxes of ammunition.

'They didn't find this,' he said softly, lifting the bag. 'We can share the money,' he added quickly.

'*Tobie będą bardziej potrzebne,*' Jan replied. 'You might need it more than me.' Sensing that it was up to him to take charge, he went on, 'We have to bury Father and Aniela. I'm going to find something to wrap them in – I seem to remember there was an old canvas cover in the barn. I'll find a knife and make two shrouds, then we can dig a grave and put them to rest side by side. After that, we need to talk about what we are going to do. In the meantime, I want you to go and choose somewhere not too far away that we can think about and remember, as time passes.'

It was a bit feeble, but Jan knew that Tadzio was not in a good state of mind. At least it would give him something to do. Hours later, they settled to sleep in the barn. Their mother's larder had been denuded by the invaders, so they consumed the last of Frau Brantis' rations. In the morning, they would have to go hungry.

'Thank God she was away,' Tadzio had told him. 'Mother went to visit her sister because our Aunt has not been very well lately. I can write to tell her what's happened and to stay where she is.'

After some discussion, they decided to return to the Raschdorf estate the following morning. Tadzio was of the view that he would eventually remain in Poland. 'We knew what was coming,' he said sadly. 'But we have a treaty with England and France. I think this means a European war, in which case I am going to stay here. We Poles have not been completely idle. There are partisan camps already prepared deep in the forests. We don't have many weapons, but these we can capture. The locals will help us – I don't think we will go short of food or information. For my part, I don't really care what happens to me, but I intend to kill as many of those bastard Nazis as I can.'

Jan was not sure what he would do, but for now there was clearly nothing left either for him or Tadzio on the farm. At first light the following morning and leading Kary they crossed – in Jan's case back – into Hitler's Germany.

Jan managed to show Tadzio to his accommodation without anyone seeing them, after which he went to find Johann. The older man could see the grief etched onto Jan's face. 'It's not good news, is it?' he asked softly.

Despite his best efforts, Jan felt his eyes welling up. 'They killed my father and sister and burned our house,' he told him, leaving it at that. 'I need to go and see the Boss,' he added tearfully.

'I think Herr Raschdorf's in the house,' Johann told him. 'You go, and I'll see you later. I'll telephone to say you are on your way.'

Günther met him outside the front door. 'I've spoken to Johann...' he began, putting his arm round Jan's shoulder to lead him into the house. 'I'm so, so sorry.'

'They...' he stammered, 'my sister – she was...' Günther knew what the lad was trying to say and could offer only a squeeze of sympathy. Again, Jan was forced to dry his eyes, but he had regained a measure of control by the time they entered the study. Only twenty-four hours ago, he realised, he had been in this same room, anxious, but looking forward to seeing his family. Now it seemed as if his life was in ruins. Jan told him about Tadzio.

'I have some news, too,' Günther replied. 'I have been ordered to set up a vehicle repair facility for the *Wehrmacht*. It looks as though you will have to move out, although there are some empty cottages on the estate now that we have mechanised. But that depends upon what you decide to do, in the light of what's happened.'

'We had plenty of time to talk, last night and on the way here this morning,' said Jan. 'I want to join the Army and fight for Poland. I hope you won't be offended, Herr Raschdorf,' he added, 'because I'll be on the other side – which is a shame, because you have been very good to me.'

'What about your brother?' asked Günther, seemingly unconcerned by Jan's announcement. 'What will he do?'

'Tadzio will go back to Poland,' he said simply. Jan thought it politic not to mention that his brother would probably join the partisans and finish up killing Germans. 'But if we could stay here, just for a couple of days, that would be appreciated.'

'We'll sort something out,' Günther told him. 'Helga's not working here any more, and Gudrun and Frau Brantis can be trusted not to say anything.'

'That's not a risk you should take, Sir,' Jan replied. 'I'll carry on as normal, and it would be better if Tadzio just stays in my room till he's ready to go. I think it'll be sooner rather than later. We brought our farm horse with us, so he'll probably ride him home – or to what's left of it,' he concluded sadly.

'You can put him in the stables,' Günther offered, 'but you'll have to look after him yourself now that young Karl has gone off and joined the Army.'

Their discussion at an end, Günther undertook to listen to the news and from time to time update Jan and Tadzio on the progress of the war, so that he would know when it might be safe to return. Jan knew his brother would go as soon as possible, not least because they had left the Dragant concealed in the roof of the barn. He left the following morning, choosing Sunday the third of September. As Günther and Jan had found, there was a fair amount of vehicle traffic on the road, but riding cross-country, it was clear that an Army had passed through and the land to the south of the supply route was empty. Avoiding all farms and villages, Tadzio arrived to find the barn still in one piece and apparently untouched, the Dragant still where he had left it. He decided to make himself a temporary base inside it until he could make contact with some of his fellow countrymen.

Jan spent most of the morning watching military traffic as it drove past the bottom of the estate drive. But when he went to the house for his main meal that lunchtime, approaching the barn he was surprised to be met by Renate Raschdorf. 'Guten Tag, Fraulein Raschdorf,' he said politely.

To his surprise she walked up to him and placed her hand tentatively on his arm. 'Good day to you, too, Jan,' she replied, returning his greeting. 'I have heard about your family. I just wanted to say how sorry we all are, and for what it's worth to offer you my deepest sympathy. I shall understand if you can't accept it. After all, my fellow countrymen are responsible. But what's happened was certainly not done in my name, nor that of anyone on this estate.'

Jan found himself too upset to reply, so he just lowered his head in acknowledgement.

'Father said can you come to the house later this afternoon and he'll tell you what he's heard on the wireless? Because things are not looking good for your poor country. If it's all right with you, I'll be there as well. So, I can make sure we have coffee and a piece of cake,' she finished with a hesitant half-smile.

'*Danke,*' was all he could manage, before walking on to a meal for which he knew he had absolutely no appetite. Fortunately, Frau Brantis had already said how sorry she was, so he was spared further words of well-meant, but for him very difficult, consolation. Although he was surprised that Miss Renate had spoken to him, not least because they had barely exchanged more than a few words in almost three years he had spent on the estate.

Jan changed into his Sunday best before walking the half kilometre or so to the house, arriving at about twenty past four. Renate herself met him at the door.

'We'll use the dining room,' she told him, 'so that we can all gather round. Frau Brantis has finished for the day – we have a cold collation on Sunday evenings, and Gudrun's gone home, so we won't be overheard.' Jan wasn't sure what a "cold collation" was, but he followed Renate into the dining room anyway. Herr Raschdorf rose to greet him. His wife, whom Jan knew less well, remained seated but smiled sympathetically. A large map of Europe had been unfolded on to the dining room table. Jan could not help looking round at the beautiful wooden furniture, shining with a gloss patina from years of polishing. There was a faint hint of lavender on the air and a bowl of roses had been moved to one end of the table, making room for the map. Jan had never seen such a luxurious room. 'Would you like some coffee and apple tart, Jan?' asked Frau Raschdorf gently.

'Just coffee please,' he replied. He would have liked a slice of tart as well, but he wasn't sure what to do with the strange little forks with two normal tines and one wide one.

Renate sensed his reluctance. No strapping young man of Jan's age turned down a slice of Frau Brantis' Sunday tart. She pulled out a chair alongside the foot of the map and asked Jan to sit down. Then she moved to the sideboard. 'Milk?' she asked. Jan shook his head, he preferred his coffee black. She poured him a cup then took a plate and cut a slice of tart. Making sure he could see what she was doing she used the edge of the cake fork to cut off the tip, then pushed the ends of the tines into the small piece. She then set the plate, cup and saucer in front of him. Then she set two arrangements in front of her parents, cut and served in precisely the same way so that Jan would not be embarrassed. Lastly, she served herself.

'I'll tell you what I know,' Günther began. 'I've been pretty much glued to the radio all weekend. I'm not sure whether I believe everything that's being broadcast in Germany. I suspect there's at least an element of propaganda with the Government's hand all over it. So Johann came over this morning. He knows a fair bit about radios from his time in the marine. We beefed up the short-wave aerial and we have good reception of the British Broadcasting Corporation's Empire Service. For some time now they have sent out news in German, but mostly it's in English. My wife is an excellent linguist, Jan – she puts me to shame.' Frau Raschdorf smiled and inclined her head, both to acknowledge the compliment and to confirm that indeed she did know the language.

'It seems that in the early hours of Friday morning,' Günther went on, 'the battleship *Schleswig-Holstein* slipped her moorings and began bombarding *Westerplatte* Polish positions in the Free City of Danzig. Soon afterwards, Army Group North, part of which was almost certainly what we saw a few days ago, crossed the border and pushed into the Pomeranian corridor. The Polish garrison is now bottled up inside their *Westerplatte* base. The *Luftwaffe* have been in action, but we know that because we have seen their planes, particularly the Junkers JU-87 Stuka dive-bombers, although at first, they were hampered by early morning mist. There has also been heavy fighting further south. As far as we are concerned, just over the border, as of now we are being told that the 27th Division is moving into Bydgoszcz,' he indicated the town on the map with his finger, 'which means that our leading elements are at least eighty kilometres into Poland. At the same time, the German Third Army is pushing south from East Prussia, on the Baltic coast, towards Warsaw, although details on their progress are a bit sketchy.

'And finally,' he concluded, 'I should tell you that today, because Hitler ignored an ultimatum for his forces to leave Poland forthwith, both Britain and France declared war on Germany.'

CHAPTER 11

Jan realised that all three members of the Raschdorf family were watching, to gauge his reaction. Clearly Frau Raschdorf and Renate had already been aware of the news he had just been given.

'What do you think will happen, Herr Raschdorf?' he asked eventually. 'Presumably this means that Germany is now at war with Britain and France, as well as Poland?' he added.

'Sadly, this is indeed the case,' sighed Günther. 'I think Herr Hitler has miscalculated badly. Somehow he has managed to plunge us into a European war.'

'I wonder who will win,' Jan mused out loud. He felt bewildered.

'As far as Germany and Poland are concerned,' Günther replied, 'I fear there can be little doubt as to the outcome. Your country was only half mobilised, because of pressure from Britain and France not to upset what they hoped would be a peace process. Added to that, Germany's army is much bigger, the *Wehrmacht* is more mechanised and the Polish army does not have enough tanks. Most of them are only tankettes, anyway, which are little more than mobile machine guns. In the air, your obsolescent P.11 fighters are no match for our modern Messerschmitt Bf 109s and I fear the Stukas will wreak havoc on your ground forces. I pray to God that Hitler will not use bombers such as the Heinkel He 111 on Polish cities, as happened in Spain, but I fear the worst.'

'It doesn't look good,' Jan concluded sadly.

Günther shook his head. 'Poland will almost certainly cease to exist in the not-too-distant future,' he observed. 'I have heard that Hitler is boasting of a victory parade in Warsaw some time in October.'

Jan sat for a minute or so, deep in thought. 'I wonder what will happen to our soldiers,' he said at length.

'Some might escape south, into Hungary or Romania, then maybe join up with the Allies in the west,' Günther replied. 'But I can't see how you can do that when every inch of ground between here and Poland's southern border is occupied by German forces.'

'Johann once told me,' Jan said eventually, 'that after the last war you travelled home from the front by riding cross-country. Do you know what's happening in the west? Maybe I could join up with the Allies by going in that direction.'

Günther was surprised that Johann even knew of his journey. Presumably his father must have mentioned it. He thought for a moment.

'It might just be possible,' he admitted reluctantly. 'Although Britain and France have declared war, both have barely embarked upon mobilisation. The French have apparently reinforced the Maginot line, and we have done the same with our new Westwall. Most of our forces are fighting in Poland. But once your country is occupied, I would assume many of those divisions will be diverted to the western front – where I believe there is something of a stalemate now, with neither side taking any significant offensive action.'

'I'm thinking out loud,' Jan admitted, 'but just supposing, do you think it would be possible for me to cross over?'

'You could try for Switzerland,' Günther responded. 'That way, there would only be the border guards to consider. If you could get there, I have relatives who would help, but even then, your next choice would be either Italy or France. *Il Duce* and the Italians are not exactly on the side of the Allies, though, and by the time you reached Switzerland, France might be embroiled in conflict. Also, without a passport, leaving Switzerland might not be so easy.' He paused for thought. 'I admire your wish to help your country. It might be dangerous, but if your mind is made up then crossing into France or Belgium whilst there is still a phoney peace might be your best option. Equally, you could just stay here. You're a skilled worker, contributing to the war effort. You should be all right and we would never do or say anything to put you at risk.'

'You said that I would have to move out of my room and that some sort of military workshop will be established,' Jan responded. 'How much can you tell me about what's likely to happen?'

Günther gave him the bare outline. A German engineer would be in overall charge. Polish labour would be provided. The *SS* or the *Wehrmacht* would supply a few guards. The building would need to be expanded and they would probably throw up a security fence around the facility. 'I'm not looking forward to it,' Günther concluded, 'but I don't have a choice. I think the engineer is due to arrive the day after tomorrow.' He did not mention the threats that had been made, although both his wife and daughter were aware of them.

Again, the room fell silent for a full minute. 'Sir, I have to think,' Jan said eventually. 'Would it be possible for us to talk again in the morning?'

'Of course,' Günther replied immediately. 'Don't eat in your room. I'll ask Frau Brantis to make you a decent breakfast and you can come through to the study immediately afterwards.'

Jan turned to Frau Raschdorf and thanked her for the coffee and cake.

'Poor Jan – so much has happened to you, at such a young age, and now this…' her reply tailed off sympathetically. 'But you mustn't feel that you are on your own,' she went on, trying to sound a little more optimistic. 'You still have us, and we will help you in any way that we can.'

'Would you mind if I walked with you back to the workshop?' Renate asked him. 'After all this, I could do with some fresh air.' In truth, she did not need a walk, but she was concerned for Jan. Brave as he was, to go into Poland and back, she knew that a dreadful tragedy had fallen onto his young shoulders.

They set out, side by side, walking slowly and without speaking. Jan could not help thinking about what he had found in Poland. At the vision of his father and then Aniela he couldn't help himself: embarrassed, he covered his eyes with his right hand as tears coursed down his face. Renate stopped, then turned to face him. He wiped his eyes on his sleeve. She stepped closer and gently brushed away what was left of the dampness, moving her thumbs outwards over his cheeks. Then she put her arms right round him and gave him a huge squeeze of sympathy and support.

'Come on,' she said quietly, clutching his left arm with both hands and walking again, 'or you'll have me at it as well.'

He felt a little better now and they finished the journey in companionable silence. When they reached the workshop, they stopped at the foot of the staircase. 'Will you be all right?' she asked.

'*Ja*, and thank you for your kindness,' he told her.

To his surprise she stood on tip toes and kissed him gently on the cheek. 'Try to sleep well. See you in the morning,' she said, and turned to walk back to the house.

With a heavy heart Jan climbed wearily up the metal steps. But the Raschdorf family had been very decent. His life might just work out, he thought to himself. There was a glimmer of hope – things could only get better – but there was a lot to mull over.

He was not a drinker. Back in his room, however, he reached into his cupboard for a bottle of schnapps he kept for emergencies, poured a stiff measure and collapsed into his armchair. Outside, the birds were still singing. A couple of hours later he pulled back the covers, fell fully clothed into bed and for the first time in days enjoyed a good night's sleep.

Fortunately, he was young and fit enough to have only the semblance of a hangover next morning. Conscious that he had eaten nothing since the slice of apple tart, he dived into the huge plateful of ham, eggs and fried potatoes that Frau Brantis proudly presented. She poured them both a cup of black coffee and sat opposite, watching him eat. She had grown very fond of the young Pole, but had taken some comfort from a conversation with Miss Renate earlier that morning, when she had politely been asked to make Jan's breakfast. Despite her years, Renate was no longer a girl – definitely an astute young woman.

'*Danke, Frau Brantis,*' he told her. 'That was the best breakfast I have had in a long time.'

'I'm to tell you to go through into the hall. I think the master's already in the study,' she replied.

Jan knocked and opened the door.

'Sir, I spent a long time thinking things over, last evening,' Jan stated, once they were seated. He didn't mention the schnapps. 'You have been so kind to me, my first choice would be to stay here. But realistically I don't think that it's an option,' he concluded.

'Why so?' queried Günther.

'You said there would be Polish workers,' Jan replied. 'They are not going to be volunteers, are they? More likely at best prisoners of war and at worst pressed labour. You also said the guards will be *Wehrmacht* or *SS*. I'm Polish, even if I have been working here for a few years. They might leave me free to walk home each evening but I wouldn't, in their shoes. I think they would probably throw me in with the labour force and I would finish up a prisoner like everyone else.'

Günther had to concede that Jan had a point. He had also

considered the possibility. If it had been raised, he would have objected, but at the end of the day there was always a chance he might be overruled.

'So, what do you propose?' he asked Jan.

'I want to go west,' he replied. 'I know that you crossed from Belgium into Germany after the Great War. I'm hoping that you will share the benefit of your experience. I prefer to take my chances and hopefully fight for my country, rather than risk finishing the war here in a forced labour team.'

Günther moved to a side table and poured two glasses of Armagnac from a decanter, handing one to Jan. 'It's early,' he told him, 'but I think we are going to need this. Is your mind really made up?'

Jan confirmed that it was. 'Absolutely, Sir,' he said. 'I don't see that I have an alternative.'

Günther took a small sip to give himself time to order his words. 'You are in for a few surprises,' he told Jan eventually, then held up a hand to forestall any questions.

'I'm going to offer you a proposal,' he went on eventually. 'I don't see it as acting against my own country, rather I am doing everything I can to protect my family. I am going to share a lot of information with you because I believe we can trust each other. And believe me, I am going to entrust to you one of the two most treasured loves of my life. First of all, did you know that my wife, Hannah, is Jewish?'

Jan could only shake his head in amazement.

'I thought not,' said Günther. 'Hardly anyone does. Although Helga found out, when she was working here. And she told her husband, who is now an *Unterscharführer* in the *Allgemeine SS* – the racial division unfortunately,' he added. 'That is why I had to agree to setting up the workshop.' He did not spare Jan the details of the threats made by Gross.

'When Renate got back last evening,' he went on, 'we opened a bottle of wine and the three of us sat talking for hours.'

'I sat for hours too,' said Jan, 'although on my own. And mine was schnapps.'

Despite the seriousness of their situation, Günther had to smile. 'Anyway,' he resumed, 'I tried to persuade Hannah and Renate to move away from here, for their own safety. My wife turned me down flat. She feels it her duty to remain, and that provided I am contributing to the war effort, and also because I am an Aryan German, she should be all right. And if I say so myself, we are a prominent family in this part of the world, which is probably why we have not otherwise been harassed by the authorities. But we both want to protect Renate. If she stays here, the Nazis will always have a terrible hold over us. Eventually, and with considerable difficulty, we have persuaded her that if it is at all possible, she should leave.'

'Sir, does this involve me?' Jan asked, 'because if there is anything I can do to help, I will.'

Günther gave a heartfelt sigh. 'You don't know what it means to me, to hear you say that. I'm going to tell you a bit of a story,' he went on. 'I won't bore you with all of it, but in nineteen eighteen, on the way back from Belgium, I needed to shelter from the weather. I arrived at a farmhouse, just inside our German border, and prevented a couple of deserters from violating a young widow living on her own in an isolated farm cottage. I stayed there to rest up and recover for a few days, and well…' he tailed off. 'Think of me what you will, and I only told Hannah and Renate of this last night, but our daughter has a half-sister.'

'What did your wife say?' asked Jan, then immediately regretted his impetuous and probably rather impertinent question.

'She is a generous and warm-hearted person,' came the reply. 'It happened before her time, so she simply said that she wished I could have shared it with her years ago. But the point is, although last evening we had not decided how Renate would travel, I managed to put a telephone call through to the lady in question. Her name is Meta. She knows that Renate's mother is Jewish. And she has agreed to offer Renate sanctuary and a safe home for the duration of the war... no more, she said, than the repayment of a long-standing debt. She will pass off Renate as a distant relative, and in a small country community nobody will have any reason to suspect that she is not an Aryan German. Meta remarried: her husband is a retired bank manager and they have a comfortable home. If you intend to try for the western lines, at some stage you will not be too far from where she lives. You would earn our undying gratitude if you would take Renate with you.'

'Of course I will,' Jan responded immediately. 'But how would we travel? What about the risk, because I don't even have any papers?'

'As for travel, I'll spare you over a thousand kilometres on horseback,' Günther said, remembering his own sufferings all those years ago – the wind and the rain, and begging accommodation or sleeping rough. 'I don't think trains are the answer, either. They'll be full of troops, there are bound to be a lot of inspections, and you will be asked why you aren't in uniform.'

He paused for another sip of Armagnac. 'I think you should take my wife's Opel. It's not new, but it's in excellent condition. Renate has her passport, and we ignored last year's diktat that it should be stamped with a 'J'. So far, we seem to have got away with it, because we hadn't been bothered until that bastard Gross turned up the other day.'

'What about me, though,' said Jan, 'with no papers? Even if we go by road we are bound to be stopped at some stage or other.'

Günther walked behind his desk, opened a draw and placed a document next to Jan. It was a German *Ausweis*.

'That was Karl's,' he said. 'When he jumped ship to join the *Wehrmacht,* he obviously packed in a hurry, because he left that in his bedside draw above the stables. Didn't even bother to say "goodbye". I kept it in case he came back or wrote and asked for it. He hasn't, so now we can use it. And he's a couple of years older than you, which might not be a bad thing.'

Jan opened it. 'But the photograph doesn't look anything like me,' he pointed out.

'Nor does it,' Günther agreed. 'But look at the two stamp marks that are mostly on the *Ausweiss.* See how they overlap only the corner of the photo - two circles round the edge with writing in between? And you can hardly see any writing on the photo itself.'

Jan studied the document. Herr Raschdorf was absolutely right.

'There's a photographer on the way to Stettin - I know him quite well,' Günther went on. 'The estate has given him a lot of business in the past, when we were manufacturing the tractors and printing brochures, and we still use him for family portraits. Later today I suggest we drive over. He can take a photograph of you and we'll wait whilst he develops it. Hannah is pretty artistic. She says she can make a rubber stamp with two concentric circles on it, and the right colour of blue ink we have already – given half an hour with her stamp and a very fine pen, you won't be able to tell the difference.'

For the first time Jan began to have a glimmer of hope. This might just be possible. 'The sooner you leave the better,' Günther told him. 'There's bound to be a certain amount of chaos on the way, now that the war has started, and you want to get there whilst the front is still quiet. Once the fighting starts, crossing the line will be more difficult. Also, it might be a good idea not to be here when this engineer arrives, whoever he is. How would you feel about tomorrow morning?'

The decision taken, Jan announced that he would be only too pleased to get started. 'I'll ask Johann to spend the rest of the day on the Opel,' said Günther. 'I want him to go over it with a fine tooth-comb. And will you come and have a meal with us this evening? We need to talk through your plans, and what you will both say if, or when, you are stopped en-route.'

Once Günther and Jan had departed, Frau Brantis was asked to prepare a chicken casserole dish that could be reheated later. On the pretext that Frau Raschdorf would do this herself, because she had no idea what time her husband would return, Frau Brantis and Gudrun were let off early.

Dinner was a subdued affair that reminded Jan of the meal he had shared with his family before leaving Poland. It was agreed that if asked, Jan would be passed off as Herr Raschdorf's chauffeur under orders to escort his daughter to visit relatives on the other side of Cologne. Although in practice they had no intention of trying to drive through the city.

'Sir, how will you explain Renate's absence?' Jan asked, thinking of how Helga's husband had threatened his employer.

'We'll say she is staying with her grandmother in Berlin,' Frau Raschdorf replied for her husband. 'I doubt they will bother to check up, particularly as I shall still be here, which is another reason why I have to stay. If neither of us were still around, the odious Gross might just get suspicious.'

'And if they do check, we'll just report that she left, and my mother can say that she never arrived,' Günther concluded. 'But I doubt it will ever be an issue. If my wife and I are still here, I suspect the *Allgemeine SS* will have enough to do without worrying about the whereabouts of one young female.'

Günther poured each of them a glass of white wine, and Renate smiled when Jan lightened the mood by confessing that it was the first time he had tasted it. She admired his honesty – he hadn't tried to put on sophistication that he just didn't have. Sad though she would be to leave her home and parents, in a way she was quite excited at the prospect of driving across Germany with Jan. She announced that she would be happy to share the driving.

Günther pointed his fork at Jan. 'Watch her,' he said, 'and keep the Opel around fifty kilometres an hour. It has to take you a long way.'

He took a sip of wine. 'I let her have a go in my Mercedes once,' he recounted. 'Before I knew it she had the speedometer over a hundred Ks – and that was still only in the drive, before we even reached the main road!'

The rest of the evening passed pleasantly. Jan thanked his hostess and announced that he would start packing and then have an early night.

In truth, he was still not entirely comfortable as a guest in the main house, although they were very kind. He would rather sit by his open window for a while, perhaps finish off his schnapps, and wonder what the morrow would bring.

Hannah Raschdorf's Opel was a rather shoe-boxy shaped motor car with a fairly long bonnet. Its brilliant cherry-red paintwork and solid, matching wheels sparkled in the early morning sun. It was also a fine-looking vehicle, with the spare wheel attached to the bodywork at the rear of the contrasting, black clam-shell front wing on the passenger side. Günther had paid two thousand marks for it in nineteen thirty-one. The one thousand, one hundred and ninety-three cubic centimetre four-cylinder side valve engine could push it to over eighty kilometres an hour but, as Johann pointed out, driven gently she would run all day. There was no synchromesh on the three-speed gearbox, but Jan had manoeuvred the vehicle countless times in and out of the workshop, as well as collecting and delivering it from and to the main house. He was a master at double-declutching and well able to drive it on the open road.

In response to a telephone call from the main house, they walked up the drive. Johann insisted on carrying Jan's haversack, which he had provided. 'After all,' he had pointed out, 'you can hardly cross the lines carrying a suitcase. And here's a souvenir,' he said, handing Jan a Breton fisherman's cap. 'It doesn't have a shiny peak, but if you stick it on your head you will look a bit more like a chauffeur.'

The roof of the two-door cabriolet had been folded back. On the rear bench seat was a strip of canvas – 'useful if you have to camp out for the night' said Günther, as well as a couple of folded blankets. They put Jan's rucksack and Renate's case on top. There were two spare cans of fuel on the luggage rack. 'And I've put a bag of tools, a funnel and a siphoning tube behind your seat, plus a few spares that I had in the workshop,' Johann told him, 'just in case.' Frau Brantis came through the front door with a large hamper which she placed on top of Renate's case before giving her a quick hug. Wishing them good luck she retreated indoors, wiping her eyes as soon as her back was turned. Günther handed Jan a bulky item wrapped in cloth.

'It's a Webley point four-five-five that I acquired in the last war,' he told him, 'as well as a box of ammunition. Keep it hidden but close at hand. It might just come in useful. Also, I have given Renate enough marks to see you through the journey.'

Jan extracted the revolver from the towel cloth and looked at the chambers, which were empty. He gave the cylinder a quick spin. The weapon was as well-oiled and slick as the day it left the factory. Quietly, he thumbed in six rounds then opened the driver's door and placed it under the seat. 'Let's hope I won't need it, sir,' he replied. 'But thank you, anyway…'

Tearfully Hannah Raschdorf hugged both her daughter and Jan. Günther embraced his daughter and shook Jan's hand. 'I know you will look after her. God go with you both, my boy,' he told him.

Jan engaged first gear and they set off down the drive.

CHAPTER 12

It was a lovely, late summer morning as Jan drove westward at a steady fifty kilometres an hour. The roof was down but Renate had dressed warmly in jodhpurs, riding boots and a thick cardigan. Mid-morning, as the sun rose higher, the latter came off to reveal a modest, crisp white blouse. She was sad at parting from her home and parents. But perhaps the war would not last for long. Despite her privileged upbringing, at the age of seventeen Renate was not much travelled – only as far as Berlin from time-to-time to shop with her mother. She began to enjoy driving across Germany and looking at the passing countryside.

They had decided to use main roads, rather than byways, but they would avoid the *Autobahnen,* over two thousand kilometres constructed under the orders of Herr Hitler so that his troops could move rapidly from one side of the country to the other. They would more likely be heavy with *Polizei* patrols and military traffic. As of now, it was fairly light in their direction but heavy going towards the front, much of it army vehicles. Several times they had to pull over to let lorries and the occasional half-track trundle past.

At lunchtime, they pulled off on to a narrow lane leading to woodland and then reversed well back between the trees to enjoy a picnic. On opening the hamper, Renate found sandwiches on top, with more durable food underneath: cheese and a ham in the middle, tinned food on the bottom layer. To one side she found a bottle of wine and, thoughtfully, a corkscrew and two glasses, plus a bottle opener and two bottles of *Pilsner* beer onto which had been pasted a small notice that read "For Jan, from Frau Brantis".

'She really likes you, you know,' commented Renate.

It was warm in the dappled sunshine between the trees and it would be even hotter, later, in full sun. After they had eaten and replaced the hamper Renate lifted her case from the car. 'I have to change into something a little cooler,' she told Jan. 'I put these on,' her hand indicated the boots and jodhpurs, 'because there wasn't much room in the case and I wanted to have them with me, but I'll just have to squash them in and put on a skirt. Wait for me in the car, please, and I'll change behind it.'

So Jan waited. Not realising that she had to partly unpack before taking out a skirt and a pair of sandals, and then put her things carefully back again, Jan wondered why she was taking so long. Wanting to check that she was all right he risked a glance in the mirror set onto the frame round the top of the windscreen. The reflection literally made his heart skip a beat. She was facing away from the car, wearing her blouse and a pair of what he could only assume to be French knickers, the hems trimmed with a band of lace. He had seen women's undergarments before, of course, but only his mother's and sister's blue flannelette bloomers blowing on the clothes line, elastic round the waist and legs. The creamy-white silk made absolutely no secret of Renate's pert bottom, firm and toned from years in the saddle. He looked away guiltily as she turned to reach down for her skirt.

They drove on through the afternoon and by early evening found themselves just south of Stettin, Berlin's Baltic seaport. Jan was tired. The sky had clouded over, so the cabriolet's hood was now up, but he had opened a window to blow humid air onto his face. And his shoulders were beginning to ache. They came to a small hotel set well back from the road but advertised by a sign with an arrow.

'Let's see if we can stay here for the night,' Renate suggested. 'I know you are tired – I've seen how you're trying to rotate your shoulders. Stay with the car,' she offered, 'and I'll go and see what it looks like inside.'

She was back after a few minutes. 'They are pretty full,' she told him. 'A lot of people are on the move, waiting to take ship in the port. There's only one room.'

'We'll have to drive on, then,' said Jan wearily.

'No, we won't,' Renate replied. 'I've taken it. The idle woman behind reception barely glanced at my passport, and I told her that *mein Mann* would bring in the luggage. You probably know that in German that phrase is often used for a husband. I doubt she'll bother to ask for your papers.'

'What if she does?' queried Jan. 'After all, our names are different. Won't she be suspicious?'

'I'll tell her we are not long married,' said Renate, 'and what with the war and everything I haven't had time to apply for a new passport. Come on, load yourself up with some baggage. She doesn't look the conscientious sort who is going to make you set everything down and put you to all that trouble.'

Renate already had a room key. In the event they walked through the entrance area whilst the receptionist was busy explaining on the telephone that they were absolutely full and there were, unfortunately, most definitely no rooms available.

There was a wash basin in their room, two comfortable chairs, a small table and just one large double bed. It was basic, but clean. Renate sat and then bounced on the bed. 'It feels comfortable,' she announced.

Jan was embarrassed. 'This is a bit difficult for me…' he began.

'It's a bit strange for me, as well,' she interrupted. 'But after the last few days, and now all that driving, you look shattered. Besides, perhaps we wouldn't have found another inn for miles and even then it might have been full.'

She stood and moved to look out of the window. 'There's a war on, you know,' she said pensively. 'I suspect the old ways are gone forever. I know what you are thinking, sharing a room with your employer's daughter and all that, but we can't live in the past.'

She turned to face him. 'We'll be all right, Jan,' she said kindly. 'I'll sleep between the sheets and you can cover yourself with the eiderdown. My father gave me some money, quite a lot of it,' she went on before he could reply. 'I'm going to give some to you – not only will it be safer that way, also it will look odd if I have to pay for everything. Then we'll go downstairs and see if we can find some supper.'

The bar had a bare wooden floor and several old wooden tables. 'A bit rustic,' commented Renate drily, 'but it'll do.' Jan bought them two beers and asked the barman about food. There was no menu, but he was offered a mutton stew and some vegetables, brought on a tray by a serving girl who also set down two large *Brötchen* and a crock of butter. The rolls were still warm. Jan thought that he might as well drag himself up in the world, and he didn't want to embarrass either of them, so again he copied carefully the way in which Renate held and used her knife and fork. They finished the stew, which was surprisingly good, although he was a bit taken aback when she grinned and said, '*Mutti* would tell me off for this', then used the last of her bread to mop up the gravy.

They sat for a while over a second beer but they were both tired after a day in the fresh air. Jan waited in the bar for ten minutes to give Renate time to undress and go to the bathroom, then it was his turn. She was in bed when he went back to their room, her dressing gown draped over a chair. He could see the top of her nightdress above the bedclothes.

'I have never owned a pair of pyjamas,' he told her, so she turned away to spare his blushes. Jan took off his jacket and trousers and slipped beneath the eiderdown. It felt very strange, hearing Renate's soft breathing, and he could smell the perfume of her soap, but he was asleep within minutes.

They breakfasted on ham and eggs. 'Good,' Jan told her, 'but Frau Brantis's are better.' She smiled wistfully at the thought of home. 'You carry the bags, then wait outside,' she suggested. 'I'll pay the bill, so she won't have chance to ask you for any identification.' Minutes later they were on their way.

Jan's main worry was petrol. He had used both cans and they were running low. But most major urban conurbations had several garages by now, and they came across one just before leaving the greater area of Stettin.

Jan pulled up beside the single pump and a mechanic in greasy coveralls came out, wiping his hands on a piece of rag.

'Sorry,' he told them, 'but I'm under orders to fuel only military vehicles.'

Jan thought for a moment, then without letting the attendant have sight of what was in his wallet he extracted one of Günther's *Reichsmark* notes. 'I also need fuel,' he replied, holding out the note. 'But you might not need to look for any change.' The note was worth more than a few times the cost of the petrol. The man eyed it carefully.

'All right,' he said at length. Moving to the pump, he turned a handle that raised a weight which in turn sucked several litres into a glass cylinder. The weight at the top began to fall, pushing the contents through a hose and into the Opel's tank.

Whilst he was doing this Renate, who had seen and heard the exchange, got out to stretch her legs. Günther took the two cans from the luggage rack and put them on the ground by the pump. 'And these, please,' he requested.

The man looked down. 'Cost you the same again,' he said greedily.

Renate waited until he had filled the Opel's tank. 'If it does,' she said sweetly, 'then we'll do without. But before we leave Stettin I shall phone the local SS office and let them know anonymously that in exchange for a bribe you have filled our tank. Your choice,' she concluded, walking back to her door. He glared at her, but wound the handle again and started to fill the first of the two cans.

'Thanks for your help,' Günther said amiably to the attendant when the refuelling was finished. 'And don't worry, there will be no phone call.' With that he re-started the Opel and they drove off. 'I think in future,' he told her, 'we should look for petrol *before* we use the cans, and not after, so that we always have a reserve.'

It was later that day, north-east of Berlin, when they came across their first roadblock. As they approached, Renate handed him Johann's cap. 'Slow down,' she said, 'then stop a few yards short and wind down your window, as if you are quite happy to talk to them.'

Fortunately, they were civilian police, not military. Renate undid one more top button on her blouse, clutched her passport, then opened her door and walked towards them. Both men eyed the rather pretty young woman.

'Good day, gentlemen,' she greeted them. 'What can we do for you?'

'Good day, *Fraulein*,' one of them replied quite politely. 'May I see that passport, and where are you going? What is the reason for your journey?'

Renate smiled at him and handed it over. 'My name is Renate Raschdorf,' she told him confidently, whilst he studied the document. 'Karl, in the car, is my father's chauffeur. *Vati* is the *Kommandant* of a military workshop that has been set up on our estate to support the *Wehrmacht* in Poland. But we are right on the border. I can give you the phone number if you want to check. I am to stay in Berlin for a few days, until the campaign is over. Then it will be safe for me to go home. Karl has been instructed to drive me, in my mother's car.'

The words "chauffeur" and "*Kommandant*" were not lost on the policeman. Neither was the reference to an estate, nor her mother's car come to that. Hardly any families had one car, yet here was the inference that there were at least two. And he had no wish to tangle with the Prussian military. They could be very prickly. The policeman saluted. 'Thank you, *Fraulein*,' he responded. 'That will be all. I hope you have a safe journey.'

Renate smiled at him, murmured her thanks and returned to the car, moving her hips just ever so slightly more that she would normally. She knew without looking that they would be watching her and not Jan or the Opel. She waved politely as they drove past.

'Phew,' Jan exclaimed as they drove away, putting his cap back on the luggage behind them, 'you were pretty good back there,' he added in admiration.

'A girl has to make the most of her assets and know how to handle you men,' she said enigmatically, smiling to herself.

Tadzio was, as usual, up with the daylight. He had made himself a shelter in one corner of the barn, at the other end from the door, with bales of hay. But there was a gap between two of them, giving a clear field of fire to the entrance. He had also created an emergency exit flap behind him. Having removed the stove from his mother's kitchen and installed it crudely in his "room", at least he had heat and could cook. These days, he slept on the floor with the Dragant by his side.

The kitchen sink could still be used, although it was open to the elements. It was whilst he was washing that he heard someone call out… in Polish. In the yard stood a slightly older man he recognised vaguely from a local farm, although he could not recall the fellow's name.

'Józek Kowalski,' his visitor introduced himself. They shook hands. '*Przyjechałem zobaczyć, jak sobie radzisz i co zamierzasz?*' he said. 'I have come to see how you are managing, and to ask what you are going to do?'

'*Gospodarstwo jest w ruinie,*' Tadzio told him. 'The farm's a complete mess. They killed my father and my sister, there's no livestock left, and I shall probably have to survive the winter on what's left of some earthed-up potatoes and a few carrots. Oh, and I have swedes and turnips,' he added with a wry smile, 'as well as the odd cabbage. *To luksus.* There's luxury for you.'

'*Możemy ci pomóc,*' came the reply. 'We could help you.'

'And who is "we"?' asked Tadzio pointedly.

'*Partyzanci,*' said his former neighbour. 'Partisans. We live in the forest. Some of us are the family of those killed by the Germans on their way through. Others are just Polish patriots. We have a few pigs and chickens, but not the right land or facilities to keep them.'

He paused. 'Have the Germans been here yet, and spoken with you?' he asked.

Tadzio explained that he had been back only for a few days, so he hadn't been contacted.

'*Przyjdą,*' came the reply. 'You will be. And you will be told that if you work the land, and supply the German garrisons, you will be allowed to stay. Otherwise, they will threaten to send you to Germany as slave labour.'

'But...?' queried Tadzio.

'*W tej chwili naszym największym zmartwieniem jest zaopatrzenie,*' he was told. 'At the moment, our biggest problem is supplies. We want to know if you will farm for the Germans, but also take some of our stock and farm for us as well. It's not ideal keeping livestock in the forest. Provided we have food, then when we have captured enough weapons – we have only a few at the moment – we can take the fight to the Nazis. But if they find out what you are doing,' he finished bluntly, 'they'll put you against a wall and you will be shot.'

It took Tadzio less than a second to think of his father and Aniela. '*Zgadzam się,*' he replied. 'I'll do it. The pig pen is still here and so is the chicken run. I can take maybe fifty birds, which will give you eggs and meat.'

'*Poczekamy aż do ciebie przyjdą,*' said Józek. 'We'll wait until you have been visited, because that's what's happened to every other farmer in the area. The Germans will probably provide you with some starter stock to replace what's been looted. Obviously, we don't know what we can add until after they have been.'

'How do I get in touch with you?' asked Tadzio.

'*Nie będziesz się kontaktował,*' came the reply. 'You don't. We'll know, then once you have your replacement stock I'll be back.'

They shook hands again. His former neighbour left the farmyard and walked across Tadzio's field towards the woods.

His next visitor, later that morning, was also a fellow Pole who drove into the farmyard in a battered old van. Not someone Tadzio knew, but seemingly a collaborator who said he came from Chojnice.

'*Gdzie byłeś?*' asked the stranger, who didn't even bother to introduce himself. 'Where have you been?'

'My mother went to visit her sister and stayed there,' Tadzio replied, deliberately not answering the question. 'When I got back, my father and sister had been murdered and our house burned down. I buried them on the farm,' he added. 'At the moment, I'm camping out in the barn. Quite honestly, I don't know what I am going to do.'

'That is regrettable,' came the bland reply. '*Nie chcesz wstąpić do armi?*' he was asked.

'No, I'm not thinking of joining the Army,' Tadzio replied. 'I'm a farmer, not a soldier. And in any case, this is our land and I'm the only one left to look after it.'

'*Będziesz prowadził dla nas gospodarstwo,*' his visitor responded. It was a statement, not a question: 'You will farm for us. I can arrange for a pregnant sow and a few birds to be delivered, probably later today. They were taken from other farmers who have proved less than co-operative. Is that understood?'

Tadzio tried to look as simple as possible. '*Mogę to zrobić,*' he replied, 'provided I can keep the farm.' He hoped his confirmation that yes, he could do that, in exchange for keeping the farm, would satisfy the collaborator. It seemed that it had.

'Maybe I can get you some canvas to put under a new roof,' his visitor replied, his eyes lifting to the cottage. 'You need a market for your produce and we need loyal suppliers.'

Tadzio pretended to be grateful for what was, in effect, a small bribe, and thanked him profusely.

There was still some seed in the barn, so he was ploughing an adjacent field with Kary when he saw a large civilian van drive into the yard. By the time he got there Collaborator, as Tadzio thought of him, was standing by the passenger door, cigarette in hand, together with a uniformed *Wehrmacht* non-commissioned officer. The driver was still behind the wheel. Two soldiers with rifles stood at the rear, one either side. The back doors were open. There were several baskets in the back from which emanated the clucking of chickens. They had also offloaded what looked to be several large sheets of folded canvas.

'We have put two pigs in your pen,' Collaborator told him, still without offering his name. 'And we have some birds here for your chicken run. We have taken them from one of your neighbours who is no longer farming. '*Opróżnij koszyki,*' he instructed, 'empty the baskets, then bring them back, so that we can be on our way.' He nodded towards the folded sheets that had been thrown on the ground behind the van. 'Those might help for now. Maybe later you can re-thatch.'

'And please be aware,' the NCO added, 'that whilst we accept you must eat, we also demand a very full and fair return on this investment. Those in the baskets are this year's birds, so they will not start to lay until spring, then someone will return regularly for the eggs. When we are ready, we will butcher the pork ourselves. You will not see either of us again for a while,' his hand waved to include Collaborator, 'but one of my men will make regular inspections, so don't imagine that you will not be watched. It would be *most* unfortunate,' he emphasised, 'were you not to keep your side of the bargain.'

He had spoken in German. Tadzio knew enough to understand what had been said, even though he did not have anything like Jan's fluency.

'*Danke,*' he said simply, and hefted the first two baskets.

A few minutes later he returned the last of them to the back of the van and one of the soldiers closed the doors. With a curt nod Collaborator stubbed his cigarette underfoot and he and the Germans drove off.

Tadzio went back to Kary and his plough. Ten minutes later, Józek emerged from the line of trees - clearly he had been watching the farm.

'I reckon you could overwinter another five or more pigs for us,' he said, 'as well as maybe thirty birds. They're laying already, but not very well, and we are desperate for the eggs. But what will you do if they are seen by the Germans?'

'Not really a problem,' Tadzio replied. 'I'll tell them I went round all the other farms in the area and several of them were deserted, presumably because people fled from the *Wehrmacht*. Obviously, I collected all the stock I could. And in any case, whoever comes to keep an eye on me might not know exactly what was put here in the first place.'

'*Najgorsze co mogą zrobić, to cię okraść.* The worst they can do is steal from you,' he offered doubtfully, as if trying to convince himself, 'but that's a chance we have to take. We can't winter our stock without shelter underneath wet trees.'

He looked round at the house, the barn and the farm. 'There's a lot to put right here, and now you have the stock as well as your fields and a fair-sized chicken farm. *Jak sobie poradzisz?*' he asked.

'I don't know how I'll manage,' Tadzio replied, 'but the same thought had occurred to me. I'll not pretend that it will be easy…'

'If you don't mind giving them a roof over their head,' he was told, 'I could get someone here to help you.'

Tadzio thought for a moment. 'It'll be a while before I can make the house habitable,' he said slowly, 'and till then there is only one small room in the barn. I don't want another man living here in case the Germans get the wrong idea,' he argued. 'I have heard that they send anyone accused of being homosexual to a concentration camp.'

'They do,' agreed Józek, 'but I wasn't thinking of sending a man. 'We have a number of women in the forest, as well as a sprinkling of Jews and intellectuals.' He laughed. 'The latter two are pretty much bugger-all use at the moment, but we are training them up.' Józek paused for a moment. 'Our conditions are a bit rough,' he went on, 'and it's harder on the women, although they never complain. What I have in mind is a young girl called Hedda. She knows farming and she's about your age. You would have some help, and you would be doing her a big favour.'

Jak wyjaśnię jej obecność?' asked Tadzio.

'You probably won't have to explain her presence,' Józek replied. 'The Germans don't know who was here when they came – for all they know she could have been hiding. It's what she would have done if she had any sense.'

'But Hedda's a German name, isn't it?' queried Tadzio.

'Tak,' came the reply. 'Quite right. Her mother's Polish and her father German. Or they were,' he added without explanation, 'and she's fluent in both languages. Hedda was brought up in both countries but she's loyal to us. Believe me, I have seen with my own eyes what she can do with a machine pistol to a *Werhmacht* despatch motorcyclist.'

Tadzio thought about it. There was almost certainly no

risk, and if he was going to have to deal with the German Commissariat there could be an advantage in having someone who could speak with them more easily in their own language.

The following morning, he was pinning canvas sheets onto damaged but still useable beams when a small group of people emerged from the woods onto his field. A woman was herding pigs with a long stick. Four men were carrying a bunch of fowl trussed by the legs over each shoulder. A pity, thought Tadzio. The birds would be distressed. It would probably be days before they started laying again.

Skilfully she guided the pigs into the pen. He came down off the ladder and waited.

'*Jestem Hedda,*' she said simply. 'I'm Hedda.' Like Jan, Tadzio was a little under two metres and broad shouldered and stocky. Unlike him, Hedda was almost his height but slim. She had a handsome rather than a traditionally beautiful face, with the fairest blond hair and most piercing blue eyes that Tadzio had ever seen – perhaps her German heritage. '*Dali ci dwie maciory,*' she said. 'They have given you two sows, so the Germans will already have put them to the boar. They are not showing yet, so it would have been within the last three weeks. You should have two litters in just under 114 days from now.'

So, she really did know her farming, thought Tadzio.

Their chickens offloaded into the run, the four men gathered round her protectively. 'Witajcie,' Tadzio said simply. After Tadzio had bid them welcome, one of the men produced a bottle of *bimber* from a side pocket of his jacket, opened it, and passed it to Tadzio. Now that the birds were no longer there, Tadzio saw that each man had a machine pistol slung on his back.

'*Zdrowie partyzantów,*' the partisan demanded.

Only late morning it might have been, but Tadzio took a deep swig gratefully – it was good moonshine *wódka* – then passed the bottle to Hedda. She swallowed a slightly less greedy helping. The four men followed Tadzio's example. They had raised a toast to the resistance.

'*Powodzenia*,' said the owner of the bottle, returning it to Tadzio as a parting gift. 'Good luck, and if anything goes wrong, and you can make it, you are always welcome to join us. Hedda knows the way.'

Later in the day she salvaged some more pots and pans from the kitchen and lit the stove. 'This scrawny one is a bit of a runt,' she told him, returning from the chicken run. 'I know you are not well off for meat, so this is a small gesture of appreciation from your visitor yesterday.' A couple of hours later, they took it in turns to spoon chicken stew, potatoes and chunks of cabbage from the pot. It was the finest meal Tadzio had eaten since returning to his beloved Poland.

CHAPTER 13

They were in the general area of Celle, northeast of Hannover and south of Hamburg. It was fairly flat, open farming countryside. To Jan it looked prosperous. They had spent the previous night in a small hotel similar to the one found on the first night, but Renate had booked two rooms. Jan felt guilty that he had been disappointed but knew it was only right. Herr und Frau Raschdorf would have excused the first night, and at least now his conscience was clear.

Next morning they pushed on in the general direction of Hannover. But once round the city, they were running low on fuel.

'I don't really want to use what we have in the cans,' Jan told her, 'so the first chance we get I would like to stop and fill up.'

But it was as if the masters of the Third Reich had efficiently taken control of all war-essential commodities. The next garage they came to had two rifle-carrying *Wehrmacht* sentries standing in the entrance to the forecourt. 'Don't even stop,' Renate told him quickly. 'Just keep going.'

Eventually Jan had no choice. He had to put the contents of one of their two, precious twenty litre jerricans into the tank. 'Either we buy fuel soon, we steal it, or we start walking,' he told Renate desperately. 'Johann has given me some siphoning kit – if we can find a vehicle we'll be all right. A small country house would be best, somewhere without staff but affluent enough maybe to have a car in a garage. Safer than trying to do it on the street in some town – although if we have to, late evening or early morning would be best.'

They drove on for another hour, but by now the tank was pretty low. They passed a farm set back from the road –

it looked a very solid, comfortable house but not too grand. And there was a barn which probably housed more than one vehicle. Most of all, a large Mercedes stood in front of the double door.

Jan drove on for a half kilometre or so, then reversed off onto a forest track. 'That last place would do,' he said bluntly. 'If the tank on that Mercedes is only half full, it will fill up this Opel as well as the can we have used. I'm inclined to wait for a few hours then pay them a visit. What do you think?'

'I don't like it,' she responded anxiously, 'did you see the flags?'

'Ja,' Jan confirmed. From a pole pointing up and outwards from the house hung a red, swastika-embellished war banner. A similar small flag flew from the wing of the Mercedes. 'So he's a Nazi, but I don't see that it makes any difference. We're stealing petrol. That's all there is to it.

'You should be safe enough here,' he told her. 'And I'll leave you your father's revolver. But I need to watch that place for a while. Find out who's there – how many people. Then I'll come back and we can decide what to do. Try to get some rest,' he suggested, although he knew that would be almost impossible.

Jan was a country boy – he could poach with the best of them. In less than an hour he had moved silently through the copses and fields till he had a clear view of the front of the house. A chauffeur drove the Mercedes into the barn. Jan moved till he had an equally good view of the rear. At about half past eight a small group of people, presumably servants and the chauffeur with them, left the house. By ten, with the lights on and the curtains still undrawn, Jan had seen only one man move from room to room. He was reasonably certain that he was alone in the house.

At about half past eleven the occupant stood in a downstairs study window, brandy balloon in hand, then drained his glass.

The light was extinguished and a few seconds later another switched on in the master bedroom. Jan gave it an hour, then returned to the Opel and Renate.

'We're clear to go,' he told here. 'I watched someone put the Mercedes in the barn, and there's no lock, just a closing beam. I can put the full can into our tank, then fill both of them, although it will probably take two trips before everything is topped up and we are on our way.'

'Just be careful,' she told him.

'I will,' he replied. 'And you stay here.'

Entering the barn was as quick, silent and easy as Jan had hoped. It was dark, but with just enough ambient moonlight to make out the shape of the Mercedes. Jan took off the filler cap and pushed the length of rubber hose into the fuel tank, feeling a slight resistance when it touched bottom.

He sucked. Despite his best intentions, he brought up a small amount of fuel that he had to spit onto the floor of the barn. Wiping his mouth with the back of his hand he spat several more times, then released his pinch-grip on his end of the hose and pushed it into the empty can. There was a gratifying "swish" as the transfer began.

Jan closed the top of the second can and made ready to leave. He would have to return, but after this exercise did not envisage a problem. Not, that is, until he was suddenly bathed in light from a hand torch. Held deliberately within the beam was a German Army pistol. It would have been foolish to imagine that it was not already cocked. Also in the pool of light, on a slip lead, was a huge Alsation. The dog was silent, but his teeth were bared. It was a trained attack dog, and Jan knew that its handler had only to release one end of the leash and he would be in serious trouble – that's if he did not collect a bullet at the same time.

'*Hände hoch!*' came the brisk, confident command, reinforced by an upward flick of the end of the barrel. Even if he had not spoken a word of German, the meaning would have been clear. Slowly, Jan raised his hands and faced the light. The dog, the torch and the light were just inside the barn door. Jan was almost blinded when a powerful overhead light came on, the man's right hand leaving the switch to re-aim the pistol.

Jan saw that his captor was wearing the boots and jodhpur-like trousers of the SS. 'You are stealing my petrol.' The accusation was a statement, not a question. 'So, I have a choice. Either I shoot you, or I give you to Rolfi here. That's how you were detected – he is trained to alert me but not to bark. And believe me, if he attacked you would not survive him either.'

'Yes, I was taking petrol,' Jan told him, thinking that his only chance was to admit his crime and hope for a degree of clemency. 'We have run out and cannot buy any. But I would happily pay you… I would have left the money… I could give it to you now,' he added quickly.

'I don't think so,' came the reply. 'The automatic was lifted into the aim.'

'Please,' said Jan desperately, 'you can't murder me just for this… it's against the law.'

'Your accent says you are not from round here – further east, I would guess,' the German replied. 'Let me tell you something. Since 1934 the SS have not been under the jurisdiction of the civilian courts. We are responsible only to ourselves. And no *Hauptamt SS Gericht*, no SS main court, is ever going to convict a senior officer for shooting a thief in the night.'

His captor's arm extended, the weapon raised into the aim. Jan knew he had only seconds to save himself. He was still cursing the fact that he had left the Webley with Renate when the explosive crack of a round was the last thing he heard.

'*Dzisiaj mamy czwartek, trudno uwierzyć, że jutro minie tydzień od dnia ataku Niemiec na Polskę.* Today's Thursday – it's hard to believe that a week ago tomorrow the Germans invaded Poland,' Hedda told him, as they huddled round the stove sharing the rest of the partisan's *bimber*. They were talking well into the night. '*Co będziesz dzisiaj robił?*' she asked. 'What do you plan to do tomorrow?'

'Well, some of the fields are ploughed ready for sowing in the spring,' he told her. 'What with the chickens and pigs, plus what we should be able to harvest after the Germans have driven over our land, we have enough for two people to survive the winter. But I'm quite keen to repair the farmhouse. I don't fancy this barn, once the weather really turns cold.'

They could sleep well enough on two beds of hay within a wall of bales, but it was already cold at night and would only get worse. Washing would be primitive – either a kitchen sink open to the elements or a bucket from the yard pump when the other was outside of their "room" to offer privacy. Hedda agreed that they would probably survive the Polish winter, but in the barn it would be hard and uncomfortable. '*Niektóre krokwie wyglądają dobrze, nawet jeśli są trochę przypalone.* Some of the roof timbers are all right, if a bit burnt,' Tadzio mused, 'but several are completely gone. Somehow, I have to replace them.'

'*Przecież mieszkasz tuż obok jednego z największych lasów w Polsce,*' she chided him. 'You live almost next door to one of the biggest forests in Poland. I have seen some log splitters in the barn and a lump hammer. After breakfast, we'll take Kary and a couple of axes and cut a few trees – they don't have to be that big to make a rough replacement for the roof beams. If we split each trunk, we'll only need to cut maybe four or five young trees. Fir would be best – it won't last forever, but for now it's soft and easy to use. You can always cut some oak later, after the war.'

'Maybe there won't be an "after the war",' said Tadzio wearily. 'Perhaps we will live out our lives under the rule of Germans.'

'*Może, ale nie wydaje mi się,*' Hedda replied. 'Maybe, but I don't think so. I'm not sure Hitler expected to have to fight England and France,' she offered, 'and I would not be surprised if Russia and America were involved eventually. Our country might not exist for a while,' she admitted, 'but even if there is no Poland, there will always be Poles. Our duty is to survive and wait for the future. For now, that means we farm for the invaders, but we also farm for our own resistance. *I kiedykolwiek i gdziekolwiek zdołamy, podejmiemy walkę z Niemcami!*' she finished vehemently. 'And whenever we can, we take the fight to the Germans!'

Tadzio was beginning to realise that there was more to Hedda, in both a practical and an intellectual sense, than he had at first realised. '*Ale póki co,*' he replied, 'but for now, we will have to set aside world politics and fix the roof. In the morning we'll cut young pines, lop the branches, then split the logs and drag them back. The bigger branches we can tie together so that Kary can also pull the bundles back to the barn – fuel for the stove. After that we remove the worst of the fire-damaged roof timbers and start replacing them with our rough-hewn fir.

'What are you going to do with the tarpaulin?' asked Hedda, taking another small sip of *bimber* and passing the bottle back to Tadzio.

'Maybe thatch over it,' Tadzio replied, 'might be a good idea. But I'm no thatcher,' he added.

'*Ja mogę to zrobić,*' Hedda said simply. 'I can do it. Father taught me. He loved doing things on the farm, when he wasn't at the university.' She stopped suddenly. Tadzio realised that she had let slip more than intended.

'*To nie jest trudne,*' she went on quickly. 'It's not difficult.

You nail some battens between the main timbers, twine- or wire-in a cross layer of thatch, then put a vertical one on top. One hundred percent waterproof!' she exclaimed.

There was even more to Hedda than he had ever suspected, Tadzio realised. 'OK, but why not thatch over the tarp?' he asked her. 'It won't look so good, but it would be quicker.'

'That tarpaulin would an absolute godsend to my people in the woods. We could give it to the partisans. Otherwise, believe me, they are soaking wet under whatever they can lash up from sods, leaves and branches.'

Tadzio agreed. They would cut rushes. '*Za kilka dni*,' Tadzio told her. 'Another couple of days, and I reckon we'll have a proper roof over our heads.'

For several seconds Jan had no hearing at all, just a ringing sensation in his ears. He wiped his face – his hand came away covered in blood and greyish-white matter. But it was not his – the SS officer lay on his side at his feet. Renate stood there, frozen, tendrils of smoke whisping from the barrel of the Webley that was still clutched in shaking hands. The Alsatian sniffed uncertainly at his master's body, then slunk from the barn, tail well down. Clearly, it attacked only on command. Slowly Jan moved to one side, out of her point of aim, then stepped forward and gently took the weapon.

'What have I done?' she asked, hands covering her face.

'Saved my life,' Jan said bluntly. 'He was going to kill me. Thank god you were there – but I told you to stay with the car?' he queried.

'I did, for a few minutes, but then I thought it might be a good idea to watch the house when I knew you would be inside the barn,' she told him. 'I brought the gun because I didn't want anyone who might find the car to steal it. I never thought I would have to use it,' she admitted tearfully.

'Thank God you knew what to do,' said Jan, moving to the

door. No lights had been switched on in the house – it looked as though his deceased captor lived alone.

'You know I was brought up on a farm,' she told him, 'I have been using firearms for years. But I've never shot a human being before... you have gone all red,' she said, looking at the mess on Jan's face, then her nerves gave out and she started to laugh hysterically.

Jan held her tightly and shushed till she stopped. 'I'm going to check out the house,' he told her. 'If possible, I have to get cleaned up. We can't drive on with me covered in blood. If there's no one else here, I'll fetch the car. First we fill up, then we can think about what to do next.'

The house was empty. The dog had disappeared. Twenty minutes later Jan parked the Opel by the barn, filled the tank and the empty jerricans and stood to straighten his aching back. It was almost midnight.

'The staff won't come back till the morning,' he suggested. 'I need to take a bath – just look at the state of me, And I stink of petrol. Whoever he was, we are about the same build. Maybe I can find some clothes – mine are stained with blood and brains.'

Whilst he enjoyed the luxury of a quick soak, Renate raided the kitchen and prepared a generous cheese and ham omelette – obviously, the SS hierarchy were well provided with rations. Fuelled, fed and with a few extra provisions, not least several bottles of fine wine, they would not take the risk of staying in the house any longer than necessary. He also lifted a box of matches from the kitchen.

'Let's put forty or fifty kilometres behind us,' he suggested, 'then find somewhere to park up until it gets light. But I have to destroy the evidence in the barn, so that we delay any manhunt for a few days, by which time we'll be well away from here.'

They left the house, doors shut but not locked. Now

wearing the most expensive flannel trousers, shirt, pullover and jacket that he had ever known, in the barn Jan left the cap off the Mercedes' fuel tank, then piled straw underneath it and threw his blood-stained clothing on top. The body of the SS officer he dragged alongside the vehicle. He started the Opel, drove it a short way from the barn, then returned and set light to the straw. Just before turning onto the highway they waited until a soft *whoomph* confirmed that the fuel tank had exploded. A few metres along the road, glancing back, he could see a red glow as flames engulfed the barn.

A couple of hours later Jan thought it safe to pull off, reversing along a broad farm track. They dozed fitfully for about an hour and a half, then tidied themselves as best they could for the day ahead. 'I think we should eat and then set off about seven-ish,' Jan suggested. 'If we were stopped at a checkpoint before then, it might look a bit suspicious.'

They breakfasted well. Renate had hard-boiled some eggs whilst making the omelette and these, together with some Brötchen and butter also lifted from the kitchen, made something of a feast. She had even thought to remove a packet of salt. But it had been a desperate night. Although longing for coffee, which they could not make, they opened and drank sparingly from a bottle of wine.

They stopped driving early that afternoon and spent the night in a rather more comfortable hotel not far from Paderborn. Fortunately, Jan was at last able to buy petrol. There was one more night, somewhere in the industrial area south of Düsseldorf, where with so many commercial travellers they attracted no interest at all. On the afternoon of the following day, with Renate navigating carefully from her father's map, they were just short of the drive that led to the address of Herr Klaus and Frau Meta Holtzer.

'She would give us both a room, you know,' argued Renate.

'Best she doesn't know,' countered Jan.

'Do you want to take the car?' she offered.

He shook his head. 'I can make my own way from here. Besides, it would be a waste – I would only have to leave it somewhere nearer the front. In any case, it belongs to your family. You take it, and if you can't get fuel then lay it up for the duration. Just make sure the wheels are chocked clear of the ground,' he finished lamely.

'Dearest Jan,' she said tenderly. 'Still looking after me till the last minute.' Twisting in her seat, she pulled his head to hers and kissed him once, passionately, on the lips.

'You were always the perfect gentleman,' she said softly. 'I hope and pray that we will meet again, once this stupid war is over.' She released him, and they were once more apart.

Jan took stock of his situation. Renate would not need the Webley, and he still had a box of ammunition. He was wearing decent boots, good clothes and had a cape in case it rained. The weather was benign, so provided it did not deteriorate he ought to be all right for the few days it would take him to reach the border. Carefully he stowed some rations into his rucksack.

'I guess this is it,' he told her. 'You drive up to the house and I shall carry on. It's best this way – what the Holzers don't know, they can never tell. If I can find a way of sending word to you, I will,' he told her, before opening the door and holding it whilst she walked slowly and reluctantly round the bonnet. She stroked the side of his face tenderly then settled into the driving seat.

'Stay safe,' she told him, 'and try to come back to me.'

Knowing that she was beginning to well up, Renate started the engine, wound down the window, clutched Jan briefly on the forearm and engaged first gear. He watched as she turned into the drive, seeing her look at the last second in the mirror, then he lowered his hand, shouldered the rucksack and set off for the border.

It was a substantial, prosperous-looking farmstead. Nothing like the cottage her father had described, and where he had made such a bedraggled and dramatic arrival twenty-one years ago. But Renate could see where the original dwelling had been extended to provide a quality, country residence. A well dressed, middle-aged woman came out of the front door as soon as she drew up outside and set the handbrake.

'I know who you are,' she said, holding Renate's shoulders at arms' length. 'Let me look. You are beautiful… and I can see Günther Raschdorf in you all over again, even after all these years.'

Meta took her upper arm. She was smiling, the few wrinkles alongside her eyes clearly signalling her delight. 'I know all about you,' she said quickly, 'but Klaus doesn't. I have told him that you are the daughter of a very dear friend who is also a distant relative.' All this before they entered the spacious hall. 'He's looking forward to meeting you,' she went on, 'though he's resting at the moment. For now, we'll have something to celebrate, then later on we can have supper.'

They entered a good-sized drawing room. Meta poured two glasses of pale sherry, then sat beside Renate on the sofa. 'Was it a difficult journey?' she asked.

Renate looked around before replying. Clearly there was evidence of wealth and good taste, but not ostentation. It could just as well have been their drawing room at home. Thoughts of the estate, her parents and the events of the journey were almost too much. She had to wipe away a tear.

'None of this has been easy,' she began, 'but I can't thank you enough for taking me in. I would never have been safe on the estate.'

'Has your father told you what he did for me?' asked the older woman.

'Only that he was able to help you just after the last war,' Renate said tactfully.

They heard the sound of footsteps in the hall. 'We'll talk again tomorrow,' said Meta. 'But believe me, you are very welcome to stay here for the duration.'

Tall, slim and balding, Klaus Holtzer was clearly some years older than his wife – perhaps in his sixties. And he walked with a cane. But even so he had an aristocratic bearing and a kindly smile. 'I like your Opel,' he said pleasantly. 'I hope you will enjoy your stay with us… I am retired now, and we are simple country people. But Meta can show you to your room, and I'll have someone bring your things from the car. Afterwards, you can put it into one of the barns. We are not grand enough for a garage,' he finished, his eyes twinkling with amusement. Meta stood and took her husband's arm as he lowered himself into a chair. They clearly had a long and loving understanding and were happy and comfortable together, given that there probably never had been the first flush of romance.

Renate glanced at a photograph on the mantelshelf of a young man in the uniform of a *Wehrmacht* officer. 'That's our son, Hans,' Klaus told her. 'And we have a daughter, Gisela. She is at the university in Cologne, reading modern languages. Although she is studying in Rome at the moment, trying to perfect her Italian. She'll be back after the Spring term.' Renate glanced at the adjacent photograph. Her heart almost stopped. It was as if she had looked in a mirror. Fortunately, Klaus Holzer had been distracted by Meta, who was handing him a glass of sherry.

Jan's journey to the front proved relatively uneventful. Sometimes he walked but more often than not he was able to cadge a ride, either in a lorry or, on more than one occasion, on a horse-drawn cart. With the money Renate had given him, and showing occasionally his borrowed *Ausweis*, he was able to lodge overnight in cheap inns that at least provided a meal and bed and kept him dry. But he walked the last few kilometres to Monshau, a border village just south of Aachen.

During the first months of the war there was little activity on the western front – all the action was in the east. The borders were patrolled, but fighting units were for the most part either billeted or kept in barracks. There was very little skirmishing. Seeing a border post in the distance, he turned off the road and followed the edge of many fields, all the time heading west. When eventually he rejoined a paved highway, the number plate of the car that stopped to give him a lift confirmed to Jan that he was in Belgium. It had been that easy.

What was not so easy, however, was that the driver was French speaking and Jan knew only Polish or German. His benefactor was nervous at first, and kept poking Jan with an index finger whilst repeating '*Deutsch, Deutsch?*' – clearly one of the few German words he knew.

Jan had no choice but to revert to his own language. '*Polak,*' he replied. 'Polish.' And at last the driver understood. Jan had an idea and pointed first to himself and then west, through the windscreen. 'England, England!'

'*D'où venez-vous?*'

Jan didn't understand, but sensed that he was being asked either about his nationality or where he had come from. '*Polska, Polska,*' he replied. 'Poland, Poland.'

The driver pointed at him, then said 'England?' The rising inflexion made the question obvious.

Jan nodded vigorously. The driver was almost beaming now, from ear to ear. He took Jan's hand and shook it, pumping it up and down. '*Angleterre,*' he said to himself, putting the car into gear. They drove, although where they were going Jan was unable to ask. But as they were heading more or less in a westerly direction he was content to enjoy the ride. Eventually they came to quite a large city and the Belgian pulled up outside what appeared to be a police station, judging by the '*Politie*' sign. The driver, whose name Jan still did not know, pointed to Jan, then to himself, and finally to the front entrance. Jan thought for a moment, but realised he had little choice. Once inside, there was a torrent of unintelligible words till Jan was signalled to a chair. He felt encouraged and a little more relaxed when he was given a cup of coffee. Finally, he was called to the desk and handed a telephone handset.

'Hello?' he asked nervously.

'*Kim pan jest?*' asked a friendly voice in Polish. 'Who are you?'

Jan told him where he had come from, and that he was trying to join the Polish army in Britain, if indeed there was one. '*Lub Armia Brytyjska,*' he added. 'Or the British Army. In fact, any Army that will fight the Germans.'

'I am going to arrange for you to be given a rail warrant,' said the voice on the other end of the line. 'When you get to Brussels, ask for directions to the *Ambassade Britanique*. Remember those words, and just keep repeating them whenever you need directions. You'll get here eventually. Now, say it back to me, *Ambassade Britannique.*'

Jan complied. '*Może być,*' he was told. 'That'll do. We'll see you later this afternoon or this evening. The people at reception will know that you're coming. *Powodzenia.* Good luck. Now hand the phone back to the police.'

There was a further exchange before the receiver was replaced. Shortly afterwards a civilian clerk appeared with a book of printed warrants. Jan was handed one on which had been written the words *Liège* and *Bruxelles*. The rest he couldn't understand. His driver shook his hand once more and departed. Jan was beckoned to follow a policeman through the building to the yard behind, from where he was driven to a railway station. The policeman took him to a window and the warrant was exchanged for a ticket. Finally, he was shown to a platform and invited to climb into a carriage. It was dusk when, weary from travel, he found the *Ambassade Britannique*.

CHAPTER 14

'*Muszę mieć broń,*' Hedda told him. 'I need a weapon. I didn't bring one with me because they are in desperately short supply and our partisans in the forest have a greater need than do I. Also, I needed to find out what the situation was here.'

'How do you plan to get hold of one?' Tadzio asked. 'And what are you going to do with it?'

'*Zdobędę u Niemców,*' she said simply. 'I'll take one off the Germans. Most of the time I'll be here on the farm, but when we mount a major operation I intend to be part of it. That's why I joined the partisans. And I would rather take my own, zeroed weapon than have to borrow every time I need one. If it's all right with you, I'll be gone for one or two days at the most, then I'll be back.'

'*Na pewno nie możesz tego zrobić sama?*' he queried.

'Yes, I can do it on my own,' she replied confidently. 'It's too far to walk to our camp, ask for help with a simple ambush, then walk back here again all in one or two days. Besides, this way the risk will be all mine – no-one else need be involved. If anything went wrong, and a group of us were tracked back to our base, it would be a disaster.'

Tadzio thought for a minute or so. 'Why are you doing this?' he asked eventually. 'How come you are half German but you hate them so much?'

She looked at him for quite a while, as if making her mind up whether – or how – to respond.

'*Dobrze,*' she said at length. 'All right, you're providing a roof over my head, so I suppose you are entitled to know something about me.

'My father was the kindest, most cultured man you could imagine,' she went on. 'He taught classics at the university in Berlin. It was there that he met my Polish mother. She came from a good family and had gone there to study.'

Tadzio noticed that she had not mentioned from where, in Poland, her mother's people originated.

'They fell in love, got married, and I was the result,' said Hedda wistfully. 'But in 1933 the Nazis passed a law depriving Polish immigrants of their German citizenship. My mother lost hers. Later that same year, they said that because my father was Jewish he was not allowed to own land. My parents lost the farm that had been my childhood home – it was just taken from us. Fortunately, Father still had his teaching post, but we had to move into a small apartment in the city. It was the beginning of a very bad time for our family.

'Then two years ago, in January 1937, a law was passed excluding Jewish people from most of the professions. Part of this law said that Jews were no longer permitted to teach Aryan Germans. My father lost his job. Already our land and home had been taken from us, and now we had no income to pay for food or rent for our apartment. I used to lie in bed at night listening to my parents' conversations – they were anxious and frightened. Ashamed that he could no longer support his family, my father hanged himself. I saw his body before it was cut down. It must have been a horrible death. With not much of a drop to break his neck he slowly suffocated. *Vati* was a fastidious man, but he had soiled himself. With no prospect of employment, and me formally declared Jewish, my mother decided to take me back to her parents' house in Poland.'

'*Dlatego tak bardzo nienawidzisz nazistów.* Which is why you hate the Nazis so much,' Tadzio empathised gently. 'But not all Germans are Nazis – your father wasn't.'

'My father's death broke my mother's heart,' Hedda went on, seemingly oblivious to Tadzio's comment. 'Back in Poland, because she had been studying chemistry, she found a job in a pharmacy. One day, she couldn't take any more. Having the knowledge and access to pills she, too, took her own life. All she left was a note to my grandparents, saying how sorry she was and begging them to look after me.'

Hedda had been staring at the ground. Suddenly she looked up directly at Tadzio, her expression a mixture of hatred and resolve. 'In 1934, the Germans gave Hitler a 90 percent vote of approval,' she told him. 'My father didn't vote for him, but I hold that country entirely responsible for the death of my parents. Now the Germans have invaded Poland. Quite honestly, Tadzio, if it were in my power, I would kill every one of them that I could lay my hands on.'

She walked away for a few steps, then stopped to wipe away tears. Embarrassed, Tadzio followed to put a tentative, comforting arm round her shoulders.

'*Muszę mieć broń,*' she said bluntly. 'So I need a weapon, and tomorrow I am going to set about finding one.'

Tadzio thought of Aniela and his father. '*Jeśli mi pozwolisz,*' he said gently, 'if you'll let me, I want to come with you. Perhaps I can help.'

They were no longer living in the barn. With the roof repaired, Tadzio had put on a new door, replaced some window glass and made the rooms habitable, although everything still smelled of smoke from the fire. He walked to the barn and retrieved the Dragant from the rafters.

'You shouldn't have kept that there,' Hedda told him, appalled. 'What if the Germans had searched the farm and found it? You might have been shot.'

'It's years old,' he told her, 'and I could have explained how my father acquired it.'

She shuddered. 'Even so...' she insisted, 'put it away for tonight, then tomorrow or the next day we'll hide it properly.'

'It's important not to do anything near the farm,' she

explained to him the following morning as they walked along the edge of a field towards the forest, 'because the Germans usually mount some sort of follow-up operation.'

They were several kilometres away before she found what she wanted, an unpaved track emerging from a good-sized copse, with mature trees on either side of the road. The undergrowth between the trees gave excellent cover. They settled down to wait.

Several groups of military vehicles passed in both directions. But eventually a motor cycle and side-car combination appeared, a lone despatch rider returning from the front. Slung on his back was an MP 38 "Schmeisser" sub-machine gun. *To też ulubiona broń partyzantów.* It's a favourite weapon with the partisans,' she told him. 'Our leader said that with a folding stock and a magazine of 32 rounds, it's a standard item of equipment with the *Wehrmacht*, alongside the rifle and heavier machine gun.'

They waited several hours, till later in the day a combination passed by travelling in the other direction. *'Myślę, że to to,'* Hedda observed. 'I think that's it. The Germans are creatures of habit. It looks as though there is one courier every day, both ways.' Brushing themselves down, they turned to walk back to the farm. Hedda set about preparing an evening meal whilst Tadzio cleared the remaining rooms of the last bits of ash and debris. They had rescued an old table from the barn that was now in the kitchen, and as she had pointed out, they were not short of timber. As soon as he could, he intended to fell a few more young trees and construct some basic chairs and a couple of beds.

The following morning, they set off again. This time Hedda had a length of coiled bailing wire over one shoulder. In her left hand was a metal crowbar. Tadzio carried the Dragant, assembled and loaded but wrapped in cloth. Not far from where they had waited yesterday, he stood a little to one side, listening for any sound of approaching traffic, whilst Hedda wrapped one end of the wire around the trunk of a tree before leading it down to the ground. Next, she used a stick to quickly fashion a shallow trench in the dirt road, before setting in the wire and covering it over. Patted down by hand, the excavation would be invisible to approaching traffic, least of all a rider on a vibrating motor cycle and wearing goggles. Finally, she selected another tree where hefty branches stemmed from the main trunk and then forked, one branch high above the other. The wire she passed down through the fork on the upper branch, then attached the crowbar.

'When the time comes,' she told him, 'all I have to do is pull the bar down, which raises the wire up from the road, and then jam it under the lower fork.' She demonstrated, checking the height of the wire, then re-buried it. Tadzio settled down nearer the track to watch for traffic. Later, if all did not go according to plan, he would be on hand to try to cover their withdrawal. Although with any luck, he pointed out, their victim would be hard pressed to follow them on foot through the trees.

At about the same time as yesterday a motor cycle and side-car appeared, travelling at around sixty kilometres an hour. Unlike yesterday, there was a passenger in the side-car, an officer, judging by his uniform, although Tadzio was not familiar with *Wehrmacht* rank insignia. There was no other traffic in sight or hearing. Tadzio shouted to Hedda, knowing that he would not be heard above the noise of the machine. The wire lifted, as if by an unseen hand, and stretched taught across the track. The rider had no chance of avoiding it. In fact, Tadzio doubted whether he even saw the danger. It struck him high in the chest, before lifting to cut deep into his throat. In microseconds, the head snapped back to a horizontal position, breaking the spinal column. Finally, as the wire lifted over the rider's face, stripping skin and tissue, there was a loud twanging noise as it parted under the quantum strain of mass times velocity. But the damage had been done. With its rider barely in the saddle, the combination turned from the road and hurtled into the undergrowth for several metres before striking a tree stump and overturning.

Both rider and passenger had been thrown clear. Whilst Tadzio covered them with the Dragant, Hedda checked each in turn for a pulse. But it was clear from the angle of their heads that they were both dead – the rider as a result of the wire, his passenger from being thrown against a tree.

'Mamy szczęście,' she told him. 'We're lucky. This is far enough from the road not be seen by passing traffic. So, when he doesn't arrive, they won't know where to search. Quickly, help me – the passenger's a bonus. He's wearing a Walther.'

Tadzio undid the officer's belt and took the pistol, still in its holster. Hedda removed the P38 from its now blood-soaked sling. Both magazines were loaded and a quick search of the bodies yielded more ammunition. From a distance came the rumble of one or more lorries. 'Probably a convoy,' she said urgently. They had just enough time to remove the wire before Tadzio picked up the Dragant. Carrying their additional weapons, they ran from the scene. Not until they were well away from the road did they ease the pace.

'We can't hide this lot in the barn,' she panted, 'it's too dangerous. The Germans probably won't find the wreck, but if they do, they might well make a sweep of the area. Later on it might be useful to have the Walther in the house. But for now, as soon as we get back we'll oil the weapons then wrap them in sacking. We can bury them well away from the farm but it will have to be in a wood.'

'Dlaczego?' asked Tadzio. 'Why so?'

'Because if the Germans search from a light aircraft and take photographs at first or last light,' she told him, 'fresh digging usually creates a faint shadow. But in the woods, they won't see it.'

Tadzio could only wonder at the knowledge she had gained from bitter experiences in so short a lifetime.

The receptionist held up an out-facing index finger, indicating that Jan should wait whilst she picked up a telephone. A few moments later a young woman looking very business-like in a pencil skirt and white blouse smiled and beckoned him to follow. She held open the door to a small office, just a short way along the corridor. A man stood and came out from behind a desk, offering his hand in greeting. He was wearing a beautifully tailored grey suit, his snow-white double cuffs and gold links visible at the wrists. His hands were immaculately clean and manicured. Jan felt rather dirty and travel-stained by comparison.

'Jan Janicki?' he queried, raising his eyebrows. 'We spoke on the telephone. My name is Major Władysław Miecznikowski.' His Polish was fluent – very cultured and upper-class. 'Do you perhaps have any means of identification?' the major asked pleasantly.

'Only this, Sir,' Jan replied, handing over his German *Ausweis*. 'But it's a forgery – my photo, but it belonged to somebody else.'

'I see,' said the officer with a smile. 'I think you had better sit down and tell me your story. But first, have you had anything to eat or drink?' – he glanced at an expensive looking gold wristwatch. 'At this time of an evening probably the best we can do is something fairly basic.'

Jan had eaten the last of his rations hours ago, just before crossing the border. 'Shall I tell you my story first, sir?' he offered. 'Then I would be very grateful for some refreshment.'

Major Miecznikowski settled behind his desk and waved Jan to a comfortable chair. Taking a few moments to collect his thoughts, he set off. 'My people farmed near Chojnice in Pomerania, although I was actually born in Bydgoszcz.

In nineteen thirty-six,' he went on, 'when I was sixteen...'

He spoke for about ten minutes, describing his life in Germany, his return to Poland, the death of his father and sister and briefly of Tadzio, his surviving brother. The officer occasionally asked a question but for the most part he was content to let Jan speak, although he made a few notes from time to time, particularly when Jan mentioned the workshop facility. Finally, he described the journey across Germany with Renate. 'And that's about it, sir,' he concluded. 'I left Fraulein Raschdorf with friends, walked and hitched rides to the border, and here I am. And as I said on the phone earlier today, my wish is to try to reach England, join an Army, and fight the Germans.'

'Do you speak fluent German?' the officer asked, switching seamlessly to that language. Again, he was well spoken, definitely *"Hochdeutsch"*. 'I would like to think so,' Jan replied in the same language, 'although I have a trace of an eastern accent. But that's not unusual, so do lots of people from the border regions.'

'Hmmm...' came a thoughtful response. 'Most of your countrymen arrive with fellow soldiers who can vouch for them. I can authorise your passage to England, but you will be taken somewhere and detained, perfectly pleasantly I can assure you, whilst we check out your story.' He smiled, 'Or as best we can, anyway. After that, we'll decide what to do with you. Would you be happy with that?'

Jan confirmed that he would. 'I shouldn't need too much training, Sir,' he went on. 'I forgot to mention it, but I'm familiar with firearms. And I can take out a boar with a head shot at two hundred yards...' he tailed off, not wanting to appear boastful, 'but the Dragant's a good rifle,' he added quickly.

'Yes, it is, isn't it?' the major replied with a smile. He stood up. 'Come on,' he said, 'let's find you some food and accommodation.'

The small detachment of military guards at the embassy were billeted in a nearby terraced house. A middle-aged woman, a local employed by the embassy, showed Jan to a small single bedroom. With the major translating from French – his third language Jan noted – he was invited to take a bath, if he wished, and then to come down to the kitchen, where he would be offered something to eat and drink. 'Please return to the embassy in the morning, about half past nine,' he was told, before the major wished him goodnight.

Jan blessed the fact that he had saved his last set of clean clothing and a small towel. He found the bathroom and enjoyed the luxury of his first soak in days. There were two other Englishmen sitting round the kitchen table, and the Belgian woman set about making something in a frying pan. Soon, two plates were set before him.

'Bacon and eggs,' said one of the men, pointing at first to one plate and then the other, 'and bread and butter.' Jan had learned his first words of English. Finally, her sloping hands together at an angle with her head resting against them, his hostess indicated that it was perhaps time to retire. Jan undressed and got into bed. Not realising how much stress he had been under since the first day of September, he was asleep in seconds.

The next morning he was offered three crescent-shaped loaves, fatter in the middle than at the ends, that seemed to have been rolled up. They were still warm. 'Croissants,' the housekeeper said, pointing at the bread whilst she set down a dish of jam with a spoon in it and a crock of butter. They were delicious, as was the bowl of fresh black coffee that came with them.

'Have they looked after you all right?' asked the major, once Jan had been conducted to the same room as yesterday.

Jan confirmed that indeed they had. 'I am grateful. I learned a Belgian word this morning,' he went on by way of making polite conversation: 'croissants. They were delicious.'

'They use two languages here,' Major Miecznikowski told him, 'but one is Flemish, not Belgian, and the other is French. *Croissants* is a French word, and I like them too.'

The ice politely broken, Jan was waived to the same chair. 'I want to start by listening to your story once more, the one you told me yesterday. There are two reasons – first, you might have missed something out that you remember the second time around, and second, I won't hide the fact that it is a checking-up process, to see if there are any discrepancies of detail.' Jan repeated his story. There were neither.

'*Dobra robota,*' said the major after Jan had finished. 'Well done, it's quite a story. But tell me, I am interested in farming. How long did it take you to make the first Raschdorf 30?'

Taken aback by the question, Jan answered automatically. 'It was before my time, sir. I don't think we ever made a 30, only a 35 and then a 40, but that was much later. Herr Raschdorf made the first one, the 35. I don't know how long it took for the prototype, but I can remember Herr Johann, the chief engineer, telling me that the second one took about three weeks. After that production was much quicker. That must be right, because I have worked on lots of 35s as well as 40s, but I have never come across a Raschdorf or a Derresford 30.'

Clearly the major was engaged in a mild form of probing. 'You said you could hit a boar in the head at two hundred yards,' he went on mildly. 'Why yards? Surely that should have been metres?'

'Ours was one of the American ones,' he replied immediately. He spoke the oft repeated words... '"*Dużo lepszy*"– much better quality, my father always said, '*niż te produkowane przez Rosjan...*' His voice tailed off, the memory still too fresh and painful.

'I'm sorry we had to ask,' said the major with something of a sigh. 'For what it's worth, I believe you. But it would help us if you wouldn't mind handing over that forged *Ausweis*.

We'll provide you with something else, but it will be genuine.' Jan didn't see how it would help, but he handed his identity document over willingly enough.

'I think you should take the rest of the day off,' the major told him. 'We will make arrangements for you to travel to England. Brussels is a lovely old city – take a walk, have a coffee or a drink somewhere. Do you have any money?'

Jan told him that he still had quite a lot of Renate's marks. 'Do you want us to change them for you? Might be difficult at the bank if you only speak Polish and German.'

With a bundle of strange notes and coins in his pocket, Jan marvelled at the sophistication of the old part of the city – the architecture, the narrow, cobbled streets and the shops, cafes and restaurants. By pointing he managed to buy some potatoes cut thinly lengthways and then fried – *frittes*, they seemed to be called – from a stall in the streets. Later he sat outside a cafe and having studied a metal advert on the wall, he pointed to it and enjoyed a beer in the autumnal sunshine.

That evening he sat round the kitchen table with more unknown companions whilst the housekeeper served a simple casserole of leg of lamb cooked in stock and wine above a garlic and herbed bed of potatoes and other vegetables. It was different from Frau Brantis' style of cooking, but it was delicious. 'Stew,' one of his companions announced, pointing at the pot. '*Agneau Boulangère*,' the housekeeper corrected contemptuously, rolling up her eyes but smiling nevertheless. She wagged a finger at Jan's English companions. 'Is lamb. In ze old days, baker cook only once on Sundays. For a few coins put villagers' pots in ze 'ot oven.' To Jan's surprise, she translated for him into heavily accented German. Obviously, there had been communication from the major. 'By the way, you are to go back to the Embassy in the morning,' she finished.

Whilst she was carving the meat, one of the British men left the table and returned a minute or so later with two bottles of wine. The housekeeper quickly set out small glasses. She waved a finger, encompassing them all. *'Prosit,'* she said, looking at Jan, who responded by raising his glass as the Englishmen shouted 'cheers!' Jan realised that they were all trying to make him feel welcome. There wasn't much more conversation – they had exhausted their limited language skills, but even so he passed an enjoyable and convivial evening. Perhaps the future might not be too bad after all.

Major Edward Władysław Warren-Miecznikowski, known as "Bunny" to his colleagues, discussed Jan's case with Colonel (acting Brigadier) Quentin Parry-Davies. 'I told him I was in the British Army,' he confirmed. 'English mother, attached at one time as a personal assistant to the embassy in Warsaw, and a Polish father. Therefore, I have dual nationality. I added that I had been attached to this embassy to look into any cases of Polish nationals, military or otherwise, seeking to reach the United Kingdom.'

'If you had been,' said the brigadier with a smile, his Welsh lilt faintly noticeable in his otherwise impeccable public-school English, 'the last couple of days would have seen the first honest work since you arrived!'

'I saw no reason to tell him otherwise,' said the major.

'So, what *do* you think?' asked the brigadier, who was genuinely the defence attaché at the Embassy.

'We have no assets in that part of the world,' came the reply. 'What's more, he also speaks German. And exceptionally well, I might add. He could be invaluable. We know there are partisan groups. They are tying down quite a lot of German troops and a liaison officer would help us enormously, getting supplies to them and so forth. Also, in time we will desperately need someone to identify targets and report afterwards on any bombing or raids.' He opened his hands deprecatingly. 'All right, I know it's early days and we are not ready yet,' he confessed, 'but establishing an asset like Janicki at this stage might yield a huge dividend later on. If we are going to win the war, we shall need people like him. If we lose, it won't matter anyway. I say we give it a try.'

The Brigadier steepled his fingers. 'I agree with you,' he said eventually. 'Best we send him over to UK. Meanwhile, we'll check him out more thoroughly. After that, if he agrees to go back, we can start the training. Even if he doesn't, I reckon one of the Polish units we are thinking of forming up would be only too glad to have him.'

Jan was a little surprised to be told that like yesterday, the rest of his day would be free, but that he would be flying to England tomorrow. He would be met off the aircraft, he was told, and taken to a holding centre. But he would not be free to leave until after a few more checks into his identity had been carried out.

Tadzio was surprised when a stranger walked into the farmyard. 'I used to be the honorary British consul in the Free City of Danzig,' he told them, although he sounded Polish. 'I worked in the port's shipping office. Mainly my diplomatic duties were to sort out problems with drunken British merchant sailors who fell foul of our police. Now I have had a communication from their Embassy in Stockholm. I want to show you a piece of paper, and if you can identify someone for me I would be extremely grateful.'

It meant nothing to Hedda, but Tadzio gasped when he saw the photographed document. Instinctively he trusted his visitor. *'To mój brat,'* he said without thinking. 'He's my brother. But that's not his name. Where is he, what's happened to him?'

'Last I heard,' Tadzio was told, 'Jan was in Brussels, but I think he is probably in England by now.'

'Thank God,' he replied, with a heartfelt sigh. 'I have been worried. It's the not knowing…'

'Let's be absolutely clear on this,' the man went on. 'It's not his name, but the photograph on this document is definitely of your brother, Jan Janicki?'

'*Tak,*' said Tadzio firmly. 'Yes, it is. If you can get a message to him, tell him I am well, please. And I am over the moon that he has arrived safely.'

'I think we can do that,' said their visitor with a kindly smile. 'I'm not sure whether we will meet again,' he added, 'but if you think about it you will realise that we had good reason to make this enquiry. Thank you for your help, and good luck to you both.'

Hedda and Tadzio could only stare in disbelief as he turned and walked back towards the road. 'Well, well,' she said, clutching his arm. 'At least you know that Jan is alive and where he is. But you took a risk, answering his questions like that.'

'*Raczej nie,*' Tadzio replied. 'Not really, it was no more than the truth, no matter whose side he was on. But I think I knew instinctively that he was on the level, and that it was important for Jan.'

Renate was almost back at the farm, walking the mount kindly loaned to her by Meta to let it cool down. A man stood to one side on the track. Politely he raised his hat. '*Fraulein Raschdorf,*' he said gently, looking up at her, 'might I please have a word?'

Renate was not alarmed, but she took the precaution of backing up the mare so that she could either turn and gallop off or ride the man down. 'Please don't be alarmed,' he told her. 'I am here to help – I mean you no harm. '*Wollen Sie Deutsch, Englisch oder Französisch sprechen?*' he asked her. His German was serviceable enough, but there was a faint, underlying accent that she could not trace.

Renate was proficient in both other languages. But she was astute enough to know that he was telling her, in an oblique sort of way, that this was a little more than a matter related solely to Germany. She suspected strongly that this might have something to do with Jan. 'German will do fine,' she told him.

'I want to show you a photograph,' he went on in that language. 'All I ask is that you confirm a man's name.'

She indicated a tree with a forked branch, about shoulder high. 'Fold it and put it there,' she pointed. 'Then step well away. I'll look at it and give you an answer.'

The stranger did as he was bid.

She nudged up her mount and unfolded the document. Realising that no matter who the stranger was working for, she was unlikely to be condemned for honesty, she gave him her answer. 'That's Jan Janicki,' she told him. 'He's Polish. I don't know where you got it,' she held up the piece of paper, 'but that's not his name, on the document. Although it's definitely Jan,' she concluded confidently.

'*Danke.*'

This time she handed back the document. 'Do you know where he is?' she asked him. 'Last I heard, in Brussels,' came the reply with a smile. 'But perhaps he's in England by now. Thank you for your assistance. I'm sure you will understand why I needed to ask the question.'

Raising his hat once more, the stranger walked the few metres back along the track to the lane. She heard a car engine start and the vehicle pulled away. Renate thought fondly of Jan. She knew that what she had done might not be in Germany's best interests, but she didn't care. Not after the threats that had been made to her family. Most of all she was overjoyed. Her lovely, brave, decent and kind Jan had made it to safety. She longed to see him again.

CHAPTER 15

Despite what Günther Raschdorf had been led to expect, it was over a week before anyone arrived to do anything about the workshop. In the meantime, Johann and Günther worked long hours to catch up on all their clients' tractor repairs. He was in the drawing room, taking a morning coffee, when a motor cycle puttered cautiously up the drive. Its rider, wearing a long tan leather coat, matching leather helmet and large, round goggles climbed stiffly from the machine and set it on a stand. Hands on his lower back he stretched, arching his spine to ease stiffened muscles. Curious, Günther walked into the hall and opened the front door.

The rider had removed his helmet and goggles and smiled politely as he clicked his heels and bowed slightly to Günther. 'Herr Raschdorf?' he enquired pleasantly. Ever a fan of all things mechanical, Günther was more interested in the motor cycle, one of the latest BMW R12s. 'Nice machine,' he commented. 'But what can I do for you?'

'It's the latest two-cylinder boxer engine with twin carburettors, she's good for well over a hundred kilometres an hour,' came the enthusiastic reply, followed immediately by: '*Entschuldigen Sie mich bitte,* please excuse me, my name is Hartmann Schultz. I have orders to report here to set up a workshop facility for the *Wehrmacht.*'

Schultz was a younger man, probably in his late twenties, thought Günther, but rather spindly-looking, with an academic but permanently puzzled expression. Also, he walked with a slight limp.

'Are you in the Army?' Günther asked.

'*Nein,*' Shultz replied immediately. 'I am not medically

able to serve, but I am a qualified engineer. So, the *Wehrmacht* have drafted me as a civilian to set up a facility here.'

For all that, he seemed to Günther rather a pleasant individual. 'I was just having coffee,' he said to his visitor. 'You had better come in and I'll order some more. I'm sure you would welcome a hot drink after your journey.'

'*Das wäre sehr nett*, that would be very kind,' his visitor replied.

'I find myself in an embarrassing situation,' Schultz began, once coffee had been served, together with a plate of Hannah's homemade oatmeal biscuits. 'I am told that I am to be billeted in your house,' he paused, waving an arm to encompass the building, 'which is very fine, and much more so than the accommodation to which I am accustomed. But I fear that this is on the orders of the Army or the Party, and I do not wish to be an uncomfortable imposition. I should like to tell you,' he went on, 'that I am first and foremost an engineer. And although I would like to think that I am as patriotic as the next man, I am a member neither of the *Wehrmacht* nor the Nazi Party.'

Günther had a feeling that this was a decent man with whom he could work. 'I was told by the Party that this is where you would live,' he responded, 'and it was made clear that I had no choice in the matter.' He decided not to go into the threats that had been made against his family. 'Please,' he invited Shultz, 'enjoy your coffee. I would like my wife to join us.'

He knew that Hannah would be in the kitchen with Frau Brantis. She came as soon as he called. The introductions completed, Günther gave Hannah a brief account of their conversation thus far. 'It seems to me,' he went on, looking to both Hannah and Hartmann Schultz for approval, 'that we have all been somewhat pushed into a situation. Therefore, I propose that we try to make the best of it.

'Herr Schultz,' he went on, 'this is quite a large house. The ground floor we use during the daytime, and there are family bedrooms, including our own, on the first floor. We no longer have any living-in staff, but there are several more rooms on the level above. I am going to suggest that initially I have two of them converted for you to use as a sitting room and a bedroom, and you would have your own bathroom. Later, if you wished, another small bedroom could be converted into a kitchen. But for now, you would be very welcome to join us for meals in the dining room. We are somewhat solitary, these days, so it would be a diversion for Hannah and me. And Frau Brantis is a very good cook,' he finished with a tempting smile.

'I cannot believe my good fortune...' began Schultz. 'That is so incredibly kind. Thank you. But there is one more thing I must tell you,' he added. 'My first task is to make a report on what the workshop can do now, and what might need to be done to enlarge the facility. Although I don't have a timetable, at some stage the SS will send back Polish workers to staff this facility. These, I believe, are to be accommodated in the floor above the workshop. But they will also send a small detachment of guards, together with a team of either military engineers or, more probably, civilian contractors to construct some sort of fence around the workshop and accommodation. I don't know about the engineers or the contractors, but I am told you will be expected to accommodate the SS guards.'

'Something that had also occurred to me,' said Günther. 'And I have given it some thought. If we try to cram everyone, less the workforce, into this house,' he reasoned, 'no-one is going to be particularly comfortable. And socially,' he looked pointedly at Schultz, 'it is not going to work. Least of all with the SS. But this estate is now mechanised. We no longer employ so many workers on the land and as a consequence we have a number of empty cottages. I can make available as many as it takes to provide a comfortable billet for the guards, and I am sure they would rather do their own thing than have to live under the immediate attention of their superiors.'

He stood. 'Let's get you settled in, then this afternoon I can show you around. We'll both talk to whoever is in charge of the SS when they arrive.' Günther looked at his pocket watch. 'Hannah can show you a few rooms, and I'll have your things brought up. You might like to unpack and freshen up, then join us for an aperitif just before one o'clock.'

Hartmann clicked his heels and made a bow. He could still hardly believe his luck. But neither could Günther. Schultz might have been imposed upon his household and business, but he was neither *Wehrmacht* nor Party and above all he seemed a very pleasant young professional.

After a light luncheon of cold meats and salad, Günther, with Johann in tow, showed Hartmann Schultz the facility that had been developed on the ground floor of the converted barn. 'We don't yet know what our workload will be,' Schultz observed, but almost certainly we will have to extend. And we will need more machinery.' They looked at the upstairs accommodation so recently vacated by Jan. 'It won't be that comfortable, just a dormitory,' he observed, 'but it will probably be enough for the workforce they initially send us.'

'What about my own business?' queried Günther. 'The Third Reich will need food, food means farmers, and farmers need tractors. Am I expected to fold-up a busy civilian farming workshop and just repair military vehicles?'

'That would not be sensible,' Schultz replied with a smile. 'We might have to give priority to the military, but we should be able to run the two facilities side by side. That way you would not be disadvantaged, financially, and I shall discuss with my superiors the remuneration and compensation that you will need to receive in exchange for what you will be undertaking for the military.'

It had been a sound move to make the engineer welcome into the household. Hartmann Schultz, Günther affirmed to himself, was indeed an intelligent and fair-minded man. Which was more than could ever be said for the senior occupant of a *Kübelwagen* that braked to a halt outside in a cloud of dust. The two of them went to meet their visitors.

Gross was extracting himself slowly from the front passenger seat, self-importantly flicking scraps of dust from his uniform. 'Good afternoon, *Herr Unterscharführer,*' said Günther evenly. An *SS-Rottenführer* stood by the driver's door. Two *SS-Schützen,* being private soldiers, remained seated in the back, weapons held vertically between their knees.

Gross ignored the greeting. 'His name is Neumann,' he said abruptly, indicating the corporal. 'I shall return to my headquarters, but he and his two men have been assigned to assist the engineer, and of course to report back to me on your progress. Later there will be *SS* guards, as it becomes necessary. My orders are that they will also be billeted with you.'

'Welcome to the estate, *Herr Rottenführer,*' said Günther pleasantly. The corporal did not reply but stood rigidly to attention. Clearly, he was considerably in awe of his *Unterscharführer.*

'Very well,' Günther went on, deliberately addressing the junior non-commissioned officer. 'There is a choice. I have made accommodation available to Herr Hartmann on the upper floor of our house. Which means that there are only two small rooms left.'

'The billeting arrangements are your concern, not mine,' broke in Gross rudely.

Günther ignored the interruption. 'However,' he turned back to Gross, 'now that the farm is mechanised, we employ fewer men on the estate, which means that there are a number of empty cottages in an excellent state of repair, and one of these could be made very comfortable.'

'You are questioning my orders?' demanded Gross accusingly.

'Not at all, *Herr Unterscharführer,*' Günther replied smoothly. 'Please, let us walk inside for a few moments. I have one or two points that are perhaps best for your ears only.'

Once inside the workshop he halted and turned to face Gross. His tone was different now, not unpleasant, but determined. 'I'm not going even to try to guess at your motives,' he began directly, 'but you have invested your reputation in this project. However, without my cooperation and that of Johann and Herr Schultz, you will find it very difficult to deliver. Which will not, I expect, please your masters. So, I think it would be in both of our interests if you leave me to organise and run this facility, and in return I will keep my part of the bargain. I hope,' he concluded, 'that we have an understanding.'

Without waiting for a reply Günther returned to the small group outside, leaving Gross to follow. '*Herr Rottenführer,*' he began, speaking so that the two privates in the back could also hear him, 'this afternoon Frau Brantis, my cook and housekeeper, will show you a cottage that both the *Unterscharführer* and I feel will provide you with accommodation that will prove both private and comfortable. I will leave you to sort out the provision of rations and so forth with your *Unterscharführer.* But you should be very self-sufficient and, I would suggest, a lot better off than your comrades on the other side of the border. For this evening and breakfast tomorrow, if you will report to the barn alongside the main house I will ask Frau Brantis to ensure that you are given a hot meal.'

Turning to both Gross and Neumann, Günther added, 'I am returning to the house now. This afternoon Johann and Herr Schultz can have a preliminary discussion, then if you will join us tomorrow morning, *Herr Rottenführer,* we will draft a preliminary plan for turning this building into a top-class workshop for the *Wehrmacht.*' Günther turned on his heels and stalked off.

Inwardly fuming, but without another word, Gross settled himself behind the wheel and started the engine of the *Kübelwagen*. As he drove away, Günther was so disgusted he did not even bother to look back and watch.

Soon after dinner Hannah announced that she would like to retire early and read. Günther seized the neck of a decanter and set two brandy glasses on the table.

'What makes me think,' said Hartmann after they had raised a silent toast, 'that you have not exactly made a friend at court with the *Herr Unterscharführer?*'

'Gross used to work for me,' Günther replied. 'But he left to join the *SA*. Last year, he managed to get himself transferred to the *Allgemeine SS*. His wife still lives in one of the cottages on the estate, but we have never seen eye-to-eye.' For now, he decided to leave it at that.

'I think there are many such people,' Hartmann commented sadly. 'They are uneducated and jealous of the professional classes but now, suddenly, they have authority – and they are prepared to abuse it.'

If the sentiment was genuine, thought Günther, and he was pretty sure it was, if gave a vital insight into the young engineer's political thinking. More than that, he knew he had taken a chance standing up to Gross that afternoon. But with Hartmann onside, Gross could not afford to cross them both. Which in turn, Günther was utterly relieved to believe, gave him a fighting chance of protecting his family and for all of them to survive this war.

Jan was informed that later that day he would take a flight to Croydon on board a British Imperial Airways four-engined Armstrong-Whitworth European class aircraft capable of carrying 32 passengers. He was handed a Polish passport which, he was told, was genuine, and escorted through the airport to the plane by a member of the embassy staff. Major Miecznikowski had told him that he would be met at the other end by a military police escort and taken to a holding centre whilst his identity was checked and a decision taken over his future. To a country boy who had, until recently, hardly travelled at all, the flight was an amazing adventure. Equally impressive was the fact that the aircraft had a butler's pantry from which he was offered refreshments, and there were no less than three lavatories. Fortunately, using one of the few English words he had learnt, he managed to ask for a coffee and had not needed to use the other facilities as he would have been embarrassed to ask how to operate them.

All too soon they were crossing the coast and the aircraft settled onto the ground. A steward asked him to remain in his seat whilst the other passengers left the aircraft. Finally, two men approached, one in a uniform, which he took to be that of a military policeman, and the other in plain clothes.

'Pan Janicki,' said the latter, speaking in Polish, 'we have come to take you to your destination.' Jan was escorted not through the public area but via a small, separate building that avoided all customs and passport formalities, and behind which was parked a medium sized black saloon. He and the plainclothes escort sat in the rear seat, whilst the uniformed soldier settled himself behind the wheel. With the sun on his shoulder, Jan knew that they were heading in a northerly direction. He was utterly fascinated to look at the English towns, villages and countryside, and from the occasional conversation with his fellow Pole, he gathered that they were on their way to somewhere near the city of Nottingham, which was part of the eastern area of somewhere described as the British Midlands.

He was taken to a large country house which seemed to have been converted to provide accommodation for a number of visitors, although as far as Jan could tell from Christian names on a pigeon hole rack he was the only one from Poland. He was shown into an office where he was met by a middle-aged, Polish speaking man in civilian clothes who introduced himself as Pan Szerezewski. 'Yes, I'm Polish,' Szerezewski replied, in response to Jan's question. 'Been here for nearly twenty years now. I'm Jewish and a refugee from the pogroms that started after the last war. Now, I work for the British government.'

He invited Jan to be seated then moved to sit behind a desk and opened a folder. 'They are still checking you out,' he told Jan, 'but it's looking good so far.'

'What happens now?' Jan asked him.

'Well, in a minute I'll show you around – where you can eat and sleep, as it were. Then whilst we are waiting for clearance, you need to start learning English. We have a particular way of doing it here – a sort of crash course, if you like, for specially selected people.'

Jan was not sure what to make of being "specially selected", but he let that pass. 'It's a one-on-one method of instruction,' Szerezewski continued, 'and once you meet your instructor tomorrow morning, you'll see what I mean. He'll be fluent in both languages, but whilst you're under instruction the only language you will use is English.' He smiled. 'Don't worry – it's very efficient. Believe it or not, you'll be chatting away after a couple of weeks.'

Jan was shown a dining room, the lounge, and a small single bedroom. Notices in English and several other languages including Polish proclaimed a few basic rules and the all-important mealtimes. But on every notice, a point emphasised to him by Szerezewski, he was instructed not to share any personal or military information about his background with *any* of his fellow inmates, of whom he counted five more. Neither was anyone, under *any* circumstances, to use their real name. He was at all times to use only a first name, Karol, an instruction emphasised repeatedly by Szerezewski.

Pan Aron Goldek was an ageing, rather short and thin individual who wore round, metal-framed glasses that gave him the appearance of an old-fashioned schoolmaster. His clothes looked to be English, if a little worn and frayed. But he was a master of his craft. Pointing at himself, he gave his full name. Then he pointed at Jan, who realised that he was required to do the same. 'Karol,' he replied. When Goldek smiled approvingly Jan knew he had given the right answer.

Pointing and speaking, at first it was only single words. But gradually they progressed. Already fluent in Polish and German, Jan now discovered that he had a flair for languages and he picked up a basic use of English relatively easily. But one session rather puzzled him. He spent half an hour with a different instructor, who did not introduce himself and spoke to him about anything and everything, but the entire conversation was in German. Afterwards the individual contented himself with *'Danke,* Karol' before shaking hands and leaving without further explanation.

He had been at the house for about a week when Aron Goldek announced that instead of their usual first session that morning, Jan would have an interview with Szerezewski and the Commandant. This latter introduced himself as Lieutenant Colonel Bray, although he wasn't in uniform. 'The colonel does not speak Polish,' Szerezewski informed him, 'so I shall translate.'

After a few desultory questions about how Karol was finding life in England, clearly designed to try to put him at ease, Colonel Bray took a folder from his in-tray. It was the same one that had been on Szerezewski's desk during his initial interview, but now considerably thicker. The British officer opened it and flicked through a few pages, as if to remind himself of the contents.

'I am pleased to tell you,' he began, 'that we are completely satisfied regarding your identity.' He paused whilst Szerezewski translated. 'Tadzio sends his regards, and he was both overjoyed and relieved to learn that you are safe.'

Jan was taken aback. How on earth, he wondered, had the British managed to speak with this brother? But before he could ask a question Colonel Bray went on, 'Fraulein Raschdorf has also confirmed who you are. She is still safe and well, and knows that you are, too. She was too taken aback to send a message, but I am given to understand that when she heard the news she was clearly both relieved and delighted.'

'I'm sorry,' he added, as Jan struggled to come to terms with the news. 'That's all I can tell you. But I am only too happy to pass on the information.'

Jan tried to take it in, emotionally, and the other two men were considerate enough to wait for a few moments. Eventually, the British officer broke the silence.

'Karol,' he began gently, 'may I ask, have you wondered why you have been brought to an establishment such as this?'

Jan admitted that it was all rather new and strange, and he realised that he had to be held somewhere whilst his identity was confirmed, so he hadn't given it much thought.

'More and more of your fellow countrymen are arriving every day now,' Colonel Bray told him. 'Usually they go to a training unit – mostly to learn English and to familiarise themselves with whatever weapons or equipment they are likely to use. But this facility is for a different class of immigrant. Essentially, it is for someone who we believe *might* be useful to the war effort in an entirely different category of work.'

A frisson of excitement fluttered somewhere inside Jan's head, but he wanted to hear more. 'Please go on, Sir,' he requested. Szerezewski dutifully translated.

'Very well,' responded the Colonel, rotating a pencil between the fingers of his right hand. 'I am going to ask you a question. You will have to give me a "yes" or a "no" answer for now and then confirm it again shortly afterwards. But think carefully, because after your final reply, and once you embark on this course, there will be no going back.

'Whatever you decide,' he went on, 'no-one will think any the worse of you. Already, you have proved to be a remarkably brave and resourceful young man. If your answer is negative, we will assign you to the regular army, in a Polish unit. Considering your engineering expertise, it will be something to do with vehicles, probably an armoured fighting regiment – tanks or reconnaissance.

'But if you say "yes", there will be a very different future, both in terms of training and operations. Listen carefully, Karol,' the colonel was speaking more slowly now, 'and take as long as you wish before you answer. The acid question is this: would you be prepared to return in order to operate on your own, behind enemy lines? And I have to tell you,' he added quickly, 'that if you are caught you will almost certainly be tortured and shot.'

'You want me to be a spy?' Jan asked, almost aghast.

'That's not a word we would use,' the colonel told him, 'although the Germans would. To us, you would be an invaluable asset. We have no-one in your part of the world, yet we know that there are partisans living in the vast Polish forests. They are desperately short of weapons and ammunition, yet they are capable of tying down hundreds of German troops and completely disrupting the enemy supply chain. Someone on the ground to liaise with them and assist with supplies would be an enormous asset. Also, you could operate on either side of the border – I'm told that even with a slight accent, which is not unusual in that part of the world, your German is so fluent you could pass as a native. That's perhaps all I should tell you for now.

'But let me give you one last piece of advice,' the colonel

said gently. 'If your heart is not fully in it, then don't volunteer. I tell you that from personal experience. If you are not utterly committed, eventually you will almost certainly be caught.' Jan was not to know that the colonel had spent nearly two years behind the German lines during the first world war, earning the Military Cross. 'But if you accept,' Jan was told, 'you will be making a far greater contribution to the war effort than you could ever make in a regiment of the field Army.'

Jan looked down at the desk, silent for a full minute. Finally, he raised his head to look directly at the colonel. 'Sir,' he said firmly, 'they killed my father, raped and bayoneted my sister, and threatened to make Renate Raschdorf a sex slave in a concentration camp. I know the countryside, both sides of the border – which in any case I can cross at will, and with the contacts that I already have I am confident that I can survive. Plus, as you have said, I have the language skills, Polish and German. I volunteer,' he finished bluntly.

There was quite a pause, the colonel looking at both Jan and Szerezewski in turn. 'Good man,' he said at length. 'Do you know,' he said slowly, and with a slight smile, 'I never thought for one minute that you would say anything different.'

'So, what happens now, Sir?' asked Jan.

'Well, you're not a lot of use if we can't talk to each other,' the colonel replied, seeking to lighten the mood. 'You'll be here for as long as it takes. But from what I hear, you are good at languages, so let's say about another six or eight weeks. After that, it'll be somewhere else, for a few skills you don't have at the moment - weapons, explosives, communications, field craft and so forth.' The colonel's face broke into a comradely, rather conspiratorial grin. 'And I hope you're not afraid of heights,' he added, 'because we are going to strap a parachute on you and chuck you out of a perfectly serviceable aeroplane! We have a joke about that,' he concluded, grinning mischievously. 'You don't have to worry about whether the damn thing opens or not, because if it doesn't, it's only the last half-inch that hurts!'

Jan was a bit taken aback but smiled politely. 'Go and find a cup of tea,' he was told, 'and think things over. Then let Mr Szerezewski have your confirmed answer. And remember what I said earlier, nobody will think any the worse of you if you change your mind. But if you want to do that, please be quick about it. And by the way,' he continued, 'whilst you are being trained, you will be paid. Also, assuming your answer is still the same, from now on you are free to leave the house whenever you are not under instruction. There's a village about half a mile from here. Go and practice your English in the pub. But don't bother asking for vodka or schnapps, because they won't have any. My advice is to try to develop a taste for good old English bitter. But if you want something stronger, you'll have to ask for scotch!'

'He won't change his mind,' Szerezewski opined a few seconds after Jan had closed the door.

'Nor will he,' agreed the colonel. 'Quite the opposite. I like the cut of his jib. To mix metaphors, if you ask me he's champing at the bit. He can't wait to get started.'

CHAPTER 16

A few days after Schultz's arrival a convoy of about twenty civilian vehicles arrived unannounced. At its head was Gross in his *Kübelwagen*. The rest were lorries and flatbeds loaded with people, building materials and heavy machinery.

A short, well-muscled and rather elderly man stepped down from the vehicle behind Gross' and stood next to him facing Schultz and Günther. 'This is Herr Maurer,' said Gross, rather rudely not bothering to introduce either Günther or Hartmann Schultz to the stranger, whose portly frame and a face and nose well lined with blue-red veins suggested that his time was divided between building and enjoying food and alcohol – this latter probably during the daytime as well.

'And to what do we owe all this?' asked Günther evenly, his arm swinging to encompass the convoy.

'They will be here for as long as it takes,' Gross replied. 'Your workshop is too small.' He made it sound as if this were both an accusation and a failure for which Günther was personally responsible. 'Herr Maurer's civilian construction company has been seconded to the *Wehrmacht*. They have plans for an extension to this building,' his hand indicated the workshop, 'plus they will add hard standing and finally put a fence around the whole facility.'

'Herr Raschdorf,' said Maurer pleasantly, as if embarrassed by Gross' tone of voice, 'if you wish, we can live under canvas, but I am told that there is an accommodation area above your workshop. If you would allow my men to use it, we would be most grateful. This is not,' he finished with a smile, 'a particularly warm September.'

Günther thought quickly. Gross was, as usual, obviously intent on being unpleasant, but the more he could encourage Maurer and Schultz to be on his side, the less would be Gross' influence. And the harder he would find it to be confrontational.

'Herr Maurer,' he replied, 'your men would be most welcome to use the upstairs accommodation. Floor space will be a bit tight, but I am sure that Unterscharführer Gross can organise some bunk beds, which would be ideal.'

Maurer just looked at Gross and nodded, as if to say, 'get on with it'. Clearly annoyed at having to take instruction, Gross tried but failed to hide his displeasure.

'Herr Maurer,' Günther went on, as if to twist the knife, 'I don't know what personal arrangements you would prefer, but if you wish there is a spare room on the upper storey of my house. Alternatively, if you would prefer something more private, you are welcome to be my guest in the house tonight and I will have a small cottage prepared for you on the estate – you would be able to move in tomorrow morning.'

'That really is most kind,' said Maurer, 'but we are quite used to being self-sufficient on a building site. We have our own rations and my men will soon have a field kitchen up and running. If it is all right with you, I will stay with them tonight and accept gratefully your offer of a cottage in the morning – perhaps I might share it with my foreman, which would give the men a break from the pair of us?'

Once more, Gross tried and failed to hide his irritation. He managed a half-hearted nod then stalked off towards his *Kübelwagen*. 'Herr Gross,' called out Hartmann, rather imperiously, thought Günther. The SS man paused and turned to face them. 'When you get back,' Hartmann went on, 'please give my compliments and best wishes to Willi. And tell him that we will do everything in our power to make this venture a success for the *Wehrmacht*.'

Rather than reply, Gross simply resumed his march to the vehicle. 'Who is Willi?' Günther asked Hartmann as the vehicle was driven off.

'Not his boss,' replied Hartmann with a grin, nodding towards the departing Gross, 'more like his boss's boss, *SS Hauptsturmführer* Willi Richter. We go back quite a way. Family friends – his are party, mine aren't, but same hometown, same university. It was through Willi's father that I got this job. *SS Brigadeführer* Richter was involved in the planning for the *Lebensraum* move on Poland. He knew I couldn't serve in the Wehrmacht but thought I would be a good choice to run this workshop – save having to appoint a military man and all that. Even though he's party, he's quite a decent chap, and so is his son Willi. It won't do that pompous little prat Gross any harm at all to know that I, and therefore we, have friends in places higher than those to which he will ever aspire.'

'Gentlemen, I look forward to working with both of you,' said Maurer, now sporting a huge grin. 'I think we have the measure of that silly little Nazi, *nicht*? Now,' he rubbed his hands together enthusiastically, 'I have some cold beers on ice in the back of my wagon. Let us enjoy a toast to friendship before my men set to work!'

Maurer and his team proved themselves to be a highly effective construction unit. By the time Hitler was reviewing a *Wehrmacht* victory parade in Warsaw on the fifth of October, they had dug and concreted the foundations of an equally sized workshop attached to one of the long outer walls of the existing one and extending into the field behind. The following day, they laid the floor. The walls were built and beams supporting a tin roof took another week. Additional machinery that had originally been stacked in the old workshop was secured in the new structure. Next, a generator building was constructed to house the heavy-duty electricity supply that would be required for the considerably enlarged facility. Outside, what had once been a productive field was converted to hard standing. It was whilst a substantial two metre fence topped with barbed wire was being set up that Gross returned in his *Kübelwagen* followed by two lorries containing twenty men, six guards and more basic stores and rations.

The "*Untermenschen*", as Gross referred to them, were all Poles, clad only in the clothes they had been wearing when they were rounded up. They were dirty, unshaven and from the smell had clearly not been allowed washing or bathing facilities for many days. Gross had the Poles herded into a small group whilst they were surrounded by the armed guards, rifles at the ready.

'You have been brought here to work,' he told them in German, 'and you are fortunate. The alternative would be a concentration camp. All of you have some mechanical experience. You will work under the direction of Herr Schultz. In return, the *Reich* will provide food and accommodation. As you can see, this facility is being enclosed. If you try to leave, you will be shot. The same will happen if you do not work to our satisfaction. I know some of you speak German, so one of you can act as interpreter after I have spoken, and then help Herr Schultz determine how best you will be employed.' With that he turned on his heels, as if abrogating all responsibility for the project, and strode back to his vehicle.

The *SS-Rottenführer* in charge of the guard detachment addressed Günther and Hartmann Schultz. 'I will settle them into the workshop, and they can make themselves something to eat. They will have to sleep on the floor downstairs until the construction is finished and Herr Maurer's men leave. I expect that later on,' he turned to Hartmann Schultz, 'you will wish to interrogate them and decide how best you can make use of their abilities. Any you do not want or cannot use,' he said evenly, 'just let me know and we will take care of it.'

It did not come across as an order, but neither was it presented as a basis for discussion. Günther decided that for now it would be better to avoid any hint of confrontation. '*Ach so,*' he replied pleasantly, 'perhaps you and Herr Schultz here would simply settle the men in for this afternoon, and perhaps find out what qualifications and experience they have between them. Tomorrow morning, the three of us should have a meeting, to agree how we will proceed. *Herr Rottenführer*, perhaps you and your men would billet underneath the construction team tonight, and we will try to make more comfortable accommodation available to you in the morning.'

It was early evening before Hartmann Schultz returned to the house. 'There's good news and bad,' he told Günther as they enjoyed a cold *Pils* before dinner. 'Two of those men are graduate mechanical engineers and four more of them have worked as foremen, either in a factory or within a machinery repair business. The rest are all basic vehicle mechanics. But it's better than I would have expected. Quite honestly, considering what we are going to have to do, we have the making of quite an effective workforce.'

'And the bad?' Günther queried.

'I had a long chat with two people,' Hartmann replied. 'First with one of the qualified engineers who speaks pretty good German – like you he studied in Stettin before the war. He knows they are slave labour, but he and his men are also aware that the alternative could be a hell of a lot worse. And to a man they are worried sick about their families. But they are also realistic – they wouldn't stand a chance if they tried to escape, and accept that the best chance of survival is to barter their engineering skills in exchange for food and accommodation for the duration.' He set down his tankard on a side table. 'I can form two good teams, with a German speaking supervisor in charge of each.'

'That doesn't sound too bad,' Günther responded after a moment's thought. 'But what's the downside? I sense that something must be worrying you?'

'It's the *Rottenführer*,' Hartmann replied. 'His name's Bauer by the way. I don't think he's as bad or as stupid as Gross, but he's a committed Nazi and doesn't give a damn for the Poles. And he's not the sharpest knife in the drawer. But he knows he and his men are on to a good thing, guarding a few workers instead of being on the front line, so I don't think he'll give us too much trouble. My recommendation would be to treat him and his men as well as we can. That way, they will all want to stay here and we'll get at least some co-operation.'

'Agreed,' said Günther without hesitation. 'But what about the Poles?'

Hartmann ticked off an index finger. 'One, they are skilled men, but all they have is the clothes they stand up in. Two, they are filthy. Some of them have lice. Soon, they'll all be the same. Three, it never occurred either to Gross or Bauer that we would need some basic form of accommodation for our workforce. They can't sleep on a concrete workshop floor for too long. And finally, there's the question of rations. I got Bauer to show me what he's been given to feed twenty-odd men for the next week. I'm no expert, but it's barely a quarter of what they need to keep them reasonably well-nourished.'

He paused. 'I think the SS intention is to work them to death, then just provide replacements. But that doesn't take account of the fact that once we have trained them up into an efficient workforce we would have to start all over again a few months down the line. And in any case,' he concluded, 'the last thing I want is to behave like a Nazi. It's inhuman and it's indecent. I know we are at war, but I just won't do it!' As if for emphasis, his hand slapped down on the arm of the chair.

Günther sat quietly for several seconds, deep in thought. 'Here's how we might proceed,' he suggested eventually. 'My problem, as you have realised, is Gross. And it's personal. But we have him in a pincer movement. Below, there is Bauer. He doesn't want to be sent to the front, so even if he's scared of Gross, he'll want this project to succeed. He'll be reasonably co-operative.

'That's from below,' he went on. 'But above Gross, we have the huge advantage of your friend Willi. He also needs the workshop to succeed. So, this is what I suggest.

'We'll have a meeting tomorrow morning, you, me, Maurer and Bauer. We'll invite the other two to the house. I don't think it will apply to Maurer, but Bauer will definitely be out of his depth. Could you, this evening, make a list of what humanitarian supplies you will need for the workforce? Bedding, clothing including overalls, extra rations, bunk beds and mattresses, soap and towels and so forth?'

Hartmann, sensing where this was going, nodded that he could.

'I'll get Maurer to agree to build a small outside latrine and shower block. I don't think that will be a problem. We'll also explain to Bauer that the only way we are going to succeed here is if we retain a skilled-up workforce. If we fail, I'll tell him that we will in all probability be closed down, which leaves him and his section on the way to the front line.' Günther smiled. 'You say he's not that smart, but he's not stupid either. I think he'll see things our way. Afterwards, you go and see Willi and I tell Bauer what we need. He'll tell Gross, and Gross won't like it, but I think he will finish up with pressure from below and above. And knowing his talent for self-interest, I think he'll cave in.'

Two days later a second lorry arrived with more bunk beds, clean palliasses, clothing and personal items – even down to a box of toothbrushes. Of Gross, there was no sign. Maurer was as good as his word and built a basic but hygienic shower and latrine block, the cost of which was hidden in the overall invoice to the *Reich*. They had to cook for themselves, but the Poles also inherited a good field kitchen, not to mention a diet that would just about sustain them – one with several times the calories meted out to thousands of their fellow countrymen being enslaved in the Third *Reich*. And Günther resolved to supplement his workers' diet from the farm as and when he could. By the end of October the workshop was receiving a steady flow of damaged vehicles and equipment. It was thriving and efficient.

It took Jan six weeks to learn English. '*Nie musisz mówić płynnie*, you don't have to be fluent,' Aron Goldek told him from the outset, on one of the few occasions when he addressed Jan in Polish. 'After all, there's no need for you to try to pass as an Englishman. Your cover language will be your native Polish, although we'll also give you a set of German papers. The instructor who interviewed you in that language was impressed – a slight border accent,' he said, 'but if you needed to enter Germany, you could pass for a local any day of the week.

'So, all we now need to achieve,' Goldek went on, 'is for you to have a good enough command of English so that you can live and work with us.' Clearly, thought Jan, Goldek now considered himself to be British.

The instruction was intensive but effective. For two one-hour sessions in the morning and one in the afternoon, Jan was bombarded with questions, all a mixture of sign language and spoken English. For the rest of the day, armed with the thickest dictionary Jan had ever seen, he was given written work to complete: verb tables to study, next simple sentences to translate, and finally newspaper and magazine articles or passages from a book – occasionally, but not always, a military manual. These latter introduced him to English arms and equipment at the same time, most importantly the Lee Enfield

Mark 3 rifle, with its bolt action and ten round magazine carrying point three-oh-three inch rounds out to a range of 2000 yards.

From the manuals he had been given, the Enfield and Webley and Scott revolvers seemed remarkably simple. But Jan was fascinated by the mechanics of the BREN Light Machine Gun, or LMG – also a three-oh-three like the rifle, and with the same range, but a fire rate of five hundred rounds a minute from a thirty-round magazine. Intrigued by its gas driven operation, he learned that the weapon had been introduced into service with the British Army only the previous year.

By late October Aron Goldek could report to Colonel Bray that Jan Janicki would be able to live and accept instruction using only the English language. 'He's still got a marked Polish accent,' he concluded, 'but he's a quick learner and he understands pretty much everything that's said to him.' In his final interview, Jan learned that he would be travelling by train initially to Manchester and then on to Scotland for further training.

Ringwood, in Manchester, proved a rude awakening. After the comfort of an English country house, Jan's new facility comprised two Nissen huts, one for men and one for women, and between them a third hut separated in the middle with a door at either end – showers and toilets. Next to the huts stood a huge hangar, in which half a dozen of them gathered the following morning.

'My name is Sergeant Hathaway,' said a track-suited non-commissioned officer bearing parachute wings on his arm. 'If I hear any of you referring to me as "Sergeant Anne" or "Mrs Shakespeare", you will spend every hour of your waking time running round the perimeter track of this airfield.' Jan suspected that it was an old joke, designed to break the ice, but there was an element of steel behind the remark.

'We only have a few days,' Hathaway went on, 'but my job

is to train you lot to be qualified parachutists. And we are in a hurry. Please follow me outside.

'There are only two tricky bits,' he continued, as they stood in a semi-circle, 'the first is leaving the aircraft, and the most important is landing. If you mess up the first, you become what is commonly referred to as strawberry jam. To me, this is mind over matter. Which is to say, I don't mind and you lot don't matter. But if you mess up the second part, the landing, you will find yourself in enemy territory with a sprained ankle or a broken limb. That way, you could be captured and interrogated. So, this training is going to start with the really serious bit – hitting the ground.'

He indicated three wooden platforms on the grass. One was barely three feet high, the second came up to Jan's waist, the third to his shoulders. 'Watch and learn,' said Hathaway. 'This is how you land.' With his knees together, he demonstrated the landing roll. 'If you don't roll as you touch down,' he confirmed for emphasis, you could well break something. You are now going to demonstrate five perfect, consecutive landing rolls from each of those platforms in turn. One mistake, and you stay on the same box to start your five all over again.'

Sergeant Hathaway did one more demonstration from the lowest box, then stood to watch as they filed up make their first "landing". A couple of people did not meet his exacting standards and had to restart their five, but by mid-morning all six of them had progressed to the third box. A van appeared with a counter flap cut into one side. 'It's the NAAFI wagon,' he told them without explanation. Each of them received a mug of tea and a "cheese wad" – a thick slice of cheese inside a bun of buttered bread, which Jan rather liked.

After the boxes came a period of classroom instruction. They were shown the diagrammatic construction of a parachute, and the importance of rolling and gathering the canopy before they were dragged helpless across the DZ by the wind. 'That's the Dropping Zone to you lot,' Hathaway explained. He also demonstrated the chest release mechanism in case they came down in a tree.

'We are going to have a light lunch now,' he went on. 'It's just a sandwich and a drink. Because this afternoon you are going to experience "the contraption". You will put on a harness and jump from a platform right at the top of the hangar. The harness and friction device will ensure that you hit the ground at roughly the same speed as you will from a genuine jump. So, don't be nervous, just think of it as another box job. At the end of the day, all I want from each of you is a few successful landings. For now,' he added with a wicked grin, 'please fall out and enjoy your lunch.'

Hathaway formed them in a semi-circle, then made the first descent. He did not, Jan observed, ask them to do anything that he was not prepared to demonstrate himself. One woman, Jan thought she had maybe a French accent, twisted her ankle slightly as she rolled, but the rest of them made it through without incident.

'So far almost perfect,' said the Sergeant at the end of the afternoon. 'I have contacted the Met office and it's looking good. Tomorrow you will each make two jumps on a static line from a balloon. Thank you for your attention today, and I will see you all, ladies and gentlemen, in the morning.'

That evening they decided to walk to the nearest public house. But after a day's exercise and fresh air they stayed only for a couple of drinks. Besides, conversation was difficult when you couldn't use your own name or talk about your background.

The following morning was cloudy but still – ideal for a first jump, Sergeant Hathaway told them. They were driven a short distance from Ringwood to a grass strip in the countryside. On the ground were two flatbed lorries parked well apart, each with a winch and cable drum on the back.

Taught lines led to two enormous barrage balloons beneath each of which a rectangular wicker basket was tethered to the ground. Jan found it difficult to take his eyes off the square opening cut in the end of the nearest one. But he was pleased to be selected to jump from Sergeant Hathaway's basket, rather than from the second one with an instructor they did not know.

'For this jump,' he told the three of them, 'just concentrate on your technique, and for God's sake remember what I told you about the landing. You'll be jumping from about eight or nine hundred feet, so you can't miss the field. You don't have to worry about coming down too near the lorries, as they will be driving slowly upwind, so you should be well clear.'

Sergeant Hathaway entered first and waited for his group to follow. Jan found it extremely cumbersome to walk with a chute on his back. Once inside the three of them sat on a canvas bench that ran along each side, then Sergeant Hathaway clipped on their static lines before taking his own place by the exit. An officer on the ground gave an order to the winch crew, their basket was released and the balloon lifted it into the air. As they began to rise, the officer bent down and picked up a megaphone. Jan realised that his heart was thumping.

All too soon a metallic voice came from the ground – 'Ready to jump'. As they had been briefed, Jan stood at the opening. Sergeant Hathaway waited for a few seconds, then with a pat on Jan's shoulder shouted 'Go!' To his credit, Jan managed not to hesitate. He was out and falling, feet and knees together till his harness lurched into his crotch as the chute opened. His hands went to the lines. Suddenly it was deathly quiet, with just a faint hiss of air and the rumble of the winch lorry barely audible as it crawled across the field. But the stillness and the view were absolutely fantastic. Jan realised that he was heading towards a clear patch of field and all too soon he was double-checking his stance for the landing. It was textbook, the grass actually softer than the landings they had practised. A vehicle was crossing towards him. As he had been taught, he hauled on the lines to steer the chute into what little wind there was then hurried to gather everything in. A small, open four seater saloon drew up alongside – a civilian model, hastily brush-painted khaki.

'Well done youngster,' the driver shouted, 'and congratulations. How did it feel?'

'It was wonderful, very wonderful!' Jan shouted, almost screaming with adrenalin.

'Well hop in,' came the rather prosaic answer, 'and make sure nothing can tangle with anything else.'

Sergeant Hathaway, who had jumped last, had them seated on the grass in a semi-circle. 'Karol, nice jump,' he told him. Most had the same comment, although Marie, the one Jan though might be French, was told that her exit was a bit untidy. 'Legs together straight away,' he told her, 'so you can be stable as quickly as possible. But otherwise a good effort.'

He glanced at his watch. 'We'll take a late lunch,' he told them, 'because I want to put in one more jump this morning. The wind's just a little bit stronger, so we'll get the second one in before it rises out of the envelope.'

This time round Jan was the third to jump, and found himself drifting toward the side of the field. But apart from a scramble to gather in on the ground in a rising breeze all went well. 'Get a good night's sleep,' Sergeant Hathaway told them before they were dismissed. 'No expense spared – I have laid on a private aeroplane for you tomorrow morning. Same routine as today – two jumps, and you'll have much more time to enjoy the view on the way down.'

Next morning he briefed them inside the hangar. 'We will fly out of Ringwood in a Mark IV Armstrong Whitworth Whitley twin-engined medium bomber,' he told them. 'This is good news – when the aircraft was originally introduced into service its nickname was the flying coffin. But the pilot told me that this aircraft has Rolls-Royce Merlin engines and is barely a year old. Like yesterday,' he went on, 'you will be on a static line. But this morning we will jump from about three thousand feet into the same DZ.

'Two major differences, though. First, you will exit the aircraft through a hole cut in the fuselage floor. Remember this, and remember it well. When the time comes, make sure you are well forward, cleanly into the hole. If you don't, your pack will catch behind you and the resulting forward pivot will smack your face into the edge opposite. Almost certainly, you will break your nose.' He looked at Marie. 'If you don't want to finish up looking like a retired boxer, Miss, you must make a clean exit.' Most of them nodded their understanding – they had all taken the point. 'Second,' he went on, 'your chute will deploy more quickly than it did from the balloon jump. This is due to the slipstream created by the aircraft as it flies forward. So, make sure you are in a stable position immediately after leaving the aircraft.' He paused. 'Packs on and good luck.'

They were driven out to the aircraft. Once seated inside, the Whitley taxied round the peri-track and paused at the beginning of the runway. The engine noise rose almost to a scream and they were off. But the smell inside the fuselage was awful – apparently, the bomber had been sprayed with some sort of chemically treated lacquer. Jan hoped that he would jump before the ignominy of being airsick. As the aircraft approached the drop zone, Sergeant Hathaway attached the static lines, then moved back along the fuselage double-checking each connection. Overhead, two red lights came on. The Whitley turned in a gently bank – Jan guessed that they were circling the DZ, and the lights changed to green. There was barely any time to register the view to earth. As quickly as they could, they jumped. Jan was about halfway along the stick. And they were all out, canopies open.

Jan picked out the DZ. But unlike yesterday, when some sounds had drifted up from below, the world underneath was silent. Despite the thrill of the jump, these were the most peaceful moments that Jan had ever experienced. After what seemed an eternity, he made another good landing more or less mid-field.

They made another jump that afternoon. Finally, Sergeant Hathaway gathered them in the hangar. 'Well, congratulations to all of you,' he began. 'Just a few words, as you will be leaving here in the morning. First of all, well done. My job was to get you through these few days without anyone being injured. You have had only the most basic of training, but if you have to jump again, there is a reasonable chance that you can reach the ground in one piece. But only if you remember everything we have taught you. I would like to have added a night drop, but we just don't have the time or the resources, so if you are up for one of those, listen carefully to the extra briefing before the flight. Second, there is a little tradition that we follow here at Ringwood. Get yourselves fed and watered, then be outside your accommodation at seven o'clock this evening. Transport will be waiting.'

'What are we going to do?' asked Marie.

'Miss,' said Sergeant Hathaway, 'we will be driven to a very nice country pub. Where I, and you, will celebrate what you have all achieved. And best of all,' he grinned at them proudly, 'although we shall never tell him, the bill will be picked up by His Majesty and we will all get ever so slightly pissed.'

The last word was not within his vocabulary. To the amusement of the others, Jan had to ask what it meant.

CHAPTER 17

Two large stuffed exercise mats about four inches thick lay side by side on the lawn in front of the house. Staff Sergeant Hardcastle had already taken them for a gruelling five mile run, after which they had been given time for a quick shower and breakfast. Now, at half past nine in the morning, they were beginning the first instruction period of the day – close-quarter unarmed combat.

Having spent the entire previous day on trains, they had arrived at a station somewhere in the Scottish Highlands late in the evening. A canvas covered lorry collected them from the station, and after a drive of about three quarters of an hour, they debussed outside a large country manse. At least, they agreed, as they were shown to their rooms before being offered a late snack of sandwiches and cocoa by a lady housekeeper, it was better than the Nissen huts at Ringwood.

The following morning, they watched as their instructor called forward a young woman called Giselle, the only other female member of their group. She was handed a knife – this one made of wood, blunt, and with the pointed end ground off so that it would harm neither the instructor nor his pupil. Under orders to attack, Giselle gave it her best shot: she moved bravely towards her opponent and with surprising speed tried to stab him in the chest. Her reward was a quick arm-lock movement smoothly converted into an over the shoulder throw and Giselle was thumped onto the canvas mats, flat on her back. At least she had the good sense to roll away, not giving the enemy a chance to drop a knee into her chest or stomach. She was allowed to stand, and Hardcastle repeated the move in slow motion, without actually throwing her, so that they could all see what he had done.

'Give the knife to Karol,' he told her, 'and we'll go through it again. Then I will attack, and one of you will defend.'

George Hardcastle watched as the young Pole faced him. But all too slowly an instinctive feeling made the hairs rise on the back of his neck. The lad was seemingly a left-hander, but he was not holding the knife by the handle in his fist, blade pointing down, as beginners usually did when attempting a stabbing movement. Rather, the knife was held low, with the blade horizontal and moving from side to side. 'Watch the eyes,' he would tell his pupils. 'They will always be your first warning.' But it was much more difficult when there was a knife swinging low in front of you. And this one, even if only a practice blade, was poised to strike either in his crotch or stomach. Somewhere along the line, Karol had been taught how to fight with a knife.

Clearly, the Pole had not been concerned when called upon to take his turn. He was just concentrating intensely on the exercise in hand. Suddenly Jan lunged, the blunt tip aimed at his opponent's lower stomach. Hardcastle read the intention to gut him, so that for real he would spill his entrails and bleed out. He started to go for a standard grip, twist and elbow break, although he would not have followed through to shatter the joint.

But the Pole didn't press home his attack. Instead, he pulled back from the feint and stepped sharply to his left. Hardcastle, committed already to defence, could do nothing as Jan's right fist caught him in the solar plexus. Not wishing to cause embarrassment, he pulled the punch, but even so it was enough to knock the wind from his opponent, who realised only too well that he had been let off lightly. With a half-skip further to the left, Jan pushed the sole of his right foot firmly against the outside of Hardcastle's right knee. At the same time, he flicked the knife from his left hand to the right, where it could have been used to finish his opponent in any number of ways. The staff sergeant realised that had this been for real he would have been on the ground, totally winded and with a leg probably crippled for life. With a knife strike on the way down, it would have been game over.

Jan retreated to the edge of the mat, arms down, hands by his sides, offering no threat. Staff Sergeant Hardcastle was still on his feet but breathing deeply, recovering. 'All right, youngster,' he said quietly, 'where and what have you been taught and who was your instructor?'

'First, my father,' said Jan evenly. 'He was sniper behind lines when we fought Russia. I don't know where he was trained, but he could fight and he taught me. Especially after some boys taunted my sister and I used my fists. Father said there were better ways of winning and he passed on everything he knew. Shooting also,' he added.

'Much later,' Jan went on, 'I went to work in Germany. My master was older than me, but he had been *Stosstruppen,* special forces, in the last war. His name was Herr Raschdorf. His father died of a stroke. Herr Günther wanted to keep fit, so we used to spar and wrestle at least twice a week. He showed me what I have just used against you.' He stopped speaking, already somewhat embarrassed and tongue-tied.

Hardcastle put his arms around Jan's shoulders and turned to face the others. 'We can all learn important lessons from this,' he told them. 'And at some time in the future, they might just save your life. 'What did I do wrong?' he asked the group. It was a rhetorical question, he was not expecting a reply.

He took his arm from Jan. 'First,' he went on, ticking off one thumb with the other, 'I under-estimated my opponent. It was a classic, stupid, schoolboy mistake. Karol here is probably the youngest of you all and I just assumed he would not be trained. In fact, he's young, strong, fast and very good. Next,' he ticked off an index finger, 'he fooled me completely. Only a trained knife fighter holds a weapon the way he did. I was too slow to pick up on this. Then I saw the knife in his left hand and assumed that he was not right-handed. Wrong! I followed the knife, expecting the attack to come from that direction. He pulled back from the feint and landed a punch from his dominant side. Had he used full force, I would have been on the ground. On the way down I could have lost all use of my right leg. And finally, for real, he could have finished me with the knife – because of my mistakes, he won fair and square.

'For now,' he told them, 'I'm going to leave Karol out of this part of the programme, because the rest of you are still on the basics. But he and I will train separately in our own time: I think I have more to offer and I'm interested to know if there is anything I can learn from him.'

It was, thought Jan, a very honest and fair assessment.

That evening they exercised in private. After an hour's workout, during which Staff Sergeant Hardcastle honed some of Jan's skills and taught a few new ones, Jan reckoned that honours were about even. The next morning Hardcastle announced a new method of instruction. He and Jan would demonstrate each move, with Jan acting as the attacking student, after which Jan would also act as defender to his fellow students. That way, the instructor told them, they could double the amount of one-on-one instruction and practice time.

'You throw me too hard,' Marie told him with a mischievous grin the first time they faced up, 'and I'll kick you in the balls.' Jan smiled wickedly. She was a good looking young woman, probably a year or two older than him, with an athletic figure and an impish face, framed by straight dark brown hair cut to just below her chin.

'And I'll buy you a gin and tonic for every time you succeed,' he replied, still grinning. But for the duration of the course, Marie bought her own drinks.

The training continued. There was range work with a variety of weapons, from handguns to machine pistols, light machine guns and even a light mortar. The three other men on the course all had some military experience but Jan was more than their equal. Eventually, they could strip and reassemble everything, even wearing a blindfold. The two girls, however, had the edge in first aid and radio operator skills, although they all mastered Morse code and attempted to transmit without trailing a "fist".

The same sergeant instructor, a rather schoolmaster-ish looking individual with round glasses, also taught map reading, although the other three men had some experience already. 'Remember,' he told them 'when you give a grid reference, the top line figures come first and the ones up the side – second.' He demonstrated. 'You give the two figure number of the vertical grid line to the left of your position first, taken from either the top or the bottom of your map. Then on a scale of one to ten you estimate how far into the square you think you are. In this case it's six-five,' he pointed to the row of figures along the top of the map, 'then as we are nearly up to the next vertical grid line, it's six-five-eight. Now go to the line below your position, take the number from the vertical scale on the left or right side of your map, and like before, estimate how far you are towards the next line above. In this case not far, so the second three numbers are four-seven-three. Therefore the full reference is Grid 658473. Got that?'

There was a general murmur that they had. 'Good,' he went on, but sooner or later one of you might forget and do it the wrong way round. So, to make sure that you won't, remember to ask yourself where the toilet is.' He smiled at their puzzled expression. 'It's along the passage,' his hand swept slowly along the top line of figures on the map, 'and then up the stairs.' His hand moved up the vertical numbers. 'Along the passage and up the stairs,' he repeated for emphasis, 'say it to yourself every time you take a grid reference and you'll never make a mistake. Better still, you won't ask some poor pilot to make a drop when the prepared DZ is miles away.'

For the next two days, they put everything into practice – contours, inter-visibility, the lot – including running all afternoon, following their map from point-to-point.

It was back to Staff Sergeant Hardcastle for the explosives module. They covered the use of both dynamite and TNT, and all the various means of initiation, from fuse cord to electrical ignition, when a precise timing of the explosion was required – 'for instance when you are blowing up a locomotive,' added Hardcastle. Jan noticed that he said "when", and not "if". 'Everyone loves blowing things up,' he told them before they were due to set off and destroy a short length of railway line set on sleepers well away from the house. 'You will be using electrical detonation,' he said, 'but remember, when it's a fuse, walk, don't run. Embarrassing if you fall over on the way out. Although I bet the first time you do it for real, you will ignore my advice and at least trot away, only to lie on the ground for ages till the device cooks off.'

Field craft was another major subject. How to check for a tail and how, where and when to lose one. They covered message passing – dead letter boxes and person-to-person. But finally, just before Christmas, the course was finished and they were pronounced trained. 'You will now go to a house in the south of England,' they were told, 'until your first assignment.'

They spent another tortuous day on trains. But late that evening they were driven to a country house in a county called "Hampshire". Someone in civilian clothes introduced himself as James Stanton-Harris, the chief administrator of the establishment. 'Those of you with homes to go to in this country will be given leave for Christmas,' they were told. 'Otherwise, let me know, and we'll sort something out.'

The three British men all had family to visit for the festive season, as did Giselle, who let slip that her mother was French but married to an Englishman. Marie and Jan were the two "orphans". 'This place pretty much closes down,' Stanton-Harris told them, 'from just before Christmas Eve till the day after Boxing Day.' He looked at Marie. 'If we make sure that the kitchen is well stocked with food and drink, would you be able to look after yourselves?'

Marie affirmed that they could. 'I'm a Frenchwoman,' she said with a cheeky smile. 'Unlike you English, I know how to cook!'

Stanton-Harris laughed at the leg-pull. 'Even so,' he said, 'there is no question of you two being left alone on Christmas day. You will please join us for Christmas lunch. For security reasons, it will have to take place here but my wife, Marjorie, will organise everything. We'll arrive at about ten and lunch will be at three.'

Jan and Marie enjoyed a walk early on Christmas morning to the local Catholic church. When they returned from Mass, Stanton-Harris's Humber staff car was in the drive. They entered via the back door. Marjorie Stanton Harris was in the kitchen, about to put a huge goose into the oven. She was a tall, rather imposing lady who introduced herself with the typical hearty courtesy of an upper-class Englishwoman.

'No staff today,' she told them with a twinkle in her eye. 'It'll have to be you and me, Marie, if I may call you that?' she asked.

Marie affirmed that it was fine. 'What can I do, Mrs Stanton-Harris?' she asked.

'Start on those, my dear,' came the reply as she nodded at a pile of sprouts, potatoes, parsnips and carrots on the table. 'And it's Marjorie, by the way.

'Karol,' she said imperiously, 'go and join that husband of

mine in the drawing room. Tell him to crack open the *fino* and we'll be through for a glass as soon as we have done these vegetables.'

Jan did not know what *fino* was, but he passed on the message anyway and was pleasantly surprised at the result. 'What do you do at home for Christmas?' he was asked.

'We have our main meal on Christmas eve,' Jan told him. 'Traditionally it is carp.'

'Wish I'd known,' came the reply, 'Would have organised some for you. But hope our English fare won't disappoint.'

Stanton-Harris had a very crisp way of talking. Almost certainly it came from a military background. 'It is most kind of you and Mrs Stanton-Harris to do this for us,' Jan told him. 'But don't you have family for all-together at Christmas?'

'Jimmie's in France,' Stanton-Harris told him. 'Armoured Corps – second in command of a tank squadron. Juliet's fled the nest. Married to a Hurricane pilot. Decent sort of chap. They have two young children. But they are stationed up north.'

'You must miss them, at this time of year,' Jan offered.

'We do,' came the reply, 'but to tell you the truth, Marjorie has taken to today's lunch thing like a duck to water. In a way, old chap,' he said, wiping his moustache left and right with an index finger, 'you are doing us a favour. If we try to give anyone forced to stay here for Christmas a good time, the old girl and I are not left sitting at home just looking at each other. Much better all round, don't y'know, what?'

Jan sipped his drink reflectively. It was a fascinating insight into the British psyche. Clearly as a nation they were generous and hospitable. And they were undeterred by events, obviously intent of making the best of things no matter the circumstances. In a way, he felt reassured. Herr Hitler might have started this war, but Jan had a feeling that the *Führer* might not be too happy when it ended.

Somehow the meal was a triumph, although Marie conceded afterwards that *chère* Marjorie, as she called her, *était un peu pompette*. The French words meant nothing to Jan, but Marie's hand held an imaginary wine glass and she mimed tipping it towards her lips several times in quick succession. Marjorie had obviously been a little tipsy. So, Marie had settled her at the kitchen table with just a half-glass more of wine whilst she made a rich sauce reduced in the French fashion. The Christmas pudding was an anathema to Marie but she followed Marjorie's instructions. Stanton-Harris implanted a sprig of holly and poured on far too much brandy, nearly setting light to the tablecloth. After the meal, he complimented both ladies generously. All four of them settled into armchairs in front of a blazing log fire and dozed off to the wireless.

Late one evening in the first week of January, there was a knock on Jan's bedroom door. It was Marie. 'I am leaving tomorrow,' she said simply. 'But perhaps we could meet, after the war? Marjorie said that her husband would be able to put us in touch.'

Jan hoped that he would have a friend for life. He readily agreed. Marie put her index finger to her lips and then touched Jan's. Without another word, she turned and left his room.

'*Chciałbym, żebyś została.* I wish you didn't have to go,' Tadzio told her, as they sat at the kitchen table after supper. 'We have a life here. Look what we have achieved. The farmhouse is almost as good as new. We have made furniture and even managed to find some whitening in the village to repaint the walls.'

Tadzio had used rough-hewn green timber from the farm to make very simple furniture – including two beds, now covered with palliasses and blankets salvaged from locally abandoned homes. Farms in the area had yielded a small but invaluable supply of animals – a few cows, all of which, when found, had been in desperate need of milking – plus a flock of sheep and quite a few extra fowls that were already in lay. They even had a young bull, found tethered in a barn. When they put two lengths of rope through the ring on its nose it allowed them to lead it away as if it knew that rescue was at hand. Tadzio had worked non-stop to improve a fence around one of his small fields. Compared with most of the population, they were well off, and what they could not provide for themselves they obtained locally by bartering their small surplus of food – a commodity in increasingly short supply.

That Saturday evening, they were seated on benches at their kitchen table – Tadzio had thought that chairs might take too long and challenge his fairly basic carpentry skills. Supper had been simple fare but adequate – sausages, cabbage and potatoes, with a bottle of home-made blackberry and apple wine also exchanged locally for a few precious eggs.

'*Muszę iść*, I have to go,' she told him. 'The partisans are desperate for food. I'm sticking to cross country and forest tracks. I don't expect to meet any Germans and even if I do they won't see me as a threat. *And* I'll be carrying a *Schmeisser*. I'll put a saddle on Kary, then load him gently as a pack horse. I'll not mount him unless I need to move in a hurry, and even then, only for a short distance. The Germans won't be able to follow me, either on foot or in a vehicle.'

Tadzio wished he shared her confidence. 'When will you be back?' he asked.

'I'll be away for a couple of days,' she replied. 'Out tomorrow, because it's quiet on Sundays, then back on Monday. That'll be quicker, because I can ride.'

She might as well have said 'away to the market,' thought Tadzio. Except that she would be making her way alone across country and if she were caught going in either direction… he tried not to think about it.

There was a human whistle from outside. Someone was in

the yard. Tadzio quickly turned down and blew out the oil lamp but not before Hedda had taken the Walther from a drawer. She seated herself again at the table, holding the weapon in her right hand on her lap. There were no curtains, so it was possible that they had been overlooked for some time.

'Pan Janicki,' called a voice softly. *Jestem przyjacielem. Już się spotkaliśmy.* It's a friend. We have met before.'

Tadzio recognised the voice. It was the man claiming to be a former consul who had asked him to identify his brother's photograph. He took the weapon from Hedda, checked that it had a round chambered and stood to one side of the door. Just to be sure, Hedda sat on the floor, completely shielded by the table. Tadzio stood to one side, unlatched the door and with one finger swung it slowly open. Their visitor stood just a pace outside in the moonlight.

'I think you know who I am,' he said softly. 'I'm alone, and I have a weapon but not in my hands. I would like to talk to you again, Tadzio,' he went on, 'but the only things I'm carrying that you can see are this carton and a bottle of *wódka* in my right hand.'

He could indeed see a cardboard box balanced on the stranger's forearms and a bottle glinting in the moonlight. His visitor's other hand, clearly empty, was in plain view.

'Stay there,' instructed Tadzio. 'We'll re-light the lamp. After that, you walk in and I shut the door. I'll still be behind you. Anything else happens after that, you won't be alive to see it. Hedda…' he called.

She struck a match and adjusted the wick. The stranger took a few slow paces into the room then turned to face Tadzio. 'I would like to put this box and the bottle on the table, with your permission,' he said, 'and then take off my overcoat. I, too, have a pistol, that I will also place gently on the table next to the lady using only my thumb and one finger. Then perhaps we can talk?'

He was as good as his word, pushing his weapon over towards Hedda so that it would take him time to reach it. Tadzio kept the Walther trained in the right direction.

'First,' he asked, looking towards Hedda, 'may I ask whom I have the pleasure of meeting?'

Rather than give her name, Hedda asked who he was and what he wanted.

'Is she secure?' their visitor asked Tadzio.

'Totally,' came the reply.

'Very well, then,' he answered after a moment's pause, 'I shall have to take that on trust.'

He turned to Tadzio. 'First of all, your brother sends his best wishes,' he began. Before Tadzio could burst into questions he held up a hand. 'Jan has just completed a training course. He is about to return to Poland. We know there are partisans in the forest. We need a liaison officer to link up with them, provide training, organise supply drops and generally help us disrupt the German war effort as it spreads east. We think his best chance of success would be if he could blend into his former background. We have already surveyed your farm. Would it be possible for him to return here, at least at first?' He paused. 'I have to tell you,' he said finally, 'that if his cover is blown, and you were caught helping him in any way, you would almost certainly be shot.'

'How do we know you can be trusted?' Tadzio replied. 'So far you have asked me to identify my brother from a photograph, but that doesn't prove anything. I answered truthfully, but you could be working for either side.'

'My name is Tomek,' he told them, using the diminutive form of Tomasz. 'I was born and educated in Poland – Polish father, English mother. Then I studied German at our university in Warsaw. My mother used to work for your trade mission there and we spoke English at home. As I told you last time we met, I was formerly the honorary British consul in the Free

City of Danzig. My main employment was in the shipping office. When Poland was invaded, I left my job and changed my address, just as a precaution. I am still based near Danzig but I undertake small tasks for London from time to time. Usually I am contacted through Stockholm. I also have communications,' he added rather vaguely. 'If you have doubts, ask me a question to which only you and your brother would know the answer. I will return with it inside twenty-four hours.'

Tadzio looked at Hedda, who nodded her agreement. 'Ask him *what was my father's most treasured possession?*' he replied.

Tomek smiled. 'We took the precaution of asking Jan for the answers to some of the most obvious ones. He said he hopes that you still have the Mosin-Dragant, and he added the words "Tukhachevsky" and "nineteen-twenty".

Tadzio thought this over for several seconds. Finally, he reached a decision. 'We can trust him,' he told Hedda.

Hedda stood and opened the door of a newly built cupboard set above the stone sink. 'We don't have any glasses,' she said apologetically, setting three enamel mugs on the table, 'they were all lost in the fire.'

Their visitor poured three generous measures. It was *wódka*, not *bimber*. *'Za Polskę!'* he said formally, raising his own. 'To Poland!' they echoed.

'What do you want from us?' asked Hedda, as they replaced their mugs on the table.

'First, you know that fairly large field to the north of here – the one leading to the wood?' he asked. Tadzio nodded his agreement. 'Jan said if you are in any doubt, it's the one where he shot the boar.'

Tadzio smiled at the memory, but only briefly. That had been in the happy days, before the Germans murdered his father and raped and killed his sister. 'Can you cut down the oak in the middle of that field,' Tomek went on, 'and level the stump to the ground?'

'*Da się zrobić* – easy enough,' Tadzio replied. 'I could use the timber anyway. Take me at least a couple of days, though, one to fell the tree, another to take off the branches and haul them away with Kary – that's the horse,' he offered by way of explanation. 'Probably have to cut the trunk a couple of times, too,' he added.

'There's still plenty of time,' Tomek told him. 'Do you have mains electricity here?'

Tadzio laughed. That was not a luxury out on the farm.

'Very well,' came the reply. 'Inside that box I've just put on the table is a radio, plus a supply of lead acid batteries, which are already charged from a rectifier. Each evening, after the news, the BBC sends out a stream of messages. I want you to listen, once a day. You have enough batteries there to last about three weeks. After that you can get rid of everything, if you wish – Jan will have his own communications. Although if you would rather, I can arrange for you to receive freshly charged replacement cells. That way you can keep up with the news from London. I probably don't need to tell you,' he concluded, 'that even to possess that equipment could be dangerous. You *have* to keep it extremely well hidden, and don't ever get caught listening to it.'

'And then?' asked Hedda. Tomek noticed that she seemed to be taking over the negotiations.

'One evening there will be a message. It will simply say "coming home", in English, and it will be repeated. The following night, I want you to light three fires in the field just before dawn is breaking and only when you hear the sound of a light aircraft. Two fires should be upwind, where the plane can touch down, and the third at the other end of the field, so that the pilot will know where it is.'

Hedda smiled. Tomek looked at her with a quizzical frown. 'Jan's hardest part will not be contacting the resistance,' she told him.

'Why so?' he responded.

'I am already partisan,' she replied with a hint of pride. 'I will speak with them tomorrow. They can help us to secure the field. If there is any danger, we won't light the fires. But if we do, Jan's pilot will know that he can set down safely.'

Jeszcze po jednym, another,' said Tomek, grinning enthusiastically at the news and splashing a generous top-up into each mug. 'Then I must leave you. I have a small motorbike hidden in your wood.'

Soon afterwards, he left. The wine and *wódka* had made them both sleepy. 'But I have to say,' she told him, putting the now empty mugs in the sink to wait till morning, 'there can be no more argument. I have to leave first thing tomorrow.'

CHAPTER 18

His initial briefing was in Stanton-Harris' office. Two others were present, a man introduced as Colonel Ives and a lady who called herself Mrs Jackman, although whether those were their real names he had no way of knowing.

'We want you to return to Poland,' Ives told him. 'Jan, we need a liaison officer with the partisans. Your cover will be that you have returned home from working in Germany but you have been lying low and just helping out on the farm since the invasion. Your brother and a young woman called Hedda will back you up, and she will be able to put you in touch with partisans hiding in the forests but quietly giving the Germans a hard time behind their own lines.'

'My name is Karol,' he corrected automatically.

'Not any more,' said the woman with a smile, 'that was for when you were in training. Now you are going operational. You will become Jan Janicki again, not least because if the Germans check you out everything can be verified. You already have a genuine passport in that name and the records, in the unlikely event that they have survived, will show that it was issued in Warsaw – even though we gave it to you in Belgium.'

'We will also give you a set of German papers,' Ives went on, 'as well as a background brief on your identity. You will have to study this till you know it like the back of your hand, but it might come in handy if you need to find yourself on the other side of the border. Once you are home, hide the German documents somewhere safe. They are inside a waterproof oilskin wrapping.'

'How am I going to get there?' asked Jan. 'Surely not back the same way I came to England.'

Ives shook his head. 'Via Sweden,' he said bluntly. 'The Swedes are neutral, but that doesn't mean they are not concerned by the outcome of the war. Privately, our intelligence is warning that it can be only a matter of time before the Germans invade Denmark and probably Norway. Sweden fears that if that happens their country will be almost engulfed. At the very least they would fall under the Third *Reich's* sphere of influence, even if they were not in their turn invaded. So, although on the face of it they are putting on an act of strict neutrality, in practice they are prepared to – shall we say – help out a bit and turn a blind eye to anything that can't be traced back to their country. I think the American word for it is "deniability".'

'So how do I get to Sweden?' asked Jan.

'Let's start from the beginning,' Ives told him. 'Train from London to Liverpool, then we'll book you a cabin on the overnight ferry to Belfast. From there you will be met and driven to Dublin in southern Ireland. They are also neutral but the border is very porous, although if necessary, your driver will have papers for you to pass through. In Dublin, you can stay for a couple of nights at the embassy, till you will be shipped out in a small fishing vessel based in Dun Laoghaire, near Dublin, to meet with the cargo freighter *SS Stockholm Star*. She is Swedish flagged, on the way home from Boston in the United States of America, so the Germans will leave her alone. The Captain does us the occasional favour. He will slow the vessel just outside Irish waters and you will board via a pilot ladder. Once in Stockholm, stay on board till we send someone to collect you.'

'And then what?' queried Jan. 'How do I get from Sweden to Poland?'

'A few months ago,' Ives continued, 'we persuaded Westland to sell one of their Mark Two Lysanders to the Swedish government. If anyone inspects the manufacturer's records, it's all there in black and white. As are details of the shipping arrangements, plus information on the engineer and rigger who met her at the other end and supervised the re-assembly. The aero engineer was a young pilot himself in 1918 and he has personally test-flown the re-assembled aircraft. But the important thing is that like the ship, she is Swedish registered. Do you know anything about the Lysander?' Ives queried.

Jan had to admit that he didn't.

'All right, just the basics then,' came the reply. 'It's a fairly new high-winged monoplane with a powerful nine hundred and five horse power Bristol Perseus engine. It's a two-seater, so you will be in the rear observer's seat with a rather large kit bag between your legs. Best of all, the Lysander has a very short take-off and landing run – it can be off the ground and climb to fifty feet in an incredible three hundred yards. The landing length is even shorter. This one has all the weaponry removed,' he went on, 'and a drop tank between the wheels. It just about has the range to take you there and back from the southern tip of Sweden to a field that is being prepared on your farm.'

He paused, then went on: 'We don't intend to file a flight plan. The pilot will fly in under the German radar, drop you off, then return to Sweden. If the fuel situation looks marginal on the way back, he will divert to Bornholm where the Danes are building a new airfield – the refuelling facilities are already in place. Obviously, you'll be met once you land and after that it will be up to you.'

Jan couldn't help a wry grin.

'Something amusing you?' asked Mrs Jackman.

'All that terrifying parachute training,' Jan replied. 'And now it looks as if I won't be needing it!'

'Don't count on it,' came her reply. 'We probably won't leave you in Poland for the duration. The longer you stay, the higher the risk. One of your tasks will be for you to train up a local successor, so it might yet come in handy.'

'OK, let's wrap this up for now,' said Ives. 'Jan, take a day to become word perfect on your German cover. All your Polish clothes and additional documents will be given to you in Dublin. Weapons, radio and a final briefing you will receive in Sweden. You travel the day after tomorrow. You will need about two days to reach our embassy there, then probably another day waiting to rendezvous with the *SS Stockholm Star*. It's just over fourteen hundred nautical miles to Stockholm. She might look a bit of an old freighter, but she has been re-engined and can cruise at fifteen knots, so the voyage will take about four days. You should be back in Poland in just over a week from now.'

Colonel Ives and Mrs Jackman both shook his hand. 'We are not going to wish you good luck,' she told him. 'It's a superstition that we have. But we do admire you. Take care of yourself.'

With that the visitors left the office.

Afterwards, looking back, laughing, they agreed it was the pigs' fault. Mucking out the sty was never one of Tadzio's favourite jobs – but it had to be done.

He must have got too close to the sow, whose newly born offspring, just suckled, were sheltering under a board behind her so that she could not lie on them. Whilst his back was turned the sow rose and pushed him, hard, with her shoulder. Tadzio was knocked to his feet and slithered on his side and back across the sty, towards the entrance. Now covered in slurry, he was disgusted at the state he was in. Hastily finishing off, he stripped in front of the pump in the farmyard. His heavily soiled clothes he threw into a barrel that collected rainwater from the barn roof – they used the contents for the vegetable garden anyway, so the addition would do no harm. But despite washing himself vigorously all over he still did not feel thoroughly clean. Which was when Hedda, who had walked to the village to barter their eggs, butter and cheese, turned the corner into the farmyard.

Seeing Tadzio in his birthday suit she placed a hand over her mouth and nose – not her eyes, he noticed – and asked with a barely concealed grin what on earth had happened.

'*Maciora mnie przewróciła* – the sow pushed me over,' he said crossly. 'Clothes are in the water barrel, and I'm going to need a hot bath.'

To his surprise, she burst out laughing. '*Ależ z ciebie rolnik*, some farmer you are,' she said eventually when her giggles subsided. But seeing that he was still furious, if only with himself, she offered to fetch him a towel. Also, if he sat in the kitchen, she would heat some water. 'Don't worry about your clothes,' she added, turning towards the back door. 'When you have sorted yourself out I'll boil them up for you – they won't smell once I have finished with them.'

Somewhat mollified by the offer of help, Tadzio followed her indoors and restored his modesty with the large bath towel that she hung up in front of her, averting her eyes till he was settled on a bench behind the table. The huge tin tub she took off an outside wall and settled on the floor in front of the range. Half an hour later it was two thirds full of hot water taken from their largest pot heated several times over the fire. Hedda left him to it.

In truth Tadzio had cleaned himself up pretty effectively in the yard, but even so he soaped thoroughly – neck, face and hair included – till he was absolutely satisfied with the result. Lying back in the still warm, now soapy water, he began to relax. Hedda knocked then opened the wooden door from the corridor and walked into the kitchen. She dipped one hand into the suds and sniffed carefully, first above his head and then at her hand. '*Może być*, you'll do,' she said. 'You don't smell at all! Neither does the water.'

The towel he had thrown over a bench by the table. It wasn't within reach. He thought of asking Hedda to pass it to him, then became aware of a rustle of clothing behind him. Out of the corner of his eye he watched as her skirt, a blouse, and finally her undergarments settled on the floor. 'Budge up,' she told him, her hand on his back pushing him forward. Naked, she stepped into the water behind him and, still pushing with her body, sank down into the water. Her legs lifted and moved forward, over his thighs. Her arms encircled his waist. Hedda stroked his back with the sudsy water, then his chest. Finally, her hands slipped beneath the surface and she caressed him again. Tadzio thought he was about to burst.

Just when he could bear it no longer she tapped him on the shoulder. '*Moja kolej*, my turn,' she announced abruptly. 'You can get out and wash my back.'

Tadzio managed to find the soap and step out of the bath without exposing his erection, which remained whilst he soaped first her back and then, as she lay back, her breasts. They were not huge – she was lithe and fit and carried no excess weight – but they were firm and excited him even further. Finally, she stood and faced him. Each took full view of the other. Stepping out of the bath she picked up the towel and wrapped it round both of them as they pressed together, front to front. '*Zabierz mnie do łóżka,*' she said simply. 'Take me to bed. *Pospiesz się!* Now – don't wait – quickly, quickly!' Tadzio took her hand and they almost ran into his room.

Afterwards, she rolled him onto his back and lay on her side facing him. Elbow on the mattress, Hedda used her raised left hand to support her head whilst she studied him. Neither of them spoke for quite some time.

'I decided,' she said eventually, softly into the silence, 'that our chances of surviving this war are at best fifty-fifty. As you now know, I was a virgin. But I was not going to die without experiencing what we did a few minutes ago. And,' she told him, 'I shall want to do it again in the morning.

'You know what your next job is, don't you?' she queried as she stood by the bed watching the sunrise, a sheet draped around her, not from modesty but because it was a little chilly.

'*Co takiego?* What's that?' asked Tadzio, still drowsy but wondering what was coming.

'Jan can have my room, if he wants it,' she said evenly, as if it were all planned out. 'And you can make this into a double bed.'

Adel Nilsson met him at the top of the ladder half-way up the ship's side. As they shook hands Jan took in a rather rotund, jovial man – grey hair, grey beard and medium height with a face weathered and tanned from a life at sea. 'Best you use my cabin,' he said having beckoned for Jan to follow. 'The crew have been told that now Britain is at war we are picking up a pilot for the passage through UK waters. I think I can trust all of them, but in your profession "think" is not good enough. I shall use the day cabin behind the bridge. My steward will bring you meals – I *know* I can trust Bernd, he's been with me for nearly thirty years.'

The cabin was well stocked with books and Bernd appeared at the appropriate times with a tray, but even so, it was a boring four days. Jan was grateful for Adel's company from time to time, particularly in the evenings when they shared a bottle of good wine. Otherwise he spent most of his time listening to the BBC, mainly with the aim of polishing his English.

The night before they were due to dock, Adel asked him to stay in his cabin until someone came to collect him. Most of the crew, it seemed, were to have shore leave. The following day, his meals arrived as before. Early that evening there was another knock on the door. His visitor was about thirty years of age, definitely on the short side but slim and wiry. 'Dinks

Lucas,' he introduced himself. 'Most people use the first name – you can see where it comes from. I'm officially a second secretary in the trade section of our diplomatic mission.'

'And unofficially?' queried Jan.

'I'm a squadron leader in the Royal Air Force. My job is to fly you home.'

Adel, Jan and Dinks walked down the companionway to the dock, where Dinks unlocked a Volvo PV 52 de luxe saloon with diplomatic plates. 'Great motor,' he remarked as they climbed aboard. Dinks was behind the wheel, Adel in the front passenger seat and Jan in the back. 'She has a massive three point seven-litre engine and a three speed manual with overdrive,' Jan was told. 'She's fast but heavy, which is all I need.'

At the gate to the dock Adel wound down his window and chatted to the security guard. Jan couldn't understand a word but the conversation ended in a laugh and a wave and the gates were opened. 'They know Adel and I are friends,' Dinks told him over his shoulder. 'When the *Star* is in port I come here quite often and Adel and I go out for a meal. They know Adel, they know the car and they know me. Adel told them that you were one of his crew. There was absolutely no reason for them to be suspicious.'

They enjoyed supper in a restaurant not far from the docks, then Jan was left nursing a brandy whilst Dinks took Adel back to his ship. 'I'm a bachelor,' he told Jan on his return, 'so you can stay in the spare room in my apartment. Feel free to go out in the daytime, but bear in mind that you don't speak Swedish and technically you are an illegal immigrant. I can get the embassy to swing it if ever there's a problem, but if you keep a low profile you'll find that the locals are a pretty friendly bunch.'

'Where did you learn to speak Swedish?' Jan asked.

'In this country,' Dinks replied with a laugh. 'Pater was

a diplomat. When he spent three years here just after the beginning of the last war he had the good sense not to pack me off to school in England. I was educated in Sweden for the duration – the only problem was day one, when I didn't know how to ask where the lavatory was. But by the end of the war, I was fluent.'

The next day was fine and sunny and Jan thoroughly enjoyed being a tourist in the Swedish capital. But when Dinks returned in the evening he told Jan that they would be leaving the flat at first light. 'Pretty full moon and good Met,' he commented, 'so reception has been arranged and we are set to take off early on the day after tomorrow.'

Jan enjoyed an interesting if uneventful car journey. Their destination was a hangar on an isolated estate on the south coast of Sweden, only a kilometre or so from the Baltic. Dinks unlocked a side door and switched on the overhead lights. Inside stood a gun-metal grey aeroplane with Swedish markings. 'Great machines, these Lysanders,' enthused Dinks. 'They can get knocked down by the German fighters, but for our purpose she's ideal. We'll take off well before dawn. For tonight, there are a couple of camp beds at the back of the hangar and I have a hamper of food and drinks in the Volvo. Managed to get you some vodka, old chap, just in case you need to settle a gippy tummy!'

Early next morning, and a bit stiff from the cold, Jan climbed the ladder on the port side of the aircraft and settled into the rear observer's seat. He was comfortable until Dinks stuffed an almighty canvas kit bag containing his clothes and a lot else besides between his knees. The pilot opened the hangar doors and climbed aboard.

The engine noise was deafening inside the hangar but the squadron leader obviously knew his way round the field. The lights in the wheel nacelles helped to guide them over the grass till they were in one corner. In good moonlight, Dinks turned the aircraft into wind and let the engine warm up for a few more minutes, then held her on the brakes whilst he plied on more power. Jan felt a strong push in the back and they were bouncing across the grass, but in seemingly no time, the Lysander took to the air and Dinks climbed gently away on instruments.

'We'll cross at about a thousand feet,' Dinks' voice came over his headset.

'Nearer their radar, provided I can see the surface, we'll drop to about five hundred. Then we fly low over the land, circle the field, and if everything looks all right I'll set her down. You chuck the bag over the side and scuttle out as fast you can. Then run for the side of the field. Don't forget to take the bag with you. I'd rather not spend more than a minute or so on the ground.'

Dinks executed a wide, low circuit. Jan could see his old home. It was just half-light, the ground barely visible in the pre-dawn. There were three small fires – no smoke, so someone had the sense to use dry wood. A strip of cloth had been attached to a small pole, giving Dinks the wind direction and its strength.

'We have to come in over that hedge,' he told Jan, 'so it'll be a fairly steep descent and a bit sideways, but don't worry, I've done this a few times already.'

From a thousand feet, control column well forward, Dinks pulled opposite stick and rudder into a side-slip and port-side on the Lysander fluttered towards the ground. At the last minute he straightened out, brought back the stick to flare gently and the wheels kissed the grass. It was a perfect landing. He gunned the engine to speed progress back to the hedge behind them, then again to kick on full rudder for the one-eighty turn from which he would take off.

Jan pulled off and stowed his headset, threw his kit bag out, scrambled onto the port side ladder and remembered to re-clip his now empty harness. He was immediately surrounded by hands helping him to the ground. One of them picked up his kit bag. Dinks' head turned back to check the canopy and rear seat and he gave Jan, who by now was outside the wingtip, a thumbs up. Seconds later the engine roared and the Lysander was airborne. Dinks waggled his wings as he climbed away.

They ran to the edge of the field where it met a small wood. Just into the trees were Tadzio and beside him a young woman carrying a machine pistol. The brothers rushed to embrace. It was an emotional moment. *'Dzięki Bogu jesteś bezpieczny*, thank God you are safe,' Tadzio told him, his face softened from damp eyes. Jan found that he, too, was welling up. *'To jest Hedda*, this is Hedda,' Tadzio said simply, indicating the young woman beside him. After a few seconds, there was a cough from a small group behind him and one man stepped forward.

'Józek Kowalski,' the man introduced himself, offering his hand, which Jan took. 'I lead the local partisan group. We prepared and secured the landing strip for you. I have an outer cordon in place, so we know we are safe for the moment, but I want to be away from here and into the forest as soon as possible. I suggest that you go home with your brother for now and, before long, we will meet again. Just in case the Germans heard the 'plane, which I doubt, we'll wait a few days so that they will have given up sending out patrols. Go now,' he went on, 'my men will remove all evidence from the field then we'll be away.'

'Jak się z wami skontaktować, how do I reach you?' asked Jan. It felt wonderful to be speaking his own language again.

'Przez Hedda,' Kowalski replied. 'Through Hedda. She knows what to do.'

'Sooner rather than later,' Jan requested politely. 'But we'll move out now as you suggest.'

Shouldering his kit bag, Jan set off with Tadzio and Hedda to his old home.

It was fully daylight by the time they were seated round the kitchen table. Jan could see that the once badly damaged house had been repaired, but questions could wait until later.

'*Co jest w torbie*, what's in the bag?' asked Hedda bluntly.

'Clothes – all Polish, a radio and code books and a few weapons and some ammunition,' Jan told her.

'Take out what you need,' she instructed, 'but anything compromising I'll wrap in something waterproof and hide with our radio and weapons. Whilst I'm doing that, you boys can be alone to talk.'

Tadzio told Jan all that had happened since they last met. Jan gave an account of his journey with Renate and his passage to England and subsequent training. 'You can base yourself here,' Tadzio told him, 'or Hedda says that if necessary you can join the partisans in the woods. But conditions there aren't good and it takes her all day to make the round trip, even on horseback.'

'Living here might be safest,' Jan offered, 'but how do we explain my presence – if we get asked by the Germans, I mean?'

'I suggest we stick as close to the truth as possible. Tell them that you were working in Germany, but that you left as soon as possible after the invasion. If they talk to this Herr Raschdorf, everything will check out – he's not going to incriminate himself by telling anyone that you took his half-Jewish daughter to safety. And if the Germans ask where you were last time they called, we simply say you were out working in the fields.'

'*Brzmi dobrze*, sounds good,' said Hedda, walking back into the kitchen and pouring water into the sink to wash muddy hands. 'Pick up your things,' she instructed, pointing to shoes and a pile of clothing on the kitchen table, 'and I'll show you to your room.'

'This was where Tadzio and I used to sleep,' Jan told her, noting the one single bed that now stood there. 'It seems years ago.'

'Come into the kitchen when you are ready,' she said. 'It has been kind of you not to ask, but you know that there are only two bedrooms. I should tell you that Tadzio and I share the other one.'

Somehow, Jan had taken a liking to this half-Polish, half-German girl who seemed so practical – as much at home on the farm as with a machine pistol and partisans. *'Tadzio to szczęściarz* – then Tadzio's a lucky man,' he said simply.

She touched his forearm. *'Dziękuję za te słowa,* thank you for that,' she replied quietly. 'Now,' her mood brightened, 'I'm going to tell that brother of yours to break out the *wódka* and a bottle of wine. Tonight, I think we all have something to celebrate.'

CHAPTER 19

They waited for two days but there was no sign of Germans. Hedda left on the third morning and returned late afternoon with Kowalski and two other partisans, all three of them armed. The other two did not offer their name.

'*Jak pewnie wiecie*, I am here, as you probably know,' Jan told the visitors once they were seated round the kitchen table and nursing a generous tot of *bimber*, 'for two reasons. First, as a liaison officer between your group and England. We know you need weapons and supplies – I can organise an air drop. Second, I need to train up a replacement, then my job here will be done and I may have to move on.'

Józek did not know whether any of his partisans knew Morse, let alone how to operate a radio set and use code books. Also, he confessed, he would have to consult his members on what would be the most essential requirements. They had a doctor and he knew they were desperately in need of medicines, but what exactly he would have to find out. Some food would be a great help, but other than stipulate their numbers he would have to leave that to the English. And they had some women with young babies. Again, he would have to ask. 'But most important of all,' he finished, 'we need guns and ammunition – as much as you can send. Machine pistols are best, but also light machine guns, mortars, grenades, hand guns and any sort of smoke canisters that you have, for when we have to try to disengage or cover a retreat.'

'*Mogę zrobić wam listę*, I can make up that list for you,' Jan offered, 'and you will also need explosives. Then the people at the other end can take a view on the right mix of goodies. But come the time, this will have to be an air drop. We are looking at several parachute loads here, because there's no way we have a field big enough for the aircraft to land. And you should think about how you are going to move the supplies once they are on the ground. If the enemy hear the 'plane they could be here within the half-hour. You have to be able to move everything out and destroy all evidence of the drop within that time.'

Józek thought about this. 'Pack horses,' he said at last. 'We don't have motorised transport and in any case, neither lorries nor carts would go through the forest. But with pack horses, we could strap on the loads and take the horses on a lead rein. We would only unpack later, once we are back at our base.'

'*Macie konie?*' asked Jan. 'Do you have them?'

'Some, not enough,' the partisan leader replied. 'But we can get more.'

They were mostly locals and knew the area thoroughly. Jan didn't bother to ask for details. 'But one more thing,' he added, 'on the subject of horses. We have only one here. Hedda uses Kary when she travels into the forest, but that means that she must ride alone. It would be useful if another animal could be provided for me. Also, when I use a radio to contact London it is much safer if I don't transmit from anywhere near the farm. Sooner or later, the Germans will pick up a signal. After that they will bring in resources to triangulate my position. So ideally, I need to be miles away. And to do that and return, a good horse would be ideal. That would leave Kary behind for Hedda – she needs him on the farm. And whether I'm out there with Hedda or on my own, on horseback, we stand a good chance of losing an enemy patrol – the Germans are generally mechanised, so they can't jump hedges or drive through woods and forests.'

Józek grinned. 'Not a problem,' he answered, 'so how would a big hunter suit you? Are you a good rider?'

'If it's a horse and it's got four legs and a tail,' Jan answered confidently, 'I can ride it. But could you find a mount for me?'

'Yes,' came the immediate reply. Then another wicked grin. 'Although a certain bigwig landlord is going to miss it. But he's a collaborator – all-be-it probably unwilling. He will be told that if he reports the loss, the partisans will destroy his property and he will be executed. That should be enough to persuade him to keep his mouth shut.'

Hedda, who had been listening but not taking part in the discussion, refilled their newly acquired glasses. 'Do you want to stay here for the night?' she asked. 'We have food – you would be welcome to some supper.'

Józek shook his head. 'It will be safer to travel back in the dark,' he told her. 'But if you have a few rations that we could carry, for the women and children, that would be appreciated.'

After about ten msinutes, another glass and with bulging pockets, Józek and his two men set out into the night.

He was as good as his word. The following evening, Jan, Tadzio and Hedda were about to close up for the night when Józek walked into the yard leading a magnificent chestnut gelding. 'I put on his tack and saddle but didn't fancy my chances at riding him,' Józek confessed. The only other animal of this quality that Jan had seen was in the Raschdorf stables, but he was quite confident that come the morning he could ride the big hunter. 'Let's put him in the barn for the night,' Jan suggested. Hedda walked quickly into the kitchen and came back with a carrot. Holding it out on a flat hand she let him take it then spoke softly to the horse, gently touching his nose. To the surprise of the men it meekly allowed itself to be led off. 'I'll give him a rub down and some feed and water,' she called out over her shoulder. 'You three can go into the kitchen – and take your muddy boots off at the door.'

'*Nazywa się Huzar*, his name's Huzar,' Józek called out to her as Hedda disappeared into the barn, 'and he has almost 173 centimetres at the withers.'

'I have a list,' Józek went on once they were seated round the table. 'And I am to tell you that we have managed to gather fifteen animals to take away the supplies.'

'Fine, I'll encode the message and transmit tomorrow,' Jan told him. 'It'll be a near full moon in about ten days' time, so that's when I would expect the drop, but as soon as we know I'll be in touch.' Józek accepted gratefully a glass of wine from Tadzio but had finished it and was long gone before Hedda returned from the barn. She promised to retrieve his radio and code books first thing in the morning.

Jan fashioned a backpack with straps so that his hands would be free to guide Huzar. With the radio and a small, hand-cranked generator it was heavy, but the extra weight would not worry the big gelding. Ideally, he would have liked an assistant, but in training they had spent hours turning a handle and simultaneously keying the message or writing down a reply. Jan's set operated on a Morse key only – there was no voice facility – and its range was about five hundred miles maximum. He had no idea where his message would be received, nor did he need to have. For all he knew it could be in Denmark or Sweden. With the equipment on his back, he would take only a revolver, which he secured inside his jacket. In a perfect world he would have liked to take a practice ride on Huzar but he needn't have worried – the horse had been well schooled and seemed to sense that it had an experienced rider.

He walked and cantered for a couple of hours, by which time he was so far from the farm that any detection would be meaningless. Settling into a copse which also served to conceal his mount, nevertheless he lowered a stirrup in case he had to move out in a hurry. Calmly he rigged his aerial and cranked up the generator. Seconds after his contact "send" he had an "ack". Minutes later, message transmitted and signed off, he was ready to return to the farm. Nine days later, a BBC radio broadcast told them that the drop would take place in forty-eight hours' time.

Flight Lieutenant 'Riggers' Rigson listened to the mission briefing. Behind the squadron leader was a map of northern Europe. Riggers' other two crew members sat either side of him. His navigator/bombardier would handle the drop, with the assistance of the third crew member who doubled as telegraphist and air gunner.

The squadron leader, who had also planned the mission, knew that the Mark IV Bristol Blenheim fighter/light bomber, introduced into service in 1937, had a maximum speed of two hundred and sixty-six miles per hour and a range of just under fifteen hundred miles. 'Enough to get you there,' said the Squadron Leader, 'but unfortunately not all the way back again. So, you will take off from RAF Milltown, which is about a hundred and fourteen miles north of Edinburgh, fully loaded and armed. We have arranged for you to be refuelled as necessary by the Danish air force – they will be expecting you.' He gave the navigator the co-ordinates for the field in Denmark.

Riggers had no great anxiety about the supply drop. Making a broad northern sweep around Germany they would be unlikely to meet opposition, and although his aircraft could be vulnerable to the Messerschmitt Bf 109s and 110s, his Browning machine guns in the port wing and dorsal and under-nose blisters meant that they were not completely defenceless. 'Should be a milk run,' he told his crew after the briefing. Firing up the two Bristol Mercury XV nine hundred and twenty horse power radial engines, Riggers lifted off from the south of England for Scotland, Denmark, the Baltic and Poland. In the bomb bay were thirty packed reinforced canvas cylinders, padded at the bottom to absorb the landing and tied into pairs. Four cylinders were rigged under each parachute, except for one load of two containing the heaviest items – boxes of mortar bombs and ammunition. 'We'll make two passes,' he told them, 'one north-west-south-east, then the other in the opposite directions. After that we scoot for home.'

Flying low over the Baltic and the coast to avoid enemy radar, as they approached the drop zone the navigator instructed the pilot to bring the Blenheim up to twelve hundred feet. From just ahead came the recognition signal – the dot, dash-dash-dash for "J". A second, continuous light shone to make the centre of the target area. Riggers flicked his landing lights on and off and throttled back to safely above stall speed, automatically leading into a turn to port with a touch of rudder and stick, making a slow full circle to give his crew time to have the bomb doors opened and stand by. 'Make sure you are harnessed up,' was his last message. 'I don't want either of you doing a pier-head jump by accident.'

'Roger out,' said the Navigator.

'*A finna,* Skipper,' came the sing-song lilt of his Welsh gunner. Riggers tried but failed to suppress a grin. On their first sorties as a crew, Taff Thomas, or "T.T." as he had become known, would have added 'That's *me too,* Skipper.' Countless times, Rigby told him to stick to English. Which he always did, if the message was urgent. But if it wasn't, T.T. ignored him and started with Welsh. Eventually, and not too much against his will, Riggers began to learn a few words of the language.

Not that he minded: air gunners suffered the highest mortality rate of all crew in the Royal Air Force. ME 109 fighters usually attacked from astern. It took a lot of courage to sit in that dorsal bubble and return fire with muzzle flashes from two wing-mounted M17 7.92 mil machine guns blazing at you. And once the gunner was gone, the Blenheim was almost helpless. But T.T. was a country boy, who loved nothing more than shooting game birds on the family farm in North Wales. As such, he was a master of the "lead-off".

His rounds were aimed not at the enemy aircraft but where it would be by the time they arrived. The irrepressible Welshman already had three kills to his credit. Which meant that he had probably saved them all the same number of times. And so, in the end, Riggers was content to indulge his squadron fly-half.

'Four gone,' Riggers heard in his headset. Throttling up, he raced from the field to pull a tight one-eighty, then slowed again for the second pass.

'Good drop, mid-field,' confirmed the navigator.

Another slow pass, a second on-target drop, and it was mission accomplished. With bomb doors closing, Riggers slammed the throttles forward and dived for the coast.

On the ground men raced to the parachutes. Others led the horses, two to each drop and one hefty animal to the last. Sharp knives cut the bindings of seven loads into pairs, so that in seconds two canvas containers could be thrown astride each animal.

Józek Kowalski could scarcely conceal his excitement. Grinning at Jan and Hedda, he pumped their hands with delight. The whole operation, from the time they had first heard the aircraft to when the head of the line left the field, had taken barely ten to twelve minutes. '*Do zobaczenia za kilka dni,* see you in a couple of days,' he said breathlessly, before turning to follow the convoy of horses. Jan and Hedda walked quietly back to the farm.

Roughly half way between Stettin and the Free City of Danzig, Frederic Armbruster was on night duty. Too old to be conscripted for the front, he had volunteered to join the coast guard. All his life he had been a fan of flying – a ground-based aeroplane buff. He heard the noise, then for a few seconds it was silhouetted against a good moon. To his amazement, it was not one of their own. In fact, illogical as it might seem, he was certain it had been a Bristol Blenhiem. He knew they were making them under licence in Finland, but no way should that machine have been streaming low, without lights, out over the coast. He radioed in his sighting and included it in his post-patrol report.

A few days later Józek was convinced that the drop had not been observed. There were no additional patrols or any signs of curiosity from the invaders. He spread out a map on the kitchen table. *'Chcę z wami omówić to, o czym myślę* – I want to talk over what I am thinking,' he told the three of them.

'I didn't mention this before,' he went on, 'because there was no point. And in any case, I thoroughly approve of what you did. You might like to know that we eventually retrieved the motorcycle, and very useful it's been. But the fact is, the Germans shot four innocent men, civilians from the nearest village, in retaliation.' Tadzio and Hedda looked aghast, but Józek held up both hands, palms towards them. 'Not your fault, you couldn't have known,' he sought to reassure them. 'But we have to learn from this – in future, partisan action will have to take place as far as possible from any Polish community.' He smiled, but not warmly. 'In fact, I have a plan to teach them a lesson,' he said grimly.

'One advantage we have here is that we are not far from the border,' he said, pointing a grubby forefinger at the map. 'I want to take out a convoy – partly so that we can steal food and weapons, but even more so to make it clear that the enemy will have to use scarce troops and resources if they want to secure their MSR – the Main Supply Route. There are no Polish villages near the border, only German ones on the other side, so what are they going to do: shoot their own people?' he asked wickedly.

'Podoba mi się – I like it, said Jan. 'It's far enough away from anywhere, and the escort won't be fully alert till after they have crossed into Poland. So where do we come in?'

'We have been watching the convoys, admittedly inside our own border, for a few weeks now,' Józek told them. 'Usually there's an armoured car in the front and a half-track at the back. In total about ten soldiers in the half-track plus all the vehicle drivers, who are an unknown quantity.'

'*Ilu ludzi możesz zebrać?*' Jan asked. 'How many men can you muster?' Up till now he had deliberately avoided being too inquisitive about the partisan group, if only to build mutual trust and confidence.

'*Maksymalnie czterdziestu, może pięćdziesięciu,*' Józek replied. 'Max, forty or fifty, but I want to leave some behind with the women and children. So, I plan on an attack force of about thirty – mostly men, although some of the women are just as good and all of them have every reason to hate the Germans. But to answer your first question, we need you to guide us there. You have unique knowledge of crossing the border safely and you know the lie of the land in detail. Maybe you can help me choose an ambush site off the map?'

Jan knew a wooded area not far from the border, well north of the Raschdorf estate, where there were plenty of bends in the road.

'The convoys prefer to cross into Poland in daylight,' Józek observed, 'so we are looking at moving from here before last light and waiting to put in an attack some time the following morning.

'Can we start from your farm?' he asked. 'It's much nearer to the border and if we lie up by day we can start out rested and fresh.'

'*Nie ma problemu,*' said Tadzio. 'Not a problem. It's highly unlikely that we will see any Germans around here, but if we do all trace of them will have to be eliminated.'

'So, when do we move?' asked Hedda.

'According to my sources, the next convoy is due in three days' time,' Józek told her. 'I need Jan with us, also for the explosives, and I would like you to come too, Hedda, but I want Tadzio to stay here.'

At first Tadzio resisted. If Hedda went, he was going, and as far as he was concerned that was that. The palm of his hand slapped the table to drive home the point.

'Look, we desperately need this farm as a supply base,' Józek replied. 'In the unlikely event that you have a visit whilst the operation is under way, everything must appear normal. That won't be the case if a German patrol turns up, there's no-one here, and then all of a sudden a convoy is wiped out and you are back the next day.

'No,' he emphasised to Tadzio, placing his hand gently but firmly on the table. 'We have to have Jan with us, and Hedda is an experienced fighter which, with due respect, you are not. But it is absolutely essential that someone stays at the farm. Tadzio, that can only be you,' he said quietly. 'If we can, we should keep the farm as a secure base, not just for this operation but for the future.'

'I know you don't like it,' Hedda offered, reaching out to put her hand over Tadzio's, 'but it makes sense.' Tadzio opened his mouth to say something, but Hedda kicked him under the table and he knew he had lost the argument.

The partisans arrived at first light, having used darkness to cover their march, then settled in the barn to rest up for the day. There were five women in the attack group and they helped Hedda make an arrival breakfast, then a lunch of soup and bread, and finally to prepare some meat, cheese and more bread that they could consume on the march and in the morning. They had also brought a few pack horses and canvas containers salvaged from the drop.

At first they moved in small, well-spaced groups of three or four, in order to not attract attention from any distant glance or passing aircraft. But in deepening twilight, the partisans closed up and marched almost silently, Jan in the lead with Józek. Talk was desultory but they did discuss setting up a programme so that Jan could train some of the partisans in the use of explosives. Although this first time he would set the charge for the ambush. 'We have a middle-aged Jewish man with us,' Józek also confided. 'He's never going to be any use as a fighter but I'm told he has always been an amateur radio ham.' Jan agreed that he would be an ideal person to train up as their operator, then he in turn could instruct others.

It was about twenty-five kilometres to the site that Jan had chosen but they stopped just short in a clearing whilst it was still dark. The partisans rigged a line between two trees to which they tethered the pack horses. Józek outlined his orders. 'If it follows the usual pattern, there will be between five and ten trucks, with an escort fore and aft,' he began. 'With any luck, they'll still be fairly relaxed – they don't get nervous till they are over the border.

'The armoured car in the lead will almost certainly be a wheeled Sd.Kfz 222. Some of you have seen one before, but for those who haven't, it carries a crew of three and is armed with a twenty-mil cannon and a 7.92 mil machine gun. Jan will set the charge and detonate it remotely, hopefully right underneath. Immediately after the explosion, if all has gone to plan, I shall take the tyres out on the lead truck. My gunfire will be the signal to start the attack. If for any reason the charge fails to go off, or we fail to disable the armoured car, we abort. Because if we don't, the armament it carries will cut us to pieces. So, if you don't hear me fire within a couple of seconds of the blast, we melt back into the trees. With only about ten soldiers I doubt they'll want to dismount and follow us. Then we can always try again another day, but not if we take heavy casualties. Clearly understood?'

He looked round the half-circle of people. There were nods and murmurs of agreement.

'Right, I want us to split into three groups,' Józek went on. 'I want seven men and Hedda with Jan and me. Our job is to take out the armoured car and immediately disable the lead lorry. I want a rear party of ten to take out the half-track. As soon as you hear firing, five of the rear group open up on the occupants, to keep their heads down, and the others put hand grenades into the passengers up in the back. The last group will form a small screen, two stop groups one on either side several metres from the road. Make sure you are far enough back and watch where you are firing – I don't want any stray rounds hitting those of us attacking the convoy. Your job is to take close-range, aimed shots at any Germans who escape our ambush. When all the firing stops, come and join us.'

'Right,' he went on, 'once the half-track and its occupants are neutralised, we start on the lorries. Chances are the drivers will jump out and surrender, but if there's any opposition gun it down. Usual drill – a few rounds through the cab door, then pull it open and check. Rear group will collect any Germans who jump out of the passenger door on the right-hand side as you look forward. My group will cover the other side, moving back down convoy, to take out any drivers who try to make a run for it from their door. So, don't fire across the line of vehicles or you risk hitting each other. Once the enemy are collected or neutralised, we'll take what we want and torch the rest.'

There were enthusiastic noises from the partisans. Clearly looting was good for morale. Jan had no idea whether Józek had ever received military training, but from the use of terminology almost certainly he had. The plan was sound and he put it across in a confident, relaxed manner that suggested every chance of complete success. He was a good leader and his men – and women – were up for the fight.

They moved into position in the gathering light to the sound of the dawn chorus. Looking at the site Jan had chosen,

Józek nodded appreciatively. Roads in Germany were generally hard surfaced; in Poland, particularly in the countryside, they were not. This close to the border, the road was not in a good state of repair. Jan selected a pot hole more or less in the middle and set his explosive charge – just past a bend so that the rest of the column would not be able to see what was happening. The device and its black wires he covered with leaves and dirt that blended with the surroundings, then led the wires off into the trees so that he would be well back but perfectly able to see his target as it approached.

Sentries were set out a quarter of a kilometre at either end, so that they could warn of any enemy approaching and then run back to reinforce the ambush groups. Józek knew they had the advantage of surprise but his Poles were only thirty fighters. Everything depended on taking out the escorts.

The rear sentry ran in, breathless. A wave to Józek, who was on the road at the bend, then both he and his sentry retreated into their ambush positions. Jan heard the convoy before he could see it and wound the handle. Suddenly the armoured car was on the bend. The commander was not down in his weapons cupola but sitting up carelessly on the rim at the rear. Jan paused for a few seconds, calmly judging speed and distance. With its front end just a couple of metres from the charge, he pressed the plunger.

The ear-splitting explosion almost deafened him. The armoured car leapt into the air and crashed down on its side a couple of metres off the far side of the road. The commander was thrown by the blast and his broken body cannoned into trees. Seconds later a fire started and rounds were cooking off. The crew never emerged.

Jan, his ears still ringing, was conscious of Józek leaping to his feet and firing at the front tyres of what was now the lead vehicle, before switching his aim to the cab. Further back, out of sight, he heard the rattle of automatic fire and the blast of Mills grenades. Jan decided to follow a few yards behind Józek, Hedda and the other fighters, just in case anyone in a cab survived to leap out behind them. With Jan bringing up the rear, they ran down the length of the convoy, pouring rounds into cab after cab till there was no more resistance. Toward the rear of the convoy one lucky driver did emerge, *Maschinenpistole* in hand, but he dropped it immediately on seeing Jan and raised his hands. Their run completed, they discovered that none of the passengers in the back of the half-track had survived.

Józek's force regrouped more or less in the centre of the convoy. A few passengers had leapt out and surrendered before the rear group of partisans arrived to shoot up their vehicle. Jan's captive was shoved into their group, who were led off into the trees. Seconds later there was a prolonged burst of automatic fire.

'Did we have to do that?' Jan asked.

'They have to learn,' Józek replied bluntly. 'We are at war. They murder innocent civilians. We kill only their military. Perhaps this will make them think twice before they extract reprisals against Polish citizens.'

At first Jan had mixed feelings but when he thought of his father and Aniela he dismissed any doubts. The murdering bastards were always someone's husband or son, but as far as he was concerned they had it coming.

Two of the partisans returned with the pack horses. Into the canvas canisters from the air drop went a treasure trove of captured ammunition, food and other stores intended for the eastern front. Sadly, they could not take everything but it was still a rich haul. Finally, they torched the rest of the convoy. The Germans would find only a line of burnt-out vehicles and a pile of dead bodies – most importantly of all, inside their own border. When they set off, leading the now heavily laden animals, all the partisans had at least two weapons, one on each shoulder, in addition to their own slung across at the chest.

Jan and Józek had plotted their return route carefully. The area, when it was not wooded, was well streamed and marshy. Even the weather favoured them with steady rain from a low, clagged-in sky. There would be no foot- or hoof-prints for the enemy to follow. Not even a scent if they used dogs. It was well past midday when Jan and Hedda, by this time well beyond the more direct route from the ambush site to the farm, broke off and returned home from the other direction. The partisans carried on to their forest.

Exhausted though they were, Hedda insisted on re-burying their weapons and ammunition before they returned to the cottage, including a mint condition Walther P38 pistol she had lifted from the body of the armoured car commander. Tadzio was overjoyed to see them safely home. He hugged Hedda tightly for a few seconds before she pushed him gently away. 'Your brother saved our life back there,' she told Tadzio, putting an arm round Jan so that he, too, received a hug. 'One of the German drivers got behind us. If it hadn't been for Jan's training, he would have opened up.' For no reason at all, she started to laugh hysterically.

Jan recognised post-action stress but was too exhausted to say anything. Tadzio sensed their mood and silently put a bottle of *bimber* and three glasses on the table. As an afterthought, he added a bottle of red wine. He had made a sort of stew for their return. Hedda, calmer now and grateful for his foresight, was too kind-hearted to tell him that it wasn't very good and that the potatoes were not quite cooked properly, but they drank the homemade *wódka,* ate a little anyway, then finally relaxed as they finished off the wine. It was barely dark when all three of them staggered off to bed.

CHAPTER 20

It was a battle for survival. In the forest, the partisans' enemies were now the cold, the wet, and the conditions under which they lived in the harsh Polish winter. Their habitations were makeshift in the extreme: primitive log and branch structures roofed with thin beams, canvas and leaking sods. Mud everywhere, inside the hovels and out – ankle deep, when it rained or the snow melted, despite their best endeavours to make pathways from hewn timber. Humans and animals alike suffered from foot rot. Primitive braziers were lit for heating, but only at night and with the ever-constant danger of carbon monoxide.

The women used salvaged oil drums to heat water for washing and laundry in the pre-dawn, pounding their lice-ridden clothes, sometimes little more than rags, with a home-fashioned postle stick. Often it took days to get them dry. And they were never far from starving. The partisans did their best to help the children survive – they were the next generation, the only future for Poland. Without the meat and eggs provided by Tadzio's farm, and food and medicines either looted or from the supply drop, the situation would have been many times worse.

Jan and Hedda restored the sleeping space that Tadzio had originally made in the barn, installing a false wall at the far end and a wood-burning stove liberated from a wrecked, neighbouring property. Jan took to sleeping there, which meant that desperately ill partisans, often a mother and child, could be brought out of the forest for a few days, put in Jan's room in the cottage and treated with the few medicines they had, but at least with a chance to recover from racking coughs bordering on – and sometimes developing into – pneumonia.

On the seventeenth of September, Soviet troops had invaded eastern Poland. On the twenty-seventh of September, Warsaw surrendered and German troops entered the city on the following day. In October, Soviet forces retreated from central Poland to a line behind the Bug river in exchange for German acceptance of their interests in Lithuania, although they retained control of western Belorussia and western Ukraine. In terms of square miles, Poland was divided more or less equally, although the western half under German occupation was more densely populated. But divided between invaders from west and east, Poland as a nation state had ceased to exist.

On the farm, they got some news from the BBC Overseas Service – Warsaw went off air in the last week of September, when German artillery and bombers destroyed the electricity supply. But the BBC did not yet have detailed knowledge of what the invaders were doing to Poland and her people. This came anecdotally, in western Poland by contact with communities in Chojnice and the surrounding towns and villages, where it soon became clear that Poland was to be reduced to a source of slave labour, machinery and raw material, all to be exported to the Fatherland. Intellectuals were considered unnecessary and fit only for transportation to concentration camps. All polish secondary schools and universities remained closed. In the streets, German soldiers stripped warm clothing, particularly sheepskin coats, from passing Poles. The ghetto process accelerated, and inside and out thousands were slowly starving to death.

Although they survived better than many, that winter the partisans lost about ten percent of their number to cold, weakness and disease: mostly the elderly, women and – despite their best efforts – some children. At least now, in the early days of spring, the weather was showing the first faint signs of warmth. As Józek Kowalski pointed out, seated at the kitchen table, most of the Polish roads could not support heavy traffic in the winter months, and the German main supply routes had shifted to the few Tarmac roads further north and away to the south. Their only success over the winter had been to blow the one important railway line near the coast, sending a locomotive and its carriages to the bottom of a small river. This had been in an area heavily populated by ethnic Germans who welcomed the invaders and co-operated with the suppression of Poles, so there had been none of the hated reprisals.

'*Prawie skończyliśmy budowę drugiego obozu w lesie,* we have almost finished building a second forest camp,' he told the three of them. 'It's a bit further from the farm, but the area to the south is even more heavily forested, to the point of being almost impenetrable unless the Germans want to mount a battalion-sized operation, and even then, they would need artillery and possibly air support. Most of the non-combatants have moved already.

'*A co do naszej obecnej sytuacji,* as for where we are now,' he went on, 'we suspect they are aware of our existence but we don't think they have the resources this far behind their lines to do much about it.' He set his cup of preciously hoarded coffee on the table. 'If they attack what's left of the original camp,' he said grimly, 'it will cost them dearly. We have permanent listening posts well out from the perimeter and the camp is heavily mined and booby-trapped, plus we have a sizeable stay-behind force with mortars and machine guns. The plan is to mount a rear-guard action to hold up the German approach, then once we have evacuated, we will let them into the killing ground. These days we have enough motorcycles and horses to move the last defenders to our new position before their foot soldiers on the ground can mount a final assault.'

Discussions were interrupted by a hasty warning from one of Kowalski's sentries that a German military vehicle was still some way off but headed in their direction. It was a flatbed field gray *Werhmacht* Ford lorry, built in Cologne. There were six soldiers in the back, which had spaced horizontal wooden "fencing" all round. Not quite a fighting patrol, but a concern nevertheless. Kowalski and his sentry hurried off to the trees behind the farmhouse. Hedda washed, dried and put away his cup and frantically checked that there were no other signs of the visitor's presence. Tadzio and Jan walked into the yard.

'I'm not sure I like the look of this,' Tadzio said quietly. 'Normally, when they want to collect livestock, they send a small van or a horse-drawn cart.'

'I don't think they are *SS*,' Jan replied as the vehicle drew up and an *Obergefreiter* jumped down from the passenger seat, 'can't see any *Sichersheitsdienst* insignia.' The soldiers lined up behind their corporal, rifles held across the chest but not in the aim. The NCO barked an order and one of the men entered the kitchen, returning a minute or so later with a struggling Hedda gripped firmly by her upper arm. She was pushed roughly to stand next to Jan and Tadzio, neither of whom till now had spoken to the Germans.

'What's happening, Sergeant?' Jan asked politely in their language, deliberately upping the rank in the hope that the man would feel flattered.

'We have to make your Polish agriculture more efficient, for the benefit of the greater *Reich*,' came the reply. His voice was matter-of-fact rather than threatening. 'Smaller farmers around the villages are being set a quota of their production that they must give to the occupation. Our requirements will always come first – the villagers must accept any shortfall.'

'And will that apply to us?' Jan queried.

'*Nein,*' came the response. 'This is more of a farm than a peasant smallholding. Also, there are two adjacent farms where the owners have either died or taken flight.' Jan thought the "died" was a bit rich – a euphemism for killed by the Germans, like his father and sister, but he said nothing.

'We know you have taken livestock and materials from these two properties,' the *Obergefreiter* went on, 'and we do not mind. That in turn has made more food available for the occupation. But now we have three farms and only one of them properly efficient. Under the greater *Reich's* new policy, these three together make a good-sized estate. From now on it will be owned by Germany, and we intend to farm all three as a single unit. A German farm manager will replace the three of you to oversee this new production unit.'

Jan let this sink for a moment. 'So, what's to become of us?' he asked eventually.

'You will assist the new manager,' he was told bluntly.

'Under what terms of employment?' Jan responded instantly.

'You will not be employed – if you are fortunate, the new manager will tell you where you can live, although I suspect he will make himself comfortable in this farmhouse, so perhaps for you the barn, and in exchange for your labour you will be allocated food. But you will no longer enjoy life like contented pigs whilst our soldiers in the field struggle for rations.'

Tadzio could stand it no longer. 'My family has owned this farm for generations,' he almost hissed at the NCO. 'You have no right to take it. And I do not intend to work for your new manager.'

'*Also,*' came the reply, the "s" a long "zzz" sound, then an indifferent shrug of the shoulders. 'If you don't wish to work here, you will be taken to Germany. We need labour there, too.'

'I do not intend to work in Germany either,' said Tadzio defiantly.

'You will not have a choice,' the NCO sneered. 'If you stay here, you will work for food and a roof over your head. If you are exported to Germany, you will not be a worker. Herr Himmler has decreed that in Germany all Poles are now slaves. You will wear a large purple "P" on your clothing, and you will toil for as long as your daily calorie allowance permits. When you are no longer fit for work you will be replaced. You are a conquered people, so it's your choice,' he stated bluntly, barely masking a note of contempt in his voice. *'Alles klar?'*

'All is clear,' said Jan softly, placing a restraining hand on Tadzio's arm.

'Well it's not all clear with me,' said Hedda defiantly, speaking for the first time. 'I have a German passport. You will not treat me – or us – like this.'

Her German, compared with the NCO's rather uneducated speech, was definitely *Hochdeutsch*. 'We know who you are,' the *Obergefreiter* said unpleasantly, 'so don't try and lord it over us. You are no more than a *Mischling*, and if you choose to make your life with these Polish *Untermenschen,* you will be treated as one.'

The corporal stepped in front of her. 'But *you* will not be deported. I think we will take you with us this afternoon – there are other ways in which you can be of benefit…' His left hand settled on Hedda's right breast.

Tadzio flew at the German, who had expected a reaction. He simply took half a step to one side and jabbed the young Pole viciously in the stomach with the muzzle of his rifle. Tadzio bent over, grimacing with pain. The German took a further step sideways, out of the line of fire, and at the same time the bolt actions of six more Mauser Kar 98s chambered a round, almost in unison, as they came into the aim.

'Keine Bewegung!' Jan said softly, knowing that the others would understand and the order not to move would placate the Germans. Now under the threat of seven rifles, the three of them could only stand and wait.

The NCO seemed to think for a moment. 'We only need one person here to watch the farm till the others arrive, a new manager and some more labour,' he announced. 'That will be you,' he said simply, pointing at Jan. 'These two,' he ordered, indicating Tadzio and Hedda, 'put them in the back of the truck. Any trouble, shoot him first,' he grinned at his men, 'after all, we don't want to damage tonight's entertainment. We'll keep the girl, and you will go to Germany,' he barked at Tadzio as two soldiers, rifles still aimed from the waist, moved round behind them.

Unterscharführer Gross settled himself comfortably in Günther Raschdorf's drawing room. This time, other than his driver outside, he was alone. 'To what do I owe the pleasure of this visit?' Günther asked evenly. He had no wish to antagonize Gross even further, but that was as far as he was prepared to bend. Maurer and his construction team were long gone. They had left behind a good standard of accommodation and sanitary facilities for the twenty or so Polish mechanics who were now forced to work in the repair shop – no longer employees, of course, but labouring in exchange only for a roof over the head and an absolute minimum of German calories per day.

Herr Rottenführer Bauer's guard force of six men were accommodated in two cottages on the estate. They knew they were well off, compared with comrades stationed further east. And Bauer turned a blind eye to the additional rations from the farm that he knew were delivered to the Polish slaves. He and Herr Raschdorf had reached a guarded but polite understanding.

'The workshop is performing as intended,' Günther pointed out deliberately. 'Willi told me that our efforts are well received when he was here for dinner last week,' he added, deliberately playing the card of social status. 'And financially, the *Reich's* reimbursement is just enough to cover our costs.'

In fact, this was an understatement. What with food

production and the marks provided to fund the workshop, the estate was generating a good surplus. But Günther would not give Gross the leverage of knowing this.

'I am not here to discuss the workshop,' Gross replied sullenly, knowing that thus far he had been out-flanked. 'As you know, I am a member of the *Allgemeiner SS* – the racial division. It is my duty to know the whereabouts of all Jews and non-Aryans within my district. There remains one small outstanding matter.'

He paused to let his words sink in. Günther sensed a fear in his stomach of what was about to come.

'We know about your *Jüdische Frau*, of course.' Günther forced himself not to react to this vulgar reference to his wife. 'But you told us that your *Mischling* had gone to stay with her grandmother in Berlin.' He pointed a finger at Günther. 'We have checked. She is not there. Nor has she ever been, these past few months. 'You have lied to us,' he concluded deliberately. 'So where is she?'

Günther tried frantically to think through his options. 'I honestly do not know, for sure,' he said eventually, 'but her grandfather is now in Switzerland. I am hoping she has gone to join him… to be safe from the war,' he finished uncertainly.

Gross let the silence hang. He was well trained in the techniques of interrogation. 'I do not think so,' he said at length. 'Our information is that she left in your wife's car soon after the beginning of the war. It was driven by your Polish apprentice – Jan Janicki, if I am not mistaken. Where he is now, I admit that we have no idea. But we very much doubt that he would have been allowed to cross into Switzerland – a Polish driver with a German passenger in a German registered car? They would have been searched, their papers examined.'

Günther could hardly indicate that Jan had a false German identity document, but that was not the point. The excuse that

Renate was in Switzerland was, to say the least, thin. He was spared further thought when Gross voiced his own opinion.

'We are not interested in Janicki,' he continued without waiting for a reply. 'But almost certainly, your *Mischling* is somewhere in Germany. You would be well advised to order her to return.'

He paused as if to emphasise his last point. 'With your wife and daughter here, we are reasonably sure of your continued co-operation. This estate, and particularly the repair facility, are important to the war effort. The presence of your family would offer us a reasonable guarantee of your future support. But now that everything is up and running, we have decided that your future here, and that of your wife and daughter,' he emphasised the last few words, 'is desirable but not absolutely essential. You would be well advised to reflect upon my words.'

With that he rose to his feet. 'And by the way,' he added nastily, 'don't bother to phone your friend *Hauptsturmführer* Willi Richter – we are already agreed on this issue. I shall show myself out.'

Hartmann Schultz had, by mutual consent, taken to breakfasting in the kitchen whilst Frau Brantis made up a packed lunch. It allowed him, he pointed out, to put his work coveralls on first thing in the morning, but they were more suitable for the kitchen bench than Frau Raschdorf's damask covered dining room chairs. Some evenings they all dined together, but occasionally and usually on a Saturday he would walk to the *Bierstube* in the village for a few beers and a bowl of stew, or perhaps a *Bratwurst* with *Kartoffelsalat*. He and Johann, who often joined him, had become firm friends and Schultz learned quite a lot from talking to the marine engineer. The other benefit was that it gave the Raschdorfs the occasional evening to themselves – welcomed kindly as he had been, and although he thought he fitted in well, he was acutely conscious that at the end of the day he had been imposed upon them.

Returning from the workshop that evening he found Günther Raschdorf waiting for him in the hall. He took the unusual step of asking Schultz if he would take supper with them – the usual seven thirty for eight. Even as they started on the vichyssoise he could tell that his hosts were unusually ill at ease. Eventually he felt moved to ask if everything was all right.

'I was going to talk later,' said Günther hesitantly.

'It's all a cold collation tonight,' Hannah put in, rising to remove their soup dishes. 'Perhaps, Günther, you might speak with Herr Schultz now. I think it might help set our minds at rest. Then we can serve ourselves afterwards – it's all set out on the sideboard.'

'We had a rather disturbing visit from Gross earlier today,' Günther began. 'It concerns Renate.'

Hartmann Shultz knew they had a daughter. He had enquired after her, having seen a photograph of a beautiful young woman set in a silver frame on a side table in the drawing room. He also knew that Hannah Raschdorf was said to be Jewish, from a wealthy family in Stettin. Johann had told him, one evening over a beer, that it was village gossip. Even now, the Raschdorf's wedding feast had not been forgotten and having found the menorah, Gross' wife could not resist the temptation to gossip. But the villagers were also acutely aware of what the family had done for them during the terrible years of inflation and famine. Both Günther and Hannah were well liked locally so the news was accepted and then quietly forgotten.

'As you know, Renate is not here,' Günther continued. 'I told Gross that she was with her grandfather in Switzerland for the duration,' he went on. 'But he doesn't believe me. He's trying to make me bring her back to the estate, arguing that the presence of the family, rather than just Hannah and I, would ensure my continued loyalty. At least that's what he says. I think he has other motives. I don't trust him at all, and I am absolutely convinced that she would not be safe even if she did return. His parting shot was that your friend Willi Richter was onside. So now you know why we are so worried – we have spoken about nothing else all day.'

Schultz noted that Günther had chosen his words carefully. He had told Gross that Renate was in Switzerland but not confirmed that this was indeed the case. However, this was not a question he wanted to ask, and in any case, it was not his affair.

'So, Gross has implied that Willi is supporting him,' Schultz said eventually, toying with a fork set in front of him. 'But I have known Willi Richter for years. He might be a member of the Party but I suspect that's more of a political gesture – it's the times we live in. I also know he's a decent man. I'm not sure that he would be complicit in this.' His right hand moved to twirl the stem of his wine glass, as yet unfilled. 'I haven't seen him since the night he came over for dinner. Do you think it might help if I talked to him… find out what's really going on? It might not be as bad as you think.'

The anguish seemed to drain from Hannah's face. 'Would you?' she almost pleaded. 'At least if we knew…' she tailed off.

'I cannot tell you how grateful we would be,' Günther added. 'If nothing else it would set our minds at rest – or at the very least we would know what we have to do,' he finished without further explanation.

'If I might use your 'phone tomorrow morning,' Schultz replied immediately, 'I'll make sure he'll be available then drive over and see him.'

'No need to use your motorcycle in this weather,' Günther offered. 'Take my Mercedes, if you wish.'

'Thank you,' came the reply. 'But I'll take a *Kübelwagen*. We have several behind the workshop waiting to go back to the front. There's every reason to take one for a road test, and I won't need to explain myself to anyone here. Besides,' he added, 'might as well use the *Wehrmacht's* petrol and not our own!'

Hartmann Schultz was as good as his word and left shortly before ten the next day. Lunchtime came and went and by late afternoon Günther and Hannah were beginning to become anxious. Finally, amidst a late afternoon shower, the *Kübelwagen* scrunched to a stop on the gravel at the top of the drive.

'Sorry to have been so long,' he apologised in the hall, 'but Willi insisted on giving me lunch in the mess. Rather a long one, too, as it turned out. Had to drive very carefully on the way back, but I think I've sobered up by now.'

'Come into the drawing room,' said Hannah, taking his coat. 'We must know how you got on, but we are almost afraid to hear the result.'

'Actually, it went quite well,' Schultz told them. 'I started by telling Willi that I was concerned about the on-going efficiency of the workshop.'

'And?' queried Günther. Hannah placed a restraining hand on her husband's arm 'Let the poor man speak,' she urged him.

'Well, when he asked why, I told him that you were worried about your long-term future here. Then I told him the reason why – Gross' visit and all that. He obviously knew about it, because he didn't ask any questions.'

'So, there is nothing to be done…' Hannah's voice tailed off.

'Not at all,' Schultz countered. 'I made out that it was for my future that I was most concerned, and that depends on the success of our workshop. I then told him that you and I,' he nodded towards Günther, 'were the only two qualified engineers on the estate. I didn't mention Johann, and neither did he, but even though he knows at least as much as we do

I would have claimed quite rightly that his experience was literally all at sea.' He smiled at his own choice of words.

'Anyway, I then told him that it wasn't just a question of workload, although that alone needs two of us to supervise. I also pointed out that you were the only one with any experience of tracked vehicles, from your time on the land, and that because of your experience in the last war, you were the only one I could trust to repair or replace any weapon systems. As I said to him, we might try to keep our Polish mechanics alive, but we are not in the game of letting them test-fire a loaded machine gun.'

'And so…?' put in Günther. Again, his wife's hand rested on his arm.

'I think he rather took the point,' said Schultz, trying but not quite managing to hide a small smile of satisfaction. 'He said that whilst he was here he would do his level best to make sure that you and Hannah are safe. But he also said that – politically – it would be unwise of him to order Gross to drop the matter entirely. He was actually quite helpful, though rather I think because of our long friendship than for any other reason. His last point, however, was that he thought it would support your case if Renate could write from Switzerland and say where she was and that all is well. Any foreign mail to you is almost certain to be checked, but even if it isn't, were you to have such a letter he feels that he could tell Gross to stop wasting his time and worry about more important matters. One last thing,' he concluded. 'You and Frau Raschdorf have been very good to me since I have been here. So, I want to make it quite clear whose side I am on. If there is anything further that you feel I can do, you only have to ask.'

Hannah took Hartmann Schultz' hand in her own and squeezed it hard, her eyes glistening. Günther patted him in the shoulder in silent gratitude and moved to a decanter on a side table. 'Hannah and I will have to talk this through,' he said, handing Schultz a glass of brandy. 'But thank you, from the bottom of our hearts.'

The problem, they agreed once they were alone after dinner, was sending a letter purporting to come from Renate and from Switzerland. 'My father could arrange it,' said Hannah, 'but how can we ask him without anyone being able to monitor a phone call or intercept correspondence that the Nazis would be bound to use as evidence against us?'

In the end, and with the Raschdorfs' agreement, Hartmann Schultz broached the subject with Johann a couple of evenings later over a glass of beer. 'I need to get a letter to Switzerland,' he said simply, 'but it's very personal and it can't go through the German post. I give you my word that in no way are the contents against Germany's best interests. But you still have a lot of contacts with the shipping world. And it would be of huge service to me and particularly to the Raschdorfs. Any ideas?'

Johann had long held the view that Hitler and the Nazis were entirely mad, but these days he had learned to keep his opinions to himself. He guessed, albeit wrongly, that the letter probably had something to do with the dollars he knew the Raschdorfs had earned during the Derresford days. But he didn't hesitate. 'The Port Captain in Stettin is an old friend,' he said, 'and we both have good contacts with the shipping lines. Your letter can be posted from a French or Spanish port – might take a little while, but it should reach Switzerland safely, no problem.'

The older engineer was as good as his word. Six weeks later an envelope covered with Swiss stamps dropped through the letterbox. Günther tried to see whether it had been opened but it was impossible to tell. It was a short, newsy letter in what looked to be a feminine hand. They knew it wasn't Renate's writing, but neither was it that different, and in any case the authorities had no means of making a comparison. More to the point, it said all the right things.

They were, as Günther pointed out to his wife, safe for the time being. 'But for how long?'

CHAPTER 21

Jan could only watch as first Hedda and then Tadzio were shoved roughly onto the back of the lorry. The rest of the Germans retreated, stepping backwards to the vehicle, rifles no longer in the aim but still waist high and pointing at him. As the last man climbed up two of them already on board moved to cover him. Unarmed, he could do nothing as the vehicle reversed then drove off down the track leading to the main road half a kilometre away.

As soon as it was out of sight, he raced round the back of the farmhouse towards the copse, shouting for Józek Kowalski. To his dismay, there was no reply nor any sign of the partisans. They must have retreated to avoid the Germans. Defeated, shoulders slumped, he started back towards the house. Halfway there he stopped as a stutter of gunfire echoed from the direction of the road. It was over quickly – probably no more than fifteen or twenty rounds. Frantic with fear for Tadzio and Hedda, he broke into a run. Perhaps the Mosin-Nagant… but as soon as he reached the yard, he was startled to see the German lorry drive in from the track. The windows were shattered. He need not have worried – a grinning Kowalski was at the wheel with Hedda and Tadzio beside him in the cab.

All three jumped down. *'Co się stało?'* asked Jan anxiously. 'What's happened?'

'Wszystko dobrze, it's all right,' Tadzio sought to reassure him. *'Jesteśmy bezpieczni*, we're safe.'

'I brought a few men with me,' explained Józek. 'As well as myself, and the sentry that came to the farmhouse, I left a stop group hidden in the trees near the end of the track.

When we heard the lorry park up on the other side of the house, we moved from the copse so that we could have sight of the yard. It was obvious what was happening, so as soon as they started to arrest Hedda and Tadzio, we raced back to the stop group, then ambushed the lorry whilst it was still on the track by firing at the cab. It's still driveable, and the rest of my men took out the soldiers in the back. Hedda and Tadzio had the good sense to dive to the floor. All Germans are accounted for.' His thumb indicated over his shoulder. 'The bodies are on the lorry.'

Jan saw a steady drip of blood falling into the yard. 'We'll take the weapons and ammo,' Józek went on. 'And the uniforms as well – they could be really useful some time in the future. But we must get rid of the bodies. If the Germans find them stripped, they will guess that partisans were responsible. And we also have to get rid of the lorry – we can torch it somewhere well away from the farm.'

'How will you get rid of the bodies?' asked Hedda.

'Moglibyśmy dać ich świniom,' Józek replied with a grim smile, 'We could feed them to the pigs, they would eat the lot, bones and all. But I think I would rather bury them – they won't be found. Besides, much as I like pork, I don't fancy dead-German-flavoured offal! The lorry we'll set alight separate from the bodies and also a few kilometres from here.'

'But the Germans will know where the patrol was going,' put in Jan. 'Surely there's bound to be some sort of follow-up.'

'Let's go inside and talk this through,' suggested Kowalski. 'The sentry and stop group are still out there, but it'll be dark soon. I don't suppose anything else is going to happen today – the Germans are too scared of us partisans to risk operating at night.'

With the three men seated at the table, Hedda produced another bottle of *bimber*. At least, thanks to her bartering, they had a decent supply, even if it was homemade potato stuff rather than the upmarket grain. But frankly, after what had happened, right now they all needed a drink.

'Według mnie, the way I see it,' Jan opened, 'the Germans in Chojdnice know that Hedda is half-Jewish. They also know that a patrol was sent out here never to return, regardless of where the remains of a burnt-out lorry are found. They are also suspicious of anyone who might be able to support the local partisans. To my mind, that's quite a lot of evidence, albeit circumstantial. So far, my cover is intact, but I'm not sure how safe it would be if the three of us were to stay on at the farm.'

'I can get my man to radio for instructions,' Józek offered, 'now that he is trained up and you have given him the radio. But I think you are right. Sooner or later, the Germans are going to come back to the farm, and with a lorry and a section of men missing, you are going to find it very hard to convince them that you are innocent.

'And there's another aspect to all this,' the partisan leader went on. 'Until now, we have been reasonably close to the farm. But the old camp is in an area that is not nearly as deeply forested as the new one much further south. So not only is our dependence on this farm less important, because we can establish similar contacts nearer the new base, but as and when the Germans put in their own management, it will be almost impossible for you to support us anyway. Frankly, I think it would be safer for all of us if we closed down here and set up elsewhere.'

He drained his glass and waited for their reaction. They sat in silence for several seconds, till Hedda stood to refill their glasses.

'He's right,' she offered at length. 'Jan, we could radio for you to have a pick-up. But Tadzio and I will not be safe if we stay here. It looks as though we shall have to move to the forest.' She looked towards Józek, who nodded his agreement.

Jan thought long and hard. *'Powinniśmy trzymać się razem,'* he said eventually. 'We should stay together. I'm not going to risk a pick-up in the field that would only take one person anyway, and neither do I intend to cut and run leaving you two with the partisans. I think we should all try to reach England. There's no reason why you shouldn't both be made welcome,' he went on. 'Tadzio could join the Army if he wanted to. You, Hedda, with your fluency in both languages, would be invaluable – either to the intelligence or broadcasting services. What do you think?'

'First, we have to get there,' Tadzio put in bluntly. 'I don't mind leaving the farm, because if the Germans want it to be productive, they will need the house and barn anyway, so they should be all right. Quite honestly, we can worry about this place after the war – or not, as the case may be.'

'We can sort out the stock,' said Józek. 'I doubt the Germans will be back any time too soon, so first thing tomorrow morning we could slaughter some and drive off the rest. I could bring more men back at daybreak, plus a few pack horses, and by mid-morning we could be well away from here.'

'I don't think any of us should stay in the cottage tonight,' Jan opined. 'The risk is small, but not one that I would like to take.'

'Zgadzam się,' said Hedda. 'Agreed, so what do we do – move into the forest with Józek and his men?'

I have another idea,' Jan offered. 'But first, if we three leave,' he asked Kowalski, 'can you and your men get rid of the evidence in the yard – just in case everything doesn't work out for us?'

'Jasne, can do,' the Pole affirmed. 'As I said, we'll keep the weapons and uniforms – both are bound to come in handy at some stage. But if you are not coming into the forest with us,' he asked, 'what on earth are you planning to do?'

'I have an idea for getting us home,' said Jan, 'or at least back to England, which is the only home on offer right now. Also, I have good contacts who might well be willing to help us. In the meantime, if the Germans are searching for us in Poland, we'll go to the one place where they won't think of looking. They have invaded our country. So, we'll hide in theirs.

'Right,' said Jan, sensing that he needed to take charge. 'Józek, will your stop group warn us if any more Germans turn up?' he queried.

'Already set up,' the Pole confirmed.

'Hedda, you unearth all the weapons and equipment that we have on the farm and pile it on the kitchen table. Also, we need a few clothes and about twenty-four hours' worth of food and water to take with us. Put everything on the kitchen table. What we don't need, we can leave for the partisans.'

'What are you and Tadzio going to do?' she asked.

'*Osiodłamy Karego i Huzara,*' he told her. 'Saddle Kary and Huzar. Then we need to fashion a couple of packs for a few clothes – my old parachute bag will do for one. The sooner we are away from here, the happier I shall be.'

It took an hour, but by last light the horses were loaded and ready. Tadzio would not be parted from the Mosin-Nagant, which he strapped to the side of Kary's saddle, but he shouldered a Schmeisser from their, by now, considerable hoard. Jan and Hedda each took a Schmeisser and a Walther, together with several spare magazines. Jan tossed a couple to his brother. 'If we are stopped, we'll have to fight our way out,' he voiced aloud. 'There is no way the Germans are going to let us live, not with what we are carrying. If it's all right with you, Józek,' he turned for confirmation, 'we'll take these and leave everything else for you.'

Józek confirmed that it was. They made a hasty cold meal of what was left in the larder and by nightfall the farm – the family home for so many generations – was deserted.

Jan insisted that Hedda ride Huzar whilst he and Tadzio led the two horses. Jan took the lead, with Tadzio well behind – if they were surprised, this would give at least some chance of survival. It was a clear night, with fortunately only a waning quarter moon, but, in any case, Jan was confident of the route. By midnight they were on the other side of the border – the ground still churned up from September, he noticed. And by first light they were on the Raschdorf estate.

Here they stopped a half-kilometre from the main house amidst a few brambles and trees. Hedda produced a breakfast from their rations and a bottle of *wódka* – she had salvaged three from her larder. 'We can't have a hot drink,' she offered, 'and it's been a long, cold night – not without its dangers. We have made it this far, let's at least drink to that.'

Leaving Tadzio and Hedda huddled together, Jan moved on foot towards the house and barn complex. He was astounded by what he saw – a once single workshop building, above which he had lived happily for almost three years, was now a huge extended repair facility with an acre of hard standing partly covered in a motley selection of military vehicles and machinery, some damaged, others pristine and freshly painted, clearly ready to be returned to the front. The whole facility was surrounded by a high fence topped with inward-sloping barbed wire. Thinking quickly, he retreated back up the lane towards the village and settled behind a hedge, hoping to intercept Johann.

He normally started work at half past seven. It was a dismal morning – not that cold, but dank and miserable. Hands in pockets, his jacket buttoned up, Johann was astounded to hear someone softly call his name. Sensing that it had come from behind, he turned back towards the village. Jan stood, slowly, above the hedge.

'*Mein Gott,* Jan!' he whispered. 'Is that really you?'

'It's good to see you, my dear friend,' Jan replied without

thinking, for despite the discrepancy of years this was how he thought of the old engineer. 'And yes,' he added, 'it's really me.'

'*Was machst du hier?*' he asked, absolutely incredulous.

'I'm not alone,' Jan told him. 'I have my brother and a German lady with me. I can explain later, but we are refugees. I desperately need to talk to Herr Raschdorf, if that's still possible?'

'*Ja, ja,* he's still here. But things are not the same as when you left. There are more Germans and some of your countrymen – forced to labour. You should not come any nearer to the house or workshop.' He thought for a minute. 'Tell me, where are you now, and I can go and speak with the Boss?'

'Two fields back, in the copse,' said Jan.

'Best wait there,' said the old engineer. 'I'll make sure everything is set up at the workshop, then take a walk up to the big house. I often do that of a morning, so no-one will think anything of it. Don't use the phone much these days,' he added, 'we are not sure how secure it is. Go back to your companions – I think you'll find that Herr Raschdorf will be along within the hour.'

They watched as Günther cantered Alger gently across the field, now fallow, small clods of turf flicking up behind the big thoroughbred. He reined in at the edge of the copse, and swung his right leg over the horse, sliding down over the saddle on his stomach with the ease of a lifetime's experience and landing lightly on his toes. Jan, with Tadzio and Hedda behind him, emerged into the field.

Jan offered his hand. Günther ignored it and threw his arms round his former apprentice. 'We can never thank you enough for what you did for us, taking Renate to safety,' he said emotionally. He stepped back, still holding Jan but at arm's length by the shoulders. '*Scheiße,* you have put on some weight and muscle,' he exclaimed, looking Jan up and down. He turned quickly to Hedda, 'please excuse my language, *Fraulein,*' he said, 'but I am astounded to see Jan again and looking so different.'

She extended a hand. 'My name's Hedda – I'm with Tadzio,' she said simply in her beautiful contralto *Hochdeutsch.*

Smiling, he took her hand but inverted it, bowed and brushed with his lips. 'Delighted,' he said, with natural old-world charm. 'Good to see you again too, Tadzio,' he added.

'Please, we need to talk,' Jan broke in urgently. 'And we have two horses with us. I should tell you also that as well as a few personal items we have weapons and ammunition.'

Günther thought for a few seconds. 'Do you remember the old woodman's cottage, right on the edge of the estate next to the forest?' he asked. Jan confirmed that he did. It was the most isolated building on the property and had a small barn to the rear of the plot.

'Nobody goes there these days,' Günther went on, 'but it's safe and secluded. Not in a perfect state of repair, but habitable. You could be warm and dry. I'll need to go back to the house but I can bring over a few basics. Can you meet me there in about an hour?'

Jan confirmed that they could. They put the horses in the barn and waited off to one side in the trees, weapons ready just in case. But fifty minutes later Günther was as good as his word. He approached down the single, dead-end track driving a *Kübelwagen* that lurched and bounced over the ruts. 'Borrowed it,' he announced without further explanation. Piled high on the seats were blankets and cardboard boxes, the latter, according to Günther, containing food and drink plus a few household items such as soap, two paraffin lamps, a can of fuel, and boxes of matches. There was also an axe, plus a sack of feed for the horses and a bucket for water. 'Plenty of dry timber on the ground,' said Günther, 'but you can cut more for the nights it you need to – if you must, use green timber, no-one will see the smoke once it's dark.'

The cottage was basic – a kitchen/living room, two bedrooms and a well and pump in the back yard for water. But it was still furnished with a table and chairs and Hedda found pots and pans in the kitchen cupboard. For now, they sat round the table whilst Jan recounted their story. He gave Günther a brief account of the journey with Renate, but glossed over the rest by saying that he had been back in Poland by design rather than accident. The meaning was well taken, but drew only a slow inclination of the head by way of understanding. Jan felt confident that he could trust his former employer, who had little enough reason to support the present German regime.

'So that's it, Sir,' he concluded. 'We need to get out of Germany and, if we can, to England. I have a few ideas but I'm hoping that Johann might be able to help. As a start, perhaps we could take ship for Sweden – even if we must stow away. After that, I have the contacts to help us on our way.'

'All right,' said Günther. 'I have a lot of thinking to do and I shall need to talk to Johann – he can be trusted, he's helped me before,' he added without explanation. 'Stay here for the night – for as long as you wish, in fact. It's so isolated you should be perfectly safe, although I wouldn't stray too far. All being well, I'll be back in the morning, but it won't be first thing.'

'Thank you, Sir,' said Jan, his voice heavy with relief.

'I think we are a bit past the apprentice stage now, Herr Janicki,' said Günther with a smile that embraced all three of them. 'Call me Günther.

'*Bis Morgen*,' he concluded, pushing back his chair.

'Till tomorrow, then,' Jan replied, reluctant to use his former employer's Christian name.

As the *Kübelwagen* disappeared down the track they lifted

the boxes on to the table. Jan wondered if Frau Raschdorf had helped her husband to put the provisions together, or whether Frau Brantis had been taken into their confidence. Either way, they found a supply of stacked timber behind the cottage and soon had a good fire going in the primitive range. The beds had palliasses but they were very damp. Hedda brushed off the mould with her hands and a couple of hours propped in front of a roaring fire pretty much dried them out. At least the blankets that Günther had supplied were aired. Whilst the men fed the horses and settled them for the night, Hedda filled the lamps and inspected the supplies. One box contained only a few bottles of beer, some wine and spirits and three tumblers, which Günther had obviously guessed would not be in the cottage.

After some discussion, they decided against a sentry system – Jan felt confident that no one would give away their presence. As dusk was falling Hedda lit one of the lamps and they dined – almost royally – on a cold leg of honey-roasted ham with buttered cabbage and potatoes baked over the ashes of the fire. They took their weapons into the bedrooms, but after a night without sleep and a stressful day they slept safely and soundly till daybreak.

They breakfasted well enough on ham and eggs, with yesterday's slightly stale bread toasted on a long forked twig in front of the range. Jan and Tadzio each took a *Schmeisser* and gathered wood, some fallen, the rest freshly cut, although they were careful not to stray too far from the cottage. Hedda prepared a substantial meat broth for later in the day, but always with a Walther not too far from her elbow. They all heard the sound of hooves on the single track leading to the cottage when, towards midday, Günther cantered Alger, then slowed to a walk for the last few yards. He unslung a large shoulder bag and set it on the kitchen table.

'Decided to ride,' he announced. 'That way I can set

off in any direction and then loop round. Also, I can't be followed, unless someone else has a good horse tacked up, ready and waiting. Brought a few more supplies,' he went on. 'We can have a beer whilst we talk things over, then perhaps lunch.'

'Do we have Frau Raschdorf to thank for this,' asked Jan cautiously, 'or have you had to take Frau Brantis into your confidence?'

'Hannah just asked her to make a picnic lunch for four,' Günther explained, 'but there's no way my wife could take these provisions from the larder without cook knowing about it. As Hannah was putting things into the bag, Frau Brantis said that it wasn't her place to ask questions, but if they were for whom she thought they just might be, then "if that young man leaves without saying hello and goodbye," quote-unquote, she would be both sad and disappointed.

'Right,' he went on, 'last night Johann had supper at the house after Frau Brantis had gone home. We trust her completely, but for the moment the less that she knows the better, if only for her own safety. Hannah was there, too, of course. I told Johann that I had another problem, and he offered to help even before he knew what it was.'

'And what did he say, when he did, I mean?' asked Jan.

'The bottom line is this,' Günther replied. 'Jan, you have German papers that would almost certainly be accepted. So you *might* be allowed to take ship legally for Sweden, especially if you had a good excuse – maybe buying essential agricultural machinery or machine parts for the estate, for instance. Hedda, we know, is already documented as having a Jewish mother,' he refused to use the abhorrent *Mischling* word. 'So for you,' he looked at her sadly, 'probably not possible. They wouldn't give you permission. Tadzio,' he turned to the young Pole, 'you have only Polish papers, so no chance.'

'We can't go back, we must stay together,' Jan stated quietly, placing his palms flat on the table.

'Understood, that's what we thought,' Günther reassured him. 'So, Johann is going to Stettin tomorrow. With all his contacts, he won't have any problem getting into the port and talking to a few of his old friends in the shipping business. He said there are two avenues he wants to explore. The first is that you stow away with the help of a friendly captain on a Swedish flagged vessel. The second is that you either buy or steal a small vessel, maybe something like a fishing boat or perhaps a private launch, but one that could still make the crossing to neutral Sweden.'

'Aren't there German patrol boats or something?' asked Tadzio, who until now had remained silent.

'There are,' Günther confirmed, 'but that's also something he will look at whilst he's away. Johann will leave for Stettin first thing in the morning – he's going to take a *Kübelwagen* and we have any number of good reasons why he should want to visit the port in support of the war effort. He'll have all the right paperwork and stamps for the vehicle and journey issued from the workshop – quite genuine, by the way. He plans to return as soon as he can, but will probably need to be there for at least a couple of days.

'All right,' said Günther, 'that's probably about as far as we can go for the moment. Today's Wednesday. Hartmann Schultz is taking some leave this weekend, so he'll be away from Friday lunchtime till some time on Monday. With Johann possibly away as well, I might have to supervise the workshop, but it pretty much runs itself these days. We have some damned good Polish engineers. Would you like to come to the house for Sunday lunch?' he looked round at the three of them. 'And how about Frau Brantis,' he turned to Jan, 'she could be there or not, whatever you think best?'

She had mothered him for almost three years. Jan knew, absolutely, in his heart of hearts, that she would never betray him. 'I would love to see her,' he said quietly. 'Renate would never forgive me if I didn't.' Without consulting the others, he went on quietly, 'When we were driving to safety, your daughter opened a picnic hamper. Almost the first thing I found,' he said sadly, still touched by the reflection, 'was a bottle of *Pilsner* beer. She had put a label on it – "for Jan, from Frau Brantis". If you think it's all right, I would dearly love to see her. God knows when I'll see my own mother again, but for the last few years Frau Brantis has come a pretty close second.'

Next morning, in the kitchen, Hannah Raschdorf did not beat about the bush. 'I would be grateful for a change from our usual arrangements this Sunday,' she said to Frau Brantis. 'We will have three guests so including yourself we'll be six at the table. No,' she said firmly, holding up a palm as Frau Brantis wiped her hands on an apron, clearly disturbed by the suggestion that she should eat with the family. 'Times are changing, and on this occasion, we will cook the meal together and I shall help you bring it into the dining room, where we will set everything on the sideboard. Then we will all help ourselves and you will join us. It will be something of a celebration, as well as a reunion. I don't have to tell you that all this has to be a matter of the utmost secrecy – you can't discuss it with anyone or we shall all be in the greatest danger.'

'Who are the guests?' asked Frau Brantis nervously.

'Can't say the names,' said Hannah mysteriously, beginning to enjoy the pleasure that the possibility might be offering her longest serving and most loyal member of staff. 'But I'll give you a clue. One guest you know very well, two you have yet to meet. But the one you do know won't be satisfied unless together we can make him an enormous, absolutely splendid *Schweinshaxe*. In fact, we shall need several!'

Frau Brantis' eyes began to well up. Hannah touched her gently on the arm. 'I'll leave you to think about what best might go with them,' she said, then turned tactfully to leave the kitchen.

It was a full minute before Frau Brantis could dry the last tears on her apron.

CHAPTER 22

Saturday evening and Martha Brantis sat at the kitchen table, glass of wine to hand. Gudrun had served dinner and gone home – she would not be on duty again till Monday morning. In truth Martha, too, should have left by now. But Frau Raschdorf had always said that if she would like a drink, she should help herself. Martha rarely did, but this evening her thoughts were in turmoil.

She was, in her own mind, simply a cook in an upper-class household and the employee of a kindly family. Her parents, long since dead, had been farm workers. She still lived in the family cottage on the estate and had every confidence that she would see out her life rent-free in that accommodation on her modest savings. Perhaps her employers would even grant her a small pension. Martha felt that she had done well – at first just a scullery maid, she had advanced through a mixture of observation, application, hard work and a talent for making tasty dishes. Her proudest moment had been when Frau Inge asked her to take over as head cook for the estate. She pulled a handkerchief from beneath the wrist strap of an inexpensive watch and – not for the first time that evening – dabbed at her eyes.

She understood why Frau Hannah had been reluctant to speak his name, but equally she knew that she would see Jan again on the morrow. With no family of her own, just a cat in her cottage, she loved that boy. He had left his own country, assimilated into Germany, mastered the language, and – according to Johann, with whom she sometimes enjoyed an occasional drink – also become an accomplished engineer. What's more, she had seen him drive off with young Miss

Renate and from the reaction of her parents there was little doubt that her darling girl of the estate had been taken to safety. Martha feared for her employers because she was acutely aware that Frau Hannah came from a wealthy but Jewish family. And ironically, although she was of purely ethnic German heritage, Martha was totally unaware that her own Christian name had a Hebraic origin.

Her thoughts turned to tomorrow's Sunday lunch. She would serve *Schweinshaxen,* perhaps some red onion and cabbage, with a little cranberry sauce. And roasted potatoes and parsnips, both cooked in fat from her dripping pot, the latter drizzled for the last half-hour in honey from the farm's hives. She would need another green vegetable, too, but sprouts from the kitchen garden were still in season. They were always better after the winter frost. Much as she loved and admired Frau Hannah, she wasn't sure how tomorrow would work out with two of them in the kitchen. Eventually she set down her glass in the sink. Tired now, she would rinse it in the morning. Martha hung her pinafore on the hook next to the kitchen door, pulled on her overcoat and set off into the night.

In the drawing room, Hannah paused from her embroidery. 'That sounded like Frau Brantis,' she said casually to her husband. 'I'll go and make sure we are locked up.' These days, they did many things that formerly would have been left to the staff.

Günther, already a bit drowsy after a splendid supper and a bottle of red wine, eased himself from an armchair for a last glass of Armagnac. He was interrupted by a loud knocking at the front door. It was Johann. 'I left the *Kübelwagen* down by the workshop,' he explained, 'but if it's not too late I can tell you how I got on.' Günther, suddenly wide awake, almost pulled him into the hall, then beckoned for him to follow into the drawing room where he poured his fellow engineer an equally generous glass.

Martha need not have worried. Frau Hannah insisted that she would not be in charge, but rather she would help prepare things and otherwise do anything else to assist. To Martha's absolute delight, just after midday the kitchen door opened and in walked Jan, followed by two strangers. She was not even put off by the sub-machine guns they off-shouldered and clattered down on the end of the kitchen table. Martha grabbed hold of Jan and gave him an enormous hug. Then just as Günther had done, she stepped back and looked at him. *'Mein Gott,'* she said approvingly, 'but you are now truly a man!'

'This is my brother Tadzio,' said Jan, more than a little embarrassed, 'and this is Hedda.'

'You should have come to the front door,' said Martha, shushing them towards the hall with her hands. 'I have to finish here, but the master has been so kind as to say that we will all enjoy the meal together. You must go through and say "hello" to Herr Günther and Frau Raschdorf.'

Once introduced to Tadzio and Hedda, Hannah Raschdorf excused herself to go and help Frau Brantis. Together, they set out a huge platter of meat on the sideboard together with heaped dishes of vegetables and a tureen of gravy. Unusually, for he normally liked to serve the meat, Günther waved at the utensils and invited his guests to help themselves. Suspecting that her husband was somewhat overtaken with worry, Hannah stepped up and transferred the *Schweinshaxen* onto plates for her guests.

Gradually, over rich food and a few glasses of wine, they relaxed. 'Johann came back late last night,' said Günther suddenly. Conversation came to an abrupt halt round the table.

'Should we be talking to him?' asked Jan cautiously.

'Let's finish our meal,' suggested Günther. 'Then I'll fill you in on what he said. But right now, he's in his office in the workshop, watching the road. We agreed that there is a risk in having us all here together, so if anyone approaches he will ring me and you will have time to melt away before anyone can reach the house.'

This seemed to cast a shadow over the lunch party, so after a quick slice of *Apfelkuchen* it was not long before dishes were cleared and they settled to coffee and, for the gentlemen, a glass of brandy. Hannah and Frau Brantis left the others at the table and took their coffee into the drawing room. Hannah closed both doors behind them.

'Johann had no difficulty getting into the port,' Günther began. 'There was an armed soldier on the main gate, but the civilian watchman recognised our man from the old days. The bottom line is that this is not an entry you can use,' he waved a hand to indicate the three of them. 'However, whilst I don't want to compromise Johann's sources, if you can get into the port itself there are a number of Swedish flagged ships that will leave you an entry ladder down the seaward side, where you are unlikely to be seen from the dock. In fact,' he went on, 'you won't be the first to leave in this way, and I suspect you wouldn't be the last.'

'But first, we have to get into the harbour itself,' observed Jan quietly.

'*Ja,*' Günther replied. 'But there is another complication. Apparently, the authorities know that people are leaving the country illegally. So now they search some of the outbound merchantmen. Not all, so it's a matter of luck. But to cover themselves the captains have to insist that any "passengers" hide as stowaways. Maybe in a lifeboat or something like that. It's the only way they can deny all knowledge, otherwise they, too, risk arrest and even having their ship impounded. Jan's contact at the port also added that none of the "stowaways" that have been discovered have ever been seen again.'

He paused to let this sink in. 'So as things stand,' Hedda said gently, 'we have a chance of making it to Sweden, but perhaps an equal chance that we might not. And you don't need me to tell you, Herr Raschdorf, what they would do to Jan and Tadzio, not to mention a Polish-German Jewess, caught in a German port trying to take ship illegally for Sweden.'

'Johann and I are only too aware of what could happen,' Günther said quietly. 'Which is one of the reasons why he is helping me. But he also mentioned that there might be another way. First, we have to get you into the port. Johann finished at the docks on Thursday evening. That night he slept in a local tavern where he has often stayed before, then on Friday spent most of the day driving upstream alongside the river Oder, away from where it flows into the port. As you leave the city, there are any number of substantial riverside residences, and many of them have a boat-house set into the river bank. Johann reckons that there are a number of possibilities.' Günther ticked them off on his thumb and two fingers. 'One might be that you steal a small vessel – quite honestly a rowing boat would do. In the meantime, we make arrangements for a Swedish vessel to put a boarding ladder along the seaward side, away from the dock. Then with the help of the captain you stow away.'

'Which gives us a chance of escape,' observed Jan, 'but only a chance – no guarantee of success.'

'Second,' Günther continued, ignoring Jan for the moment, 'you try to find something in one of the larger boat sheds that would take you to Sweden, or at least to the off-lying island of Öland. But you would need a big-ish motor cruiser with enough range – we are talking something like two hundred kilometres here. We might be lucky, but there's no guarantee of finding the right craft. Also, the Germans patrol the harbour with launches and in their coastal waters they have converted fishing boats armed with cannon and machine guns. You would have the advantage of speed if intercepted, but a luxury peacetime power boat would stick out like a sore thumb. If seen, it would bound to be challenged and assuming you don't stop they would certainly open fire. Perhaps you could take evasive action, but there is still quite an element of risk.'

They waited, sensing that there was more to come. Günther paused to sip his brandy. 'What Johann suggests,' he said eventually, 'is that you find something small and inconspicuous that has a good chance of floating down river, into the harbour, and alongside a fishing boat without being seen. After he had spoken with the port captain Johann strolled round the harbour on his own – for old times' sake, he told him. There were a number of fishing boats obviously still going out into coastal waters under the supervision of the *Kriegsmarine*.

'But there were also quite a few,' Günther went on, 'that appeared to be laid up – in mothballs, if you like, probably because their crews have been drafted into the Navy proper and there aren't enough men left behind to man them. Johann noted several that looked to be seaworthy. He thinks the best chance might be to take one of these, go to sea one night with the rest of the fleet, then try to sneak away for Sweden. With luck and perhaps a bit of foul weather, he thinks that overall this idea could have the best chance of success. But that said, at this stage he doesn't want to rule out any of the options. His advice to me was that we need to do some further reconnaissance before coming to a decision.'

'Who would do that,' asked Jan, 'and when? After all, grateful as we are, there is a risk in hiding here.'

'Agreed,' Günther affirmed. 'Johann wants to stay here tomorrow, then take a couple of days off and spend Tuesday and Wednesday looking round the river and harbour area – mostly during the hours of darkness. He would like you to go with him,' he added, looking at Jan. 'Johann has all the papers to take a military vehicle like last time, and you can use your *Ausweis*.' Jan did not see the need to let on that he now had a German passport that would pass muster – he would tell Johann about it once they had set off. 'Johann can always explain that you are working for the *Wehrmacht*,' Günther concluded, 'so even if you are stopped, there shouldn't be a problem.'

There was little point in prolonging the afternoon. Frau Brantis bustled off to prepare another basket of provisions, including the remains of the apple cake because she knew it was one of Jan's favourites. 'Just in case it's not safe to say goodbye later,' she said after the three of them had shouldered their weapons, 'I'll give you a big hug now. But be careful and try to stay in touch – if only when this ghastly war is over.'

Hedda and Tadzio tactfully turned away but then they, too, were tearfully embraced. Frau Brantis quietly closed the door behind them and with a heavy heart turned to the washing up. Frau Raschdorf was already at the sink. 'Come on,' she said quietly, putting a sudsy arm round the older woman's shoulders and giving her a squeeze, 'let's get this lot done then we'll go back into the drawing room, have a few more drinks and forget about the war.'

Frau Brantis did not leave the house that evening. She woke up early next morning fully dressed on the *chaise longue*, just her shoes on the floor, with two soft pillows beneath her head and an enormous eiderdown keeping her warm. For the first time in her life, Frau Brantis had a hangover.

They took a *Kübelwagen* on Tuesday morning. Johann drove Jan to the same small inn that he had used on the previous trip, explaining that he had known the owners for years and there would be no questions asked when a seafarer appeared to keep strange hours.

'There's no point in trying to find something from the road,' Johann explained. 'Most of the river bank is taken up with the grounds of expensive private property. Many of them have their own boat-house, or at least a small pier or jetty.'

After an early supper, they drove to the southern outskirts of the city, where the occasional field or park gave access to the river. Walking downstream along the river bank, for the most part they had to cross the grounds of substantial residences, almost all of them in darkness. 'Most of the owners are so rich they live in Berlin and only come here for weekends and holidays,' Johann told him, 'but it helps that all the big houses are set well back from the river in case of flooding.'

It was not long before Johann found what he wanted – a boat-house, but also a small jetty on which lay an inverted, clinker-built rowing boat. 'There are no oars,' Jan whispered, although they had to be a good three hundred metres from the house, which was in darkness anyway.

'They'll be inside the boat-house,' Johann told him, walking to a side door at the rear of a long shed and unrolling a canvas strip wrapped round a selection of tools. It was a clear night and there was just enough ambient moonlight to see what he was doing. It took only a few minutes to extract a hacksaw blade and split the arch of a rusty padlock. Inside, Johann switched on a small flashlight and searched around. The boat shed housed a luxury open motor launch covered for the winter with a huge piece of canvas. 'No use to us,' he said quietly to Jan, 'but this is what we need.' Resting on twin brackets screwed to the wall were two oars, obviously for the tender.

Back outside, Jan waited whilst Johann wrapped a small strip of tape round the cut section of the padlock. 'Doubt they'll notice until summer,' he said quietly. 'In fact, they probably won't even notice that the dinghy is missing – at least not for weeks, anyway.'

They set off downriver, keeping as close as they could to the bank. Most of the bridges were guarded by a single sentry, rifle slung over one shoulder, standing at one end or the other – doubtless with a half section of men keeping warm nearby. Well short of the first bridge Johann nudged the tender into the bank and watched patiently. Occasionally the sentry walked from one side to the centre. But for the most part the guard spent long intervals at one end. 'Probably trying to keep warm,' Johann whispered quietly. 'More wind and a lot colder mid-stream,' the old mariner observed. As soon as the sentry settled down Johann let the tender drift downstream hard under the same bank. 'If we had floated downriver opposite,' he said quietly to Jan once they were safely away, 'he might have seen us. But hard up in the lee of the bridge and the bank we were pretty much invisible.'

Finally, Johann rowed gently into the channel that led to the port area. Here he stopped for a full minute and listened. 'No engines,' he said quietly. 'I think they only patrol at intervals, so if we follow the line of the dock and just leave it to go round any shipping we should be fine – if we hear a patrol launch we just melt into the darkness between a ship and the jetty.'

Gradually Jan's tension eased. Johann obviously knew exactly what he was doing and thus far no alarm had been raised. Unbeknown to Johann, Jan had a Walther in his jacket pocket, but this would be absolutely a last resort. If he had to use it they would probably finish up dead anyway.

After what seemed an eternity of crawling round the edge of the port and the occasional merchantman, they came to an area reserved for the fishing fleet. There were empty spaces alongside, and vacancies on the mooring buoys, which suggested that quite a few of the fleet were at sea. But one vessel swinging to her mooring was in darkness. Johann rowed gently to her stern ladder and threw a practised hitch with their painter. He leant towards Johann, still seated in the stern.

'There's no gear or nets on deck,' he told Jan, 'so she's

almost certainly in lay-up. Don't be put off by the rust streaks – that's superficial. She's about twelve metres, made of steel, and if she's fuelled up, more than capable of taking us to Sweden. Let's climb aboard and find out.'

The wheel-house door was not even locked. 'Nobody ever steals a fishing boat,' Johann said with a grin. Once inside he ran his flash lamp over the console. A narrow companionway led below to a small saloon and the engine compartment. Jan was out of his depth, but Johann was clearly in his element. Back in the wheel-house he hot-wired an ignition switch and flicked over three orange circuit breakers. Instruments glowed dimly and Johann studied them intently before disappearing below again. 'As I expected,' he enthused. 'Both tanks are full of fuel.'

'How come we are so lucky?' asked Jan.

'You leave big tanks half empty,' Johann explained, 'and you get condensation. Also, at the interface water and diesel produce a bacteriological fungus. It clogs up the fuel filters. So, in the long run it's much better to diesel up if she's going to be left for any length of time.'

'I have opened the seacock for the generator,' he told Jan. 'The main engine battery is no more than half-charged so there probably won't be enough to fire up the big diesel. And the house batteries are a bit low. But the generator battery has held its charge – more than enough to start the 'genny's small diesel. If we run it for a couple of hours the main and house batteries should be fine. I'll switch everything else off, and it's going to be boring, but all I need you to do is keep a look-out for any patrol launches. Almost certainly they'll be showing navigation lights, so you might see them before you hear them. If so, we'll just shut down till they have gone away.' With that he pressed the starter button, and when the little diesel coughed to life he moved another switch to initiate the charge. The diesel slowed as the electrical load came on then settled to a steady hum. It was not that audible on deck.

They were not disturbed. By two in the morning Johann pronounced himself satisfied with the state of all batteries. With the 'genny off and the engine seacock open he selected a quarter throttle and pressed the starter button. The first time, the diesel coughed and died. Jan realised he was holding his breath. 'Might need to bleed the system to the injectors,' Johann muttered quietly, almost to himself. But the second time she coughed, missed, cough-missed, then settled into a steady rumble, just a small cloud of grey-white smoke followed by spurts of cooling water from the exhaust near the water line giving away the fact that the engine was running. Johann throttled back to tick-over at eight hundred revolutions a minute then left her to warm up. An hour later he pressed the shut-off button and the diesel went quiet.

'That'll do for now,' he told Jan, turning off the electrics. 'We'll close up here then row to somewhere a bit nearer where we can hide the rowboat and use it again another night.'

'Then what?' asked Jan.

'Then, my boy, we have to collect the *Kübelwagen*. At a guess, it's going to be a good ten kilometres. If we step out and keep an eye open for any police patrols, we should be able to get back to the inn soon after daybreak.'

The innkeeper and his wife seemed to take no exception when Johann and Jan turned up looking oil-stained, unshaven and grubby just after eight in the morning. But they were starving. Johann ordered a hearty breakfast of ham, eggs, fried potato and dark bread. Instead of just coffee he also asked for a couple of decent brandies. The requested checking-out time was midday, so they set the alarm clock for eleven-thirty, slept for a couple of hours and left on time. It was late Wednesday afternoon when they arrived back at the estate. Johann dropped

Jan off within walking distance of the cottage, then parked up the *Kübelwagen* and walked to the main house.

They reconvened at lunchtime the following day, this time at the cottage as Hartmann Schultz was back in residence. 'So we go tonight,' Günther concluded after some discussion. 'Johann says the fleet will be out on Friday night, but then back in harbour until Monday – there's no fishing on Saturday night through to Sunday, so there will be more boats out on Friday than at any other time in the week.'

'There's one thing we haven't made clear,' said Jan. 'I realize that Johann has to be on board when we make a break for Sweden, but I would be interested to know what he will do afterwards, assuming we arrive there safely?'

'*Ja, ja,* I have to come,' Johann confirmed. 'I could give you a course to steer and you might make it, but if anything happened on the way, like a blocked fuel filter, or there were signals from other ships, you would not have a clue what to do. I have talked this over with Herr Günther,' he went on, 'and he has kindly agreed to leave it to me. Assuming we make it safely to Sweden, I'm hardly likely to steam the fishing boat back to Germany. I could take ship commercially, but in truth I am not happy here. I don't like working for the Nazis and even less so having to use slave labour. If I don't come back, and I doubt if I will till the war is over, Herr Günther will inform anyone who asks that despite my age I have volunteered again for the merchant navy or the *Kriegsmarine*. We doubt that anyone will bother to check, because in any case that will still leave two fully qualified German engineers in the workshop.'

'One last thing,' said Günther. 'Weapons – I assume you'll take with you the ones you arrived with, but Johann feels that they won't be enough if you are challenged by a German patrol boat. Cannon would be too heavy for the rowing boat,' Günther went on, 'but I could lift a couple of 7.92 mil machine guns from those taken off in the workshop, together with a few belts of ammunition. It might give you a fighting chance, as a last resort.'

A *Kübelwagen* would have been too small, so from several on the park Johann chose a commandeered civilian delivery van repainted in *Wehrmacht* livery. They could take only one vehicle because Günther would be the sole person available to drive it back to the estate. They set out late on Thursday evening, Günther and Johann up front, Jan, Tadzio and Hedda in the back, together with weapons, ammunition and yet another hamper of rations. They found the rowing boat where they had left it, just outside the port area.

Günther shook hands then embraced all of them, adding a kiss on both cheeks for Hedda. 'Let us pray that we meet again,' he said softly as they pushed off, 'and may God look after us all.'

Once loaded, there was not much freeboard, more than a gentle rocking and water would slop over the side, but fortunately it was flat calm. They followed the same procedure as before and reached the fishing boat without incident. 'It's going to be a long day,' said Johann, 'but once it gets light we can't afford to go on deck – we have to stay below.'

Jan raised an eyebrow – not sure why this was necessary.

'It's like this,' Johann explained, 'people scan the harbour, often with binoculars, all day long. Usually just for interest. Also, there is the returning fleet. But you only need one person to see that there is activity on this boat when there hasn't been any for months and we could be reported.' Jan nodded his acceptance. As it got light they closed the wheel-house door and went below.

Johann found a pack of cards in one of the lockers and they took it in turns to play from time to time. Meals also provided something of a break, but in truth time passed interminably. Finally, in the gathering dusk, crews boarded other boats where deck, cabin and navigation lights came on. Johann turned to Jan. 'Please take the dinghy, and row to the nearest empty fishing boat,' he requested. 'They all have nets, buoys and fishing gear on deck. Take a knife. I want you to stay low, but cut away a few items, load them in the dinghy and row back here.'

'What's that for?' asked Hedda curiously.

'This vessels' been laid up,' Johann explained. 'We have no fishing gear on deck at all – it's probably stowed safely ashore somewhere. But if we set off with the fleet, and we're the only boat without any, we will stand out. We have to blend in with the rest.' Jan came back with a small mountain of bits and pieces that he piled haphazardly on deck. They were now indistinguishable from the rest of the fleet.

A coastal patrol boat appeared near the harbour mouth; its deck lights ablaze. One by one, the fleet started engines. So did Johann. As their escort turned to leave buoys were slipped. Johann released their chain and Jan secured the dinghy astern. Together, as the bows were beginning to pay off, they returned to the wheelhouse where the other two were waiting, their faces just visible in the glow from the instruments. Johann shoved the gear lever from neutral to ahead and the screw began to bite. Outside the harbour, the fleet formed into a loose convoy formation. Johann managed to position his boat so that they were port side and rear. The first turn in an easterly direction and they would be well placed to fall back to a position from which they could cut and run.

CHAPTER 23

Late into the afternoon Doreen Jackman relaxed in her chair whilst Colonel Bill Ives, elbows on his desk in front of her, went over the latest messages from Poland. He was a widower, she a spinster – although she had enjoyed her moments. Both lived only for their work. It was Friday, the beginning of the weekend, but neither was in a hurry to go home.

'Bit confusing, really,' he said quietly. 'We had that broadcast from Jan, saying that he was nearly ready to hand over the radio duties to the partisans. Then not long afterwards one from a different "fist" – *farm compromised, partisans moving south, returning to UK with two relatives.*'

He steepled his fingers. 'Trouble is, the sender didn't say when or how. Come to that, we don't know where the partisans are now, either. But if they are on the move, that might explain why there hasn't been another message.'

'I think, Bill,' she offered, 'this is one of those times when what's needed is masterly inactivity. If I know Jan, unless his luck runs out, he'll turn up sooner or later and probably where we least expect it. Come on,' she urged, 'first round's on me. Let's go and spend an hour in The Sherlock Holmes.' Together, they set off for Baker Street.

In contrast to the balmy evening in London, it was blowing a good force four in the Baltic, white caps cresting the waves. Johann had told Jan to keep his eyes as much as possible on the horizon. So far, he felt fine, as did Hedda, but Tadzio did not seem to be coping so well – twice he had rushed out of the wheel-house to retch over the rail, although he had not actually been sick.

'It'll wear off,' Johann advised him, 'but drink plenty of water. Don't get dehydrated. And if you can, you'll be better off staying up here in the fresh air than down below on your bunk.'

Tadzio nodded, still looking uncomfortable. The old mariner couldn't resist a grim smile. 'Try to put something in your stomach,' he advised. 'I saw some oats in one of the lockers. You only need to add milk or water.'

'What do they do for seasickness?' asked Tadzio.

'Not a lot,' came the reply. 'But if the worst comes to the worst, it's one of those foods that tastes the same in either direction!'

Although they couldn't be seen in the faint glow of the wheelhouse, both Jan and Hedda attempted but failed to hide something of a grin. Tadzio suppressed another heave then opened the door to the side deck and rail.

'So far, we're steaming north, out into the Baltic,' Johann observed once Tadzio was back, wiping his mouth. 'We're port side rear, so ideally, we need the fleet to make a turn to starboard before it starts fishing. That would put us in the ideal position to fall back and break for Sweden.'

But the patrol craft turned west and they found themselves on the inside of the fleet nearest to the German coast. 'Damn,' said Johann. 'Too risky to break now – the fleet's spreading out so we would have to cross all the way over. The patrol boat's bigger and faster than us, so if we were reported trying to make a run for it they would only have to steam north to make an intercept. We are far enough from the others for them not to see what we are doing, so we won't bother to stream nets – just put the deck lights on to make it look as if we are working.'

For a nerve-racking hour, the fleet steamed slowly west just outside German waters. Finally, the patrol craft, all lights ablaze, executed a wide turn away from the shore and settled on an easterly course. The rest of the fleet followed.

At the rear, and with further to travel on the outside of the turn, it was logical that Johann's vessel would take the longest to change course and take up station. They were now well into the manoeuvre and therefore at forty-five degrees north-west of the fleet.

'Here goes,' said Johann grimly, simultaneously turning off all deck and navigation lights. In pitch darkness, he opened the throttle and turned to port, directly for Sweden. Anxiously they watched as the lights from the rest of the fleet dropped astern. There was no sign that their break for freedom had been observed.

Finally, the lights of the fleet faded into the night. Johann throttled back to about eight knots and their mood brightened as the distance from the fleet increased. In the pre-dawn, entering their dead-reckoning position on the chart, as he had done every hour on the hour, he told them that they were over a third of the way to their destination.

Daylight brought a calm sea with only a light breeze. They steamed on through occasional wisps of early morning mist but there was only patchy cloud – for the most part visibility was excellent. They heard it before it was in plain sight – the buzz of twin BMW engines on a Heinkel HE 59 flying boat. The biplane circled low, inspecting them.

'Damn,' said Johann. 'I thought we had got away with it. The patrol boat probably decided to stay with the fleet, in case there were any more defections, but they must have radioed our likely course and speed.'

The aircraft passed low overhead then waggled its wings and turned back onto a course for Germany. The message was obvious: they were being ordered to follow.

'We can't go back,' said Hedda.

'Not going to,' Johann replied, holding his heading. 'Legally we are in international waters and not flying an ensign. If he fires on us it will be an act of piracy. Jan, Tadzio,' he added urgently, 'get those machine guns up into the wheel-house, just in case.'

The maritime patrol craft completed a half circle and came on again from their stern. This time, as it neared the fishing boat, there was a burst of fire from its nose machine gun, the rounds deliberately aimed about two hundred metres in front of their bow. The message could not have been clearer, but as if to emphasise the point, the seaplane executed a turn to make a low pass, just ahead of the wheel-house. They could see the pilot frantically stabbing a forefinger to drive home the order that they must reverse course. Finally, he made another quarter turn and flew back towards his original position, well aft of their stern.

'Keep low, but move out on deck and cover it,' Johann urged them, jabbing his right thumb over his shoulder. 'The steel bulwarks will give you some protection, but rest the machine guns on the capping rail and sight on the 'plane. If it opens fire again, so do we.'

The aircraft was still travelling away from them as Jan, Tadzio and Hedda scrabbled aft along the side deck.

The pilot of the Heinkel was over-confident. Convinced that he had nothing to fear from an unarmed fishing boat, he decided that a burst onto his deck would persuade the skipper to change course. The dorsal gunner relaxed to watch the show.

'If they open fire, take the port engine,' Jan commanded. 'I'll take the starboard. As soon as we think we have a hit, switch to the cockpit.'

The Heinkel was not a modern aircraft – designed at the beginning of the decade, its wings were covered in a mix of plywood and fabric whilst the fuselage had just the latter covering a steel frame. Only the tail was protected with lightweight, metal sheeting.

The pilot had not seen the three of them take position.

Neither had he noticed two small heads behind machine guns now steady in the aim.

Even as the first flashes from a 7.92 mm machine gun appeared from the muzzle, Jan and Hedda returned fire with two weapons of the same calibre. They had the advantage of a more stable platform. They could hear rounds thudding into the vessel behind them, but almost immediately the Heinkel's port engine emitted a plume of black smoke. Seconds later, Jan's target leaked a trail of light-coloured vapour – presumably from the cooling system. As soon as they switched their aim, the cockpit erupted in a shower of glass, metal and fabric. Then the Heinkel was overhead. As they watched it climbed into a vicious stall, a sure sign that the pilot was hit, before turning over a wingtip and diving almost vertically into the sea. They watched, spellbound, as it disappeared beneath the waves. Only when they turned to look forward did their relief turn to dismay. They were way off course. The wheel-house had taken a number of hits. Frantically they wrenched open the door. Johann lay face up on the wheel-house sole with sightless eyes – a round had smashed into the old mariner's head.

Tadzio hunted through the lockers till he found a small anchor with a couple of metres of chain and about ten metres of light warp attached – presumably for use with the dinghy. Jan wrapped Johann's body in a blanket then bound it with the anchor, chain and warp.

'You need a hand?' Tadzio asked as Jan collected the shrouded corpse in his arms.

'He was my friend, I'll do it,' said Jan, ignoring the tears that threatened to blind him. All three of them stood silently at the rail as Jan, elbows on the mahogany capping, lowered his left forearm to drop Johann, feet and anchor first, reverently into the sea.

Turning back to the wheel-house he wiped his eyes with a

sleeve. 'Hedda,' he asked, 'I would be grateful if you could try to find a mop and bucket so that I can wipe the blood off the wheel-house sole.'

She returned a few minutes later, a stiff brush together with a mop and bucket in hand. This latter had a long lanyard attached to that it could be filled with seawater. It was already half full. 'Let me,' she offered, 'you have done enough for your old friend.'

Whilst she removed the worst of the stain Jan studied the chart, which was undamaged on the navigation table alongside the wheel. Johann had ruled a compass line to pass from where they had left the fleet into the channel between the outlying island of Öland, off the south-east coast of Sweden, and the mainland. He had circled the port city of Kalmar on the mainland, opposite and about half-way up the length of the island.

'Looks like this is where we were heading,' Jan observed, tapping the end of a pencil on the chart. He'd written °K after three numbers adjacent to the course line. 'Presumably that's degrees *Kompass*,' Jan said quietly, 'which means he's made all the corrections he can and that's what we have to steer.' Turning to head just west of north, he settled the fishing boat onto Johann's course. Neither he nor Tadzio had any experience of steering a boat, but they soon learned to anticipate the effect of the waves and within a few minutes either of them could hold a more or less steady course.

Jan was particularly worried about the possibility of another air attack, but as the morning wore on they steamed under an empty sky. 'From the way it went down,' Tadzio suggested, 'it could be that there wasn't time to send a Mayday.'

Hedda produced a meal from Frau Brantis' hamper. The bread was stale, but moistened with some oil from a tin of canned fish, the sandwiches were eaten gratefully. As the day wore on it became obvious that they would not make the

Swedish coast before dark. Jan decided to throttle right back and wait till dawn, but not before they were cloaked in the protection of twilight.

At first light, they could make out both Öland and the mainland, their course taking them pretty much mid-channel. *Thanks, old friend,* thought Jan. *Well done, and rest in peace.* He had no difficulty in identifying the harbour and its entrance, the latter evident from several smaller vessels and one large freighter following the channel. Slowly, Jan eased back the engine revs till they barely had steerage way, then nudged the fishing boat into a space alongside the dock port-side-to in the southern area of the harbour.

Initially, they seemed to have attracted no attention, but Jan was still trying to work out what best to do when a bearded, late middle-aged man in what looked to be a harbourmaster's jacket and cap appeared on the dockside. It seemed polite to move out onto the side deck to greet him. The official uttered some words, presumably in Swedish, that were completely unintelligible to Jan, but probably a question about who they were and where from. Instinctively, Jan decided not to reply in German.

'Do you speak English?' he asked quietly. Judging by the raised eyebrows, this had taken the harbourmaster by surprise.

'I speak English,' came the reply. 'I learn when I was many years at sea.'

'Can you help us, please?' asked Jan. 'I need to contact the British embassy as a matter of urgency.'

'You had better follow me to my office,' came the reply. 'Your two companions must stay here, on the boat.'

Jan translated very softly. Tadzio and Hedda nodded vigorously to confirm their agreement.

Jan walked with the Swede along the dockside and into the port administrative office. It was empty save for a huge rather battered desk, a few chairs, a large cupboard and two filing cabinets. There was a metal pot on a wood burning stove set in one corner. 'Would you like some coffee?' came the unexpected invitation.

'I would be extremely grateful,' replied Jan.

His host produced two tin mugs from the cupboard and set the steaming drink on his desk in front of Jan. 'Please,' he invited, 'then you had better tell me who you all are, where you have come from, what you are doing here in my port and why you need to contact the British embassy in Stockholm. After that, we'll decide what to do with you. And by the way,' he added, 'I want the truth. And in case you were wondering, I heard your translation into Polish back there.'

Despite the assertion, the Swede's tone of voice, Jan noticed, was in no way harsh or threatening. If anything, he detected a hint of sympathy. Jan decided to tell the truth – or at least some of it.

'I was born in Poland,' he began, 'and I have genuine papers to prove it. Tadzio, on the boat, is my elder brother. He and Hedda have been running our family farm since the Germans invaded. On the way through they killed our father and sister. Fortunately, our mother was away visiting her sister in Bydgoszcz at the time. Hopefully she is all right, but we haven't been able to contact her.'

He paused to let this sink in. The harbourmaster had listened intently but did not ask any questions. *Now comes the real bombshell,* thought Jan. The Swede's reaction would probably decide their fate for the rest of the war.

'I have to tell you,' he went on, 'that I was not in Poland when the war broke out. After some training in England, I returned there illegally a few months ago. I would prefer not to go into detail, but I can tell you that we are we no longer safe at the farm. Also, that the Germans are aware Hedda's father was Jewish. At the time we fled Poland, they were in the process of deporting Tadzio to Germany as slave labour and

Hedda off to their local barracks for a fate even worse. I think you understand what I mean…' he tailed off.

The harbourmaster nodded sympathetically. 'So, you have stolen a fishing boat and escaped to Sweden,' he surmised.

'We had some help,' Jan confirmed, 'a dear old friend who had been a professional mariner. But we were attacked by a flying boat on the way. Johann was in the wheel-house, which is made of wood. As you will have noticed, it has a lot of holes in it. Poor Johann died in the attack. We buried him at sea yesterday.'

'But you survived,' came the observation.

'We did, the 'plane didn't,' Jan said bluntly. 'But if it worries you, there are two machine guns and a few other weapons on board that we brought with us. And that's about it,' he concluded. 'So now you know why I am desperate to contact the British embassy.'

The harbourmaster said nothing for several seconds. Finally, he seemed to come to a decision. Rising from his battered captain's chair, he walked slowly round the desk and extended an arm. Jan stood automatically to shake the offered hand. 'My name is Carl Magnusson,' he said.

'Jan Janicki,' he replied automatically, taking the introduction as a good sign. Magnusson returned to his chair.

'We Swedes are supposed to be neutral,' he went on. 'In reality, we are a nation living in fear. Most of our merchant fleet was caught outside of the Baltic at the outbreak of war, which personally I think was a good thing. But we can't trade much with the outside world any more, so we have no choice but to trade with Germany. If our economy is to survive, we must import German coal. And they are desperate for our high-quality iron ore and ball bearings.

'We have our protocols for dealing with foreign nationals,' he went on, 'but that does not mean that as ordinary citizens we don't have our own feelings. German arrivals would be free to conduct their business in our neutral country. I don't know what the correct procedure is for Polish nationals, but perhaps it might be better not to ask.'

At all costs, Jan had to avoid internment. 'If it helps,' he said quietly, 'I also have German papers and so does Hedda – she is half-German through her father.' It was a last throw of the dice.

Carl leant forward, his arms on the desk. 'I want to say something,' he replied, 'and it's an observation not a question, so I don't want a reply. But I think you are either a member of the British armed forces, or you are working for their government – perhaps both.'

Jan nodded slowly to indicate that he had taken on board the question, but said nothing.

'Our government is neutral,' Carl told him, 'but many of our people are not. Carla – my wife – and I have been blessed with only one child. Gustav is now twenty years old and a third officer in our merchant marine. His ship was caught outside the Baltic and is now on charter to the British merchant navy. Carla and I are entirely content with this, but we fear that in this war casualties, not only in the Royal Navy but also in those ships flying the red ensign, will be very high. Perhaps it will be the merchant marine who will suffer the most. Every day we pray that we will not receive a telegram with devastating news. So, in case you were wondering, Jan Janicki, I am going to help you.'

Jan felt an overwhelming sense of relief. 'Thank you,' he said with heartfelt sincerity. 'So, could I use your 'phone to contact the British embassy?'

'Too risky,' came the reply. 'We are never sure which of our lines might be monitored. And besides, unless you speak Swedish, you would never navigate our telephone system.

'Give me a number,' Carl offered, 'and tell me what you want me to say. I'll go to a public phone in the railway station and make the call. It would be better if, before I do that, we walk together back to your boat, and then please wait for me there.'

Carl Magnusson was as good as his word. An anxious hour later he returned with a satisfied grin and arms laden with shopping, which he dumped on the cabin table. 'These will see you through till tomorrow,' he told them, 'you can't have much if you have been at sea for a couple of days.

'I got through all right,' he told them, 'although when I asked to speak with "Mr Dinks" the receptionist was a bit stupid at first, until she spoke with one of her colleagues.' He paused, milking the moment. 'She asked for my name. I just told her that I had information Mr Dinks would be desperate to receive, and if she didn't put me through she would be looking for another job before morning.

'Anyway,' he went on, 'Like you said, I told this Mr Dinks, although that's obviously not his real name, that I had a message from a passenger he delivered last autumn who is now back in this country and anxious to make contact. I also told him that in total it was a party of three.'

'And ?' asked Jan anxiously.

'We were both playing things pretty much by ear,' Carl admitted, 'but he suggested that we meet early tomorrow afternoon in the station car park. He said someone would be driving Adel Nilsonn's taxi, and unless I recognised the vehicle that you could describe to me, I was not to make contact. But assuming that all went well, I would then guide the driver to where you could be collected.'

Jan had no difficulty in recalling the Volvo PV 52 de luxe saloon with diplomatic plates. Carl delved into his packages and produced a bottle of *bränvin*, or Swedish schnapps. Hedda produced four mugs and the Swede poured – *generous measures*, thought Jan.

'Can I pay you for all this?' asked Jan. 'I still have some

German marks that you could exchange.'

Carl shook his head. 'But tell me,' he asked, 'What do you want me to do with your boat?'

'My boat?' queried Jan.

'Well, I assume it wasn't yours originally, but it seems to be now,' came the reply. 'You are going to be collected tomorrow, and please stay on board overnight, but you will be leaving in the morning.' He waved an inverted hand to encompass the vessel. 'What do you want me to do with her?'

It was not something Jan had even thought about. 'What I could do for you,' Carl offered, 'is register her in Sweden. Not difficult for a harbourmaster and port captain with my contacts. None of us know what the war will bring, but for now she could be chartered out as an inshore fishing vessel – after all she's pretty much a going concern.'

'Could I leave all that to you?' asked Jan. 'If you can take care of the boat, we'll split the profit fifty-fifty. If I can collect her again after the war, so much the better. If I can't, I suspect it won't matter anyway.'

'Consider it done,' said Carl, pouring another four measures.

He arrived early in the station car park and had no difficulty recognising the vehicle Jan had described to him. Although as he approached he was surprised to see an attractive young woman step out from behind the wheel. 'I'm Mrs Dinks,' she introduced herself and offered her hand. 'Climb in, and you can guide me to my passengers.'

Seeing Carl in the front right hand seat, the Volvo was waved into the port. She parked, as directed, outside Carl's office, where she waited until a few minutes later he returned with Jan, Tadzio and Hedda. From the brief conversation Mrs Dinks held with Carl Magnusson, she was obviously fluent in Swedish – probably a national.

Jan took the front passenger seat, Tadzio and Hedda in

the back. 'I'm afraid we might be a little fragrant by now,' Jan apologised in English, 'but we have been at sea for a few days and then not allowed off the boat.'

'Don't worry about it,' she replied easily in the same language and with a musical laugh. 'We can always open the windows.'

Jan took another glance at their driver. She had the Nordic good looks of blonde hair, ice-blue eyes, high cheekbones and a film-star figure. If she really was Mrs Dinks, then she was a good three inches taller than her husband.

'I didn't know Dinks was married,' he said casually.

'He wasn't then,' she said, indicating that she knew Jan's history as she flicked expertly through the gears and cleared the suburbs. 'But he is now! And by the way, he told me to ask you what type of aircraft was it in which you last flew together?'

'A Swedish registered Lysander,' said Jan with a smile. She reached inside her tailored jacked and produced a small revolver. 'In which case,' she said with a quick smile to her right, 'you can put that in the glove box. I won't be needing it, and it's bloody uncomfortable tucked into my skirt!'

The car was waved through the embassy gates and they were shown to Dinks' office. Jan gave the so-called second secretary a more detailed account of his time in Poland and their subsequent escape. Dinks made a few notes and asked questions – mostly directed at Tadzio and Hedda. Jan translated.

'I'm going to send a message to London,' he said at the end. 'There's nothing more I can do till they reply.'

'So, what do we do in the meantime?' asked Jan.

'Well, you can't stay in the flat like last time,' Dinks replied with a friendly laugh. 'For a start, there are too many of you, and second, I don't think Mrs Dinks would be too pleased!'

'Congratulations on your marriage,' said Jan quickly, remembering his manners. 'She is a lovely lady.'

'We met in the line of duty, as it were,' Dinks offered, 'although I had better not tell you what she does for a living. But believe me, you were in safe hands. These days the Germans follow me every time I leave the embassy, which is why I asked Mikaela to pick you up. She often drives my car. Her people agreed to the request without asking questions, and she knows how to make sure there was no tail.'

'So, Mikaela is Swedish?' Jan asked.

'She is,' came the reply. 'Don't get me wrong, I love my wife dearly, but the fact of life is that it makes for a useful two-way exchange of information within our host country – and one that the Germans don't know about.

'Which brings us back to what we are going to do with you,' Dinks went on. We have a couple of safe houses not too far away, and we'll put you in one of those. It's well stocked with pretty much anything you might need, and I'm authorised to give you some *kronor* in case you want to take a walk and perhaps have a coffee or a beer. But same rules as last time, Jan – best you just point, but if you have to say anything use German or English but on no account Polish.'

That evening Mikaela drove them in her own car, a rather smart Ford, to a small, terraced house in a quiet, leafy suburb of Stockholm. Before they left the embassy, Dinks told them that he hoped to have news within two or three days.

He was as good as his word. 'London has agreed to your travel,' he told them at the safe house. 'This time we don't want to risk a Swedish vessel – it's ever more difficult for them to leave the Baltic these days, if not impossible. Instead, you will be taken to the UK on board an American flagged freighter. The Germans won't stop her – they wouldn't risk doing anything that might alienate the U.S.A. and tempt them into the war. Once near British waters, the ship won't dock. You will disembark somewhere off the coast of Scotland

and you should be in London twenty-four hours later. At some stage, expect to be questioned in some detail,' he told Tadzio and Hedda, 'but frankly my people don't expect any complications.'

CHAPTER 24

Dinks stopped his car at the entrance to the port. As he wound down the window, the guard made a show of looking inside, then opened the gate and waved them through.

'That was easy enough,' Jan remarked. It seemed only yesterday when he had arrived on the Swedish freighter.

'He claims to be pro-British, plus he has expensive tastes,' Dinks told them laconically, 'that can't be satisfied on a security guard's pay. Our arrangement works both ways.' He did not offer any further explanation.

The car edged slowly along the dock till it stopped at the bottom of a gangplank leading up into the hull of a good sized cargo vessel. Carrying small cases containing a few clothes and toiletries provided by Mikaela and Dinks, they followed him on board till they were met at the top by a rather young-looking officer in the dark blue livery of his shipping line. 'Welcome aboard the *Memphis Pearl*,' he drawled, saluting then offering his hand to each in turn. 'Earl FitzHoward Junior. Call me Earl or Junior – either's fine. And good to see y'all – you again, Dinks,' he added. A white jacketed steward hovered in the background. 'Benson here will show the lady and gentlemen to their cabins. Dinks, come with me, if you will, and we'll take a drink in mine. Fortunately, we're not the U.S. of A. Navy,' his grin embraced them all, 'so we don't sail dry.'

At the stern of the ship, main deck level, were a number of cabins. Benson showed Hedda and Tadzio to a double, with vertical bunk beds, whilst Jan was offered a spacious single. Both had an en-suite head. 'This is very pleasant,' Jan said easily to the steward.

'The Pearl Line vessels all have guest accommodation, Sir,' he replied. 'We are primarily freighters, but often take paying passengers who enjoy a voyage at much less than the cost of a conventional liner. I trust you will enjoy a pleasant passage.' He looked at his watch. 'We sail at six, Sir, and I shall collect you at a quarter to eight for dinner. We do not dress – on the Pearl Line we dine well but not formally. In the meantime, there is a bell over there –' he indicated a brass fitting next to the bunk, 'so should you require my assistance you have only to ring. You might kindly mention this to your colleagues. They have the same facility.'

With just the faintest nod of his head Benson left the cabin. Dinks returned a few minutes later and all four of them convened next door. 'You're absolutely safe now,' he told them, 'Earl has been briefed on all that he needs to know and he's quite happy, so just enjoy the trip.'

'This is rather more than I was expecting,' Hedda told him in German.

'I hope you have a pleasant few days,' Dinks replied in the same language, his proficiency surprising Jan. 'We know you have all had a hard time of it over the winter, so hopefully this will come as a small reward with the compliments of His Majesty's grateful government. And the food should be good – things won't be quite the same once you are back in wartime Britain!' With that he shook hands with Jan and Tadzio, made Hedda blush with a kiss on both cheeks, and waved goodbye. Shortly afterwards a quiet vibration underfoot suggested that they were about to be underway.

Dinner was not in a wardroom but a spacious dining area adjacent to the captain's cabin. They were the only guests. In response to a query from Jan, Earl explained that when they had official "government guests" as he called them, they did not take other passengers.

'Captain Earl, this must be costing a fortune,' observed Jan.

'Please explain and translate to Tadzio and Hedda for me,' Earl replied, 'because I don't speak Polish. The owner of this line is second generation American,' he went on, 'but the founder, his grandfather, came from Scotland. My country is neutral, but some of us help out the old country a bit more than others. And money doesn't even come into it.

'Now,' he said, as soon as Jan had translated, 'what will you have to drink before dinner?' Benson appeared as if on cue to take station next to a well covered sideboard. Sensing Hedda's uncertainty, Earl suggested they open a bottle of white wine.

'You seem young to be the captain of such a fine ship,' she said, having taken her first sip.

'Aw, you got short-changed,' Earl replied with a grin. 'The captain was taken ill soon after we arrived. Normally we would have waited till he came out of hospital, but because of the uncertainty in Europe the owners cabled to sail soonest. So, we're in ballast. I'm only the first officer really. But not to worry,' he added with a laugh, 'I think I can find my way home.'

Dinner was a revelation to all three passengers. A creamy soup made from fresh tomatoes was followed by a dish of huge prawns in an oriental sauce of fresh ginger, soy and garlic. 'One of our cooks is 'Frisco Chinese,' Earl told them. 'His chow is something of a favourite with the crew.'

But the main course surpassed anything they had eaten before. They were each served a huge rib-eye steak with what Earl referred to as a "side order" of French fries and a bowl of salad. There was a sauce with the steaks that tasted of red wine, cream and brandy. Hedda had never eaten meat so tasty, tender and succulent, she informed him.

'Ma'am, we invented fast freezing back in the twenties,' he replied, 'so these steaks came over in our on-board freezer and were defrosted today. The salad and vegetables we bought in Sweden.' Finally, the chef had prepared apple pie and ice cream, with cheeses and fruit to follow. Earl offered them all a glass of port or Madeira, although Jan noticed that their host consumed only one glass of red wine. 'Please excuse me for a few minutes whilst I visit the bridge,' he told them rising from the table. 'Be back soon, although I have to stand a watch later. But in the meantime, please ask Benson for anything you might need.'

'That was absolutely fantastic,' said Hedda, setting down her napkin. Again, Jan translated.

'The Pearl line is perhaps noted for its cuisine,' their steward observed softly. 'Captain FitzHoward is determined to follow the family tradition.'

'The family tradition?' queried Jan.

'Yes, sir,' came the reply. 'He would be too modest to mention it, but this line has been owned by the FitzHoward family for several generations. Captain Earl is a fine officer, and is shortly to take command of his own vessel anyway. He is more than capable of taking your good selves back to the United Kingdom, and the rest of us on to the United States.' He paused. 'If you have all that you require, and you are happy to make your own way aft to your cabins, I will leave you now, lady and gentlemen.'

'We'll enjoy our nightcap and wait for the captain,' Jan told him, 'but thank you, I don't think any of us could manage another thing.'

Back in their cabin, Hedda eyed the sleeping arrangements. 'I'm tired and full to bursting,' she told Tadzio. 'So, they'll do for now. But we might have to be a bit snug in just my bunk tomorrow morning.'

At breakfast on their third day at sea, Earl announced that they were off the northwest coast of Scotland and would rendezvous with a Royal Navy vessel later that morning. Hedda confessed that she had grown accustomed to waffles and maple syrup, bacon, eggs, hash browns and fresh-baked rolls. Earl grinned appreciatively and gave each of them his card. 'You have my office and home contact details there,' he told them. 'Any time you think there is something we can do for you, just call.'

Later that morning Jan thanked him profusely for their passage before they descended a pilot ladder into a blue-ensigned motor torpedo boat. They docked in northwest Scotland and just made the overnight sleeper to London. By midday, travel-weary, grubby and almost exhausted, they were shown into Bill Ives' office. Doreen Jackman was already there.

'Welcome to England,' he greeted Hedda and Tadzio. 'And thank God you are all safe.' Jan translated. 'Full debrief in the morning,' the colonel went on. 'For now, we'll take you to a safe house and let you rest overnight.'

Dinner, their first meal since that morning, was something of a contrast. The housekeeper served a thin brown soup followed by a vegetable pie. London, it might have been: the *Memphis Pearl*, it certainly wasn't. 'We should have stayed on board,' Tadzio observed dryly, setting down his knife and fork.

Next morning, they were taken to separate rooms to be debriefed. Hedda's interrogator spoke excellent German, but Tadzio, in an adjacent room, spoke through an interpreter. Jan's interviewer was Colonel Ives, but they were joined by another civilian who hoped that Jan would not mind if he did not give his name. But, he confided, he had the ear of the First Lord of the Admiralty and many expected that Mr Churchill might soon become Prime Minister. His visitor was acutely interested in the activities and morale of the German Army in Poland and the plight of the local population. He enquired in great detail about the resistance movement and the extent to which they were able to interdict the German lines of communication. Jan gave both men as much detail as he could, not forgetting to mention the need to supply arms and other matériel to the resistance by whatever means could be established. Importantly, he was able to confirm that the new "fist" operating the transmitter was genuine.

It was almost lunchtime before they were finished. His visitor thanked Jan profusely for what he had achieved and also for the invaluable first-hand evidence he had been able to provide. Once they were alone, Jan asked Bill Ives what would happen next.

'For you, personally?' the Colonel asked.

'For all of us,' Jan replied. 'Me, my brother and Hedda. I will translate for them later.'

'First,' came the reply, 'I want you all to have another night of relaxation. One of my staff will make a reservation at a restaurant not far from your safe house. Then we'll leave the three of you to make your own way home. Come back in the morning, all of you. About ten-ish, if that's all right?'

Jan confirmed that it was.

'Fine,' the colonel thanked him. 'That will give us time to go over the results of the debriefing. I don't want to say too much before tomorrow, but we have a position in mind for Hedda, not to mention a few options for Tadzio.'

'And me?' Jan responded.

'I shall be able to confirm things in the morning,' the colonel said guardedly, 'but I think we are going to ask you to undertake another mission. Let's leave it at that for now, please. And by the way, you have a considerable amount of back pay in an account with Coutts' Bank that has been opened in your name, but I am authorised to give you an additional sum that will cover any reasonable expenses for the next few days.'

They sort of enjoyed what Hedda pronounced to be something of a plain meal in a rather ordinary restaurant, but the adventure of the night – for Hedda and Tadzio – was to call in at a local public house on the way home. Jan chose a corner table where they could speak softly in their own language, although at the end of the day he did not think that being a Polish-speaking member of the British armed forces would be a problem. In an atmosphere thick with smoke, and accompanied by an out of tune piano, they drank English beer, two of them for the first time, that both Tadzio and Hedda pronounced initially to be disgusting. But it didn't stop them finishing their pint, Jan noticed, and then accepting another. Finally, arm-in-arm, they made their way back to the safe house.

Their meeting next morning was with both Bill Ives and Doreen Jackman. 'We have discussed all three of you at great length,' he told them. 'You have unique experience and abilities. So what I am going to suggest is a request only. If you do not wish to accept our recommendation, we will try to come up with another solution that would be mutually agreeable.' Jan translated.

'Tadzio,' Bill Ives turned to face the young Pole. 'Let's start with you. You mentioned yesterday that you would be willing to volunteer for the armed forces. We would like you to attend a short course so that you can learn English, then we want you to volunteer for one of the embryo Polish military units that are being established in England. We can go into detail later, but in view of your background, we are probably thinking infantry, or maybe armoured corps. How does that sound?'

Through Jan, Tadzio replied that in principle it sounded fine, but he and Hedda wanted to marry, so they needed to know what would happen to her and if they would still be able to see each other from time to time.

'Hedda,' Doreen Jackman began, and again Jan translated. 'Because of your language skills, we want you to work with one of our intelligence services. The less I say at this stage the better, but you would be based not too far away, north-west of London. We will arrange billeted civilian accommodation and when he has leave Tadzio can stay there too. How does that sound?'

Hedda thought for a few seconds, then nodded her acceptance.

'All right,' resumed Bill Ives. 'Tadzio and Hedda, tomorrow you go your separate ways. Doreen will set up postal addresses and contact telephone numbers so that you can stay in touch both with us and with each other. But for now, just enjoy the spring weather. For once, it's a sunny day in London. Do you have enough funds left over to see you through?'

Having translated all that, Jan confirmed that they had, and arranged to meet them later back at the safe house. 'Well now,' said Bill Ives, once the other two had left, 'we want you to volunteer for another mission.'

Doreen Jackman took over. 'Because of your recent history, Jan, you may be uniquely well placed to help us in an area where we are desperately short of assets.' Having assumed originally that she was the colonel's junior, Jan began to wonder whether it might not be the other way round – that she might be considerably higher up in the government pecking order than he had at first suspected.

'We have every reason to believe,' she went on, 'that now he has conquered half of Poland in the East, Herr Hitler is poised to invade the West. Intelligence is vital,' she continued, 'but beyond the French, Belgian and Dutch borders we have hardly any people on the ground. And virtually none that are able to report back to us independently. And that said,' she paused for emphasis, 'at this stage it would be extremely difficult to insert someone able to fit in locally unless they had at least a measure of support. Some sort of base in the area, if you like.'

It began to dawn on Jan what he was about to be asked to do. 'You think...' he hesitated, 'that I have this – what would you call it – this facility?'

'Renate Raschdorf,' she said bluntly. 'You have a long and deep affiliation with the family, she probably owes her life to the fact that you smuggled her to safety right across Germany,

334

she is half Jewish, and after the threats made not just to her but also to her family, we believe she must have absolutely no love for Hitler and his Nazi Party.' Her hands turned palms uppermost, as if in a gesture of honesty. 'To what extent she might help you, we don't know,' she admitted, 'but we think that in all probability, she would. And from what you have told us, even if not, there is no way she would ever betray you.'

Jan tried desperately to think this through, but try as he might, too many thoughts were tumbling in his head. Seeing Renate again… back to Germany… how would he be able to operate, alone and without the backing of any resistance organisation? Not very coherently, he tried to put these points to the two of them. It was Doreen Jackman who replied.

'We know it's all a bit up in the air,' she responded, 'and that it's a lot to ask. But we feel this has to be a risk worth taking. Having someone such as yourself to report on troop movements in the border area just inside Germany could be an enormous bonus for this country.'

'All right,' Jan said eventually. 'Supposing that this all goes to plan – then fine. But suppose that it doesn't. Let's say I get there, but Fraulein Raschdorf either doesn't want to or just isn't able to get involved. What happens then?'

'We can't answer that,' said Bill Ives honestly. 'If that's the case, and the Germans haven't invaded, maybe you could try coming back the same way you did previously. But if they do attack, then you will find yourself behind enemy lines with no obvious means of getting home. It's a hell of a risk, I grant you, and not one to be undertaken lightly. But if it comes off, the information you might be able to provide could save thousands of Allied lives.'

'Put like that,' Jan said eventually, 'you don't really give me a choice.' For several seconds, he studied the toecap of his shoe, moving slowly almost on its own accord from side-to-side. Finally, he looked back at both of them, although there was neither mirth nor humour in his smile. 'To me it seems a pretty mad scheme,' he said dispassionately, 'almost one of desperation. But just assuming that we are prepared to give it a try,' he went on, 'in practice, how do you see things working out?'

'We have given this some thought,' replied Doreen Jackman. Jan sensed that she was trying hard to sound reassuring. 'You could probably cross the border without too much trouble, but this time you will have to carry a certain amount of equipment, none of which would bear scrutiny. So we think a parachute drop, fairly close to the farm. That might be safest, after which it would be up to you to make contact. How would you feel about that?'

'The plan or the para-drop?' mused Jan, speaking softly, almost to himself. 'Obviously I'm going to need a certain amount of equipment – a radio, some emergency shelter kit, a weapon and ammunition... the jump doesn't worry me, at least not too much,' he added with a smile, 'and presumably everything I need could be in drop pack. They mentioned on my course that it could all be stuffed into a sort of canvas kit bag that could be lowered to hit the ground just before I did. Never tried it though, nor jumping at night...' he trailed off.

'Spoken to Ringwood,' Bill Ives pressed on, trying to sound as confident as he could. 'Sergeant Hathaway sends his regards, by the way. Delighted to see you back safe, and all that. If you agree he's looking forward to meeting up again. I'm told to tell you there's still a bit left in His Majesty's ale fund, whatever that means.' Jan could not help smiling at the private joke.

Back at Ringwood, they discussed a night jump over a cup of tea in Hathaway's tiny office. 'We can give you a practice run,' he told Jan. 'But basically, it's all pretty much the same. You'll have a fairly heavy kit bag clipped on at the waist, and once you are out of the aircraft and stable you lower it away on a few feet of strapping. It's a bit hard to see the ground, but at least you will feel a bit of 'give' when the kit touches first – only a couple of seconds, though. Then you are straight into the landing roll. But you have done all that before...' he finished off, hoping to sound reassuring, thought Jan.

'You must be quite important,' Hathaway said almost respectfully. 'Crab Air have laid on a Whitley for you to have a practice jump tomorrow night, and apparently you will fly in the same aircraft over Germany before it goes on to do a leaflet drop on Cologne.'

'Crab Air?' queried Jan.

'Ah, bit of British military humour,' came the response. 'The Royal Air Force came into being on the first of April nineteen eighteen. As if the date wasn't enough,' the point was lost on Jan, 'the colour of their uniform was exactly the same as the ointment the Navy dished out to its sailors, when they got infected with nits and other things in their private parts, in cat houses and such in the more dubious ports of the world. "Crab ointment" they called it. Hence the nickname for our colleagues in the Royal Air Force. Wouldn't use it in their hearing though,' he advised with a grin.

'Come on,' he urged. 'Enough of this. Let's go and enjoy a couple of jars. We'll do another jump together tomorrow night, then you can go back to your bosses in London as a fully trained, super-expert night time parachutist!'

Which is far from how I feel, thought Jan, a week after his visit to Ringwood. Again, the sickly smell of the Whitley almost overwhelmed him as they droned away from the airfield in southern England. He had managed to pinpoint the farm on a map accurately enough, but as the pilot explained, they would be relying on dead reckoning, so when he landed – assuming he did so safely – he might well be a few miles off target.

The light changed from red to green. Trying hard not to

think about what might go wrong, Jan closed his eyes and dropped into the void. His 'chute opened with a reassuring crack and he found himself busy lowering the heavy kit bag to the length of its strap. Despite patchy cloud there was just enough ambient light to distinguish between woodland and fields. He would land alongside a dense copse, although at this stage he had no idea where he was, or in which direction lay the farmhouse. One problem at a time, thought Jan, as he slowed momentarily, the kit bag hitting the ground before he, too, made a perfect landing. *'Hathaway,'* he thought to himself, *'I've done you proud.'*

There was nothing to be achieved till daylight. Jan dragged his kit into the copse. It was a mild night, no rain, so he checked his side-arm before wrapping himself in silk, covering up with a raincoat and enjoying a few hours of surprisingly sound sleep. It was almost a shock to wake at first light to the dawn chorus. Instinctively his hand moved to the grip of the pistol at his side, but there was no need.

He breakfasted on a ration bar and a mouthful of water from his canteen. At sunrise, Jan suspected that he was a little west and maybe a kilometre or two north of the farm. All in all, his aircrew had done a pretty fine job. He decided to establish a temporary base in this isolated spot and then explore on foot. Jan wrapped the pistol inside his raincoat and placed it alongside the kitbag. If he were stopped, he would rely on his documents rather than risk the discovery of an illegal firearm. An hour later, his leaf- and sod-covered position inside the woodland could not have been seen from more than a couple of yards away.

After half an hour's walking, he finally came to a lane. It was hauntingly familiar – where he had stepped out of the Opel cabriolet what now seemed a lifetime ago. Keeping well to one side of first the road and then a track to the farm, Jan settled behind a clump of bushes to watch the dwelling. It was maybe a hundred metres away. His heart skipped a beat when he saw Renate at the kitchen window.

Sometimes it was good to be careful. But Jan sensed that right now he had to throw caution to the wind. There was a light on in the kitchen, but he was not in Renate's line of sight as he walked slowly towards the door. Jan stepped sideways to tap very lightly on the window pane. Seconds later, her hand covering a mouth agape, she was lifting the door latch. *'Mein lieber Gott, Jan,'* she exclaimed, 'but what on earth are you doing here?'

She threw her arms round his neck, hugging him and pulling him into the kitchen at the same time. Strangely, Jan felt that he had come home.

CHAPTER 25

Glancing round quickly to confirm that they were the only occupants, Jan allowed himself to be drawn into the warmth of the kitchen. Renate took his face in both hands. Suddenly she kissed him once, briefly but hard on the lips, then released him and stepped back, at the same time looking him up and down.

'You've changed,' she said abruptly. 'You look bigger... heavier, I mean. You really are more of a man than the person who drove me across Germany!'

'It's good to see you again, too,' he chided gently. 'But are we safe here?' he added urgently. 'Who else is in the farmhouse?'

'Just the two of us,' she answered. 'Old Carl, who comes to help out each day, is on the farm, but this morning he's hedging and ditching two or three fields away. Sit down,' she told him, pulling out a chair. 'Would you like some coffee?' Jan told her that after a night in the open a cup of hot coffee would be a godsend.

He watched as she turned the handle, tipped out the ground coffee and poured on boiling water. Renate was wearing jodhpurs that made no secret of her figure and a plain white blouse. Jan had not forgotten that she was a beautiful young woman. He could hardly take his eyes off her as she poured two cups, set them on the table and sat opposite. He warmed his hands around the hot drink.

'So, tell me,' she said simply. 'Where have you been, and what have you been doing?' Jan knew he couldn't dissemble. Not with Renate. She had to know, if only for her own safety.

'I made it into Belgium then with the help of the British embassy back to England,' he began. 'Once there, I spent some time under training,' he went on, deliberately not going into detail, 'then returned to Poland for a while to liaise with the partisans. Unfortunately, through no fault of our own, we were compromised. The group moved on and I took my brother and a young woman called Hedda back to the United Kingdom. Johann helped us to steal a fishing boat, but when we were about half-way to Sweden a German flying boat opened fire on us. We managed to shoot it down... your father had given us two machine guns. But I'm very sorry to have to tell you,' he said as gently as he could, 'that Johann didn't make it. We buried him at sea.'

Renate gave a small gasp at the news. Jan could see that she was upset, even though she had not had all that much contact with Johann. He waited whilst she sat quietly for several seconds, looking down at her hands. Eventually she lifted her head. 'Please go on with your story,' she said in a small voice.

'The British intelligence people think that Germany will invade France and the low countries any time soon,' Jan told her, 'and as we have virtually no assets in this area I am ordered to find out as much as I can. That's about it,' he concluded. Jan had deliberately not asked her for assistance.

'So you're a spy,' she said slowly and deliberately. 'You know that if they catch you, it will be an execution?'

He looked into her eyes. 'And for anyone caught helping me,' he added bluntly.

Renate stood and walked round the table, obviously thinking about what she had just been told, and where she stood in all this, before sitting down again.

'Jan, if it had not been for you, I would not be living here in comfort and relative safety,' she said at last. 'I'm not stupid. This farm is near the Belgian border and all of us round here know that the *Wehrmacht* is gathering in assembly areas. You haven't asked for my help as such,' she went on, 'but I bet it's no coincidence that you were deliberately chosen for this mission in precisely this part of Germany.'

They looked at each other for several seconds. 'You're right,' he said eventually. 'But much as I wanted to see you again, I can complete this mission without any further contact between us. Just forget that I was ever here. And thank you for the coffee.' He smiled and set both hands on the table, obviously about to rise and leave.

'Stay there,' Renate commanded sharply, quickly placing both hands over one of his. 'First, you know what the Nazis threatened for me. Second, I have had hardly any news from my parents, but I do know that my father is being forced to work for the regime and my mother is seriously at risk because she is Jewish. And now they have killed Johann. So, if you were to ask me if I supported Herr Hitler, the answer would be absolutely not.' She sighed. 'I love my country, but not what is happening to our poor Fatherland. We all know there is a bigger war coming. If we win, God help my people and God help me. So much as I love Germany, I have to hope that we lose...' she tailed off softly.

Renate tried hard to inject a sense of brightness and optimism into her voice. 'So, tell me how I can help you, Jan Janicki. If I am caught, then I'm lost. But if the Nazis win, I'm probably lost anyway. So, whatever I can do... I will.'

Jan thought quickly. 'Who's living here at the moment?' he asked.

'Just me and *Tantchen* Meta,' she replied. 'That's Frau Holzer, but she asked me to call her Auntie Meta. Her husband, Klaus, was a lovely man, but he was a lot older and not in good health. He died just after Christmas. Meta has a daughter, Gisela, who is a student in Cologne. After all the legal things were settled Meta told me that she had been well provided for – her Klaus was eventually a bank manager before ill health forced him to retire, and he and his family were quite well off.'

She paused for several seconds. 'They were hoping for a few more quiet years on their small place in the country, but sadly things didn't work out like that. Meta went to Cologne last week to stay with Gisela. Now that the will and the finances are all in order, she was thinking of buying a small flat so that Gisela wouldn't have to rent and they could spend more time together.'

'Any other family?' asked Jan.

'Just an older brother, Hans, named after Meta's first husband who was killed at Verdun,' she told him. 'Hans is in the *Wehrmacht*, on the staff of some senior officer, although he joined a *Panzer* regiment originally. For all I know, he might not be stationed too far from here, but Meta hasn't heard from him for a while. I'm not sure how well they get on – he didn't take it too kindly when his mother remarried. I have only met Hans a couple of times,' she concluded, 'but I think it's fair to say that I don't much like him. He's very Nazi – probably a party member.'

'So, you are here on your own at the moment?' Jan confirmed.

She nodded. 'I don't know when Meta is coming back, but I don't think she'll be away for long. The flat buying aside, she just needed a break from here, after the funeral and everything. In the meantime, I'm sort of in charge...' she tailed off. 'So, what can I do to help,' she asked, with what Jan recognised as an attempt at normality.

He thought quickly. 'Just in case anything goes wrong, for instance I am discovered,' he told her, 'there has to be no evidence that you have been involved in any activity not in the best interests of your country. Weapons and equipment I can hide, well away from the farmhouse. But two things would really help. First, I need some form of shelter – I *could* survive in the woods, but it would not be easy. And second, ideally I need some means of moving round the local countryside other than on foot. The Opel would be too conspicuous and in any case, it would lead straight back to you. But perhaps I could steal a bicycle or even a small motorbike. That would be best.'

Renate thought for a few minutes. 'Petrol's not easy to come by, these days,' she said. 'The *Wehrmacht* has priority. A bicycle wouldn't be a problem. You can still buy one, and if I did it for you, no-one would think anything of it. If asked, I could easily claim that I bought it because the Opel has been laid up and then the bike was stolen – so no problem there. But as I see it, the first difficulty is to find you somewhere to stay. The estate doesn't run to farm cottages; it's much smaller than home.'

'Perhaps one of the outbuildings, then?' asked Jan. 'The stable or the barn? I have German papers, so you could reasonably explain that I turned up here looking for work, and because so many young men have joined the *Wehrmacht*, including Hans, and because Frau Holtzer's husband died recently, you were only too pleased to take on someone you assumed to be an itinerant farmhand. I can build myself a shelter in one corner of the barn. All I would ask from you is the occasional hot meal and perhaps the luxury of a bath. You would not be out of pocket,' he hastened to reassure her. 'I am well provided with money.'

'That would work,' she said pensively, a forefinger resting on her lower lip. 'But it still leaves the problem of how you are going to travel around. A bicycle isn't going to be very efficient and it wouldn't be much use if you were challenged. But you could ride.'

'You have horses?' he asked.

'Three,' she explained. 'There is our old plough horse. Then Meta's mare – I exercise her most days, but she is getting on a bit and in any case she couldn't carry your weight. But Herr Holzer bought a grey gelding about eighteen months ago, before he was taken ill. He and Auntie Meta used to ride out together, but Gunnar's only been in the stable or the paddock for the past few months, although the tack is all there. I think it would be safe enough if you stayed here tonight – I can make up a bed and I'm sure you could use a hot meal. When we have had coffee, we can look over Gunnar, then perhaps make a plan.'

Later that morning they saddled up Gunnar and Jan took him for a gentle trot and then a canter, first round the paddock and then over a couple of fields. The horse was a little out of condition but well-schooled – he took a couple of jumps easily enough. Jan was careful not to let him anywhere near being blown, but Gunnar seemed to relish his first proper ride out for quite some time. Not a challenging horse, maybe, but a good, serviceable mount – just the animal a responsible dealer would sell to a not very experienced and elderly rider. Jan was confident that after a few hacks to improve Gunnar's fitness, the horse would take him round the countryside at a respectable clip. He was well pleased as he slid off the saddle and led him back to the stable.

Jan rubbed the horse down and gave him feed and water. In the twilight of late afternoon, he returned to his bivouac site in the wood and buried his weapons, radio and parachute, after which he re-packed everything that wouldn't be compromising into a small rucksack and returned to the farmhouse.

He knocked quietly on the kitchen door. Renate opened it immediately. 'Come on in,' she urged, 'Carl has gone home for the day, so we should be alone till morning.'

Renate disappeared into an adjacent scullery. Through the open door, Jan could see a marble cold-slab and on it a meat safe. She returned and set a bottle of *Pils* before him. 'Drink that, then perhaps you would like a hot bath. Do you have a change of clothes?'

Jan told her that he had only clean underwear and a shirt. 'I'll sort something out for you in the morning,' she told him. 'Between what Hans has left behind and Herr Holzer's wardrobe, we ought to be able to find enough things that fit.'

Jan flipped the bottle top and drank deeply. 'As well as extending the property, Herr Holzer installed an upstairs bathroom,' she told him. 'I have made up a bed in the room next door and put a towel on it. Whilst you are having a bath – we have the luxury of an electric boiler these days – I'll put out a warm dressing gown for you.'

Renate, too, had changed into a dressing gown whilst Jan was enjoying his bath. It seemed strangely intimate as she served a chicken casserole at the kitchen table. Several times the neck of her gown fell open, showing the swell of a breast. Jan tried not to stare as she immediately adjusted the gown and re-tied its cord. But finally, after a night parachute drop, not much sleep in a strange wood, a day in the open rounded off with a fine meal and two glasses of wine, Jan's chin was nodding onto his chest.

'Bed,' she said firmly, as not for the first time he opened his eyes and lifted his head with a start. The dishes were in a stone sink full of hot, sudsy water. 'We are all locked up and I'll sort that lot out in the morning.'

She turned at the top of the stairs. 'Sleep well, Jan,' she said softly, before putting one hand alongside his cheek and brushing his lips gently with a kiss. 'It really does my heart good to see you again.'

Less than a minute after his head hit the pillow Jan was sound asleep.

Over breakfast they agreed that at least for now Jan would sleep in the same room. 'I'll also set up a makeshift sleeping area in the barn,' he told her, 'so that if asked we can claim that's where I'm staying. Because,' he added, 'you are hardly likely to invite someone with my cover to sleep in the main house. Just a precaution,' he told her. 'If I am questioned I'm bound to be searched, perhaps the farm as well. Our best chance is to rely on my cover story – Dietmar Hofmann, an itinerant farm labourer medically unfit for the armed forces – and my German documents.' Over a second cup of coffee they co-ordinated the final details, including when he had arrived, how and why he had been engaged, and so forth. As with any good cover story they kept as close to the truth, or what could reasonably appear to be true, as possible.

His sleeping area in the barn constructed, Jan rode out that afternoon to look at the surrounding countryside. Eventually, following Renate's instructions, he came across one of the main supply routes. It was clear from the volume of traffic heading towards the Belgian border that a major military build-up was underway. A peacetime army did not require the massive tonnages of fuel, ammunition and miscellany of equipment transported in convoy after convoy of heavy military vehicles. This could only be the preparation for an invasion.

Choosing his moment, he guided Gunnar over the road and pushed further north, looking for the railway line that Renate had described. He came across it quite suddenly, where it emerged from a tunnel into a deep cutting that ran on for several hundred metres. Backing well off from the lip, he tethered the horse to a fence then returned to lie down overlooking the two tracks. He did not have to wait long. A passenger train passed from east to west; its carriages crowded with men in uniform. Ten minutes later a second train laboured slowly in the same direction, two locomotives in tandem pulling a long line of flat cars each carrying 25 tonnes of a menacing-looking Panzer Mark IV medium tank. An anti-aircraft gun of some sort was mounted on the final car.

The two trains confirmed what Jan had already been told. It would be useful to know where the armour was headed, but it was late afternoon and he still had a good hour's riding back to the farm. As the train disappeared along the track, he rose and returned to Gunnar.

It was dark by the time he had groomed and fed the horse, who showed no signs of discomfort after a gentle if longer than usual hack into the countryside.

Wearily, Jan settled himself at the kitchen table. Renate was busying herself with the preparation of vegetables. 'Something smells good,' he told her. She opened the range door and took out a roasting tin, before basting the contents and tipping the vegetables around the meat. 'A large *Schweinshaxe*,' she told him proudly. 'One of our own pigs, so it should be all right. I remembered that it was always your favourite. I can't promise that it will be up to Frau Brantis' standard, but I'm doing my best.' She returned the heavy tin and closed the door with a cloth-wrapped hand. 'Now, what would you like to drink?' she invited. 'Supper will take another hour, so beer or wine?'

They talked contentedly whilst the hock of pork finished roasting. He told her about the main supply route and the trains. 'What I would really like to know,' he added, 'is where those flat cars were going. The *Wehrmacht* won't offload them till they are pretty close to their destination.'

She thought for a moment, then set down her glass. 'I can't say for sure,' she replied, 'but I have ridden out that way a few times. I think I know where you were this afternoon, and if you ride further west for a few kilometres there's an airfield. The *Luftwaffe* use it as a training base. But there are quite a few hangars alongside the field. If I wanted to find a temporary assembly area for an armoured unit and its personnel, that's the sort of place I would choose. Wait a minute,' she added suddenly, leaving the kitchen to walk across the yard. Through the window Jan saw a light come on in the barn. She returned clutching a folded map.

'Klaus had a draw full of them – I should have thought of this earlier,' she admitted, 'but you said all you wanted were directions to the main road and the railway line beyond.' She carefully unfolded the map onto the kitchen table. 'It's not marked,' she told him, tapping the paper with her forefinger, 'but it's about here – a couple of kilometres north of the village. You could head west of today's route. In a straight line, it's not much farther and it's mostly flat farmland, a fairly easy ride.' Jan decided that he would rest Gunnar for a day, just as a precaution, then take a look at the airfield.

The map refolded and set aside, Renate produced her meal and asked him to carve. 'That,' he told her afterwards, 'was every bit as good as Frau Brantis used to make.' They were both quiet for several seconds, each thinking of their former home right at the other end of Germany. She smiled. 'I'm glad you thought so,' she said eventually, 'and thank you for telling me. But actually, I can't take all the credit. It was her recipe. When I was about fourteen I persuaded her to teach me how to make it, then she made me practice until she was happy to serve it to my parents. I remember the time, it was a Saturday, when mother said that obviously it was Frau B's. I was so thrilled, because it was *mine*. I dashed back into the kitchen in triumph to tell her. I remember dear *Mutti* saying that when Frau B. retired, she wouldn't have to pay for another cook – I could do it instead.'

Jan looked away tactfully, to give Renate a moment to wipe away a tear.

After dinner, she washed and he dried, for the most part in companionable silence. Afterwards he returned to the table. Renate produced a bottle of brandy. 'I don't have any plans for tomorrow,' he told her. 'Is there anything you want me to do around the farm?'

She shook her head. 'Meta hired someone to do the spring planting,' she said, 'and we're only a small estate farm so Carl can manage the rest. But you could try your hand at hunting, if you wish. There are deer in our woods and extra meat is always useful.'

'But that would mean retrieving a weapon,' he pointed out.

She shook her head. 'Meta keeps a *Gewehr 98* in her room,' she told him. 'My father left it with her after The Great War, on his way home from the front. I'll go fetch it.'

Renate handed over the rifle. Jan quickly checked that the internal magazine was empty then flicked back the bolt to confirm that a round had not been left 'up the spout'. Finally, he set the weapon down on the table, making sure that the muzzle was pointing safely away from both of them. The whole process had taken barely a couple of seconds.

'I don't know what instruction you were given in England,' she observed shrewdly, 'but you seem very familiar with firearms all of a sudden.'

'I was hunting with my father's rifle,' Jan told her with – hopefully – a disarming smile, 'when you had not long finished playing with dolls.'

'There's also these,' she added, ignoring him and opening a cloth bag. She tipped several five-round clips of ammunition onto the deal surface. Jan looked at them and again at the rifle. 'There isn't a hint of rust anywhere,' he told her. 'Someone has gone to a great deal of trouble to look after this weapon. It was a great rifle twenty-something years ago and it's still a fine weapon today. *Ja,* we can hunt with this.'

'That was Herr Holzer,' she told him. 'Klaus always said that working in a bank all day was just accounts and talking to customers, so when he wasn't doing that he loved to potter about the estate doing practical things. As far as I know, he never fired the rifle, but he seemed to take pleasure in stripping and cleaning it from time to time.'

'Perfect condition,' Jan affirmed, setting it down.

He left soon after breakfast the following morning and did not return till late afternoon. She was at the window when he walked wearily into the yard, the *Gewehr* at the trail in his right hand. His left held a fine hare by the hind legs. But over his upper back and shoulders lay a small buck. As she ran out from the kitchen he lowered it gently to the ground and with an effort straightened his back. Looking at the kills, Renate clapped her hands in delight. 'All we need are a few vegetables from the farm,' she enthused, 'and we have enough meals to last for ages.'

'I'll gralloch it now,' he offered, 'then it can hang for a few days. If you can find me a decent knife, I'll do it over some straw in the stable. After that, I shall need another hot bath, if that's all right.'

Back in the kitchen, his boots left at the door till morning, Jan gave her back the clips of ammunition. One held three rounds, the rest were full. 'Two rounds, two kills,' she said in a matter-of-fact voice. 'You certainly didn't waste your time back in England.'

'I told you, I was hunting as a teenager,' Jan reminded her. It was no more than the truth, but it deflected any further enquiries.

Renate had prepared a simple sausage casserole with root vegetables and served with sauerkraut. 'Do you still intend to look at the airfield tomorrow?' she asked anxiously.

He nodded, in the process of forking up a generous helping of cabbage. 'I have to,' he told her, 'so I'll be away for most of the day. I don't want to ride Gunnar too hard. Then Wednesday, I'll probably be out again – I'll have enough information to send back to London.'

'Please be careful, Jan,' she urged. 'If they catch you...' she tailed off, the thought and the consequences too dreadful to put into words.

Jan leant across the table to place his hand on hers. 'I will be careful,' he told her. 'I know you haven't been fishing, but more than once you mentioned my time back in UK. The less you know the better, but please try to take comfort from the fact that I'm not the same person you knew last year. Since then, I have been very well trained. And I have just spent months with the partisans in my homeland. So, don't worry too much – I'll be back tomorrow evening.'

Renate rose from the table to clear the dishes, but paused behind Jan to put her arms round his shoulders. 'I thought I had lost you for good, last year,' she said softly into one ear. 'Now that I have found you again, I'm hoping against hope we can have some sort of future.'

With that she took his plate and stood at the sink. Lost for words, his heart thumping, Jan moved to stand behind her. He curled one arm around her waist, his other hand giving her a reassuring pat on the shoulder. Reflected in the window, Jan couldn't help but notice two moist eyes and the hint of tears that she tried hard to blink away.

CHAPTER 26

The ride to the airport proved uneventful. Jan had memorised the route from Herr Holzer's map, but left it behind. If he were stopped, he was carrying only his German papers, which he was confident would pass muster.

The area was flat, which he had expected. Surrounding hills would have presented an unwanted complication for pilots. But at least it was farmland, so he judged it safe to ride round the airfield perimeter, albeit a field or so away. The edge of the airfield was packed with tanks, all carefully camouflaged with a double layer of netting. Some were side on, against bushes that were clipped to the height of the fence. Others were under brick-coloured netting and hard against buildings. There were probably more inside the hangars. From the air, it would be obvious that there was something on the ground, but only from an aircraft flying almost over the field and at a fairly low level. Had he not been this close, Jan would not have known that there was a tank under every hide. He recognised a number of Panzer Mark IIs and IIIs, as well as the latest Mark IVs he had seen on the train. Light aircraft almost covered the apron – perhaps to make more room for the Panzers or their crews inside the hangars.

Jan counted about one hundred tanks, although there were probably more under cover inside. He knew from his pre-mission briefings that this was a build-up of at least regimental strength. But if Panzers were still arriving, then more likely he was looking at a Division being assembled of anything up to more than three hundred fighting vehicles, not to mention headquarters, reconnaissance, signals and logistic support transport. A number of lorries, not camouflaged and parked in small groups all over the airfield, gave credence to this.

The size of the formation suggested to Jan that the main invasion thrust might not be to the south. The presence of a full armoured division might also mean that any southern advance could just be a feint, and that the full force of the invasion would be more to the west, through Belgium and Holland – information that had to be passed urgently back to London.

Thus far he had bordered three sides of the field, but not the one facing the road and the main gate. This, thought Jan, it might be wise to avoid. Besides, he had found out what he needed to know, so at the end of the third side of a rectangle he turned right, away from the field, and led Gunnar in a round-about route to where he had originally arrived. So far, he thought, the mission was going well. A couple of hours later, after a good walk and the occasional canter, he guided Gunnar back into the farmyard.

The kitchen door opened, but before he could dismount, instead of Renate a German officer emerged and looked him disdainfully up and down. He was tall, a little more so than Jan, but wiry rather than stocky and well-muscled. His black hair and regular features were almost handsome, but thin lips suggested a less than kindly disposition. 'Who the hell are you,' he barked sharply, taking a couple of strides forward, 'and why are you riding my father's horse?' His hand moved to the flap on his holster, although he did not draw the weapon. Jan reckoned this was more a gesture of intimidation than any real threat.

He decided to play the subservient farmhand. 'Good afternoon, sir,' he replied. But before he could go further Renate emerged to stand alongside the *Hauptmann* and place a restraining hand on his arm. 'It's all right, Hans,' she said urgently. 'This is Dietmar Hofmann. He works for us... Carl can't cope with everything now that your father is no longer here and the estate was too much for just your mother and me. Dietmar is very good with horses, so I asked him to help exercise Gunnar, who was getting out of condition.'

Jan was ordered abruptly to dismount. 'Yes, Sir,' he said, sliding quickly from the saddle.

'Where does he come from?' Hans snapped at Renate.

'Originally, I am from northeast Germany,' Jan replied, speaking up for himself. 'I tried to join our armed forces, but my health is not good. I have a weak chest.' He tapped himself to emphasise the point. 'Then I tried to find a job in the industries of the *Ruhr*. But the doctors had already told me that I should try to find something in the fresh air, so I also looked for farm work, thinking that this, too, would help the war effort. My people lived on the land, so I went from farm to farm, and eventually Fraulein Raschdorf was kind enough to give me a chance. I am happy here...' he added lamely. 'I have my papers, Sir, including my medical report.'

'So where are you staying?' asked Hans, in a harsh voice.

'I am kindly allowed to sleep in the barn, Sir,' Jan responded. 'I have a small sleeping place prepared there. I work for my food and accommodation and just a small allowance,' he told the German, 'Sir, you can ask Fraulein Raschdorf...'

'Take good care of my father's horse,' the German interrupted bluntly, 'then stay out of my sight for the rest of today.'

Jan bowed his head and led Gunnar off to the stable. It was cold in the barn, but with forethought Jan and Renate had included a few blankets. He thought he would have to do without supper, but around seven that evening, Renate opened the door and hurriedly handed him a plate of sandwiches. 'He's having a bath,' she told him, 'but I have to get back. With luck, I don't think he'll stay for long. Just a day or so – two at the most.' With that she hurried back.

Some sort of premonition told Jan that it would not be wise to get undressed and go to bed on his straw palliasse. So, he lay there fully dressed, under the blankets, taking off only his riding boots. An hour and a half later, he thought he heard raised voices. Pulling his boots back on, Jan crossed the small yard and stood to one side outside the kitchen door. He recognised Hans' voice, now slurred from whatever he had been drinking.

'Don't be a frigid cow, Renate,' he was shouting. 'You should be grateful. You're safe and comfortable in my father's house. Ten days from now I'll be at war. You can't deny me something to remember from a pretty German *Mädchen*.'

There was the sound of furniture being pushed to one side, a scraping of wood on flagstones, then something of a struggle. A glass shattered, presumably on the floor. Then came Renate's cry of *'Nein!'* followed by a scream. Jan opened the door.

It took only a second to take in the scene. There was broken glass on the floor and an almost empty schnapps bottle that had rolled on its side across the table. Hans had Renate pinned against the sink. Her clothing had been pulled down, she was naked to the waist, and one hand was pawing at her breast.

'Sir, please do not do this,' said Jan mildly, but at the same time taking a step forward. Distracted, the German turned from Renate. Dishevelled, he was wearing only tunic trousers held up by braces over a half-undone shirt. Unfortunately, his holstered pistol was immediately behind him on the table. Spinning unsteadily, he managed to draw the weapon and before Jan could reach the two of them it was pointing towards him, albeit in a shaky aim.

'I told you to stay out of my sight,' Hans shouted, his voice still slurred heavily from drink.

Jan was about two metres away. Leaving Renate to the German was not an option, but rushing his enemy and hoping to brush the weapon aside offered at best an outside chance. If the *Hauptmann* got off a round, it might not be fatal, but he might well take a hit in the shoulder. He watched as Hans swayed slightly from side to side, his aim wandering all the time. Picking his moment, when he watched the muzzle beginning to drift off-line, Jan made his move. A shot rang out, and rushing forward, Jan knew that the German had missed. But as they closed the pistol pointed straight at his chest. Jan was not sure if he had time to push the muzzle aside and prepared himself to take a round.

The second shot, when it came, went over his shoulder and into the ceiling. The weapon clattered on the floor and seconds later a trickle of blood escaped from Hans' mouth to run over his chin. Then he slumped to the floor. The knife Jan had used to gralloch the buck had been on the draining board. Now, only the handle protruded from the German's back. Renate slumped to her knees, her face in her hands. 'He would have killed you,' she sobbed. Jan put two fingers to Hans' neck. He was dead.

Jan lifted Renate to her feet and first eased her back from Hans' body, then around the table to sit on the other side. He pulled her clothing up and she tugged her blouse together. From here she couldn't see what was on the floor between the other side of the table and the sink. 'Do you still have any brandy?' he asked.

She could only nod towards the larder. There were shelves at the end above the meat safe and along both sides. On one of them was an almost-full bottle of cognac. Taking it into the kitchen he opened cupboards till he found a glass and poured her a stiff three fingers of the spirit. When he pushed it into her hand she was shaking so much that the liquid threatened to slop over the side. Putting his hands round hers, he guided it to her lips. She managed a small sip at first, then a larger draught that made her cough. Jan kept his hands near hers as she set the glass back on the table. Perhaps it was the burning jolt from the alcohol, but she had stopped shaking.

'What will we do?' she asked.

'First, I'm going to get rid of what's down there,' he told her, inclining his head towards the sink. 'Then we'll talk. Will you be all right for a couple of minutes whilst I go outside to the stable?' Renate nodded that she would.

Jan moved quickly to find an old horse blanket that he had noticed a few days earlier. Back in the kitchen, with Renate still seated where he had left her, he withdrew the knife. She had put a lot of force into the blow and he had to twist from side to side to let in air round the blade, which was not grooved like a bayonet, before he could pull it free. He wrapped the corpse in the blanket together with the rest of Hans' uniform, although he kept the automatic and ammunition, plus the documents he found in the German's jacket pocket. The knife he threw into the sink – he could worry about that later.

'Close your eyes,' he ordered.

The blanket covered nearly all the body, although Hans' feet stuck out from one end. Jan dragged the shroud and its contents into the yard, then hefted the bundle over his shoulder. After a short walk, he was able to set down his burden inside the stable. Closing the door, he returned to the kitchen.

Telling her not to watch, he rinsed the knife clean and searched under the sink for caustic soda. Finding a metal bucket, he made up a strong solution deep enough to cover the weapon, which he dropped in before setting the bucket outside the kitchen door. Finally, using a strong, fresh solution of soda, he cleaned the kitchen floor. With everything rinsed away there was no sign of the recent carnage.

'What will we do now?' she asked anxiously, looking up as

he settled opposite and poured himself a glass of cognac. She had stopped crying but the whites of her eyes were streaked with red.

'There's nothing we can do, before daybreak,' he told her. 'Then I can get rid of the evidence. You saved my life back then, you know,' he added gently, placing his hand over hers, which were clasped together on the table, still clutching her glass.

'On the way here was bad enough,' she said softly. 'But that was just some anonymous Nazi. Here, it was *Tantchen* Meta's only son... it was horrible,' she finished with a convulsive shudder.

'Renate, you would have been raped,' he said gently but firmly. 'He was drunk and his blood was up. Had you not done what you did, I would probably be dead and then you would have been violated anyway. You cannot possible blame or reproach yourself.'

'What will we do,' she asked yet again, 'and what on earth can I say to *Tantchen* Meta?'

'First things first,' Jan replied. 'How did Hans arrive here?'

'He walked from the station,' she replied automatically. 'He was angry, because he had told someone to phone and tell his mother to pick him up. Meta wasn't here, and either they didn't bother to phone or I missed the call. And in any case, Meta's taken the Mercedes to Cologne. But it's a good two or three kilometres from the station, so he was already in a foul mood when he arrived. Then you came back on Gunnar, which set him off all over again.'

She paused. 'He had a couple of drinks,' she went on, 'then went for a bath. He was annoyed because he couldn't find his dressing gown – I didn't think he would need it any time soon, so I gave it to you. Then he got dressed again, came down into the kitchen, and literally ordered me to make him some supper. I was just making a start when he...' she hesitated. 'Thank God you came in when you did.'

She took another sip of cognac. 'I think you should try to eat something,' he told her. 'If you tell me what to do, I'll put something together.'

'I don't know if I can cook,' she said hesitantly. 'But I was going to do something with a chicken. Maybe you could cut off a few pieces, dust them in flour, and fry them in a pan.'

'That's probably all I could make anyway,' he told her, trying to lighten the mood if only just a little.

'That's too strong for me,' she told him, pushing her drink aside. 'But could I have a glass of wine? There are some bottles of red on the floor in the larder.'

Jan finished off her cognac, then fetched and opened a bottle. As he fried the chicken, Renate felt well enough to walk round the table and throw in a few herbs, although he caught a frightened glance at the now cleaned space on the floor, as if there might still be something there. The bottle was almost finished before the chicken was ready so Renate went into the larder and brought out another.

By time they had finished and the new bottle was half empty, Jan could see that Renate was suffering from shock, not helped by the drinks she had consumed.

'It's been a horrible day,' she slurred, 'I just want to go to bed and forget about it.' She reached out for his hand. 'Jan, I'm frightened. Could you...' she hesitated, 'would you keep me company, just like you did on that first night on the road? So that I won't be on my own?'

Jan locked up and found Renate in her night-dress and under the covers. He lay alongside her fully dressed, Hans' side-arm on the floor beside him. She tossed and turned for quite some time but eventually fell into a troubled sleep. Carefully, so as not to disturb her, Jan opened the curtains. He needed to be up and away before dawn, but despite the vicious events of the evening he did manage a couple of hours' sleep.

It was still pitch dark when he left a sleeping Renate and

let himself out of the kitchen door. There was a shovel in the stable. Hans' body he tied across the plough horse, judging him to be the most placid of the three. In the half light of pre-dawn, he headed off to the wood, not far from where he had first slept and then buried his equipment. It was just light as he led the horse into the trees, but he was confident that they had not been seen. An hour and a half later, Hans was interred in his last resting place, the grave smoothed down and covered with dead leaves, immune to any inspection.

By the time he got back to the house the sun was up. Renate was re-lighting the kitchen range, a dressing-gown now over her night-dress. 'I should have banked this up last night,' she said matter-of-factly. She put a match to the paper and sticks and stood up.

He turned her to face him and put his hands on her shoulders. 'Are you all right?' Jan asked anxiously.

'I think so,' she said slowly. 'And thank you again for looking after me. Have you...?'

'All taken care of,' Jan broke in. 'So try to put your mind at rest. Now,' he said firmly, 'we have breakfast then we put our story together. You may be contacted in a day or two, or maybe even not at all, but for now we just carry on with our lives. I have to be away for a few hours, but I'll be back as soon as I can. I have some information for London that needs to be transmitted as soon as possible.'

Renate bustled about making *Speck und Ei* which she served with buttered toast and coffee. Jan always enjoyed bacon and egg, but also recognised that keeping busy was a defence mechanism, a way of taking her mind off things.

After breakfast, they put together a version of events. Having reassured himself that she would be all right for a few hours, Jan saddled Gunnar, retrieved his radio and code books, transcribed his message and then set off to be well away from the estate. Despite having ridden that way yesterday, knowing the lie of the land he went more or less in the general direction of the airfield. Perhaps a kilometre or so to the east, he found a suitable copse, tethered Gunnar, and set to work.

Oberleutnant Erdmut Kühn loved flying the Fieseler Fi 156 *Storch* – the Fieseler Stork. Trained to fly gliders in order to circumvent the prohibitions of the Versailles treaty following Germany's defeat in the Great War, he was perhaps a little old for fighters. But he loved the almost glider-like simplicity of the Army's general purpose, high wing monoplane light aircraft, with its long stick-like undercarriage and fabulous short take-off and landing ability. Earlier in the day he had taken a senior officer, in the passenger seat behind him, to a grass field near Cologne and now, with the aircraft to himself, he was thoroughly enjoying a leisurely ride home in the late morning sunshine. Humming contentedly, he scanned his instruments and then, as he always did, the ground as it passed under each side of his aeroplane. The Argus As 180kW engine hummed smoothly as he held her at just under seven hundred metres – low enough to give him a chance to dive for cover in the unlikely event that he encountered a stray reconnaissance machine of the Royal Air Force. The light wind was pretty much on the nose, but he looked forward to landing back at the strip and a good if late breakfast – or perhaps it would be an early lunch with a glass of beer – in the mess.

Something moved between the trees. In a two-second gap as he flew over a small break in the canopy he thought he saw a grey horse. But why would it be tethered in the middle of a small wood, he wondered?

Instinctively his left hand moved to the yellow knob on the throttle and he pulled back smoothly to reduce power, at the same time leading with a touch of rudder before pushing over the stick to execute a gentle turn. As he circled the wind set the *Storch* back the way it had come. At this height, with the revs now set so that the engine was barely ticking over, he knew that downwind he would be pretty much inaudible to anyone on the ground.

Wearing headphones and concentrating frantically on taking down a message, Jan was totally unaware of the sinking, circling aircraft. On his third turn, and at barely four hundred metres, Kühn risked a quick leg back towards the trees and caught a glimpse of a figure on the ground. He was hunched over some sort of box, and... just before the man on the ground disappeared again behind the canopy... Kühn thought he was wearing headphones. He had, he realised, almost certainly caught someone in the act of making an illegal transmission: a traitor – perhaps a spy.

This time he broke off from his circle and headed away downwind. Not until he was barely above treetop height did he risk feeding the power back on. Gently the *Storch* responded, levelling out at first then starting to climb as Kühn gradually pushed the knob forward for more revs. He reached for his radio telephone. Flying one-handed, he opened the map and reported what he had seen to the tower, giving both the co-ordinates and a geographic description of the copse, with reference to its position both from the airfield and the nearest village. He was ordered to hold station and observe. This, Kühn calculated, would best be done at a good height and just downwind. Throttle well forward now, the *Storch's* willing little engine pulled her in broad circles to settle at eight hundred meters.

As Jan switched off and began to pack his equipment it was Gunnar that drew his attention to the faint buzz in the sky. The horse turned his head, ears flicking. Jan watched and listened for several seconds before catching a brief flash of reflected sunlight as it caught the wings of a light aircraft. He watched as it circled. It might be a coincidence, but there was only one way to find out.

Hastily he gathered everything together, shouldered his

pack and remounted. He would not set off in the direction of the farm, but neither could he move nearer to the airfield. If the pilot had radioed in a report, he had no wish to meet up with the inevitable follow-up patrol.

He rode gently, as if out for a pleasure hack rather than fleeing an aerial pursuit. The circle pattern of the aircraft moved with him, always high, and always downwind, but following him nevertheless. Jan knew now that he was being hunted, and soon the aircraft would be joined by other assets on the ground. What they might be, he had no way of knowing.

Erdmut Kühn checked his fuel state. Unfortunately, he had been almost at the end of his filed flight plan before the sighting, and he now had barely enough to make it back to the field. But when he requested permission to abort and return it was flatly denied. He was ordered to continue surveillance, and if necessary to make a dead-stick landing and await further supply. To Jan's immense relief, the sound of the aircraft's engine died before he encountered any form of ground patrol.

Kühn was not particularly concerned when the buzz of his engine became a cough, to be replaced by a rush of wind. The *Storch* had a reasonable glide angle and its speciality was a short field landing – and take off for that matter. Besides, it was fairly open country below, and selecting a field and making an engine-off landing was part of the trade test for any aspiring pilot under training. Often, when flying alone, he would practice the selection and approach, only pushing on the power at the last minute when he was certain that the landing would have been successful.

He had already chosen a field. It was easily long enough for the *Storch*. Flaps set, he turned onto a parallel downwind leg off to one side, but because of the steeper approach from an engine-off powered aircraft, he went past what a glider pilot would call "the box" somewhat higher, at almost four hundred meters. Turning base leg, he set himself up for a landing just beyond the low hedge. He smiled – power pilots were sometimes challenged by a dead stick landing. After all, a misjudged approach meant either hitting the hedge or landing way down the field, with the possibility of running into whatever was at the other end. But as a glider student, Kühn had learned to do this consistently, time after time, with no margin for error. One last application of rudder and stick and he was committed to finals. He had allowed for the steeper glide angle of the heavier aircraft and passed over the hedge with perhaps ten metres to spare. No need to side-slip off any height. Just into the field he checked back, then as the wheels neared the ground he eased the stick back even further and flared out. *The Storch* brushed the stubble in a perfect three-pointer.

Minutes later, pleased with himself and still grinning, Kühn climbed through the door on the starboard side of the Fieseler and stepped down onto spring wheat. He had reported his position as soon as the engine cut out, but like as not, he would be here for some time. There was a small village only a kilometre or so away. He lit a cigarette. He had played his part. Now he would enjoy a walk in the spring sunshine and hopefully, at the other end, something to eat and – never mind the regulations – that glass of beer.

CHAPTER 27

Jan guessed what had happened. Almost home, the pilot was probably low on fuel. But Jan's description and general direction would have been passed back to base. The airfield lay to his west, the farm to his south and east. He had been heading back east, deeper into Germany, but that had to change. He could go north, but that would eventually leave him with a longer ride home, together with more chance of being stopped after dark. In the end he headed south, to put himself on a different position line before finally turning east again for the farm.

He rode gently for about twenty minutes. Jan had no idea what the Germans from the base were doing, but he and Gunnar might need to make a run for it at any moment. He couldn't afford to have his horse half-blown – all Gunnar's speed might be needed later, at a moment's notice. There was probably another hour of daylight left.

He led Gunnar on foot into the next field to save his stamina, rather than take the jump. Jan was closing the gate behind him when he heard the roar of engines. Two motor-cyclists were a couple of fields away, on a narrow lane. Quickly he led Gunnar behind the hedge but the horse had not been trained to lie down. Although he stooped to hold his mount steady it was obvious from the way the riders stopped and the shouting that followed – Gunnar had been spotted. Jan mounted, knowing he would have to ask a lot of his horse.

At first it was barely an even chase. Jan could jump from field to field. His pursuers had to find a gate. Jan and his mount began to pull away, but eventually Gunnar would tire. Jan knew he could not let that happen. He was still carrying a radio on his back and a German officer's weapon concealed beneath his jacket.

Eventually he found what he was looking for – a field with a taller hedge, interspaced with trees. There wasn't time to dismount and open the gate. Gunnar had a lot of heart and was still game. Jan set him at the jump. They floated over, then he pulled him up short, turned Gunnar quickly to his right and walked the horse back to where several trees and bushes offered a good spread of branches overhanging into the field – pretty much blocking the view from the other side. The reins secured, he left his pack alongside his mount, ran back to the gate and waited, just to one side. Pressed into the undergrowth, he was barely visible from a few yards away, but he was acutely conscious that Gunnar was less well concealed by the overhanging foliage.

The bikes roared up to the gate then both engines dropped to a tick over. Jan heard shouts of 'Can you see him?' followed by a 'Nein!' They had made the mistake of assuming he had fled to the next field.

One rider dismounted and rushed to the gate. Pushing it open, with Jan and Gunnar now behind him, he had eyes only for the far end of the field and did not think to look over his shoulder. With the gate almost open his companion roared through, to stop, facing into the field, just clear of a patch of churned mud. Jan took aim at the rider still at the gate and loosed off two rounds. Switching aim he fired again. Whether his second target ever heard the first two shots, through his leather helmet and above the noise of his machine, Jan had no way of knowing. Either way the threat, for now, was over.

Jan dragged both bodies – they yielded two MP 38 Schmeisser sub-machine guns together with a pair of extra thirty-two round magazines for each – then pushed them as far as he could into the hedge. Setting his haul aside, he leant the two bikes over the bodies of their riders. Working quickly, he ripped a few branches from the nearest bushes, which were just in leaf, and threw them on top of the machines. The camouflage wasn't perfect, by any means, but the branches would break up the shape, shine and silhouette from any distant inspection.

It was then that he heard it – in the silence following his hasty action and before turning back to Gunnar. There was just the faintest buzz somewhere in the sky, way to the north. Jan couldn't see anything, and for a few seconds the sound died away, only to return. There was another light aircraft somewhere in the distance. It was no coincidence that it was flying a circular search pattern over where he would have been had he not changed direction.

Daylight would fade soon and cloud base was fairly low, but Jan knew that if the aircraft widened its pattern he would almost certainly be spotted. There had to be radio contact between the plane and its base, and almost certainly between the base and whoever was commanding the troops on the ground. Jan knew that if the plane found him, he would be hunted down.

Briefly he considered dumping the damning evidence, the radio and his weapons, and just riding for it. But this was not really an option. If he were caught the area would be searched, with every chance that the two dead Germans, their motorcycles, and whatever Jan left behind would be found – even if he left his own equipment in a different hiding place. To be arrested only a few kilometers away would be as good as a death warrant. And besides, without the radio his entire mission would be over. Jan rode gently south for about ten minutes. The sound of the aircraft engine mercifully died, but then returned, if anything a little more loudly than before.

Jan knew that he had to find shelter, if only for another three quarters of an hour or so till last light. Thinking furiously, he realized that he could not be far from the deep railway cutting that he had found only a few days previously. Turning in what he hoped was the right direction, Jan was relieved to meet a fairly familiar landscape. This time he came to the cutting from the north, with the farm way beyond on the other side. Jan dismounted and led Gunnar down the bank. Pausing at the mouth of the tunnel he listened carefully. For the moment, there was no sound of an aero engine.

Kneeling beside the tracks, he placed a hand on both sets of lines to feel for the vibration that would warn of a coming train. There was none, and he probably only needed this refuge for a half-hour or so. Gunnar was reluctant to be led into the dark mouth of the tunnel, and he didn't like having to step carefully over the sleepers, but eventually Jan had him far enough inside and turned around. He just had to hope that if he heard a train coming, particularly from the direction of the airfield, there would be time to lead his horse out of the tunnel and up and over the embankment.

Once or twice he thought he heard the faint buzz of an engine, but his luck held and there were no trains. As the dusk of last light faded into darkness they emerged, climbed the left hand bank and set off for the farm. It was difficult, with low cloud, to follow the way home, but Jan was happier to have the cover. A bright, starlit night and a bomber's moon might just have been sufficient to persuade the Germans to fly another sortie.

Mindful of his arrival when Hans had unexpectedly opened the kitchen door, and in case Renate had other visitors looking for him, Jan tethered Gunnar a field or so from the house, offloaded his radio and captured weapons and walked, carefully, automatic in hand, to the kitchen window. As she was in an isolated farm dwelling, Renate did not usually draw the curtains and he could see her, seated facing the window, a glass of wine to hand on the kitchen table. He stepped back and watched for a minute or two, till he was fairly certain she was alone, then moved forward and tapped, lightly on the window pane. She looked up immediately and almost ran to the door. Jan knew that if there had been anyone else there, Renate would have waved him away. She opened the door and he stepped inside – he was safe.

She threw her arms round his neck. 'Jan, I was so worried… what happened… where have you been?'

'I was seen using the radio,' he told her. 'Tell you the full story later, but a *Storch* flew over the wood when I was transmitting.' She looked puzzled. 'It's a small light aircraft,' he explained. 'It wasn't looking for me originally, but it must have radioed my position. After that, I spent the afternoon playing cat and mouse with the German army – with me as the mouse. But we managed to lose them, well to the other side of the railway line, before it got dark. Only then was it safe to ride home. But if you are all right here, I have to see to Gunnar.'

He gently eased her arms from his neck – although it had been an enjoyable welcome – and returned to his horse. The weapons and radio he wrapped and buried in his shallow hide, not without difficulty in the dark. He didn't think anyone would arrive to make a morning search of the farmhouse, but that wasn't a risk he was prepared to take. Finally, with Gunnar rubbed down, fed and watered, it was well over two hours before he returned to the kitchen.

Renate poured him a glass of wine. He washed his hands, which were still grimed with soil, then took a sip and collapsed gratefully onto a chair. Over a couple of glasses, he told her what had happened from the time he had signed off, having sent his message. She was visibly shocked at the shooting of the two motorcyclists. 'Didn't have a choice, though,' he explained. 'With what I was carrying it would have been a firing squad for me. And even if I could have held out under interrogation they might have traced the horse back to you – if they had just turned him loose he could even have found his own way home. Then it would have been the end for both of us.' Jan refrained from telling her that if capture had seemed imminent he had resolved to shoot Gunnar and then take his own life.

Renate had a pot of meat and vegetables simmering on the range. Jan realized how hungry he was, not having eaten since breakfast. 'It's the hare you shot the day before yesterday,' she said flatly. Jan suspected she was still shocked by his account of the day's events.

'I'm filthy and I probably stink of horse sweat, not to mention my own,' he said gently. 'Do I have time for a bath?'

She seemed to gather herself together. Lifting the lid, Renate stirred the pot. 'Go on,' she invited, 'this will take another half-hour.' When he returned to the kitchen wearing a dressing-gown that had belonged to a man now no longer alive Renate didn't bat an eyelid. She, too, had changed into her night-robe, tied firmly at the waist. They sat at the table and sipped their wine, waiting for supper to be ready. Eventually she stretched out her arm and placed a hand over his.

'We have to talk...' she said softly, 'about what we are going to do. If we carry on like this, it's dangerous here for both of us. And besides, *Tantchen* Meta will be back any day soon. What are we going to tell her?' Hans' name had not been spoken, but the question was very much there. 'And where will you sleep after that?' she went on. 'You are supposed to be an itinerant farmhand, but I don't want to see you sleeping in that barn. It might be all right for a few months over summer, but not when we go into winter.'

'We can talk some more in the morning,' he suggested. 'I don't think I'll still be here come winter, so maybe it'll have to be my cover story. If only because she will know that the person who brought you here also went on to England?'

'Meta knows your real name,' Renate told him. 'So perhaps

you are right. And at least you have German papers to support a different identity. But what about Hans?'

Jan thought for a minute. 'I think we have to be kind,' he said at length. 'You can hardly tell Frau Holzer that her son was a drunken Nazi thug who tried to rape you and is now well under the turf somewhere on her own farm. Perhaps it would be better to let things take their course. From what he said – and I have passed this on to London, by the way – it looks as if Germany will invade the low countries and perhaps then France in the next ten days.'

He shrugged. 'Let's stick with what we agreed: Hans was here but left to return to his unit. I suspect there will be only a fairly cursory investigation, assuming there is one at all. With the opening of a second front, the whereabouts of one missing *Hauptmann* is not going to be a priority in the greater scheme of things. I think that eventually both the *Wehrmacht* and Meta will come to accept that he was just lost in the early days of the war.'

She was silent for a while, thinking this over. 'You're right,' she said at length, 'although we are going to have to talk about this some more tomorrow.' Renate set the pot and two bowls on the table. 'I know today has been bad for you,' she said matter-of-factly, 'but I have also been out of my mind…' She paused. 'We have to eat,' she went on, 'then I think I am going to have a few more drinks. After that, we worry about all this in the morning.' The first wine bottle was empty. Renate walked into the larder and returned with another, together with the remains of the cognac.

To Jan the meal that she ladled into the bowls was superb. Afterwards they sat at the table till the wine was finished and the spirit bottle almost empty. Renate checked the kitchen door and stood behind him, her hands on his shoulders.

'Come on, Jan Janicki,' she said softly, 'it's time for bed.' Jan followed her up the narrow stairway. But she caught his arm as he turned towards his room. They had both been drinking, but her voice was perfectly clear. 'You told me about Hedda,' she said, 'and she was right. We might survive this coming war, but perhaps we won't.' She opened the door to her room and took his hand. 'You have always been the perfect gentleman,' she told him, 'and I think I fell in love with you that first night, when we were on the road – perhaps even before. And I'm not stupid. I know you feel the same about me – you're just too decent to take advantage.' With that she led him by the hand into her room.

'We are living in bad times,' she said, walking round the bed and throwing off her robe. In just her nightdress she threw back the covers and lay on the sheet, patting the space beside her. 'There is about to be a war in the west,' she went on. 'And from what you have told me, I agree with Hedda. I have no intention of departing this world a virgin. So come here, Jan Janicki. I'm going to love you, and give you the most precious gift that I have.' She pulled off her nightdress and dropped it onto the floor.

Jan took off his own dressing gown and lay beside her. They were both naked. Renate pulled up the covers, threw one leg over his and snuggled up, her arm over his chest. Jan had never been more aroused. His hand cupped her breast. But the anxiety of the day, plus the meal and drinks of the evening, had extracted their toll. Warm and beautiful as she was cuddled beside him, Renate was purring softly. She had fallen asleep.

Drowsy and never more content, his arm around her shoulders, Jan lay on his back and listened. It was absolutely pouring with rain, the wind thrashing in bursts against the window. The weather couldn't have been better – at least it would muddy out any hoof-prints. Slowly he, too, drifted off.

It was not quite light when he woke and he could hear the dawn chorus. Carefully he tried to extract his arm, which was so numb he could barely feel his fingers, from beneath Renate's neck. There was silence for several seconds, although he sensed that she was awake. Then she eased from the bed, pulled on her robe and headed for the bathroom.

'Didn't distinguish myself last night,' she said, padding back across the room. 'I fell asleep.'

'Cognac and wine one, Jan and Renate – nil,' he said quietly, as if it were a football score. 'But we were both absolutely exhausted.'

She dropped her robe and scrambled back into the warmth. He could smell tooth powder. There was no hesitation this morning. Lying on her side, facing him, Jan felt her hand on his stomach. He turned to face her, but she pushed him back. 'You did enough riding yesterday,' she said mischievously. 'This morning it's my turn.'

With the covers slipping from her shoulders she climbed astride him, sitting on his stomach. He held her breasts, both nipples already hard under his thumbs. With one hand on his chest, the other was behind her, rubbing his penis as she pushed it against her body. Then she moved to place both hands on the bed aside him, lifting just enough to ease the lips of her sex over his. She moved gently, down just a little, then up again. Jan resisted an overwhelming urge to raise his hips and push into her. Renate wanted the moment to last forever. But neither of them could wait. She lowered herself all the way down. There was a brief moment of pain then an overwhelmingly warm, sweet sensation as she felt all of him inside her. Almost immediately they were both arching up and down, thrashing wildly, till she cried out with joy as they climaxed together. They were both gasping for breath. Eventually Renate slid off him and lay on her back, holding his hand.

'What will you do today?' she asked after a little while, speaking softly into the silence. Jan had to force his mind back to the present. 'First thing, I have to go and check the wood,' he replied. 'It was dark when I buried everything last night and I need to make sure that it's all well covered. After that I'll come back for breakfast. Think I'll spend a quiet day on the farm, so let me know if there's anything you need doing.'

Renate leant over and kissed him. 'Going for a bath,' she said, 'you have made me all sweaty!' With that she swung her legs from the bed, pulled on her robe and left the room. Half an hour later, shaved, bathed and dressed, Jan allowed himself a quick cup of strong black coffee before setting out into the morning. It was fully light now, the sky had cleared after last night's rain and it promised to be a sunny if cold spring day.

His cache was fine. He had done a good job in the dark. Jan kicked a few leaves around, but really it wasn't necessary. Hands in pockets, he enjoyed a leisurely stroll back to the farm. Heaven alone knew what the future might bring, he thought. All Jan knew for certain was that right now, he had never, in his entire life, been happier.

CHAPTER 28

'Take a walk into the village?' Renate suggested after breakfast. 'Even though he's getting on a bit, there's nothing left to do here that Carl can't cope with, and you might enjoy some time off after the excitement of yesterday. When he arrives, I'll give him our version of why you are here, then I want to get on with some housework and cooking,' she told him, 'but I need a few things from the shop, and there's a *Bierstube* where you could stop for a coffee or perhaps *Frühschoppen*.' Jan had to smile at the German word for an early-ish morning beer. 'If you are going to stay here for a while,' she added, 'it wouldn't hurt to be seen from time to time in the local community – establish your identity, as it were.'

Jan thought about this. 'Maybe it wouldn't be a bad idea to work on my cover,' he said eventually. 'Perhaps better than being a surprise to anyone who turns up at the farm. It might even forestall any gossip '

'The *Bierstube* was owned by *Tantchen* Meta's first husband's late father, the *Bürgemeister*,' she informed him. 'But now it's run by Wolfgang, his nephew. He's a nice young man. Just introduce yourself as an employee from the estate and tell him that you are staying here for a while, to help out. He'll think nothing of it – in fact he'll almost certainly make you welcome.'

She gave him a wicker basket for the shopping and he spent a pleasant forty minutes walking in the spring sunshine. He sensed that the shopkeeper and two other customers were curious, but no one asked any questions as he politely placed his order. 'It's for Fraulein Raschdorf,' he said, holding his hand out for change, then left without further explanation.

At the beer hall, he introduced himself to Wolfgang, who was behind the bar, and they chatted amiably. Jan knew that from what he had said in the two establishments news of his arrival, who he was, where he was staying and what he was doing would soon be all round the village, such was the way of country life. But equally, it would help make him accepted – to blend into this small community. Carl, too, would probably make mention of him and the information would all neatly marry up.

Walking back to the farm, he thought that the last few days had gone rather well from an operational point of view. And he was over the moon about his new relationship with Renate. He was looking forward to a relaxed afternoon – perhaps they would sit and enjoy a bottle of wine in the sunshine, followed by a delicious supper and then another night together.

He was shaken from his reverie by the sight of a black Adler saloon parked in the yard. It was a Trumpf, not the smaller Trumpf Junior, so if this was an official visit the occupant was no underling. Jan thought for a full minute but decided in the end that he had no choice. He knocked on the kitchen door and walked in. Two men were seated opposite Renate and Carl, each with a coffee on the table. One was in uniform – which suggested that he was the village policeman. The other wore a trench coat, his hat on the table – all the hallmarks of some branch of the security services. Renate looked remarkably cool and collected, thought Jan. Carl, next to her, was clearly uncomfortable wearing his working clothes inside the farmhouse.

'Herr Hofmann,' greeted the civilian, without introducing himself. 'Your papers, please.'

Jan handed over his documents, tucked into which was his medical exemption certificate. Doreen Jackman had assured him that the identity was genuine – it had belonged to a German citizen who died in the United Kingdom but whose death had never been reported to his national authorities. Only the medical certificate had been forged, but it was on the correct paper, it had the right signature and stamp, and could never be suspected.

Trenchcoat examined them carefully before placing them on the table and pushing them back towards Jan. 'We are looking for a grey coloured horse,' said the uniformed policeman. 'It was seen yesterday near a military facility well to the west of here, but I have assured my colleague that I have known this family and the estate for years, and I am sure that there could never have been anything untoward.'

'Do you ride a grey horse?' broke in Trenchcoat.

'Most days,' said Jan, 'at the request of Fraulein Raschdorf. After Herr Holzer passed away, Gunnar gradually lost condition. I am slowly trying to bring him back.'

'I told them,' broke in Carl, ignoring the seeming annoyance of the two visitors. 'I work on this farm every day. I see you riding out all the time. And I don't care what they are looking for, I watched you schooling Gunnar for a good half-hour yesterday lunchtime. You have a way with horses, Master Dietmar, and I don't mind telling you, so do I. It takes one to know one, and it was a pleasure to watch.' Jan realized that for whatever reason, old Carl had just given him a cast iron alibi.

'I don't think there is much more to be gained here,' offered the policeman, more to his colleague than anyone else. But Trenchcoat ignored him.

'Perhaps before we go,' he said, looking directly at Renate, 'I might see the animal? We have a good description, so this could rule him out absolutely.'

From elation at Carl's gesture, Jan's heart sank. Gunnar would match up precisely. 'Fine,' offered Renate, 'he's in the paddock. Let me know if you want me to put on a halter.'

Jan thought she had to be out of her mind. He wondered if, whilst they went to look at Gunnar, he could make a break for the wood and his cache of weapons. But a gesture from Trenchcoat made it clear that they were to stay together. And Jan was pretty sure that underneath his coat their visitor would be carrying a side-arm. For the moment, making a run for it just wasn't an option.

'Stay here, please,' said Renate as they approached the gate to the paddock. 'He'll be startled by too many people.'

All four of them watched as she closed the gate behind her and walked up to Gunnar. As she had expected, he shied then danced round her in a circle. Jan couldn't believe his eyes. Gunnar had two large brown patches: one on his left shoulder, up close to the withers, the other on the right side, high on his rump.

'Thank you for your cooperation, Fraulein,' said Trenchcoat, rather more politely now. 'I don't think we need trouble you any further.'

They walked back to the yard together and watched as the two visitors drove away, Trenchcoat at the wheel. 'Kitchen,' said Renate firmly, 'I think we all need another coffee and perhaps a glass of something stronger.'

Seated once more at the table, whilst Renate bustled about Jan thanked Carl for his support. 'But you and I both know that it wasn't entirely true...' he finished gently.

'Served this family and this estate man and boy,' Carl replied. 'Always been good to me and mine. I listens to the news and reads the papers, same as anyone else. Don't like these Nazi people. Not what they're doing to some of our own, nor that they're taking us into another war. I fought in the last one till I was discharged wounded. They must be bloody mad, pardon my language.' His last few words had been directed towards Renate.

'But where did those patches come from?' asked Jan. 'They weren't there yesterday.'

With a mischievous grin Renate stabbed a finger towards her feet. 'For dancing,' she said. 'For thinking,' she went on, pointing to her head then tapping the side of her brow. 'Gunnar was obviously a weak link if there was any kind of search, so I took care of it whilst you were away in the village.'

'You had me worried when you offered to show them the horse,' Jan admitted. 'Despite what Carl said, I thought we might be in serious trouble.'

She shook her head. 'Consider it *Tantchen* Meta's contribution to our war effort, although she doesn't know it yet. There was a good supply of hair colouring in the bathroom cabinet – L'Oréal, imported from Paris. It's fast, it won't wash out, and until his hair grows through again Gunnar will be a mostly grey piebald! The only thing is,' she went on, still grinning, 'unless Meta can order some more, which might be unlikely if we are about to invade, it looks as if she will have to finish up with some grey hairs of her own before the end of the war.'

They finished their coffee, downed a small glass of schnapps, then Carl excused himself to return to the fields. 'That was brilliant,' he told her, as she poured two more glasses.

'I had intended to warn you,' she said seriously, 'but as you could see there was no chance. Although I think we are off the hook, at least for now. Are you intending to do anything else that might put us at risk?'

Jan shook his head. 'I've warned London about the invasion,' he replied, 'and they'll be marrying up my message with countless other intelligence reports from a mass of different sources. It's up to them what they do about it, but although they acknowledged my message I haven't had any further instructions, other than to keep my eyes open and not transmit again unless I have anything further to report.'

'That makes good sense,' she responded, 'and besides, it's just as well. We can't have you seen riding far and wide on a piebald – not too soon, anyway, after what's just happened.'

'Yesterday was just rotten luck, that *Storch* flying over, but perhaps with hindsight it wasn't a good idea to be so close to the airfield.' He paused. 'I think that armoured formation will be moving out any day now,' he went on, 'but even so, if I have to transmit again I'll ride in a completely different direction and make damn sure that I can't be seen from above.'

'So for now, at least, we have some time to ourselves,' she said more lightly. 'I have work to do. I asked Carl to kill a chicken – it's in the larder. Tonight, I shall try to create a Frau Brantis roast.'

'I should visit the cache,' he replied. 'It's hell's damp out there, buried in the wood, even though everything is well wrapped up. I'll take some oil and a rag from the barn and make sure nothing is likely to rust. I'll be gone for most of the afternoon.'

Jan was working away with a makeshift pull-through, re-oiling a Schmeisser barrel, when there was a cough behind him. Snatching up the automatic at his side he rolled onto his stomach and into the aim. It was Carl, both hands in the air. Jan lowered the weapon, his pulse still racing. 'Christ, you nearly gave me a heart attack,' he told him.

'Didn't hear a thing, did you?' said Carl, not attempting to hide a certain amount of satisfaction. 'I'm an old countryman, Master Dietmar. You was easier than knocking off a pheasant on a black winter's night.' He eyed the weapons and equipment on the ground.

'There's a derelict old one-roomed stone dwelling not far away,' Carl went on. 'Nobody else knows about it, and I'm not even sure whose land it's on – this farm or the next. It's completely overgrown, but I made a small entrance and re-turfed the roof a while back – it's dry inside. I stays there awhile sometimes when the weather turns bad.' More likely, thought Jan, to hang the proceeds of a night's poaching. 'Better you put them there things under cover inside it,' Carl went on. 'And there would be nothing to link them with either you or the young mistress.'

Jan sensed that he could trust the old man. Together they moved everything to the new hide, before Jan scuffed over the old one for the last time. Jan thanked his helper. "Twasn't nothing,' the old countryman replied. 'Told you afore, don't hold with them Nazis and unlike some, the people on this estate have always been kind.'

The old hide was further away from the farmhouse. The sun was down and the light fading before he opened the kitchen door, to be greeted by the delicious smell of a chicken roasting in the oven.

'A quick bath, get changed and then come back down,' she ordered. 'There will just be time for a drink before we eat.'

In bed later that evening it was slower, tender and even more loving than it had been in the morning.

They enjoyed the following days of life on the estate. Jan had no immediate need to travel and spent most of his time working with Carl on the farm. In the evenings, he sat with Renate in the kitchen whilst they listened to the wireless and drank wine until supper was ready. Jan noticed that several of his favorite "Frau Brantis" dishes were also in Renate's repertoire. They had a particular celebration on Saturday, when she produced something of a triumph – the chicken recipe, with a pigeon flavoured cream sauce, that her mother had perfected all those years ago. Over the last few days they had talked exhaustively about what she would say to Frau Holtzer on her return.

They were drinking coffee in the kitchen on the morning of Sunday 6th May when a black Mercedes Benz 170V four door sedan pulled into the farmyard. Jan moved to the kitchen window, suffering a few anxious moments before an elegant older lady slid sideways from the driving seat, whilst a younger woman emerged from the passenger side.

'It's Frau Holtzer,' said Renate in surprise. 'I think the other person must be her daughter Gisela – her photo's in the drawing room, although we haven't met.'

Frau Holtzer entered the kitchen, removing her gloves. 'Renate, *liebchen*, this is my daughter Gisela. Gisela, this is Renate – I told you about her – come to stay here for a while till everything sorts itself out in the East.'

The two young women exchanged a nervous smile. Renate and Jan had agreed that he would be introduced as Dietmar Hofmann. Frau Holtzer looked at the young stranger in her kitchen then, eyebrow raised, at Renate. Clearly, she was waiting for him to be introduced.

Renate was taken aback at the sudden and unexpected arrival. 'This is Jan,' she said quickly, without thinking, and against all that they had agreed.

The damage was done – it was impossible to backtrack now. Jan knew he had to make the best of it. He stepped forward, accepted the hand offered – albeit somewhat hesitantly, clicked his heels and bowed elegantly in the best German fashion.

'Jan Janicki, Frau Holtzer,' he said politely. 'And good morning also, *Fraulein*,' he greeted Gisela, again with a courteous lowering of his head. 'Miss Renate has kindly allowed me to help her with the estate, so may I be of assistance? Perhaps you have cases in the Mercedes that I might bring inside for you?'

'*Danke*,' said Frau Holtzer automatically. Jan bowed slightly one more time and made for the kitchen door. 'Would you like coffee after your journey?' blustered Renate, to cover her hideous mistake.

'Thank you, that would be lovely,' replied Frau Holtzer, settling herself at the kitchen table. 'And in the meantime, you had better tell me all about this young man who seems to be working on my estate.'

Renate busied herself grinding beans and making coffee. Jan had deposited luggage in the hall and returned to the kitchen before Renate felt the need to launch into an explanation. It might be best, he realized, if he controlled this first meeting. He returned to sit opposite Frau Holtzer and her daughter.

'I'm sure Renate will have mentioned my name,' he began, addressing Frau Holtzer. 'As you know, I used to work for Herr Raschdorf until he asked me to bring his daughter here to safety.'

'Frau Holtzer knows that I am Jewish on my mother's side,' interjected Renate.

Jan deliberately waited for a few seconds before looking directly at the older woman. 'Yet you were content to shelter Günther and Hannah's only child, even though this would inevitably entail – in the present social climate, shall we say – a degree of risk. Was this,' he pressed on, 'because you felt obliged to repay a debt to an old friend, or because you did not agree entirely with the present regime, or perhaps both?' he asked bluntly, turning his hands palms up on the kitchen table.

'I won't be interrogated, Jan Janicki,' she responded firmly, although with something of a smile. Her tone was not unfriendly. 'But I don't mind telling you, it is probably "both", as you put it.'

'And you, Fraulein Gisela,' he went on, turning to the young woman. 'Where do you stand, may I ask, in all this?'

'I don't,' she said. 'But I would never do or say anything to hurt Mama.'

The older woman's left hand moved to rest over those of her daughter.

'I think,' Meta said firmly, 'that it is time for a full and honest exchange. I am not sure where all this is leading, but we cannot base decisions on ignorance, or even only a half truth.' Meta hesitated. 'Gisela, you have to know. I should have told you years ago, but perhaps I was too embarrassed. Renate is here because her mother is a Jewish lady, that much is true. She is also here because I am repaying a debt – happily and willingly, I might add – to her father. On his way back from the front after the Great War, Günther Raschdorf rescued me from being raped by two deserters and undoubtedly saved my life.

'He stayed with me for a short while,' she pressed on. 'But there is another reason why I am so happy to welcome Renate into my home.' Frau Holtzer looked at her daughter. 'I have to tell you that she is your half-sister,' she said, perhaps more forcefully than intended. Gisela, wide-eyed, could hardly believe her mother's words. A hand flew to her mouth. Renate sat, impassive – her father had already made her aware of this. Meta Holtzer placed a hand over her daughter's arm. 'I hope this doesn't come as too much of a shock, darling,' she finished quietly.

Renate knew she had to seize the initiative. She moved to stand alongside Gisela and leant forward to put an arm round her shoulders, giving them a gentle squeeze. 'My father only told me just before I left home,' she told her. 'It was a shock for me, too. I think that like your Mama, he was also a bit embarrassed.' She paused… 'But as soon as I saw your photograph, I knew it had to be true. We are so alike: we could even be twins.'

Gisela stood to face her mother. 'You know I have never been friends with Hans,' she said calmly to her mother. 'I don't know why – maybe he's jealous – he doesn't like me and I have never liked him. But what you have just told me… I think it's wonderful news.' With that she turned and embraced her half-sister. After a moment Meta looked away, but Jan saw that all three women had tears in their eyes.

Jan watched the two younger women embrace then coughed, gently. Renate took her chair round the table and set it next to Gisela's, which he thought was a kind touch. Now he was facing all three of them. 'My turn for a bit of embarrassing honesty,' he said to Frau Holtzer. 'Renate and

I have a relationship. If you want to know more, please ask Renate, but suffice it to say that it has been developing for a long time and it finally came to a head after I arrived here during your absence.'

Both Gisela and Renate had to suppress a giggle at his choice of words.

'I honestly think that the less I tell you, the better,' he went on, looking first at Frau Holtzer and then Gisela. 'But you do need to know that I have German papers – genuine ones – in the name of Dietmar Hofmann. Beyond that,' he added, looking at the three of them on the other side of the table, 'all you need claim to know is that I came here looking for work, I had papers declaring me unfit for military service, and I was taken on by Renate to help with the estate.'

'Jan originally set up a sleeping area in the stable, Tantchen Meta,' said Renate, 'but I told him to use one of our spare rooms.'

'Of course you did,' Meta replied, recalling what he had said a minute or so ago and with the faintest smile twitching at the corners of her mouth. It wasn't awkward, but there was a moment of silence.

'In the meantime,' Renate pressed on, 'Jan pointed out that Gunnar was not in great fettle, having been only stabled and paddocked over the winter. He is a very experienced rider, and on your behalf, I accepted his offer to take Gunnar in hand and bring him back to condition. He has been riding out from time to time... I hope that's still all right,' she finished anxiously.

'Thank you, Jan – or Dietmar –' Frau Holtzer replied quietly. 'Please continue to ride him whenever you wish. I know that my late husband would have approved.'

'If it helps,' added Jan, 'I don't think I shall be in this part of the world for much longer. I would obviously appreciate it if the present arrangement could continue, but if you are in any way concerned, Frau Holtzer,' – he looked at her directly – 'I can take my leave whenever you wish.'

Meta looked first to her daughters and then at Jan. 'A lot has been said,' she began slowly, 'and we all know that there is much that has not, but which is nevertheless understood. I think for now,' she concluded, 'we will try to carry on as we are, and wait until we see how things turn out. Are we all agreed?' she asked.

'Renate dear,' she answered into the silence, 'I think we could all do with something to drink. Would you be so kind as to bring a bottle of wine? And Gisela, we shall also need glasses.'

CHAPTER 29

It proved an uneventful Monday. Jan exercised Gunnar and helped Carl on the farm. The three "girls" spent the morning looking after the house and the afternoon in the kitchen. Jan thought he could include Frau Holtzer in that description because she had a lively personality and a great sense of fun. By late afternoon, when he pulled off his boots and asked, in his stockinged feet, if he might have a bottle of beer, he suspected that they were no longer on their first glass of wine.

Supper was claimed to be a combined effort, but Jan detected Renate's influence. There was a delicious veal schnitzel, beaten wafer thin, covered in flour, egg and breadcrumbs, then shallow fried in garlic and butter and served with a mound of sautéed potatoes and green vegetables. Frau Holtzer had made an apple tart, from what she said were almost the last of her stored crop, served with a topping of cream from their small dairy.

When they had washed up and settled to coffee and brandy, Jan felt drowsy and replete. There had been no follow-up visit either from Trenchcoat or the local police, and he quietly expressed the hope that things appeared to have blown over. He had no immediate tasks to perform for London and it occurred to him that he was being paid to live very comfortably, in a country that he knew well, with the woman he loved. As they went to bed Renate clutched his hand and pulled him into her room. 'They know,' she said softly, 'and Frau Holtzer said she doesn't mind. I think she rather likes you and Gisela might even be just a teensy bit jealous!' Jan's day was complete.

They were seated at the table with a modest Tuesday lunch

of bread and liver sausage when the illusion was shattered. The kitchen door was thrown open and two uniformed soldiers with machine pistols rushed in. Between them they were holding up a semi-slumped Carl, his face badly bruised and bloodied. Clearly, he had taken something of a beating. Behind them came the man Jan thought of as Trenchcoat. In his hand was an automatic. He flipped open a wallet containing some sort of identification. '*SS-Hauptsturmführer* Scholz,' he informed them briskly, without offering any opportunity to examine the document, before snapping his wallet shut and returning it to an inside pocket.

Jan's mind was racing. He knew they were in serious trouble, but the three intruders were too far back to give him any chance – except of being shot for his efforts.

'What is the meaning of this,' snapped Frau Holtzer in her best *Hochdeutsch*.

'No use coming the high and mighty with me,' Scholz replied, his voice almost a sneer. He pointed a finger at Renate. 'You were too smug, young lady, when I asked if I could see the horse. I knew then that you were up to something.' His hand embraced all of them at the table. 'I had to threaten that stupid policeman, back at the station, but rather than have his family sent to a concentration camp he came clean – admitted that he didn't ever remember that horse being a piebald.

'Too much of a coincidence,' Scholz went on. 'We suspected there had been a parachute drop somewhere in this area. We didn't see the plane, but plenty heard it – people who know the sound of one aero engine from another. Then someone with a grey horse is seen transmitting from a wood not too far from an airfield – one being used as a major forming up base.

'I could have arrested three of you last time I was here,' he went on, a certain self-satisfaction in his voice, 'but instead I borrowed a couple of men to watch the farm. Eventually, this old fool inspected an overgrown ruin. We let him leave, then took a closer look. So why, I ask myself, would weapons and a field radio be hidden conveniently nearby?'

'I'm sorry, Jan,' Carl mumbled through badly damaged lips, from which blood ran down over his chin and on to the bib of his boiler suit.

'It's all right,' Jan said gently. 'These women know nothing about this,' he went on, looking to Scholz, 'it's me you're after.'

'Very noble, I'm sure, but it won't wash,' mocked the *Hauptsturmführer*. 'I'll accept that the Holtzer woman here and her daughter only turned up forty-eight hours ago, but I think you and this *Mischling* were in it together.' Renate's heart was thumping – obviously Scholz had checked up on her. 'Either way, you will both talk. Rest assured, once you are in my custody there can be absolutely no doubt about that. Also,' he turned to Jan, 'you will transmit for me. If you refuse, or I have any reason to suspect that you are trying to disguise your "fist" or insert a hidden message, this woman will enjoy the longest sexual night of her life – in front of your eyes, and before she is shot. Then you will share her fate.'

'Drop this idiot,' Scholz instructed the two soldiers. Carl staggered a few paces forward then steadied himself with both hands on the end of the kitchen table. The *Hauptsturmführer* waved his automatic and pointed it at Jan. 'Arrest him,' he ordered, 'and cuff his wrists.'

Jan stiffened, but there was nothing he could do. He would be dead if he moved.

One of the soldiers handed his weapon to the other and walked the length of the table to stand behind Jan, who was still seated. It was old Carl who broke the impasse. Turning with a speed that gave the lie to his age, with an almighty roar he threw himself at Scholz. With hands hardened from years of heavy work on the land, Carl seized his throat, thumbs digging in either side, and squeezed as hard and viciously as he could.

The soldier holding both weapons turned, trying to help his officer, who was struggling to free his pistol. There was a muffled shot. Carl's body spasmed but he clung on, if anything tightening his grip. As his companion tried to prize away the locked fingers the soldier behind Jan hesitated.

Jan seized his chance. Diving under the table he snatched the *Gewehr* from its mounting. There were five rounds in the magazine. Lying flat, he put two rounds into the soldier attempting to help Scholz. Somewhere above, someone screamed. As Carl, barely conscious now, slipped slowly to the floor, but before Scholz could bring his weapon to bear, Jan flicked the bolt to chamber a third round. It took Scholz in the throat. Scrambling forward from under the end of the table Jan was on his feet just in time to face the remaining soldier, who raised both hands. There was no alternative. Jan took a half step towards him, pointed the rifle at his face and pulled the trigger. A shower of red and grey matter sprayed from the back of his skull. Flicking the safety, Jan worked the bolt to empty the magazine, which now held only one round. He snatched another five round clip from under the table and reloaded. 'There has to be a driver and vehicle somewhere,' he told them, more harshly than intended. 'Do what you can to drag this lot outside and clean up. I'll be back.'

Jan threw a saddle and tack on Gunnar in record time. It was as if the horse sensed the urgency – he stood there, solid and co-operative, whilst Jan rushed to make him ready. Finally, *Gewehr* in his left hand, reins in the right, he urged the horse from the stable. It would have been no use trying to find Scholz's transport on foot – it there was a driver, he could enter the farmhouse at any time, perhaps whilst Jan was searching two or three fields away. That would put the entire family at risk. It couldn't be allowed to happen.

He started to circle the house, at first close in, but gradually widening the distance till he was perhaps half a kilometre away. Eventually he saw the roof of a car on the other side of a hedge. It had been reversed into a track, bonnet facing the road. Dismounting, Jan secured Gunnar a hundred meters away and approached on foot, shielded by the hedge. As he drew closer he could smell cigarette smoke – the wind was blowing towards him, which would have carried the sound of shooting away from the farm, in the other direction. About fifty metres from the vehicle, Jan pushed himself through a small hole in the base of the hedge. There was a driver, weapon slung over his shoulder, leaning back on the vehicle and enjoying a cigarette without a care in the world.

Moving slowly, centimetres at a time, Jan wriggled into a prone firing position. He was not going to enjoy what he was about to do, but there was no choice. A single survivor would spell a death sentence for all of them at the farm.

There were four bodies in the farmyard, although out of respect they placed Carl away from the other Germans. They were heating a bucket of water when a single shot rang out. Such was the state of their nerves that all three women flinched. Frau Holtzer ran to the window when Jan drove the car into the yard. She moved to the door.

'Leave the vehicle,' he instructed. 'I'll sort it when I get back. Right now, I have to go fetch Gunnar.' As he left on foot she took a couple of steps forward and looked through the side windows. There was a uniformed body across the foot wells between the front and rear seats. Fifteen minutes later Jan returned and led Gunnar into the stable. All four of them assembled in the kitchen.

'One of you girls, please see to Gunnar – he hasn't been ridden hard but we need to get that saddle off him as quickly as possible, just in case. Otherwise, please carry on cleaning up in here.' It occurred to Jan that he had taken control automatically, issuing orders as if they were a military unit.

'What are you going to do?' asked Frau Holtzer.

'We have to get rid of the evidence,' Jan responded. 'Scholz might have left word where he was headed, but from the way he reacted when he arrived and found out what his watcher had seen, I rather think he didn't. He seemed keen to beat up poor old Carl and then come in here and arrest us all. He probably wanted to leave us tied up under armed guard, so that he could return with more escorts and a prison van, only to report to his superiors covered in glory. Either way, we must get rid of the evidence. And if anyone does make enquiries, we have cleaned up and no-one was ever here.'

'What do you propose to do with the bodies?' asked Frau Holtzer.

'I hate to do it to Carl,' Jan confessed, 'but I think we have to put all five of them in the car, drive it somewhere safe and set fire to it.' He looked to Frau Holtzer. 'I'll do it, but perhaps you have somewhere in mind?'

'Better than that,' she replied. 'There's an old quarry not too far from here. We used to swim there when I was a child. The water's deep. If we can drive the car over the edge, I doubt if it will ever be found. But I'll have to come – to show you where it is.'

'Too dangerous – if we are caught on the way we are both in trouble,' Jan responded.

'If you are caught on the way, we are all in trouble,' she came back sharply. 'Besides, with me alongside you can go straight there. You take Sholtz's side-arm and I'll take the Gewehr. Rest assured, if we hit trouble I know how to use it.'

Jan stripped all five corpses, removed identity documents and loaded the bodies into the back of the car, which was now well down on its springs. The weapons, with the exception of Scholz's automatic, he threw on top. Back in the kitchen, he nodded towards the range. 'Burn the lot,' he told the girls, dumping clothing and documents on the floor. 'We'll be gone for some time.'

The journey to the quarry proved uneventful, although it was late afternoon before they arrived. A wide sandy track led down into the water, presumably to where the workings had once been, but otherwise it was surrounded by an almost vertical bank at least two meters high.

'We used to jump and dive off here, many years ago,' Frau Holtzer said wistfully, standing on top of a grassy bank. Jan positioned the car several metres back from the edge, leaving the driver's door fully open, and broke off a short branch from a young tree. Snapping it to length, he wedged it between the seat and the throttle, so that the engine would be well gunned. Settling into the driver's seat he restarted the engine. It revved into life with a healthy roar. Selecting second gear, he slowly eased his foot off the clutch. The engine did not stall and the car moved forward, rapidly gathering speed. Just before it reached the bank he launched himself from the vehicle, almost leaving it too late. He had to stretch out his arms and legs to stop himself rolling over the edge. Sitting up, he watched the car arc well out above the quarry before falling, slightly rear wheels down, into the water. Within a minute it had disappeared completely. 'That was well done,' observed Frau Holtzer. 'But now we have a long walk home.'

In fact, they didn't. A third of the way back they met Gisela on Frau Holtzer's horse with an off-saddled Gunnar on a lead rein. 'I've been to the quarry often enough,' she greeted them, 'and we all need to get back sooner rather than later.' Jan and Gisela mounted Gunnar and they returned to the farmhouse at a brisk walk. It was quite sensual, her arms around his waist and the movement of the horse beneath her.

Back at the farm, in fading light, they gathered round the kitchen table. 'We found broken cotton and panel pins underneath,' said Renate, 'but when did you put the Gewehr there?'

'After Trenchcoat's first visit,' he told them. 'Early the following morning. It occurred to me at the time that if things went tits up – sorry, ladies –' he added, 'I had absolutely no plan to fall back on. And the rifle was the only weapon we could legitimately explain away, but it was no use up in the bedroom.'

'Thank God you did put it under the table,' said Frau Holtzer with a heartfelt sigh. 'Otherwise by now we would all be inside a Gestapo cell. I for one,' she said, rising to her feet, 'am in desperate need of something strong to drink.' She emerged from the larder with a bottle of schnapps and pulled a clutch of small glasses from the nearest cupboard. Once seated again, her first tot disappeared in one.

'So assuming you are right, and we manage to survive today's dreadful events, what happens now?' she asked.

'It's not safe for me to stay here,' Jan told her. And it's obvious they have been checking up on Renate, so her refuge is also compromised, to say the least.' He paused, turning the glass between his fingers. 'We have to leave, both of us,' he went on. 'First thing in the morning, I'll bury my cache. Whilst I'm doing that, Renate can sort out a few things for the journey. I've done it before – we can cross into Belgium on foot and make our way back to England from there. No absolute guarantees, but I'm pretty sure you and Gisela should be all right here, once we have left.'

'What about Carl?' Renate asked. 'Won't he be missed?'

'He lived on his own,' Frau Holtzer assured her. 'I think there's a son and daughter somewhere in the Ruhr, but he always complained that they never bothered to contact him. It'll probably be quite some time before anyone notices he's no longer around, and I suspect that by then we'll be well into the next stage of the war.'

'How will you manage on the farm?' asked Jan, 'I mean, without Carl, and the two of us no longer around?'

'In the short-term, Gisela and I will just have to roll our sleeves up,' she said bluntly. 'I did it when my first husband was in the trenches and I can do it again. After that, we'll have to see.' She paused. 'But if we are going to be at war, Gisela will be safer here than living in a city like Cologne. For us civilians, I suspect it is going to be a case of survival.'

They sat in silence for several seconds, each to their thoughts. Jan finished his drink and poured them all some more. 'I think your plan might work,' Frau Holtzer said eventually, 'but the border is bound to be much more closely guarded now that we are technically at war with England and France. These days, there is a distinct possibility that you might be caught.'

'That's probably a risk we have to take,' Jan replied, 'because I don't see that we have much alternative.'

'I think you do,' she argued. 'Listen, we don't live that far from the border and I regularly cross over to go shopping. There's an excellent market just inside Belgium – I go there most Saturday mornings. It's only a small crossing on a quiet rural road, manned by ordinary border police, not military, and I know nearly all of them. What's more, they know me, they know Gisela but not that well, and they are quite used to seeing my car.'

'What are you proposing?' Jan asked slowly.

'You have German papers, and they pass muster,' she looked at Jan, who lowered his head in confirmation. 'Renate and Gisela are very similar in appearance. You drive the car as our chauffeur, Renate takes Gisela's passport, and the three of us cross over tomorrow morning. Gisela isn't going to be on any list of Jewish people, and she has a genuine Aryan passport. Once over the border, we drive to the nearest railway station and you both take the first train for *Brüssel*. After that it's up to you, but I might suggest *Ostende* and the first ship for England.'

CHAPTER 30

After an early start, and with everything safely buried, they were ready to leave at half past ten. Renate had prepared two rucksacks with bare essentials: a change of clothing, a few toiletries and a small pack of food. 'I've put the same things in each,' she told Jan, 'just in case we have to separate for any reason.'

'And I have put an envelope into each,' added Frau Holtzer, 'with a supply of marks. The *Belgierinnen* will take them near the border – I often use marks to pay for my shopping. They won't give you a fair exchange rate, but pretend not to notice. Alternatively, you can wait till you hit *Brüssel* and find a *bureau de change*.'

Frau Holtzer had found Jan a cap. It wasn't exactly a genuine, shiny-peaked chauffeur's one, more like something worn by a Breton fisherman, but it was better than nothing. She and Renate settled into the rear seat. After only a fifteen-minute drive, they could see two guards at the border who made no move to draw their side-arms. Jan coasted slowly to a standstill, intending to stop well short of the barrier in case he had to reverse. 'We're in luck,' said Frau Holtzer quickly, 'I know the older one. His name's Rüdiger Weber.' Taking their passports, she stepped from the Mercedes and walked towards the two men.

'I'm sorry, Frau Holtzer,' said Weber, holding out his hand, 'I know who you are, of course, and your lovely daughter, but I am under strict orders to inspect all documents.' His eyes flicked sideways and there was an almost imperceptible nod towards his companion. *So*, thought Meta, *not one of the usual people*. 'Who's the young man at the wheel?' Weber asked casually.

'That's Dietmar – Dietmar Hofmann. His papers are there.'

'I haven't seen him before,' Weber responded. It was little more than an observation, no trace of suspicion.

'He's been working for me for some time,' she offered. 'Wanted to join the *Wehrmacht* but the poor man has a history of tuberculosis. His medical certificate is in there,' she nodded towards the passports. 'Now that so many young men have joined up,' she told him, 'the doctors suggested he help the war effort on the land. After my husband died I had only one farm worker, and Carl is quite an old man, so when Dietmar was recommended to me it seemed like a good idea.'

'And it's really nice to have a driver,' Weber said with a smile.

'It saves worrying about parking,' she replied smoothly, 'not to mention having someone to help carry the bags.

'How's your daughter?' she asked. On a previous trip she had stopped to chat, as country people tended to do, and he had shown her a photograph. On her return journey Meta handed over a bar of really good Belgian chocolate. 'For your daughter,' she had said simply. At the time, she viewed it as just a small kindness. Now she was beginning to think it might have been a good investment.

'She's fine, Frau Holtzer, and thank you for asking,' came the reply. 'All's well here,' he turned to his companion, 'you happy, Reinhart?' he checked with the younger man. Obviously, thought Frau Holtzer, the older guard was not in command. But Reinhart Lehmann had noticed his colleague's deference towards the immaculately dressed older lady, not to mention a motor car enjoyed only by the wealthy.

'That's fine,' he replied, turning towards her. 'Thank you for your cooperation, Frau Holtzer, and I wish you a pleasant day. But I am afraid the border is closed to all non-essential traffic at the moment.'

Meta's heart sank, but she managed to hide her feelings. 'May one ask why?' she queried, after just a moment's hesitation.

'An administrative matter,' he replied blandly. 'I am sorry for the inconvenience, but perhaps you could make your shopping trip in a few days' time?'

'I'm sorry too,' Frau Holtzer, Weber added gently. 'But kindly allow me to escort you back to your car.'

Lehmann stood watching and lit a cigarette. *If old Weber wanted to be extra polite to the local gentry,* he thought, *that was up to him.*

Back at the car she turned to face him. They were perhaps fifteen metres from the barrier pole. 'And I don't want you taking that track on the right just beyond the first bend,' he said softly. 'It belongs to a local farmer. Goes past his cottage, then comes out again on the other side. We know about it, saves him from clogging up the border with his tractor, so we turn a blind eye. I haven't mentioned it to him,' again a barely perceptible flick back of the head, 'and you didn't hear about it from me.'

With that he threw up a courteous salute and walked back to the crossing. Jan turned the car, not without some difficulty in the narrow lane, and drove back the way they came.

Seated on his tractor he saw the black Mercedes from two fields away as it drove slowly towards the border, although the farmer could barely make out the occupants. But he made no move to acknowledge them. People like him made every effort to stay away from any possible form of *Bürokratismus*.

They emerged well out of sight from the barrier. Jan accelerated gently on the cobbles, which soon gave way to a paved road leading into a small market town. At Frau Holtzer's request he parked outside the station. Meta went to the ticket office where she found enough local currency left over from previous shopping trips to purchase two tickets for *Brüssel*. They had three quarters of an hour to wait.

'What will you do now?' Jan asked.

'A bit of shopping – some vegetables, a little chocolate and I think some expensive lingerie. In the unlikely event that I am caught using the track on the way home, at least I shall have a good excuse – something to show for my journey. And if that young guard decides to check my shopping, what he will pull out of one of my bags will turn his face the colour of beetroot! At worst, I'll just get a ticking off…'

They lapsed into anxious silence, but the train was on time. 'Thank you for all you have done for us,' Renate told her. Meta hugged her tightly and planted a kiss on both cheeks. Then to Jan's surprise he was gripped by the shoulders and also kissed. But he could see tears in her eyes.

'You must get on,' she instructed. 'Have a safe journey, and if you can, let me know when you have arrived. Good luck!'

With that she turned and walked slowly along the platform towards the exit. When she didn't look back, Jan and Renate watched till she was out of sight then boarded the train.

Had he been alone, Jan would have phoned the embassy. But he didn't want any complications because of Renate's nationality. So, he simply found a *bureau de change* and bought two onward tickets to *Oostende*. After asking around, he managed to secure passage on a good sized vessel whose skipper intended to make an overnight crossing to England. Only when they had cast off did Renate truly feel safe.

CHAPTER 31

There was a long queue at Dover customs and immigration, but eventually they stood before a uniformed officer who asked briskly for their passports. Jan handed over his Dietmar Hoffman document and Renate the one borrowed from Gisela.

'German,' he observed, not very enthusiastically, thought Jan. And certainly not very welcoming.

'Yes,' Renate replied. 'But not my own. And I'm classified as Jewish, which is why I am here.' She was speaking slowly, but her English sounded proficient to Jan. 'This gentleman can explain,' she concluded.

'And I have a Polish passport,' said Jan, nodding towards the one held by the official. 'But that German one's a fake – it was made for me in London.' He had no intention of revealing his true, Polish identity to a junior official, not least because he might need it again for another mission in the future.

The immigration officer looked as though someone had dropped a bombshell into what should have been a routine day.

'You need to ring a number in London,' Jan told him. 'If you can't do that, ring the local police and ask them to send round a plain clothes officer. But either way, someone has to make that call.'

'How do I know I can believe you?' the official asked bluntly. 'So why should I do either?' Jan realized that he was just trying to save face, but after what he and Renate had been through, he was in no mood to suffer fools gladly.

'If you do not do as I ask,' Jan said through a humourless grin, 'you will be acting completely against the best interest of your own country. And mine now, come to that. Interests that

402

this young lady and I have spent a very dangerous time trying to protect, if that makes you feel any better. We are not refugees; it is more a case of having made a very fortunate escape.'

Jan sensed that the officer was wavering. 'Try and put two and two together, from what I have said,' he went on, 'because you just don't have the security clearance to know any more.' He paused… 'It will all come out eventually, at a level far above your own, so please make just one phone call. The alternative, I can assure you, is that my superiors will probably make sure that you spend the rest of the war cleaning toilets.'

Slowly, the official's hand moved to the phone. 'If you are calling London, then whoever answers, please just say that their Polish gentleman is here.'

A minute later, as instructed from the other end, he handed the receiver over to Jan. 'There are two of us,' he said in answer to the question. 'But I can't explain here, or on an open line.' He listened for a moment then handed back the phone.

'Yes, Sir,' the immigration officer kept repeating, as if they were the only words he knew. Finally, he replaced the handset.

'You must be important,' he said. 'So please forgive me for doubting, at first.'

Jan could afford to be magnanimous. He smiled, suggesting that he understood. 'I'm arranging transport,' the official told them. 'You are to be taken to a local hotel. It's a very good one,' he hastened to add, sounding impressed. 'London are sending a car for you – it will pick you up around lunchtime. In the meantime, they are arranging for a room and you are to order whatever you wish.'

It was late afternoon when Jan introduced Renate to Doreen Jackman and Bill Ives. 'I suppose you could say they are my handlers,' he told her.

'I would prefer to say colleagues,' said Doreen kindly to Renate.

'We have a lot to tell you,' said Jan. 'But Renate has been at my side from the moment the mission started. In fact, I could not have succeeded without her. She is a German national, but the Nazis have classed her as a *Mischling,* to use their horrible word, because of her Jewish mother. So, she has to be given asylum. There can be absolutely no question of internment. And that's the very least she is owed by this country.'

Doreen Jackman looked at her colleague. 'I am quite sure that we can come to an arrangement that will suit both of you,' she said gently, only too aware of what the young girl had probably been through.

'And that was a brilliant transmission,' Ives added. 'We had other intelligence, of course, and the RAF have flown some very courageous high-level reconnaissance sorties, but there was nothing to beat your description of a camouflaged-up armoured formation on that airfield, not to mention what you overheard from that officer, Hans, about being at war in ten days. It was absolute gold dust, and will save a lot of lives.'

'My dear,' said Doreen Jackman, who seemed to have taken a rather motherly liking to the young German woman, 'I give you my word that we will look after you. There is absolutely no question of internment, so you have nothing to fear.' Jan suddenly realized with a start that she was speaking to Renate fluently in her own language. 'Please come with me,' she asked politely. 'I want to hear your story. The crusty old colonel here will debrief Jan. There's nothing sinister in this – we take two separate versions, then put them together. If there are any discrepancies, we iron them out between us. That way, we make sure that the final account is as accurate as is humanly possible. You must be tired,' she concluded, 'so we'll be as quick as we can today, and we'll probably have another chat tomorrow.'

She stood. 'Would you like our English tea and biscuits, or would you prefer coffee? I'll have it freshly ground, the way you might like it.'

Renate instinctively trusted the Englishwoman. With no more than a quick, slightly anxious glance towards Jan she followed her from the room.

The debrief did not take too long. At the safe house a middle-aged housekeeper offered them a light supper and they talked over the events of the day.

'Do you know what's going to happen?' he asked her.

Renate shook her head. They were speaking in German, to the housekeeper's obvious disapproval. She stopped hovering and disappeared into the kitchen to attack the washing up.

'But Frau Jackman said that they would find some form of employment for me, and that I shouldn't worry at all about being interned. I believe her. She said it's just not going to happen and she obviously has the authority to make sure that it doesn't. Thank you for insisting on that,' she said softly, placing her hand over his. 'First, though,' she concluded, 'it seems I have to improve my English. Mine is apparently good but a bit basic. So, what about you?' she asked in return.

'The colonel said that they don't want me back in the field just yet,' he replied. 'He asked how I would feel about a course with their English armoured school, perhaps followed by a tour passing things on to Polish volunteers. Always wanted to drive a tank,' he finished with a schoolboy grin. 'But either way, the war be damned. The old colonel gave me this – said it would improve my education.' He produced a bottle. 'Apparently it's a single malt whisky. A bit peaty,' he said, in a fair imitation of the colonel's Scottish accent, 'but if we are going to be stuck here for the duration, it's a taste we might do well to acquire.'

'Pour me a glass,' she said with a tired smile. 'And offer one to that poor lady doing our washing up. Then when she's gone, take me to bed.'

The following morning, Germany invaded the Low Countries.

ACKNOWLEDGEMENT

During the early days of writing this book I was fortunate to secure the services of Agnieszka Bolek, a professional Polish/ Russian/English translator and genealogy researcher living in northern Poland.

Agnieszka far exceeded her brief, not only undertaking translation but also offering much cultural input, with valuable information about life in rural Poland during the years before the Second World War. From documents still in my possession she was also able to discover the location of Jan's original family home. Today it is the site of an evangelical church. Jan, a staunch Roman Catholic throughout his life, would not have approved!

Agnieszka's contribution has added greatly to the authenticity and atmosphere of this book, for which I am most grateful. She can be contacted at abolek1@wp.pl or www. polishrelish.com